ONE NIGHT ONLY

Sue Welfare was born on the edge of the Fens and is perfectly placed to write about the vagaries of life in East Anglia. In between raising a family, singing in a choir, walking the dog, working in the garden, taking endless photos and cooking, Sue is also a scriptwriter, originating and developing a soap opera for BBC radio, along with a pantomime for the town in which she lives.

Sue Welfare also writes as Gemma Fox and Kate Lawson. For more information on Sue go to www.katelawson. co.uk.

ID800302

SUE WELFARE

One Night Only

AVON

AVON

A division of HarperCollins*Publishers*
77–85 Fulham Palace Road,
London W6 8JB

www.harpercollins.co.uk

A Paperback Original 2012
1

First published in Great Britain by
HarperCollins*Publishers* 2012

A catalogue record for this book is
available from the British Library

ISBN-13: 978-1-84756-119-0

Set in Sabon LT Std by Palimpsest Book Production Limited,
Falkirk, Stirlingshire

Printed and bound in Great Britain by
Clays Ltd, St Ives plc

MIX
Paper from
responsible sources
FSC
www.fsc.org **FSC™ C007454**

With thanks to my fabulous agent, Maggie Phillips, at Ed Victor Ltd. and to the lovely, Sammia Rafique, and the rest of the team at Avon.

*To my family and
friends – you know
who you are.*

PROLOGUE

Now

Slowly – almost unnoticed at first – the lights in the theatre began to dim. Tucked out of sight in the wings Helen could sense the growing anticipation and expectation in the audience. The seconds ticked by. Part of the magic of good showmanship is to make an audience wait, to hold them there a few seconds longer than feels quite comfortable, so that every eye is focused on stage. That growing sense of what is *about* to happen pushes aside all the thoughts about the drive there, the queue to get in, the day they had had before the show began and so Helen waited.

In the auditorium someone coughed; there were the sounds of people settling back in their seats, their conversation changing from a noisy cheerful babble to an altogether lower, denser hum. There was a crackle of excitement in the air, an electric charge as tangible as a coming storm. It made Helen's skin prickle.

'Okay, Miss Redford?' mouthed the assistant stage manager, giving Helen the thumbs up. She smiled and nodded, all the while aware of every breath, every movement, every sound around her.

As the music began to play Helen closed her eyes, making an effort to control the panic that bubbled up inside. There was a peculiar fluttering fear that started somewhere down low in the pit of her stomach and rose up into her throat, closing it down, stealing her breath away and making her heart race. She knew that once she was out on stage it would be fine, but for now the panic crowded in on her, making her tremble, making the sound of her pulse ricochet around inside her skull like a drumroll. Deep breaths, calm thoughts; any second now the curtains would open and everything would be all right.

In the auditorium beyond the curtains the audience was still and quiet now. The hairs on the back of her neck rose.

'Miss Redford?' someone whispered. Helen opened her eyes and looked up. One of the crew adjusted the radio mike onto the front of her dress and leaning closer flicked it on before tucking the wire down in amongst the embroidery. One of the spotlights reflected in the facets of the jewellery she was wearing, projecting a great arc of rainbows into the wings. It felt like an omen.

Helen smiled her thanks and she pressed her lips together, blotting her lipstick, and then ran a hand back

2

over her hair checking it was all in place, her heart still racing, anxiety edging out all sensible thoughts.

The technician grinned. 'You look fabulous,' he whispered. Her smile held. On the far side of the stage, behind a cameraman, Arthur, her agent, raised a hand in salute, his fingers crossed. He winked at her.

A moment later and the music changed to the signature tune for *Cannon Square* and as the curtains slowly opened, the deep inviting voice of the theatre's resident compere rolled out over the PA.

'Ladies and gentlemen, welcome to this evening's show. Tonight, for one night only, we would like you put your hands together and give a great big Carlton Rooms welcome to star of stage, screen and television, our very own homespun diva, Miss Helen Redford!' His voice rose to a crescendo in the darkness.

It was as if someone had thrown a switch. From the auditorium came a sound like heavy rain and then thunder as people clapped, cheered and stamped their feet, the sound filling the theatre, a sound so loud that Helen could feel it pressing on her chest as much as she could hear the noise. The assistant stage manager waved her on and as Helen stepped out into the glare of the spotlight the volume of the applause rose.

She waited for the noise to ebb and then smiled out into the expectant darkness.

'Well, hello there,' she said, pulling up the stool that was there waiting for her centre stage. 'It's been a long time coming but it's great to be back here at the Carlton

Rooms. I don't want to think about how many years it's been since I stood right here on this stage. I've been away too long.' And as she spoke the audience roared its appreciation and Helen's nerves melted away like snow in sunshine.

ONE

Last Year

'I just wanted to tell you, Miss Redford – may I call you Helen? – how absolutely delighted we are to have you on board for next season's TV show. It's a real honour – I mean *really*. Now, before we run through a few details, would you like a drink? Tea. We've got green if you prefer? Or coffee, mineral water? We've got still or sparkling, haven't we, Jamie?'

Ruth Long, the executive producer of *Roots*, glanced across at her assistant, and then tried out a smile; an expression that didn't sit at all well on her plump, rather earnest, face. She had a face made for documentary television, her plain meaty features framed by unnaturally black hair cut into an asymmetric bob so straight and so unmoving that Helen wouldn't have been at all surprised to discover that it sat on a dummy head beside Ruth's bed at night. Certainly it didn't so much as ripple while Ruth made a show of being hospitable.

Jamie, her assistant, stood to one side of the office, skittering in and out of Helen's peripheral vision as he fiddled with his hair.

'Actually it was Jamie who suggested you for our programme – wasn't it, Jamie? He's got such an eye for a story, it's a real talent,' Ruth said fondly. 'And as he pointed out at our last planning meeting you truly are an icon.'

Helen smiled while her agent, Arthur, leant back in his bucket seat steepling his fingers, and with a sly smile said, 'Time was when people broke out the champagne when they signed an icon; a nice bottle of chilled Krug to seal the deal. Lunch at the Ivy, or the Groucho –'

For the briefest of instants Ruth looked thrown. 'Ah, yes, right,' she said. 'I'm most terribly sorry – we just thought – I mean –' she glanced at Helen, and then more pointedly at Jamie.

'You shouldn't believe everything you read in the tabloids, Ruth,' said Arthur. 'Make mine still, will you? Slice of lime would be nice.'

Helen looked at up at Jamie and smiled. 'Actually I'd love a cup of tea and what Arthur is trying to say is that I'm not a drunk and never have been, so the clause in the contract about needing a regular sobriety test –'

'To be honest, Ruth,' said Arthur, all shark's teeth and diamond-hard bonhomie, 'Helen and I were a *teensy-weensy* bit thrown by that. It could be interpreted in all kinds of ways – as an infringement on our civil liberties for a start – and just a *little* too American for our tastes.'

On the far side of the desk Ruth Long tried to wave the words away like a bad smell. 'It's standard in all our contracts these days, Miss Redford. Helen – you're happy for me to call you Helen? It's our insurers who insist on it. Let's be candid, shall we?' Ruth leant forward as if to imply she was sharing a confidence. 'We occasionally have people on the show with, what shall we say – *issues*? It's the nature of the beast. Stardom, fame – I don't have to tell you the price those things exact on a person. And you're right, it is a very American concept but so far we've sold every series of *Roots* into the States and we've got a really good co-production deal going this series, and our American cousins are very hot on that kind of thing.

'You have to see it from our point of view, Helen. We just want to make sure that if we invest in all the research, the travel, the hoopla, that our guests will be able to string a sentence together when it comes to filming. Everything's tight round here and everywhere else these days: tight budget, tighter schedule; last thing we want is a tight guest, if you follow me –' She laughed at her own joke.

Arthur eyed up the tiny glass of water he had been given. 'And so you're telling me that you breath-tested Bishop what's-his-name and that civil rights guy?'

Ruth's smile held. 'We just want the option, that's all, Arthur. Of course we don't always exercise it. But, for example, we took Lena Paige, series two, show six, all around the world looking for her mother and father – St Kitts to find her mother, New Zealand to track down her father. I don't know whether you saw it, Helen, but it made the most sensational television – not a dry eye in the house. It was nominated for a TV Times Peoples' Choice award, a Bafta – I'll get James to get you the DVD – anyway, her dad was some sort of fighter pilot and then he emigrated and left them all behind. It was all very emotional, but I wouldn't be letting any cats out of any bags telling you that Lena comes with a certain amount of history. Rehab, hospitalisation – lots and lots of counselling over the years. And of course the whole weight problem.

'Anyway, while I don't wish to be indiscreet, it was touch and go at some points, I can tell you. We had to have her sedated in Auckland. So, what I'm saying here, Helen, is once bitten twice shy. We need to know, come show time, that we'll get something we can use. A lot of this stuff is highly charged and we understand that people always come with baggage. It's what gives the show its appeal. Digging deep, shaking the dust off, getting down to the heart of our guest – however you like to express it.

'So that's why the clause is in there – we reserve the right to test all our guests because by its very nature our show focuses on a lot of –' Ruth paused, as if searching around for the right word.

'Icons,' suggested Jamie, handing Helen a cup of tea.

'Exactly,' said Ruth, pushing her designer glasses up onto the bridge of her nose. 'And you don't get to be an icon by living the quiet life.'

'When that bloody woman said icon she meant washed-up has-been, didn't she?' said Helen. She was pacing up and down in her kitchen. The sun was streaming in through the windows, picking out Arthur, who was sitting inscrutable as Buddha, at the long refectory table. He was cradling a mug of coffee. Helen was too agitated to sit down.

'You could see it on her smug little face. Icon, my arse. And she more or less came right out and accused me of being an alcoholic.'

'But you're not and it's still the most fabulous offer,' said Arthur, rolling a cigar between his fingers like a plump carrot. Helen didn't like him smoking in the house so he made do with sniffing it instead. 'And it's a real coup coming out of the blue like that. *Roots* is mainstream prime time. Right up there in the ratings and the public consciousness. I know people who would give their right arm for a shot at it. I mean this offer came in right out of left field –' he mimed.

'Okay, okay, I get it, Arthur. Right arm, left field, I should be grateful, eager and excited.'

Arthur nodded. 'And then some. We could hang all sorts of things on the back of this. I've been working on an idea –'

'He saw me, you know,' said Helen. 'That boy, Jamie,

the one she keeps as a pet? He told me when he was showing me where the loo was. He saw me shopping in Waitrose in Swaffham when he came home to visit his mother at Easter. He said he thought I was dead. Dead!'

'He's a producer.'

Helen threw herself onto the sofa under the window. 'He doesn't look old enough to have produced anything that doesn't involve glue and sticky-backed plastic.'

'He's won awards, apparently,' said Arthur wistfully, staring at his cigar.

'For what? The tidiest desk? Best guinea pig in show?'

'Most promising newcomer, and some sort of arty short on Channel 4. He's the next big thing apparently.'

Helen laughed. 'And we all know how that works out, don't we? I remember a time when I was the next big thing.'

'And it could you be again, sweetie. Remember June Whitfield in *AbFab?* You know Lena Paige who Ruth was talking about got a part in the last Bruce Willis film on the back of her being in *Roots.*'

Helen raised her eyebrows.

'Okay, okay,' said Arthur, 'So she got shot during the opening titles. But at least it was work. Second bite of the cherry. Look, Helen, speaking as your friend, you know that if you don't want to do the show then it's fine by me – it's not too late to pull out, we're not committed, nothing's signed yet. But as your agent I'm telling you, you'd be bloody mad to turn it down.

A whole hour on prime time TV? All about you? Jesus, what's not to like?'

'I know what you're saying, Arthur, but I'm not the kind of person who washes their dirty linen in public. I never have been. You know that.'

Arthur sighed. 'Yes, but when you look at what else is on offer, it's a chance in a million.'

'So what else *is* on offer?'

'Pantomime somewhere out in the boondocks. I could probably get you a cameo on *Holby City* as a down-and-out.'

'Is that chap Nettles still murdering people? Didn't their producer say that I'd make a great corpse?'

'There are always voice-overs,' continued Arthur.

'Funeral expenses insurance and female incontinence pads. I don't think so,' Helen said, taking a long pull on her fruit juice. 'I'd like some real work.'

'There's not just those. I mean the yoghurt thing was fun, you said so yourself.'

'I was a Friesian cow.'

'I know, and they loved you, sweetie, you know they did. And they're keen to use you again, so they're always an option. We've already had this conversation, petal. Getting yourself onto *Roots* is a genuine opportunity, and it's the first really exciting one that's come along in a long while. We both know that. It could be the first step on the road back home, and let's be honest: it's either this or the bush tucker route.'

'No!' Helen said emphatically.

'It can be the way into the nation's heart. Look at Christopher Biggins. And you were right up there with the best of them, Helen, don't ever forget that – remember they had an item on *News at Ten* when you retired?'

'Retired? You make it sound like I had a choice, Arthur. If you remember, the writers blew me up in a gas explosion in a specially extended episode. That woman who comes on *News at Ten* did a segment about faulty boilers on the back of it.'

'Jammed the phone lines,' said Arthur, philosophically, sniffing his cigar. 'People wrote in to the papers. And don't forget the six weeks on life support. The whole nation was totally gripped. People cared, Helen. They really cared. When they finally turned your machine off the whole country mourned.'

'Don't tell me, Arthur. I was the one with a tube stuck up my nose and that bloody machine pinging all the time. You know it took wardrobe hours to do me up like that? So yes, Arthur. I understand. Once upon a time I *used* to be big.' Helen looked heavenwards. 'And no, before you ask again: no, no bush tucker. I couldn't stand it. No moisturiser, surrounded by self-pitying whiners, has-beens and hyperactive third-raters, the self-obsessed and actors who should be in therapy. And I'm not eating anything that moves.'

'Which reminds me,' said Arthur. 'Where exactly is the boy wonder today?'

She raised an eyebrow. 'Bon? He's downstairs working out in the gym, I think. And if you're going to be nasty about him then you can leave now, Arthur. I don't have to justify my taste in men to you of all people.'

'Just as well really, isn't it,' murmured Arthur.

It was an old battle; the lines were well drawn. Helen chose to ignore him. 'He's good for me.'

'So is spinach, but you don't have to have it on your plate twenty-four hours a day seven days a week, do you? In my opinion he's not as good for you as you are for him. You're not going to marry him, are you?'

'We haven't talked about it,' said Helen.

'Well, don't. The idea of you saddling yourself with him makes my flesh creep. Your taste in men is appalling, sweetie.'

She raised her eyebrows. 'Well, you would know.'

'He's just a phase.'

'You're suggesting that I'll grow out of him?'

'You will if you have any sense. He's going to break your heart.'

'And you didn't? You're only jealous, Arthur – you've done nothing but sulk since what's-her-name ran off with that footballer. Besides, I need a new project.'

'Then do something to the house, remodel the garden, get a dog – anything.'

'I was thinking of something a bit bigger. Bon was talking about us buying a bar together, somewhere warm and sunny. Somewhere with a little stage, where we could have live music. I'm thinking about going to have a look in the Canaries. See what's on offer.'

Arthur rolled his eyes. 'What's on offer in the Canaries,

sweetie, is total bloody oblivion. For God's sake Helen, you're so much better than that. What's it going to take to get you to see sense?'

'Bon loves me.'

Arthur rolled his eyes. 'So did that Pekinese my mother used to have, but I didn't feel obliged to change my life to accommodate it.'

'You loved that dog.'

'Well, you know what I mean. You need something new to get your teeth into. Something big –'

She sighed. 'Something special.'

'Exactly, *something special*, which is why *Roots* is just perfect for you. This will get you right back where you belong, back out there in the public eye – give you the exposure you need, and maybe shake something interesting out of the woodwork. I've got a plan – I've been thinking we should get you out on the road again. You should be thanking Jamie, never mind whisking golden boy off on another jolly. And *Roots* do it so well. Have you watched any of the programmes?'

Cautiously Helen nodded. 'I think I have. I'm not sure. I saw the one about a ballet dancer. Some posh blonde girl with buck teeth whose family went back to Elizabeth I?'

'They're biking round a boxed set for you. Basic format – they whisk you back to your old home town in a limo, put you up in a luxury hotel, then you drive around and point out the sites, you go and see a few old friends and your family and then they whip out your family tree,

14

along with a few black and white photos and the odd black sheep, you ooh and ahh in all the right places, cry a bit and tell them it's been the most moving experience of your whole life.'

Helen laughed. 'You are such a cynic, Arthur.'

'And you're not?' Arthur asked, rolling the cigar for added dramatic emphasis.

'I didn't used to be. I was a nice girl when I first met you.'

He smiled gently. 'And you still are, Helen. Appearing on *Roots* will be a walk in the park for someone with your talent. Now – about my other plan. I've been thinking, while we're red hot and rolling, how about we reprise the one-woman show you used to do? I mean you don't have to be a genius to see that there's a tie-in here. You've got loads of material. Do a few songs, tell a few stories about the good old days, a behind-the-scenes look at *Cannon Square*, some jokes – and you've got those monologues you used to do. You know the kind of thing; *An Evening With* – what's the name of the town where you grew up?'

'Billingsfield.'

'Okay, well there you go then, Billingsfield's favourite daughter, Helen Redford, comes home to roost at long last. For one night only –' He lifted his hands, fingers spread to create an imaginary billboard. 'It shouldn't be that hard to find a venue, somewhere intimate and not too big.'

'You mean cheap.'

Arthur grinned. 'That isn't what I said, and that most certainly isn't what I meant, but I'm just thinking that that way we can test the waters; see what the response is. If it bombs then we've lost next to nothing and if it doesn't and we time it right then we could maybe take it on the road. I'll see if I can sort out a few dates – it can't hurt. Cash in on the TV show –'

'On the road?'

Arthur nodded. 'Yes, why not? It would be just like the good old days. You used to love it, remember? Take you right back to where you started from. Where was that place in Billingsfield?'

'The Carlton Rooms.'

He laughed. 'That's it. There you go then, that's where we should start the tour. You went down a storm there last time, remember?'

'Do you know how many years ago that was?' Helen laughed. 'Those rose-tinted spectacles are going to be the death of you, Arthur.'

'I thought I'd maybe have a chat with Ruth at *Roots* about it. See what we can organise. It would give their show a real focus too. And you never know, maybe we can work out a book deal on the back of the TV programme?'

Helen looked sceptical.

'What?' said Arthur.

'It's a bit late for all that, isn't it? Maybe ten years ago, when I was strapped to a gurney fighting for life, I might have swung it, but now? Memoirs of a has-been? The public have got a horribly short memory, Arthur.'

He pulled a face. 'For heaven's sake don't be so bloody hard on yourself, Helen; not if you're up there all over again, babe – and you could be. And let's face it, you've had an interesting life. Kids who're still wet behind the ears are writing bloody autobiographies these days – that little fat bird who got married to that footballer, and the one with the –' he mimed a pair of pantomime breasts. 'Kiss and tell, reality TV, it's all the go now, sweetie – and you'd be a natural. Everybody's doing it.'

'Doing what?' said a voice from the stairs. Helen looked up as Bon jogged into view. She could hear by the rhythm that he was taking the steps two at a time, which for some reason made her smile. Arthur rolled his eyes and looked heavenwards.

Bon was tall and blond with broad shoulders and a body that reflected all the hours of work he put in at the gym and in the studio. They'd met while she was doing pantomime in Croydon. She was playing the fairy godmother. He was in the chorus. Well, that's what they told people. Actually he had been doing the choreography for the show and had been standing in one night when one of the dancers was off sick, but it made a good story for the tabloids. He was somewhere in his late thirties but looked younger, while Helen was in her early fifties and looked well preserved.

She had never imagined ending up with a younger man. When they were alone together those things didn't matter; he made Helen laugh and she adored what they had, but in company the cliché sometimes made her defensive. It was obvious that Bon was younger than she was. She didn't dwell on exactly how many years but it was enough to be notable in the gossip columns. On the plus side, Bon was beautiful and kind, warm and funny, and he made up for all those men along the way who hadn't been, and – Helen kept telling herself – if it didn't turn out to be forever then as far as she was concerned what they had had was still worth it.

He smiled at her.

Sometimes, Helen knew, it was better to have a little drop of something wonderful than a whole lifetime of something ordinary. Two years on they were still together, although she often wondered if he saw her as a stopgap, a place marker to hold the page until the right woman came along, someone young whom he could have a family with – although she kept those thoughts to herself.

Even as the idea rolled through her head, Bon's smile broadened, and leaning closer he kissed her.

'Hiya honey,' he purred, his body language freezing Arthur out. 'Did anyone ever tell you that you look lovely, and you smell divine? I really love that perfume.'

Helen looked up at him. 'Birthday present from my lover,' she said.

From the corner of her eye she saw Arthur mime retching, and laughed, breaking the intimate connection between her and Bon. Bon glanced round and grinned. 'A bit too much for you at your age, Arthur?'

'Bit too much for anyone at any age,' huffed Arthur miserably.

'You're only jealous,' said Bon. 'So, what is it that you're up to?'

'Arthur was talking about people, more specifically me, writing their memoirs,' said Helen, as she pulled away.

'I think that you should do it,' Bon said. 'I've told you that before – you're a natural and I'm sure Arthur could get you a bit of help if you needed it, couldn't you Arthur? A ghost – I'm not saying you couldn't do it yourself –'

Helen laughed, 'Which I couldn't. But I know what you mean.'

'And how did the rest of the day go?'

'Arthur wants me to take my old show on the road.'

The words caught Bon's attention. 'Really? The one-woman show? But I thought you were talking to a television production company today, weren't you? I mean going on the road, that's great too – but it's not TV.'

'That's true,' said Helen. 'Arthur was saying we should think about touring again if the TV thing comes off – cash in on the exposure.'

Bon nodded. 'Sounds like a good idea. Okay, well if there is anything I can do to help – you know that I'd be really happy to help you rehearse.'

'Thank you.' Helen smiled. 'But never mind me. How did your meeting go?'

Bon opened his mouth to protest.

'No,' said Helen, stopping him with a gesture. 'Come on, 'fess up. I got in first. So?'

He groaned. 'So, nothing. Libby's thinking I should

19

maybe take the Dubai gig. She's really keen to get me out there; apparently she's got loads of really good contacts.'

Libby, the new agent that his old agency had assigned him, five feet two in her tiny stockinged feet and blonde and gorgeous and not a day over thirty. Helen slammed the door shut on the place her thoughts were heading and tried to ignore the giggling from behind it.

'Well, that's great,' Helen said. 'And it's well paid – I'd go for it.'

'It's a long way to go,' said Bon. 'And if you're serious about going on tour, you're going to need some backup. You know that I hate to leave you here on your own.'

'I can almost hear the violins from here. New high-lights?' said Arthur, conversationally, elbowing his way back into the conversation.

Helen sighed; at least Arthur had managed not to say that they had been touring while Bon was still in short trousers.

'Sun-kissed,' said Bon with a lazy grin, running long fingers back through his artfully tousled hair. 'It goes like that in the sunshine.'

Helen shook her head. 'Don't bait him, Bon, you know he hates it.'

Bon's grin broadened. 'You should try it some time, Arthur – get outside, get yourself a little bit of gold in the old toupee.'

'It's real,' Arthur growled.

'Real stoat?'

'Play nicely you two,' Helen said sharply.

'So how did *your* meeting go?' asked Bon.

'Not bad. Arthur has got me a job, haven't you, Arthur? *Roots*? The TV show – apparently I'm an icon.'

'Wow,' said Bon, interest piqued. 'God, now that *is* just fantastic. It's got a real following and you'll be great on there. When do you start shooting?'

'I haven't even signed the contract yet. I might not do it . . .'

Bon grinned. 'Why ever not? You'd be mad not to. You want anything?' he asked, heading towards the fridge.

'No, not for me, thanks. I've already got one.'

'Arthur?'

Arthur lifted his coffee mug instead of replying.

Bon dropped a handful of ice into the tumbler and topped it up with fruit juice. 'So when do you *think* you're going to start?'

'We're not sure yet. We'll be discussing dates next week,' said Arthur.

Helen couldn't take her eyes off Bon. He moved with a fluid grace that still made her mouth water. 'You are going to take it, aren't you?' he asked.

'I'm not sure.'

Bon pulled a face. 'Oh come on, Helen, you'd be absolutely mad not to. You'd be brilliant. They syndicate the show all over the world and then it ends up on the satellite channels.'

Arthur sighed. 'I've been trying to tell her that.'

21

'Don't tell me we've finally found something we're agreed on,' laughed Bon. 'By the way, are you staying for supper, Arthur? You're more than welcome. I thought I'd cook Thai tonight?'

Arthur sighed 'I really hate it when you're nice to me,' he said.

Helen smiled, ignoring the banter, her mind elsewhere. She'd come a long way since the Carlton Rooms in Billingsfield. Did she really want to go back?

TWO

Natalia, *Roots* resident researcher and the person assigned to *liaise* – whatever that meant – with Helen for the duration of the filming, perched on the edge of one of the big red shabby-chic sofas in Helen's sitting room, looking for all the world as if given half a chance she would be up on her toes and away. Natalia had her laptop bag balanced on her lap but so far hadn't unpacked it.

'Are you sure I can't get you a drink? A cup of tea? Herbal, green? Coffee?' asked Helen, settling herself down in the armchair opposite. 'We've got juice?'

The young woman blinked and stared at her, caught, anxious as a rabbit in the headlights. She retrieved a small plastic bottle from her handbag and waggled it to and fro, in a gesture Helen guessed was supposed to amuse.

'No, you're fine, really. I've got water, but really, thank you,' she said in her breathy little-girl voice. 'Now how we do it at *Roots* is that I'll be working with you all the way through, right through the filming and everything, so we can build up a relationship and you'll know the score. And you'll know that I know what I'm talking about because I'll have been here right from day one. So, I thought we'd just start with a few basics – get those out of the way first – and then maybe if you've got any photos? Did Ruth ask you about photos? Don't worry if she didn't, we can always get them later and we don't take them away or anything. I've brought a scanner with me.' She tapped her bag. 'And I've brought some cuttings and things for you to take a look at, you know, from the good old days.' She tipped her head down towards the bag again. 'Usually I've got this guy who comes with me and does all the technical stuff while we're talking, but he's got this bug. Jamie, you might have met him?'

Helen nodded. 'He thought I was an icon.'

The young woman smiled. 'Right, well he rang in to say he's got flu, well he thinks it's flu, but then again he is a man: probably just a sniffle. He usually does the driving too – you know if it's like somewhere off the beaten track, or the country or something –' Natalia carried on smiling; it was clear she meant a trip like this one.

Natalia, all turned out in her leather jacket, hand-knitted beanie hat, and a floral mini-dress worn over black leggings and twenty-eye black patent DMs had arrived two hours late, not so much fashionably late as horribly lost late, and from her colourful account of finally having tracked down Helen's house, she seemed to view rural Norfolk as if it was just a step away from the Amazon basin or the African veldt.

'How on earth do you manage out here?' she asked conversationally, taking a swig from her water bottle as she made an effort to slough off her oversized biker jacket. 'I mean it's so isolated; so far from anywhere.'

Helen raised an eyebrow. She lived in a handsome Victorian house in the middle of Denham Market, five minutes' walk from the town centre and two major supermarkets. It was hardly the Serengeti.

'It's an hour and a half from Kings Cross,' Helen said, pouring herself a mug of tea.

'Really?' The girl looked genuinely surprised. 'You mean like the trains come right out here?' she said.

Helen suppressed the desire to sigh and shake her head. 'Every hour.'

'*Really*?' repeated Natalia, unable to conceal her amazement, as she finally shrugged the jacket off. 'Well, wow – I mean that is really impressive. Anyway, as I said, I'm *delighted* to meet you. I'm so looking forward to working with you on your story,' she gushed. 'Jamie was really gutted that he's not here today. When I told my mum I was coming to talk to you today she was just so envious. My mum said that you were a legend. She used to watch you every week on *Cannon Square*. Right from the first episode. And Jamie's got them all on DVD right from episode one.' Natalia grinned. 'I think that the two of them were more excited than I was about me coming to meet you. Anyway, let's get down to business.'

Helen smiled at her; Natalia, twenty-six, had been best in show on her degree course, according to Ruth's latest email, which made Helen wonder whether there was anyone on the *Roots* production team who had just wandered in on the off chance of a job and got in on the strength of being nice, making good tea and being shit-hot with the filing.

'We always like to come out and see people in their own homes if we possibly can,' Natalia was saying earnestly. 'It's always nicer and makes it more intimate. I'm sure you read in the contract that we'll probably want to come and do some of the filming here too, you know, like background; give people an idea of how you live now. People are always fascinated by other people's houses, aren't they?' And then Natalia paused and looked anxiously over her shoulder. 'Do you think my car will be all right out there?'

'On my drive?'

Natalia nodded. 'I mean like it's locked and everything, but I was just wondering. You know.' Her voice tailed off. 'I was just wondering –'

'I'm sure it'll be fine. Whereabouts do you live?'

'Hackney,' Natalia said. 'We've got a flat, nowhere near as grand as this, obviously, but it's nice and really handy for work. My boyfriend and I keep saying once we have children we might like to move out – you know, to the country. Like Epping or Chadwell Heath or some-where. His mum and dad come from Cheshunt. I quite fancy Brighton myself.' She paused. 'It's the dark out here that would worry me; that and the quiet. And then you get the animals.' She shuddered. 'Me and my boyfriend went camping once, to the proper country. I wouldn't want to do it again; there were all these really weird snuffling noises in the night and then you had to go to the loo in a shed. With a torch. I still get flashbacks.

Anyway we really like to see how our guests live, see them in their own environment. And how they cope day to day, what they do, cooking and that kind of thing.' It made it sound as if Natalia was doing a home visit for social services. 'I mean this is really nice,' she said, peering around. 'Why do you live upstairs, is it like a flat or something?'

'No, I own the whole house. It's just that the main sitting room is on the first floor.'

'Right,' said Natalia, scribbling something down on her notepad. 'So, what, is the downstairs for your servants?'

Helen laughed. 'I wish. No, the kitchen is down there, and the utility room, and there's a gym and –'

'And so your staff live out, do they?' asked Natalia, pen poised above the pad.

Natalia had obviously worked with far grander stars in the past; or maybe she came from a generation that thought everyone on TV had an entourage of hired help dealing with the daily grind on their behalf.

'No, I don't really have any staff. We have Audrey who comes in to clean every day, and Bert, he comes in to help me with the garden –'

On the sofa Natalia was writing feverishly. 'And you live up here *because*?' She left the question hanging. Helen stared at her wondering what lurid possibility Natalia was considering.

'Because of the view,' said Helen, standing up and directing the young woman's attention towards the tall windows, with their plush window seats and piles of cushions. 'I really love the view from up here.'

Natalia stepped up beside her to take a look. '*The view*,' Natalia echoed.

Denham Market was built on the hill where Norfolk began to drag itself up out of the dark rich expanse of the fenland. Situated a few minutes' walk from the church, Helen's house was a Gothic gem, with a fairytale turret at one corner and huge rooms with vaulted ceilings and broad oak floors. At this time of the day the sun came flooding in through the mullioned windows, casting everything in a warm glow.

Up on the first floor, the open-plan double-aspect sitting room looked out over the gardens on one side and over the dark red pantiled rooftops of the houses in the streets below on the other, and beyond the town the glittering snake of the river Ouse, which wound its way across the flat lands of the fen. Beyond that as far as the eye could see were acres and acres of farmed fenland, flat as a billiard table, rich and fertile, lush green or black or gold, depending on the season, stretching out to Ely in the southwest and Long Sutton in the north-west.

It had been the view and the unique appearance of the house that had attracted Helen to it in the first place; it looked for all the world like a fairytale castle up on its hill close by the church. On a clear day it really did seem as if you could see forever. Compared to the tiny terraced house she had grown up in, the view alone at High House lifted Helen's spirits, the sense of space and freedom under the vast fenland sky finally letting her breathe.

'So did you always live round here?' asked Natalia, pen poised.

'No, I was born and grew up in Billingsfield. It was a factory town. It couldn't have been more different to Norfolk and this place. Number thirty-six Victoria Street; I'm sure I've probably got some photos somewhere. I remember as a little girl looking out of the front-room window of this tiny terraced house and having a horrible sense that I could easily be in the wrong one. Opposite me across the street was a house that was identical to mine, in a row of houses all identical to mine. All the doors were painted the same flat brown, all the windows had the same thick nets in the windows. Even thinking about it now after all these years it makes me shiver; it felt as if you couldn't breathe.'

Natalia nodded and made another note.

Helen didn't have that feeling living here. High House

was unique, a one-off, with no twin staring back at it, no neighbours peering in, making judgements on her family, from windows that faced each other across a strip of tarmac. No one teased or tormented her here. There was no lying in bed at night hearing the frenzied scuttling and scurrying and raised angry voices from the family whose bedroom adjoined hers. No, up here in High House there was only Helen and the people she invited in, which today included Natalia, who was busy peering out of the window, probably trying to work out what all the fuss was about.

'Over there on a clear day you can see Ely Cathedral,' said Helen, pointing into the distance.

Alongside her Natalia stifled a yawn. 'I'm not much of a one for views,' she said.

'So,' said Helen, now that it was obvious her audience had moved on. 'What else would you like to know?'

Natalia settled herself back on the sofa. 'I'm not sure how much you know about the show but in the first segment we talk about you and what you do or did. There's usually some film clips, some interviews with friends and colleagues, that sort of thing – and then we explore where you came from and we look around the places where you grew up and talk to people who knew you. And then we explore your roots.'

'Which means what exactly?' asked Helen.

The girl looked surprised. 'I'm not sure I'm with you?'

'Well, *which* roots?'

'Presumably you've seen the show. Your parents and

any interesting ancestors we throw up when we do your family tree. We've got this great guy, Alan – well, when I say *great*; he's a bit of an acquired taste – he doesn't like real live people very much. He likes to stay in the office and he wears cotton gloves and a mask a lot of the time, and he's got this whole thing about pens – but he's brilliant when it comes to research. Anyway, you see that's the thing with *Roots*; we don't just tie ourselves to the historical, that's the beauty of the format, we just follow our noses on the good stories. So, like with Terry Haslam – you know, the civil rights bloke? Well his dad, Jack, used to be a strongman in the circus, so we took a look at how Terry had grown up, and that whole nomadic circus culture. It was funny because most people talk about running away to join the circus, but in Terry's case he ran away to join the Church. Terry's heritage was amazing – his dad's family came from Transylvania and his mum came from somewhere in Somerset.

'Anyway, it was really weird; we took the crew out to this funny little village to film. I mean it was truly spooky. I've never been *anywhere* like that before – and the locals were just so peculiar, they kept pointing and laughing – and anyway Jeremy, the sound guy, bought us all these strings of garlic.' Natalia paused to take a sip of water. 'Transylvania was a complete doddle by comparison.'

'I'm not sure that there is anything that interesting in my family,' said Helen.

Natalia waved the words away. 'Oh don't worry. Everyone I work with always says that but we usually poke around till we find something, and to be perfectly honest, if Ruth's signed you up to do the show, then there's something we can get our teeth into or she wouldn't be doing it.'

The remark caught Helen off guard. She stared at Natalia. 'I'm sorry?' she began. 'What are we talking about here?'

The girl reddened. 'Sorry, but I don't suppose I'm telling you anything you don't already know, Helen. We all know that there is an elephant in the room when it comes to your past. I don't want to be tactless about it – but it's not exactly rocket science, is it? We'll start off with your parents –'Helen waited.

'Your mum? The whole motherhood, abandoned children thing, I mean I'm assuming you'd have realised what we'd be going for here – a sort of *cherchez la femme* angle. Looking at the kind of woman who leaves her child behind and the reasons why. Why? What did you think we were going to do?'

Helen couldn't think of anything to say, but it was fine because Natalia was firing up her laptop and had all the answers on hand. 'You see what I'm saying here, Helen? There's no point us dragging up some unknown Elizabethan sailor from God knows where, when we've got a story like that to unpick, really, is there? It's just too good not to use –'

'I'm sure you think I'm being naïve here, but I thought Ruth said that it would be mostly historical?'

'Well, sometimes it is, but mostly –' Natalia hesitated,

'To be honest *mostly* it isn't. The last series everything was pretty much about this generation and maybe the last one. You know, like their mums and dads – people like all that sort of stuff. And of course your mum vanished too, so realistically that is just too good a story not to go after.'

'She didn't vanish,' said Helen, dry-mouthed. 'It wasn't like some sort of conjuring trick. Are you telling me that is going to be the main focus of the programme?'

'We've got other angles too, obviously. I don't have to tell you your own secrets, do I?' She smiled. Helen stared at her; what did that mean?

'So are you saying you've found my mother?'

Totally wrong-footed Natalia stared at her, trying to compose herself. 'No, no, that's not what I'm saying at all.'

At which moment Bon came up from the gym, dressed in sweat pants and an indigo blue tee shirt. His tee shirt was soaked with sweat across the chest, underarms and back.

'Hi,' he said with a grin, wiping his hands on the white towel draped across his broad shoulders. He looked like a character from a wholesome-life advert. 'I see your guest arrived then,' he said to Helen, as he strode over and extended a hand towards Natalia. 'I'm Bon Fisher. Great to meet you. You must be Natalia, from *Roots*, is that right?'

Natalia's mouth had dropped open. 'Bon?' she managed, and for a few seconds Helen caught a glimpse of what it was others saw in him. His face, though classically handsome, was still masculine and rugged, manly rather than fey; and his eyes, bright blue and clear as high summer skies, were surrounded by a corona of laughter lines. But what made him infinitely more attractive was that he had this warm sunny aura that was hard to quantify or to miss.

'That's right, I'm Helen's lover,' he continued, without so much as a hint of hesitation, as he shook her hand. 'But presumably if you're working on Helen's life story you already know all about that. Delighted to meet you. Helen is the most amazing woman.' He turned to look at her affectionately. 'Amazing. I'm really lucky to share my life with her.' He moved across the room and brushed his lips across Helen's, which made something inside her flutter; he was gorgeous. She glanced up at him, wondering not for the first time if this was some kind of cruel trick. 'God only knows why she puts up with me.'

Natalia reddened and opened her mouth to say something, but Bon didn't pause to let her catch up. 'Anyway, I'm just going to go and grab a shower and then I'll fix us some lunch. You are staying for lunch, aren't you, Natalia? I realise it's a bit late but we've both had a busy morning –'

The girl glanced at Helen who nodded. 'Please,' Helen said. 'You'd be more than welcome, and Bon is a superb cook.'

'Well, yes then, sure, if it's okay with you.'

'Got to be better than a supermarket sandwich,' Bon

said. 'I'm thinking hot spicy shredded chicken with avocado on baby leaves drizzled with raspberry vinaigrette. Does that sound all right to you?'

'Sounds fabulous,' said Natalia.

Helen laughed in spite of herself. 'Don't encourage him,' she said and then smiled up at Bon. 'He thinks about food all the time he's working out. I have no idea why he doesn't weigh twenty stone. I keep thinking that one of these days we should open a restaurant.'

Bon bent down and kissed her. 'And how boring would that be, cooking the same thing over and over? Lunch in say, half an hour?'

'Fine by me; how about you, Natalia?'

The girl nodded.

'Great,' said Bon. 'Oh and I've got a meeting at four. Libby and I are working on the costumes for the show we're taking to Dubai –' he continued, aiming his remarks at Helen. *Libby*. It felt like he was mentioning her a lot lately.

'You're a dancer, that's right, isn't it?' Natalia was saying, pen poised over her pad.

Bon nodded. 'Yes, that's right, although I'm actually more about the choreography these days, and I've helped produce some of the shows we take out on tour.'

'We?' said Natalia, all eagerness and enthusiasm, clutching her pen. 'Is this something new for you, Helen?'

'Don't look at me,' said Helen, holding up her hands. 'I can't dance and have no intention of taking it up now. No, this is definitely Bon's baby.'

'Mine and Libby's,' Bon said. 'Libby Sherwood, she's my agent.'

There she was again.

'So how long have you and Helen been together?' Natalia asked.

Bon smiled. 'Not long enough. Now I really have to go. I'll give you a shout when food's ready. You okay for drinks?'

'I'm fine,' said Helen.

'Me too,' said Natalia brightly, doing her little trick with the water bottle. Helen watched Natalia watch Bon cross the room and head back down the stairs.

After a second or two Natalia turned back to Helen and realised Helen had been watching her watching him. She bit her bottom lip and looked horribly self-conscious.

'He seems very nice,' Natalia said with feigned casualness, turning her attention quickly back to her notepad.

Helen laughed. 'Oh, he is. And he has got the cutest arse, hasn't he?'

Natalia turned pillar-box red and was about to protest.

'It's fine,' said Helen with a smile. 'You're welcome to admire the scenery – lots of people do.'

Natalia's colour deepened. 'Where were we?' she said, faffing around with her notebook and laptop in what appeared to be a show of regaining her composure.

'My mother,' suggested Helen helpfully.

'Oh yes,' said Natalia, with equal discomfort.

'I'm not the only little girl whose mother walked out on her family.'

'I know,' said Natalia. 'But it is something that a lot of people will be curious about. It must have had a profound effect on you. On your relationships; on your own views on children and families.'

'I didn't have children,' said Helen briskly. 'So it didn't arise.'

'Was that because of your mum?' pressed Natalia.

Helen shook her head. 'No, it hadn't got anything to do with her. I suppose it must have had an effect, but I was open to the idea of having a family. I was just never with the right person at the right time.' She paused. Natalia was scribbling away furiously. When Helen stopped she looked up.

'I'm sorry,' Natalia said. 'You were saying?'

'I suppose looking back if I had wanted them enough I would have had them, but it didn't happen.'

'It didn't happen,' she repeated.

'No,' said Helen. 'There was always another job, another part, always something else coming along, and then it was just too late.'

'And so you don't think that was because of your mum?'

Helen shook her head. 'No, quite the reverse; in some ways her leaving made me make more of my life. I probably took more chances, more risks, enjoyed all of life while it was there. Her going made me realise that nothing is as safe as it first appears. But it wasn't just me, it affected my dad too, his work – his friends. I was very small when it happened, but I was old enough to know something was going on; old enough to miss her, but not old enough for anyone to explain it to me. In those days I'm not sure how much notice people took of children's emotions. I think because children hadn't got the words to express what they were feeling people just assumed they didn't feel anything – although to be fair, no-one really talked about my mum once she was gone. No-one at all. It was like a door had opened up somewhere and she just walked through it. Some days I wonder if I imagined her and that perhaps she had never existed at all.'

'Did you think she was dead?' asked Natalia.

Helen watched the younger woman's face carefully, wondering what it was that *Roots* had managed to uncover. Natalia's body language gave nothing away.

'I didn't know then, and I don't know now. I still don't have any idea what happened to her.'

'It's such an interesting thread. Weren't you ever curious? I'm sure I would have been. Didn't you try to find her?'

'No,' snapped Helen.

Natalia looked surprised. 'What, never?'

'Like I said, no one talked about her at home and back then I was powerless to look; looking or asking would have felt like I was betraying my dad. And what if me asking too many questions made him go away too? I remember reading in the Sunday papers about people losing their memories and wondered if that was what had happened to her and that maybe one day, some day she would remember us and just come home.

'I had a lady to come in and sit with me if my dad was going to be late home from work. Mrs Eades. I didn't like her very much and I was terrified that she might end up looking after me permanently if my dad didn't come back – but no, I didn't look, I didn't ask.'

Helen glanced across; Natalia was busy making copious notes.

'Please,' she pressed , when Helen stopped speaking, 'It's really interesting.'

'I did think when I was first on the TV that maybe my mum might show up then; you know: "Long-lost mother reunited with celebrity daughter". It's the kind of thing the tabloids have always loved. Real Max Clifford territory. But she didn't.'

'And you'll be happy to talk about all this on the show?' asked Natalia.

Helen nodded, 'Yes, I suppose so.'

Natalia scribbled something else on her pad. 'So you thought that she was probably dead?'

'Or that she had run off with someone, remarried and not told her new family about me and Dad; or that she'd emigrated or just plain didn't care,' said Helen, conscious of the crackle of emotion in her voice.

'Didn't you think about hiring someone? A detective or something?' Natalia pressed, with a hint of accusation in her tone. 'I don't think I could have lived with not knowing, and you had the money –'

'There is a lot more to my life than what happened to my mother. Not everything I've done is about her.'

Helen took a deep breath. 'And it might seem like a hard thing for you to understand, Natalia, but no, I didn't go looking for her. She rejected me once; I didn't want to give her the chance to reject me again.'

Natalia winced. 'I hadn't thought about it like that,' she said, before setting off on another tack. 'One of the things that struck me when I was looking through the press cuttings and what we've got on file for you, is how little there is. There is a lot about your awards and TV roles but not very much about the woman behind the actress.'

'I've always been very private.'

Natalia nodded and made a note. 'Until now,' she said, watching Helen intently.

'That's right.' Helen said. 'Until now.'

'Can you tell me why that is?'

Helen looked her squarely in the eye. 'Because you asked me – and to be honest I miss working on interesting projects with interesting people. I'm an actress. I want to work. I can't skate, I hate ballroom dancing and I'm not cut out for roughing it in the jungle. So it's this or –'

'*Celebrity Come Dine With Me?*' Natalia suggested helpfully. She pulled out a file. 'Okay, so we've got some newspaper clippings, reviews and things which we'll be using that I'd like you to take a look through. Oh and this –' she handed Helen the photocopy of a page from the *Billingsfield Echo*. 'I can't make out the date,' said Natalia. 'We'll probably need to chase that up, unless of course you can remember when it was? National talent competition, Carlton Rooms?' She leaned across, reading over Helen's shoulder. 'March the something – no, it's no good, I can't make out the year. But here we are, look –' she said, pointing to a grainy black and white photo of the contestants. 'Local songbirds, Helen Redford and – hang on I've got a magnifying glass in my bag.'

'Kate Monroe,' said Helen, tipping the photocopy towards the light. 'It was a Saturday – the 15th of March, and that was the first night we'd used our stage names; before that we used to be Helen Heel and Charlotte Johnson.'

THREE

Then

'You'll be fine, Helen,' snapped Charlotte. 'For God's sake just stop worrying, will you, and pass me the eyeliner.' Charlotte took it and then leant forward to dab concealer on her chin. 'You know, the light in this room is terrible. You should really get his nibs to get you a lamp or something for this dressing table.' She turned to face Helen. 'So what do you think? Can you still see that spot?' She tipped her chin up towards the light. 'It looks like Vesuvius from where I'm sitting.'

'That's because you're three inches away from it, anything that close up is bound to look big,' said Helen, who was sitting on the end of the bed, struggling to do her makeup in a tiny hand mirror. She felt sick.

Charlotte was right, though, the light in the bedroom wasn't good; but Helen was so full of nerves that she didn't really care. Helen took a closer look at her reflection; she was so pale and drawn it looked as if she might be coming down with something. 'And I've already told you, Charlotte, this is Harry's bedroom. The light in here is nothing to do with me. All right?'

'So you say,' Charlotte teased. 'Anyway, we could hardly get ready in your room, could we? It's like a bloody shoebox in there. How on earth do you manage? There's barely enough room for the bed. Where do you put all your clothes and shoes and things? It's a good job you're tidy; it wouldn't suit me at all,' Charlotte continued, turning her attention back to the mirror. 'The whole place would be a tip in ten minutes. A bit like this place really,' she giggled.

Helen looked round Harry's bedroom; Charlotte was right. There were things everywhere – shoes all over the floor, clothes and makeup spilling out of the suitcase Charlotte had brought with her; their coats were slung on the bed along with their costumes and handbags. Harry's bedroom looked like someone was running an impromptu jumble sale.

Getting ready for the show at Harry's flat had been Charlotte's idea.

'Anyway, it's your fault we're here. I thought that we were going to get ready at your house,' said Helen, rolling on a slick of lip gloss. 'That's what your dad said when he came into the shop yesterday. He said he'd come into town and pick me up if there wasn't a bus.'

'I know,' said Charlotte. 'There's a lot more room at my place obviously, but Harry's flat is so much nearer to the Carlton Rooms.'

'Your dad told me he was going to drive us in.'

'Yes, all right, Helen, don't keep on about it. I *know* what my dad said, okay? But he can be so bossy and so narrow-minded, interfering all the time – and *yes*, I know he's on my side and everything, but he's just so over-protective. This is better; we can please ourselves here. He's really getting on my nerves.' Charlotte screwed up her face and dropped straight into a cruel impersonation of her father. '*Don't do this, don't say that, don't you sign anything, not so much as an autograph without me reading it first, do you hear, Charlie? It's for your own good, young lady* He treats me like I'm a complete idiot. He nearly had fifty fits when he saw the costumes I'd had made for tonight. *Too short. Too low. Too clingy.* God only knows what he is going to be like when I finally get discovered, or come to that when I go off to teacher training in September.'

'You're still going, then?' said Helen, concentrating her efforts on finishing off her mascara.

'Oh yes,' said Charlotte, sagely. 'Finish my A levels and then on to teacher training, unless of course I get discovered in the meantime. Teaching will give me some-thing to fall back on if the singing doesn't pan out. I'm not totally daft despite what my dad thinks. And anyway, it's more fun being here; I wanted to see where you and Harry lived. You two, all tucked up in your little love nest,' she continued in the same teasing voice.

Before Helen could reply there was a sharp knock on the door.

'God, that made me jump,' gasped Charlotte with a nervous giggle. 'Good job I wasn't doing my eyeliner.' And then she called out, 'Hello, who is it?'

Helen rolled her eyes. 'It's Harry, who else is it going to be? It's his flat. Can you just pass me a tissue?'

'Could be the press, dahling,' said Charlotte, striking a pose and putting on a big starry voice as she handed Helen a box of Kleenex. 'Or maybe it's TV people, wanting to come in and do an interview with the next big thing.'

'*Things*,' corrected Helen, sitting down alongside Charlotte on the dressing-table stool so that she could see herself in the big mirror. 'Shift up a bit, will you. There *are* two of us, remember?'

'I meant collectively, you and me, we *are* the next big thing. I keep thinking that that is what we should call ourselves: 'The Next Big Thing'. It sounds good, don't you think? Although 'Wild Birds' has got a nice ring to it too. Sort of sexy and cheeky and a bit risqué. I'm glad I thought of it – it's good, memorable; even if I do say so myself.'

Harry knocked again.

'Hang on a minute,' called Charlotte. 'We just want to get ourselves decent.' She leaned forward again to brush away a speck of something on her cheek. 'He's keen. You did drop the music off, didn't you?'

'I've already told you. Yes. I did it during my lunch break yesterday. Front office, Mr Tully, just like you said. He said that we need to be there for a run-through and a sound check by half past five.' As she spoke Helen glanced at the clock; time was getting on. 'We should really let Harry in, see what he wants. We need to be going soon.'

'*Sound checks*. That sounds as if we've already arrived, doesn't it?' Charlotte said approvingly. 'You know we should have brought some wine or something to drink while we were getting ready, maybe splashed out and bought a bottle of champagne, like real pop stars do. So –' she said, pointing with her makeup brush to the palette on the dressing table. 'Do you think I should go with the blue glitter eye shadow or purple?'

Through the door Harry shouted, 'Are you decent in there yet?'

Charlotte raised her eyebrows. 'Depends what you mean, really, doesn't it?' she called. And then she glanced at Helen. 'Are you and him –' She nodded towards the double bed that dominated the tiny bedroom and which was currently strewn with Charlotte and Helen's clothes. 'You know.'

Helen reddened furiously. 'No. God, no,' she protested. 'No, it's not like that at all. I'm just living here because –' she hesitated, not wanting to get into any long conversations about the state of her home life, 'because, it's easier for everyone, that's all. And convenient. You know what the buses are like out our way. Five minutes' walk from here and I'm slap-bang in the middle of town. That's all.'

'That isn't how it looks from where I'm standing.

Come on, Helen, don't be so coy; you can tell me,' purred Charlotte conspiratorially. 'Harry follows you around like a dog and he can't take his eyes off you, you know that. Although personally I've always seen him more as Buttons than Prince Charming. I mean, don't get me wrong, he's sweet – but he's a bit wet, isn't he?'

Helen glared at her. 'No he isn't,' she said. 'Harry's really kind.'

'Well, you would know,' purred Charlotte. 'You'd have to be blind not to notice how much he fancies you. What do you want? A neon sign? Him down on one knee? A nice fat diamond? Oh my God, is that what you're hanging out for?' She laughed. 'Don't tell me. You're saving yourself till you're married?'

'No, don't be ridiculous,' said Helen more forcefully, feeling her face redden under Charlotte's scrutiny. 'I mean, I like Harry, but not like that. He's a friend – a really good friend.'

'So you say. If that's true why are you blushing?'

To try and divert Charlotte's attention Helen nodded towards the little pots on the dressing table. 'I'd go with the blue if I were you. The purple makes you look like you've got a black eye.'

'Oh, bugger the eye shadow. I want to talk about Harry. He's not that bad a catch when you look at it, he's quite nice looking – he's got his own flat, own car, and his dad's got his own business. You could do a lot, lot worse, you know,' whispered Charlotte. 'I'd be in there if I were you.'

'Stop it,' hissed Helen. 'He'll hear you.'

Right on cue Harry shouted through the door, 'Look, I don't want to rush you in there, ladies, but we really need to be leaving in about fifteen minutes if you want to be there by half past. It's going to be busy in town and I'll need to find somewhere to park.'

Charlotte glanced at her watch. 'Oh, come on, don't be such an old woman, Harry,' she shouted back. 'I reckon if we leave in half an hour we'll have plenty of time. Why don't you come in?' She gave Helen a long sly wink. 'Keep us company. Help Helen fill in these entry forms.'

A split second later Harry peered around the door, grinning like a loon, his expression a subtle mixture of nervousness and expectation. 'Hi, how's it all going in here?' he asked. 'You all ready, are you?'

Charlotte gave him the full benefit of her *come and get me* smile while peering up at him sexily from under her long sooty black lashes. 'Why don't you come on in and judge for yourself, Harry,' she purred. 'What do you think?' She batted her lashes like a film star.

Harry blushed scarlet. 'Lovely, really lovely,' he stammered. 'You both look amazing.'

Helen groaned and looked away. The two of them were still in their dressing gowns. In Charlotte's case a skimpy, bright, red, silky, kung-fu, just-above-the-knee number that left very little to the imagination; and in Helen's, a long tartan one that she had bought from a charity shop on the walk home from work, when she realised that she couldn't wander about in her nightie with Harry around. As it was he still went bright crimson as soon as she opened her bedroom door in the mornings, and he'd been so kind to her that she didn't want to cause him any more problems.

'I'm *very* glad that we meet with your approval,' Charlotte purred, pulling out a fold of papers from her handbag. 'Have you got a pen on you?'

Helen knew from experience that Harry was the kind of young man who always had a pen to hand. He tapped the top pocket of his jacket. 'Here we are,' he said. 'What colour do you want?'

Charlotte waved the words away. 'We don't mind what colour it is; the thing is, Harry, as you can see we're both really busy. We were hoping you'd fill in our entry forms for us, weren't we, Helen? While we finish getting ready.'

Helen looked up at him and smiled warmly. Harry's father, Helen's boss at the toy shop where she worked, had given her and Harry the afternoon off for all this. Harry grinned self-consciously and hastily turned his attention to the papers he'd been given. 'So what do you want me to do?' He said.

'We were supposed to fill them in when we went for the auditions,' said Charlotte, her gaze wandering back to her own reflection as she set about finishing off her makeup. 'But we didn't go because my dad knows the people at the Carlton Rooms and they said we didn't need to audition, but we really need all that stuff done before the show tonight. And you seem like the natural choice; Helen said you're really good at that sort of thing. You know, like organising and giving Helen a helping hand with things.'

Harry reddened furiously.

Helen shot her a look. Charlotte winked. 'So can you do it?'

Harry flicked through the forms, while Charlotte patted her nose with a powder puff and then sat back, turning her head left and right to admire the overall effect. 'So, what do you think? Perfect or what?' she asked, striking a pose.

Harry, oblivious, was concentrating on the entry form. He glanced up at Helen and frowned. 'I'm not sure about all this,' he began.

'How about you read out the questions and we'll answer them?' Helen said quietly. 'I mean it's not like it's an exam or anything.'

Harry nodded. 'Okay. Fair enough.'

At the dressing table Charlotte was adding a great gash of bright orange lipstick. 'Uhuh, and then we better get a move on or we'll be late, won't we Harry,' she said, heavy on the sarcasm. 'How old are you?'

'Why?'

'Well, whoever signs those has got to be over twenty-one.'

'I'm twenty-two, nearly twenty-three,' said Harry.

'That's okay then. So what's the first question?'

'Name of the act?'

'Well, that's easy enough, we're the Wild Birds,' said Charlotte with a grin. 'Wild by name and wild by nature, isn't that right, Helen?'

This time it was Helen who blushed.

Dutifully Harry wrote it in. 'And what type of act are you?'

'We're singers,' said Helen.

'Female vocalists,' corrected Charlotte. 'We're an all girl duo, and we're really good. I mean you've heard us, Harry? We're bloody brilliant, aren't we? They're going to love us tonight, I know it.'

Harry laughed and then bit down thoughtfully on the end of his biro; there was obviously no section set aside for boasting.

'They want to know what kind of material you do. You know, like what sort of songs you sing?' he continued, still reading.

'Carly Simon, Roberta Flack.'

'Simon and Garfunkel,' added Helen.

'Uhuh, okay,' he said, while still writing, 'And your names –'

'Wait,' snapped Charlotte, holding up her hand to stop him. 'Before you write anything down, let me think about that.'

'What do you mean?' said Helen. 'What is there to think about?' She turned back to Harry. 'Helen Heel and Charlotte Johnson.'

'Whoa there, just hang on a minute, don't write anything yet,' said Charlotte before Harry had a chance to put pen to paper. 'This is our big chance, our big moment. We could get discovered tonight, Helen. Do you want to be plain old Helen Heel for the rest of your life? Good old down-at-heel?'

Helen felt a tiny residual prickle of pain and indignation at the old playground insult.

'Well, *do* you?' repeated Charlotte, more forcefully. 'Because I sure as hell know I don't. I don't want to be Johnny Johnson's little Charlie, the girl who should have been a boy, Daddy's little girl, forever. I want to be *somebody*, not just Charlotte Johnson. *Helen Heel and Charlotte Johnson*. It makes us sound so ordinary. And we're not ordinary.' She struck a pose and then grinned. 'Well, at least, I'm not. How about Kate Monroe and Helen Hepburn?'

Helen laughed. 'Where on earth did that come from?' she said.

'I've been thinking about it for while now,' said Charlotte. 'It's time we reinvented ourselves.'

'Oh, Charlotte,' Helen said.

But Harry didn't laugh – instead he nodded. 'You know, Charlotte, you're right, that's not such a bad idea. You should really have a stage name. Kate Monroe, that sounds lovely.' To her surprise Helen felt a tiny prickle of envy. 'I'm not so sure about Helen Hepburn though,' he continued. 'How about Hemingway? Helen Hemingway, that sounds really classy.'

Both girls shook their heads.

'Too long for the billboards,' said Charlotte. 'And it's

way too fussy. People won't know how to spell it. No, we need something catchy and memorable.'

'Hang on a minute then,' said Harry, picking up the evening paper from the bedside table.

'What on earth are you doing?' asked Helen. 'Please don't tell me you're looking at births, deaths and marriages?'

Harry laughed. 'No, I just thought I'd see what was on at the Odeon.'

'You planning a trip to the pictures?' asked Helen incredulously.

'Don't be daft. I was just thinking we could look to see what's on and who's in it; see if any of the names go with Helen.'

'I'm not sure I even like Helen, not really,' Helen began, not that either Harry or Charlotte were taking any notice of her.

'How about Helen McQueen?' said Charlotte, reading over Harry's shoulder and pointing. 'Oh or how about Helen Brando, or Helen Eastwood?'

'No,' said Harry. 'You need to take this seriously. We've only got another ten minutes and then we really have to be going or we're not going to be there in time for the run-through.'

If Charlotte had any other opinion about how much time it would take to get to the theatre, this time she kept it to herself, and instead she took a long hard look at the cinema programme. 'Okay. There we are. I've got it. The Sting. Helen Redford or Helen Newman. What do you reckon?'

Harry nodded. 'They both sound good to me. Classy but of the people.'

Helen stared at him. '*Of the people*? What on earth is that supposed to mean, Harry?'

Neither of them appeared to be listening to her; instead Charlotte nodded. 'I just knew you were the man for the job, Harry. I've been thinking – if we get discovered tonight we're going to need a manager to handle all this sort of stuff for us. You know, doing the forms and the booking and sorting out the transport, and working the money out, and all that sort of thing. What do you reckon, do you think you'd be up to it?'

Helen stared at her in amazement while Harry, pulling back his shoulders and coming over all manly, appeared genuinely flattered. 'Well,' he began, 'I'm not sure – I suppose I could always give it a go –'

'Wait,' said Helen. 'Charlotte, stop it. You know what your dad said about not saying anything or signing anything?'

Charlotte laughed. 'Which is why we're here getting changed and not over at my place. And anyway this is different. This is our business. What do you say, Harry?'

'Harry, don't say anything,' Helen said quickly. 'Charlotte, Harry doesn't know anything about show business,' she protested. It sounded disloyal but she was trying hard to protect Harry from Charlotte – not that it appeared to be doing any good.

'Oh, come on, Helen, he's a natural, aren't you, Harry?' said Charlotte. 'He'd be perfect. And we both know him and we trust him, and he manages his dad's shop, doesn't he? And you're always saying what a good job he does.' Charlotte gave Helen a great big pantomime wink.

'Stop it,' Helen said, but Charlotte was on a roll.

'You can do it, can't you, Harry? I reckon you'd be ideal for the job.'

'Well, I'm not sure about that,' Harry said, wriggling uncomfortably under Charlotte's attention. Even so, Helen could see he was being persuaded by her flattery.

'Of course you are,' said Charlotte, patting him on the shoulder. 'Anyway we can talk about all that later. Back to business. Names. What do you think? Helen Redford or Helen Newman?'

Harry was busy pulling a coin out of his trouser pocket. 'Heads for Redford, tails for Newman. Okay, Helen?'

Before Helen could reply he had flipped the coin up into the air. It spun over and over, catching the light as it peaked and then began to fall. She watched it with an odd detachment as Harry caught it, slapped it down onto the back of his hand and then peeled away his fingers to reveal the coin.

'Heads,' he said. 'It's heads.'

FOUR

Before Filming Starts

'Helen? You're awake, aren't you?' Bon said, rolling over onto his side and propping his head up on his hand.

She could see him from under her lashes but lay very still and kept very quiet, keeping her breaths shallow and even, hoping to persuade him that she was asleep.

'You don't fool me, you know,' he said, when she didn't respond. 'It's no use pretending. You've been tossing and turning all night. What's the matter?'

'I'm sorry. I didn't mean to wake you,' Helen said, finally conceding defeat.

'I'm not worried about being awake. I'm worried about why *you're* awake,' he said, brushing a stray tendril of hair back off her face. His touch was gentle, his fingertips cool against the warmth of her skin, his eyes glittering like jet in the half-light of the early morning. 'I heard you wandering about in the night. Do you want to talk about it, whatever it is?'

Helen sighed. 'Not really. Oh, I don't know. I'm really not sure about all this.'

'About all what? Look, if it's about me going to Dubai, why don't you come with me? We could shut up the house. Let's face it, we could both do with some sun, and it's only for six weeks. It'll be fun. We could get a little apartment. I could talk to Libby –'

'No, no, it's not that,' said Helen, cutting him short. She didn't want Bon talking to Libby about her; she didn't want him to make her sound needy or insecure.

'Well, what, then?' He let the silence open up between them until she couldn't bear it any longer.

'It's this whole *Roots* thing.'

'I thought you were really keen on the idea.'

'No, no, I'm not, but Arthur is – mind you he's keen about anything that'll earn him a few quid. He sees it as my way back into prime time; it's just that I'm not sure that it's such a good idea after all.'

'But I thought you were happy about it. Arthur seems to think that it's the best thing that could happen to you. A new start, a ticket out – that's what he said, and who knows what it might lead to, Helen? It's a real showcase for you. I was looking at the viewing figures online – it's international, you know; it goes out all over the world and then it ends up on Dave.'

Helen raised her eyebrows. 'I know and you know as

57

well as I do that Arthur's got his eye fixed firmly on his ten per cent.'

Bon laughed. 'Come on, Helen, I think you're being way too hard on him. He wouldn't see you doing something you weren't happy with.'

'How long have you known him?' asked Helen incredulously. 'Are we talking about *the same* Arthur?'

'You know what I mean, he tempers a healthy mercenary streak with a huge heart. And he loves you; he's always loved you.'

Helen nodded. 'Yes, but –'

'Well then trust him. He wouldn't do anything to hurt you. Anyway what it is you're unhappy about?' continued Bon. 'You know your own life story. You know where the bodies are buried, and okay so it probably will be painful and I'm sure you'll shed a few tears –'

She bit her lip and Bon pulled her closer.

'Sorry, that was insensitive, but that's what *Roots* is good at. I think it'll be the most fantastic opportunity for you and you're overdue a break. You don't know what might come out of it. Film, a book? TV?'

'You know, you're even beginning to sound a lot like Arthur.'

Bon smiled. 'And I love you too, you know. But if you don't want to do it, then don't. It's not too late to pull out.'

Helen smiled. 'That's exactly what Arthur said.'

'Well, there you are, it's got to be right then, hasn't it?'

Helen glanced at the bedside clock. Another few hours

and she'd have to be up and in the rehearsal room they'd booked, putting the finishing touches to the new show she was taking on the road. The costumes had arrived, the pre-publicity had gone out and ticket sales were doing well. Helen and Arthur were just putting the running order together, finalising the script, the music and the songs.

'You'll be perfect,' Bon was saying. 'Do you want me to come to Billingsfield with you? I'm really happy to cancel –'

'No,' Helen said emphatically, cutting him short. 'You don't have to cancel anything, okay? The Dubai show is important for you, and besides, I'm a big girl now. I'll be fine. Really.'

'You know you don't have to be tough with me.' He grinned. 'Who are you trying to convince?'

Helen smiled; it felt as if Bon had been reading her mind. 'It's just that I haven't been back to Billingsfield for such long time.'

'Well, other than going home to see my mum once in a while I don't hang out in my old home town that much either. Life moves on, we grow up and we move away. That's how it goes. What are you so worried about?' He didn't say it lightly but earnestly, in a voice that made Helen turn and look at him.

The light of the new day was forcing its way between the slats of the wooden Venetian blinds, its rays creeping up and over the bed to catch the blonde in his hair, throwing his strong uncomplicated good looks into sharp relief.

Helen sighed and shook her head. 'You know, the usual stuff – there are just so many reasons: the people, the places, the ghosts from the past, all the things that made me leave in the first place. I'm not sure that I want to go back to all that again.'

This time Bon laughed. 'You should have thought about that before you said you'd do it. Where did you think they'd go back to look at your roots? Another town, another life, another Helen Redford?'

'I know you're right. I suppose I just didn't really think it through. It seemed like such a good thing and I was really flattered to be asked out of the blue like that, and Arthur was so bloody keen and persuasive, you know what he can be like – a real dog with a bone when he gets an idea into his head. And now it's almost here I'm starting to think I've made the most terrible mistake. I'm not sure that I can go back,' she said, annoyed by the emotion crackling in her voice.

His expression softened. 'Because?'

'Because I just can't, Bon, that's why. I'm going to have to talk to Arthur, ring them up, and explain. I've come a long way since Billingsfield. It's not that I'm ashamed of where I came from but it wasn't as if I lived this fabulous life there, and then went on to fame and fortune, things were – were –' She hesitated, struggling to find the right words.

'Things were what? Hard? Complicated? Difficult? You know as well as I do that's exactly what people like about those shows. They like to see how you dragged yourself up from nothing. It makes other people think that they can do it too. Inspirational, aspirational; TV audiences love that kind of thing. And then there are some of them looking at where you came from and thinking their life is damned good compared to what you had to go through and they're glad they didn't have to go through it to get where they are.'

Helen stared at him. 'And what exactly have I been through, Bon? I wasn't going to say *hard*. I was going to say boring. Okay, so I grew up without a mother but so do lots of other people. Being poor and working hard to get out of where you are is boring and tedious, and that's not what people want to hear. They want to believe in some romanticised version. They want to think it happens in the blink of an eye, some fairy godmother moment, one zap of the magic wand and everything changes forever. Well it wasn't like that –'

'I'm talking hypothetically here, Helen – I meant *one* – not you specifically.'

'I know but that's the trouble, it isn't *one,* it *is me,* Bon.'

'And we both know that there *are* moments, chances taken, people you meet, things you do that do change your life forever –'

'Of course there are, but my experience of life is the harder you work the luckier you get. Up until now I've always kept all those things to myself, all those years. I had the chance to write about all this when I left *Cannon Square*; my life, where I came from; and I didn't –' Helen paused and then said more gently, 'I didn't. And for a good reason, because it's boring.

'People have got these ideas in their head about what my life was like; what it *is* like. They make assumptions, they want to romanticise it all, make it all into a fairy story and it wasn't like that. It wasn't like that at all. It was grim and cold and I was afraid and scared all the time –' She rolled over. 'I'm just not sure, even after all these years, that I'm ready to go home.' The words were out before Helen realised exactly what she'd said.

Bon stroked her back, his touch offering comfort. 'It's okay. This is your home now, baby, not Billingsfield. You and me. We're home. You're not going home, you're just going back to a place, a town where you grew up, which you left. This is your home now,' he said, moving closer and curling up around her.

If it ever was my home, Helen thought miserably, closing her eyes and squeezing them tight to hold back the tears. There were so many emotions she felt about going back to Billingsfield that it was hard to unpick them all. One was the irrational fear that if she went back, somehow she might find that everything she had done so far – her escape, her career, her whole life, had all been a trick of the light, smoke and mirrors, and that she would never be able to get away; that somewhere back beyond the docks and the factories, down past Market Street, tucked between Jean the florist's and Ross's camera shop, she would find her real self still working at Finton's Finest Toys, still unpacking the new deliveries out in the stockroom while Harry checked them off the delivery note. And then there were Charlotte and Harry.

Bon, not privy to her thoughts, put an arm around her waist and pulled her tight up against him. She could feel the fingers of his other hand brushing her hair; feel the warmth of his strong muscular body; and she lay so still that she could pick out the beat of his heart. Whatever happened, whatever Arthur said, and even if it all ended tomorrow, being with Bon in that moment was the best thing that had ever happened to her; she had never felt so loved or so wanted in her whole life.

'I love you,' he murmured into her neck, as if he had read her thoughts.

Safe with Bon's arms around her, lulled by the gentle rhythmic sounds of his breathing, Helen realised just how tired she was. She closed her eyes, finally letting sleep wash over her like a warm sea, and did not fight it as she sank into unconsciousness.

FIVE

The Talent Contest

'I don't think I've ever seen the Carlton Rooms this busy. We're never going to get parked in their car park, it's heaving. Look at it –' said Harry, throwing his arm casually over the passenger seat so he could look back over his shoulder to reverse his Mini back out into the road. 'We'll have to go round again – or maybe it would be easier if I just parked down on the quay and we walked back?'

He didn't say *I told you so* to Charlotte, for which Helen was grateful. The last half hour had been a nightmare – Charlotte had taken forever to finish getting ready, dithering about whether they should go to the theatre in their costumes or take their outfits along on hangers and change when they got there, whether they should wear long boots or the high-heeled sandals that they had both bought the previous week, and if they went with the sandals should they stop off and get some proper tights somewhere instead of the fishnets that Charlotte had insisted that they needed the day before. And then, just when Helen thought they were ready, Charlotte had begun a big debate with Harry about the songs they had been working on for the last few weeks. Did the look they had gone with suit the music they had chosen? And then, when they had finally squashed everything into Harry's car they had got snarled up in late afternoon traffic, and had crept nose to tail towards the town centre – and now it had started to rain.

The whole of Billingsfield seemed much busier than was usual for a Friday – every junction was gridlocked, every set of traffic lights red – as they got closer to the town centre. There were roadworks in the High Street and a diversion running around by Railway Road that slowed the cars down to a snail's pace – and so now they were running late, and Charlotte was getting more and more annoyed.

She was sitting in the front passenger seat, alongside Harry, her vanity case balanced on her knees, her hair perfect, her makeup immaculate, looking as if she had just stepped out of the pages of a magazine fashion shoot, while Helen was squashed up in the back seat of the car with the costumes and bags and a cardboard box of flyers for the shop and Charlotte's suitcase, her knees folded up to her chest. Helen had known from the outset that there was no chance she'd be sitting in the front; Charlotte wouldn't have dreamt of sitting in the back.

And there was no way they could put anything in the boot because that was packed full of stock and bits of a display stand for some sort of new doll that Harry's dad had bought at the wholesalers.

'Do you think we should have worn hot-pants?' Charlotte was saying as Harry tried his best to manoeuvre his way backwards out of the car park, through the people and traffic. 'I saw some in Swanley's department store last week. I was thinking if we get through to the national finals that we really ought to get some. They would make more of a splash, make us stand out a bit more, wouldn't they? What do you think?'

'Certainly would,' said Harry. 'Especially with your boots,' and then to Helen, he said, 'Can you just tell me if anything's coming? Only I can't see round those people on the kerb.'

'We can't do anything about the costumes now,' continued Charlotte, apparently oblivious to all the manoeuvring. 'Although if we win tonight we could. I was thinking we could nip in on Monday and get ourselves a pair. What do you think, Helen? Could you nip in first thing?'

'Whoa,' shouted Helen to Harry. 'Hang on, there's a blue car right behind us, Harry. He looks like he wants to get into the car park too.'

'Well, good luck to him,' sighed Harry. 'He can have a go if he'll just let me out.'

'I don't think he's going anywhere,' said Helen nervously. 'There's another one pulled in right behind him.'

66

'This is ridiculous,' Charlotte grumbled, sighing heavily. 'We're going to be late now . . .'

The cars were nose to tail. The car behind Harry honked as Harry tried to reverse out, and then honked his horn again because Harry couldn't go forward either.

'I'll just have to drive in, get past these cars, and turn around. But don't worry, we've still got plenty of time; it'll be fine, there's bound to be somewhere down on the quay.'

'We can't do that, we can't park too far away,' complained Charlotte. 'It's nearly half past now and it's raining out there. My hair will be completely ruined if it gets wet. It's taken me hours to get these curls right. And there is no way I'm going to be able to walk back from the quay in these shoes. Why can't we just stop here?'

'Because we can't. I'm totally blocking the entrance.'

A stream of people were crossing the road in front of Harry, while beyond them a white Transit van had pulled up outside the back of the theatre. People started piling out of the back, carrying boxes and bags in through the stage doors, so that Harry couldn't move forwards or backwards. Helen glanced back over her shoulder; they were well and truly stuck. The sounds of horns honking were slowly spreading further back down the queue.

'Tell you what, why don't I just jump out here and go in and let them know that we've arrived?' said Charlotte, pushing the car door open as she spoke. 'I'll sign us in. Sort out where the dressing rooms are and everything.'

'But what about all the stuff?' protested Helen, looking around at the pile of things on the back seat.

'Oh, you'll be fine,' said Charlotte casually, waving her protest away. 'And anyway Harry will help you bring it in, won't you, Harry? I mean it's not like there's that much, and I don't want them to think we haven't turned up or anything. I'll see you in there in a minute, and don't forget the costumes. Don't be long, will you? I don't want to be singing out there all on my own.'

Watching Charlotte picking her across the cobbles towards the theatre Helen wondered if that wasn't *exactly* what Charlotte wanted. As she made her way up the steps towards the foyer Charlotte didn't even look back.

'Do you want to get out here too?' asked Harry. 'I'd be happy to bring the things in once I've found somewhere to park. Go on, out you get. I'll be fine.'

'You'll never be able to carry all this lot on your own.'

He grinned. 'Don't worry about it. I'll make two trips if I need to. Go on, just hop out here. I really don't mind. And Charlotte is right, you don't want to be late for your big night, do you?'

Helen hesitated long enough for the car behind to honk again.

'Are you sure you'll be all right, Harry?' she asked.

Ahead of them the Transit van finally moved off.

Harry nodded. 'Of course I will. Stop fussing. Oh, hang on – just let me just pull in to the side over there so I can get out of the way of this moron behind me and then you can get out, okay? Before Charlotte decides to go solo. Oh, and you'll need these.' He reached into the inside pocket of his jacket and pulled out the forms that he had helped them to fill in in his bedroom.

'God, I'd forgotten all about them. You're a total genius, Harry,' she said.

He laughed. 'I don't think so.' Behind them the car pipped again. 'We better get going before the gorilla behind us gets really annoyed.' He drove into the car park and pulled up in front of a row of parked cars, a little way past another knot of people unloading even more equipment.

'It's going to be a really big night by the look of it. Have you got everything you need?' Harry said, as Helen pushed the seat forward and scrambled out into the car park.

She nodded. 'I think so.'

It was raining harder now.

'I'll see you in a few minutes,' Harry said, leaning across the seat to close the door. 'I think there's a brolly in the boot if you want one?'

'No. I'll be fine, thanks – I'll run,' Helen said.

'Break a leg, isn't that what they say?' called Harry.

Helen laughed, pulling her coat up over her head so that it covered her hair. 'In these shoes, on those cobbles there's a really good chance you could be right. See you soon. Are you sure you don't mind bringing all our stuff in?'

He smiled back at her. 'No, now stop worrying and go or you'll be late,' he said.

'You're a star, Harry,' she said. And before Helen really

thought about what she was doing she leant back inside the car and kissed him.

It was only after she had slammed the car door shut that Helen thought about the kiss. It hadn't felt awkward and Harry hadn't blushed – in fact if anything he acted as if he deserved it. She smiled; maybe he wasn't so bad after all.

With the rain pelting down, Helen picked her way carefully across the shiny wet cobbles towards the theatre's rear doors.

It was complete madness in the car park. Cars and vans were parked haphazardly across the bays, while a few others had pulled up in a tight semicircle outside a set of huge double doors that led into the theatre's cavernous interior. There was a buzz of industry and excitement as people unloaded all manner of props and equipment, the drivers and helpers hurrying in and out of the pouring rain. A magician's cabinet was being rolled in on a sack barrow, while another man pushed in a long rail full of sparkling costumes covered over with polythene, and then behind him came a man and a woman scuttling in from the car park, each carrying guitar cases and glittering cowboy hats.

Once she was inside out of the rain Helen joined the crush of people trying to make their way through to the dressing rooms. Standing behind a trestle table was a small man holding a clipboard; he was struggling to keep order and stop people pushing their way past him. He was failing miserably.

'If I can just have your name. I need your name,' he called after the man manhandling the costume rail along the corridor. 'You can't just wander in here like that,' he bawled.' I need to check you off my list, you know. I have a list – you can't just go through there. Oh for God's sake,' he snapped as the man, apparently oblivious, just kept on walking, before pushing open the double doors at the end.

'How am I supposed to know who's here and who's not?' the little man shouted to no one in particular, and then he muttered,' I need another bloody table and some help here,' before turning his attention back to the queue. When he got as far as Helen he raised his eyebrows and smiled triumphantly.

'Well, hello there,' he said. 'And how can we be of service today, then?'

Helen couldn't decide whether he was being sarcastic or not. 'I don't know whether I should be here or round the front,' she began.

The man looked her up and down. She suspected, from the look on his face, that he thought she was someone he could manage to control without too much trouble. 'And you are *who* exactly?' he said, pen poised.

'Helen Heel.'

'And you're a performer, are you, Helen?'

Helen nodded. 'Yes, I'm singing tonight.'

'Right. Well, you've come to the right place, dear.' He said, eyes moving down his list. 'Only the nobs and bigwigs get to go in round the front. Soloist, are you?'

She shook her head.

'In that case with *whom* are you singing?'

'I'm with Charlotte Johnson. We're the Wild Birds.' Helen looked beyond him into the corridor. Now that his attention was firmly fixed on her, other people were slipping past unnoticed and making their way into the theatre.

'She should be here somewhere. She came in a little while ago,' Helen said. 'She came in through the front doors.'

'No, she shouldn't have done that, I've just told you – it's VIPs only that way,' the man said with a sniff. 'Me, I get stuck out the back here with the hoi polloi, while they get the bloody Mayor and all the celebs. How am I supposed to keep track of who's here and who's not? I warned them, I said, bunch of bloody amateurs, it'll be chaos on the night, we need extra staff on the door to help sort it out I said. And look at it, tell me I'm not right? No idea how to behave, any of them – animals –' He looked at her and sighed; Helen was quite obviously a disappointment, and then he smacked his lips before taking another long hard look at his list. 'Wild Birds, you said, didn't you?'

Helen nodded. 'That's right. We're singers.'

'So you said.' He tapped the board with his finger. 'Here we are. The Wild Birds. You're late.'

'Only by a few minutes, we couldn't get parked and –'

'It says on here that you were supposed to be on stage for a run-through at half past four.'

'*Half past four*?' Helen felt her stomach tighten. 'It can't say that. You're joking,' she said. 'The man told me half past five.'

He pulled a face. 'Do I look like the kind of man who's got the time for jokes? Have you seen how many people we've got to try and get through here tonight? Now that *is* a bloody joke. The management want shooting. They should have asked me. I was in variety for years, me – on tour with the greats. I told them. I mean this is a complete farce.'

As he spoke Helen tried to get a look at what was written on his clipboard. 'I'm sorry, but your list can't be right,' she said. 'The man at the box office yesterday told me that we had to be here at half past five.'

'Did he indeed?' The little man pressed the board close up against his puny little chest. 'And which man was that, then?'

'Tully, Mr Tully,' she said, feeling her pulse quicken. 'He told me yesterday, he said we'd got to be here by half past five.'

'Like he knows anything,' said the man with a sneer.

'He was the only one here when I got here. At lunch time. I gave him our music.'

The man snorted. 'You gave him your music, did you? Well God only know where that's ended up, then, it could be anywhere. The man is a complete nightmare. He's a glorified caretaker.'

'He seemed very nice. Very kind,' Helen said, feeling totally lost. 'He had a clipboard too. He said half past

73

five and that I could leave the music with him, and that he'd look after it and make sure he passed it on to the right people.'

'Well, you just better hope that he gave it to someone who knows what they're doing,' said the man. With that he ticked something on his board and waved her through. 'Female changing, first floor, room three. You can't miss it, up the stairs, just follow the sound of the bitching and smell of the hairspray. Go right along there. I've got a lot of people to see and you're holding everybody up.' With that the man's attention turned to the next person in line.

Helen didn't move, instead she stayed exactly where she was.

'What?' snapped the man.

'What should we do?' asked Helen.

'What do you mean, *what should we do*?' The man peered at her. 'What should you do about *what*?'

'About not being here at half past four?' said Helen.

The man pulled a face. 'There's not a lot you can do really, is there? All the acts were allocated a time slot for a run-through and sound checks. It was tight as charity without people buggering about.'

'And so you're saying that we've missed it?'

'Were you here at four thirty?'

Helen felt sick but tried very hard not to let it show. 'No. But –'

'But nothing, sweetheart,' said the man, tapping his clipboard. 'You were down for a four thirty run-through and you weren't here. End of story. All right? Mister Tully should have given you a copy of the new schedule. There's nothing I can do about it now. So if you'd just like to move along there please. Female dressing room, first floor, room three.'

She stared at him, refusing to budge. 'Is there anyone I can talk to?'

'No, now can you just move yourself? I've got a troupe of Eastern European acrobats unloading at the moment – all foreign – *vich* this and *osky* that, bloody nightmare making sure they're who they say they are.'

Helen glanced around. She couldn't spot anyone who looked as if they were anything to do with the theatre management. 'So what will happen now, then?' she asked.

'I'll count them I suppose; it's the best I can do under the circumstances.'

Helen put her hands on her hips, her anxiety rapidly turning to anger.

'I meant what will happen because we've missed the run-through. It wasn't our fault.'

The man shrugged. 'Look, sweetheart, the resident sound man they've got here is really good: he's wasted in a place like this if you ask me. But he probably took a guess at what you need from what you put down on your application form and set it up accordingly; to be honest he's not often that far out.'

The application form, thought Helen miserably, which was currently folded up in her handbag.

'And there's no one else I can talk to?'

The man shrugged. 'I don't know. God, maybe?'

At which point Helen caught sight of Charlotte further along the corridor. She was standing at the bottom of a flight of stairs, waving frantically. 'Over here, Helen, here,' Charlotte called.

'Female changing –' the man began.

'I know, I heard you the first time,' snapped Helen, pushing past him.

'God, where on earth have you been? I was getting worried; where are the costumes?' said Charlotte, all outrage and indignation as Helen hurried towards her. 'I can't believe you took so long. You knew I was waiting. Don't tell me, Harry ended up having to park right down on the far end of the quay, didn't he? I'm just glad I got out when I did. It's complete madness here and it's like a bloody cattle market upstairs. Have you been up there looking for me? I can't believe this, how come there are so many people? It's totally mad. And they've put everyone in together. I can't even find anywhere to sit down. And the toilets are disgusting.' Rant over, she looked Helen up and down. 'So where are the costumes?'

'Harry's bringing them.' Helen bit her lip, feeling a growing sense of panic. 'He should be here in a minute.'

Charlotte stared at her. 'What's the matter with you? You're not still nervous about singing tonight, are you?'

There was no point lying or beating about the bush. 'No, it's not that. The man down there who signed me in said that we should have been here at half past four;

they must have changed the times, Charlotte. We've missed our sound checks.'

Charlotte's expression hardened up. 'Don't say that, Helen. You are kidding me, aren't you?' she snapped. 'Tell me it's a joke.'

Helen shook her head. 'No, it's not. He said that the man I saw yesterday didn't give me the right schedule.'

'Oh for God's sake. How could you be so bloody stupid?' spat Charlotte. 'How could you get the time wrong?'

Helen wanted the ground to open up and swallow her whole. 'I'm really sorry but it wasn't my fault,' she protested. 'The man in the front office told me half past five. I wasn't to know there was another schedule, was I?'

'Are you serious? Of course it's your fault. For God's sake, Helen. You can't do anything right, can you?' Charlotte raged. 'I mean, what does it take to get the bloody time right? What are we going to do now? I *knew* I should have got my dad to sort it all out. I just knew. He said you'd let me down. He did, you know. He said you're a waste of space and that you'll never amount to anything, that you're just hanging on my coat-tails. Poor little Helen Heel. You're going nowhere. You work in a toy shop for God's sake. And you know what? He was right.'

Helen stared at her. 'What?' she gasped. It felt as if someone had punched her. 'Your dad said that about me? When did he say it?' She spluttered, 'He's always been nice to me. Is that what he really thinks?' Not that Charlotte heard her or had finished with her stream of venom.

'I can't believe you, I really can't. Trust you to spoil my big chance, Helen. You did it on purpose, didn't you? *Didn't you?*' Charlotte continued furiously. 'You're just jealous, aren't you? And you've always been jealous of me. *Haven't you?*' she shouted.

People were staring at them.

'Of course not.' Helen stammered. She'd always known that Charlotte had a short fuse but this was something different. She was totally stunned by the fury of Charlotte's outburst.

'I'm going to go and ring my dad; I'm just hoping he'll be able to sort something out,' Charlotte said, and stormed off back upstairs. 'He wouldn't have let this happen if he had been here,' she shouted over her shoulder.

Which was the moment that Harry arrived.

'Hello,' he said, hurrying down the corridor towards Helen. He was soaked, his curly blonde hair slicked down over his face, his jacket dark with rain, but at least he was smiling. Helen had never been more pleased to see a friendly face in her life. He'd got their costumes on hangers, slung over one shoulder, a makeup box tucked under one arm and a holdall in the other hand.

'There you are,' he said with a grin. 'Thank God I found you. Busy, isn't it? I had one heck of a job getting past that little squirt on the reception desk. Who does he think he is?' He paused. 'What's the matter? Are you okay?' he asked.

'No,' Helen spluttered and burst into tears. 'No, I'm not.'

Harry looked aghast. 'What's the matter? Here, let me put these down. Don't cry – what is it?' he said, putting his arm around her.

Helen, feeling stupid, struggled to compose herself and tried to explain between sobs what had happened. 'Charlotte is furious,' she said finally. 'But I didn't do it on purpose, I'm not like that, you know that, Harry. It was a mistake. I only passed on what the man told me yesterday at the box office.'

'I know,' said Harry, handing her his handkerchief. It was neatly ironed into a sandwich-sized triangle and although slightly damp from the rain, smelt of washing powder and sunshine. Good old Harry.

'I didn't do it deliberately.'

'I know you didn't, and when she calms down so will Charlotte. Here, you stay there and look after the costumes and the rest of the things and I'll go and see what I can do.'

'Charlotte's gone to ring her dad,' said Helen.

'Okay, well in the meantime I'll see if I can talk to someone, see if we can't sort something out.'

'Really?' said Helen.

He grinned. 'It's got to be worth a try, hasn't it? The worst thing they can say is bugger off. Just watch the bags, will you?' And with that Harry vanished into the press of people heading into the auditorium.

Helen waited. A moment or two later Charlotte stamped down the stairs and slumped onto the step alongside her; her expression was like thunder.

'Harry's just gone to talk to someone about the mix-up with the times. Did you get through to your dad?' asked Helen, hoping to make peace.

'You care?' growled Charlotte.

'Of course I care, Charlotte. I'm really sorry. Despite what you think I really didn't do it on purpose.'

'I can't get through to my dad. The pay phone up there is only taking incoming calls,' Charlotte said.

There was a tense silence.

'Harry brought the costumes,' Helen said tentatively, indicating the bags slung across her knees.

'So I see. Well, he can just take them back home again then, can't he? This was meant to be our big chance, Helen. Our big break. They've got agents coming from London tonight, you know, and someone from the Corn Exchange who is casting their big extravaganza this Christmas. And bits of it are going to be on TV on the local news. You do know that, *don't you*?'

Helen flinched. 'Of course I do, Charlotte – that's why we're here.'

'This could have been my big chance if it hadn't been for you buggering it all up.'

'We're here now, we can still go on.'

Charlotte's face contorted into a furious grimace.

80

'Without sorting the sound out, without doing a run-through? Don't be stupid. What it's going to sound like – what's it going to *look* like? Rank amateurs, that's what. We'll look like idiots, Helen. And I'm certainly not going to go on stage and make a total fool of myself even if you are. And what if that bloke you saw *didn't* give them the music? We're going to look like morons, Helen, and *it's all your fault.*'

Despite trying to keep her cool Helen could feel her bottom lip begin to tremble. 'I said I'm sorry. I don't know what else to say. I didn't do it on purpose, Charlie, you surely must know that. I –'

'For God's sake just shut up, will you? There's no point apologising now, is there? It's done. Over. And you know what? You're just totally useless,' said Charlotte, waving the words away. 'I'm going to go round to the phone box on Market Street, ring my dad and get him to come and pick me up. You can do what you like, Helen. Go home with Harry, go back to your pathetic little life. I can't believe you, I really can't – you knew how important this was.' She bent down and snatched up the costumes. 'We won't be needing these now, will we?'

'Helen! Charlotte!' Harry shouted from the double doors at the end of the corridor. He was waving frantically, trying to attract their attention. 'Come on, come on. Quickly, quickly, we haven't got much time.'

'You better run, lover-boy wants you,' snapped Charlotte, folding the costumes over her arm. 'I'd grab him with both hands if I were you, Helen, because let's be frank, he's the only chance someone like you's got. You know what people are saying about you, don't you? Moving in with Harry like that – that you're only after him for his money, trying to get yourself knocked up so that he has to marry you? And you know what? I think they're right, leading him on like that. You're a grade A bitch, Helen Heel – probably break his heart and leave him when you've got what you want. Just like your mother.'

Helen stared at her in horror, unable to believe what she was hearing. 'You don't know a thing about my mother,' she hissed.

'Everyone knows,' growled Charlotte. 'She was a tart, that's what my dad said – everyone knew about her. Ran off with some old rich bloke – didn't want to take you because you'd cramp her style. I know my mum and dad got divorced but at least I know where my mum is.'

Helen could hardly breathe for pain and indignation. Charlotte couldn't have hurt her any more if she had stabbed her.

'You can't think that,' Helen whispered. 'You can't – you're my friend.'

'*Was*,' said Charlotte icily. 'I *was* your friend.'

Harry ran up to them and caught hold of Helen's arm. 'Come on,' he said breathlessly. 'Quickly. What are you waiting for? Bring the costumes and the rest of the things with you. I've had a word with the stage manager and if we hurry then they'll let you have a few minutes to do the sound checks. They can't promise a full run-through, but at least it's better than nothing, and I checked and they've got your music. But we really need to hurry, come on –'

Charlotte's expression turned from total fury to elation in a matter of seconds. Helen wouldn't have believed the transformation if she hadn't seen it for herself. Charlotte beamed at Harry, apparently oblivious to how upset Helen was, and practically threw the costumes at her.

'Come on, let's get going. See, I told you Harry was a genius,' Charlotte said, throwing her arms around his neck and planting a great big kiss on his cheek. 'But you didn't believe me, did you, Helen? You are absolutely amazing, Harry. You see? I was right. I think he would make the perfect manager, don't you, Helen? You're a natural . . .'

Still smiling, Charlotte linked her arm through Harry's and strode off down the corridor with him, and then, looking back over her shoulder, snapped, 'What are you waiting for? An engraved invitation? Didn't you hear the man – we can do the sound checks. Bring the things, will you. Which way do we have to go, Harry?'

SIX

Filming

'Okay, so if you could just tell us again how it feels to be back in your home town –' said Natalia. Natalia was standing out of camera shot, by the hotel reception desk. She glanced down at the notes on her clipboard.

'And we need you to come in again and if you could maybe say that thing you just said about how much things have changed since you were last here? And remember when this is aired they'll be cutting my voice out. So if you could speak in whole sentences. It makes the editing a whole lot easier.' She smiled at Helen reassuringly. 'You okay with that? You're clear about what we'd like?'

Helen nodded.

'Okay, and you've got your case? And so are we ready to go again?' Natalia glanced over her shoulder towards the rest of the film crew, who were arranged in a ragged semicircle by the reception desk. Felix, who was supposed to be directing the *Roots* shoot, was watching something on the playback screen, but even so he nodded. 'Whenever you're ready,' he said, making a 'wagons roll' signal with his fingers.

Helen did as she was told and set down the suitcase she had been carrying and smiled into the camera. 'It feels great to be back. On the drive up from the station I was looking around at everything, taking it all in. It's been a while since I've been back home and at the risk of sounding like a cliché, I was just thinking how things haven't changed all that much, and of course that's the moment when the taxi turns a corner and just about everything's new. The big warehouse by the river – luxury flats now – Tilman's factory gone for a shopping mall. So, so far it's an odd feeling but it's good to be back. I'm hoping the big things haven't changed that much.' Helen glanced around the foyer of the Billingsfield Arms Hotel, catching the eye of the receptionist who was busy fiddling with something behind the desk.

'Hello, my name is Helen Redford,' she said, walking up to the desk to talk to the woman. 'There should be a reservation for me?'

The receptionist looked up and smiled.

'And *cut,*' said Felix. 'That's just great.'

Natalia turned her attention to the woman behind the desk.

'Presumably we won't be needing to book in again, so can we just go from where you give Helen the keys?'

The receptionist nodded. Felix gave her the thumbs up. The receptionist took back the set of keys that she had given Helen on the previous take and waited to be cued in. The woman was a natural, Helen thought.

'Sorry about this, but they want it to look just right,' Helen said by way of an explanation. 'The phone ringing and that guy wandering into shot last time,' she began. 'It spoils the way it looks and sounds.'

The receptionist's smile held. 'Not a problem,' she murmured, her attention on Felix, who gave her an okay signal with his thumb and forefinger.

'We're good to go, whenever you are,' he said.

The receptionist cranked her smile up a notch. 'I hope you'll be very comfortable during your stay with us, Ms Redford,' she said, handing Helen the keys to her suite. Still smiling, she waved a porter over. 'This is Christov, he'll show you up to your room and take care of your bags, and if there is anything you want, *anything at all*, then please just let us know.' She paused, turning the corporate hospitality smile up to stun for the benefit of the camera, and then added, 'And can I just say how pleased we are to have you here at the Billingsfield Arms, Helen. Welcome home. It's really good to have you back.'

Helen smiled graciously right on cue. 'Thank you. It's good to be back.'

'And cut,' said Felix. 'That's fantastic, really nice. Okay, lovely, lovely, lovely. Now am I right in thinking we've got one of the suites with the balcony? The one overlooking the quay?' he asked first Natalia and then the woman behind the desk.

They were causing a stir. People were coming in off the street to watch what was going on; people who wouldn't normally consider ever going into the Billingsfield Arms. People, Helen suspected, who the hotel management would probably prefer stayed outside, but who were making their way inside, past the doorman, past the plate glass and handsome oak panelling, to watch the filming. There were two men in anoraks, tracksuit bottoms and baseball caps standing just inside the revolving doors and alongside them two girls with babies in buggies. The girls had bare legs, their hair dragged up into topknots. Over by the entrance to the restaurant were a gaggle of women who had been shopping on the market, and were surrounded by piles of thin stripy carrier bags, the bags spilling their contents out onto the plush carpet.

The doorman stood to one side taking it all in, although from his expression it was painfully obvious he was unsure what to do. Did he throw the gawpers out or let them stay? How bad would it look for the hotel if he ended up on Youtube, hustling the hoi polloi back onto the streets?

Helen smiled at all of them. She had already done a round of autographs and hellos. One of the women, who before coming in had stubbed out a cigarette on the sole of her shoe and pocketed it, waved at her. Helen's smile broadened as the doorman looked on, narrow-eyed and suspicious, as the woman found herself a chair and started to rifle through the complimentary magazines and newspapers.

Usually the Billingsfield Arms was the kind of establishment where people – guests and staff alike – spoke in hushed tones; where hurrying or shouting, shows of petulance or bad manners, were frowned upon. It was certainly not a place for shell suits and flip-flops, puffa jackets and baseball caps. Other hotel guests – mostly corpulent men of a certain age looking up from behind their broadsheets – cast glances in the film crew's direction, making a great show of not being curious about all the comings and goings. But despite their measured indifference it seemed as if the business of the hotel had ground to a halt for the filming, as the staff crept out to join the people from the market to take in the floorshow.

'That's right. Suite thirty-four, top floor,' the receptionist was saying. 'I thought you'd already been up and had a look around?'

'I did, but we have looked at quite a few. That is the one with the balcony, right? In the middle – the one with the view of all those warehouses?' said Felix. Felix had bright red hennaed hair and was chewing gum.

'That is correct,' said the woman briskly; she didn't look like the kind of woman who took kindly to hippies or chewing gum.

'Okay, so we're sure about that, are we?' asked Felix. The receptionist's expression hardened. 'Of course I'm sure. Suite thirty-four with a balcony. Your colleague booked it.' She glanced at Natalia, who was nodding furiously.

Helen stood to one side of the melee along with her luggage. They had been in the hotel foyer for what seemed like forever, unpacking the equipment, setting up and then filming her walking down the street, looking up at the hotel, coming in out of the rain, making her way to the front desk, smiling at the receptionist, confirming her booking. All this for what would amount to a few seconds of airtime or probably be cut in the edit and not used at all. But it was getting them to bond, to gel as a team, which Natalia had explained was very important to all of them.

'We really want you to trust us and understand where we're coming from, Helen. We're here to support you on your journey and make this a great show,' she had said in a rather earnest pre-filming pep talk. Helen looked from face to face, well aware that no one else appeared to care a stuff about bonding, trust or any journey, other – possibly – than the one home.

So far their impromptu audience had hung on through it all, totally enthralled by all the comings and goings. One of the women, who was leaning against a baby buggy, blew a big pink bubble in her bubble gum.

Helen's attention wandered, while Felix, Natalia and the receptionist discussed balconies, views and who had seen what and when. The hotel hadn't changed that much since Helen had last been there. It was no less intimidating, no less grand. It stood just off the market square, no more than five minutes walk from the Carlton Rooms and the main shopping centre. Considering how far she had travelled since leaving Billingsfield it was odd to think that so many of the significant moments and events in her earlier life had been played out within a few hundred yards of each other.

The Billingsfield Arms still resembled a Victorian gentleman's club with few visible concessions to the twenty-first century. Above the huge open fire hung an ornate gold-framed mirror reflecting the wood-panelled walls, the deep buttoned leather sofas and the high-backed winged chairs arranged around low tables. The floors were covered in thick, heavily patterned wine-red carpet that deadened every sound, every footfall, creating an atmosphere that made you whisper and walk on tiptoes so as not to shatter the tomb-like silence. It was a bastion of old conservative values, of Queen and country, with an ambience that was still more colonial than metropolitan.

With the crew still wrangling over locations the little crowd finally began to get bored and wander away. The girl blew another great balloon in her bubble gum and then – as it burst with a satisfying wet pop – peeled the fallout off her face and teased it from her lank greasy hair before following the others back out into the market square.

Helen glanced up at the mirror above the hearth, wondering what she might see reflected in it. Time dragged. *Roots* had arranged the shoot; they'd promised a light afternoon schedule, a nice hotel and dinner and then a bright and early start the following morning. It had all made perfect sense at the time.

Arthur had nodded when he looked at the proposal. 'Good idea, split the days – do some of the filming on the Friday afternoon, then do the rest the next day when you're rested and raring to go, and then the show on Saturday evening. Sounds perfect to me. Oh, and don't forget you've sound checks Saturday afternoon. I've talked to the team at *Roots* and they seem to think the theatre will make a great backdrop – you know, see you in your natural environment. Your pianist will be there from three I think, but I'll check.' Arthur had sniffed his cigar. 'So let's see, train there late Friday morning, filming and your show Saturday and then back home Sunday, done and dusted.'

'You'll be there, Arthur, won't you?' Helen had said.

'For the show?' He grinned, 'Oh God, yes – of course I will, I wouldn't miss it for the world. You'll be brilliant. I know you will. I've seen the rehearsals, haven't I? To be honest, watching you work I wondered why the hell we hadn't done it sooner.'

Flattered, Helen had smiled, although she had rather hoped he'd be there with her for the filming too. As if catching her thoughts Arthur shook his head. 'You won't want me the rest of the time, hanging around getting in the way, cramping your style. You'll be just fine – you're a natural – and I'll only be a phone call away.'

Helen had sighed. 'I'm still not sure about this,' she'd said.

'What's not to be sure of? You'll be fine, honest,' said Arthur. 'They're good people, Helen. I mean they've won awards and everything. And you're an old hand at this; there's nothing they're going to pull that you won't have seem a dozen times before.' He paused. 'If you're worried I could organise someone to come with you if you like. Do you want me to book you a dresser for the show – or a driver? See if I can get Florence or Benny? I know they'd both jump at the chance.'

Helen had shaken her head, and with more confidence than she felt, said, 'Don't be silly. And you're right, I'll be just fine. Just make sure you're there for the show. All right? First show of the tour – I'm banking on you to tell me what you think.'

He laughed. 'You'll be brilliant, you always are.'

'Arthur, you are such a bullshitter.'

And so now here she was, all on her own, back in Billingsfield.

Helen glanced into the mirror on the wall; she wasn't so sure now that she wanted to spend a night in Billingsfield or the hotel. It felt like she was being surrounded and jostled by all the ghosts she had left behind. How many years was it since she had stood in this hotel foyer? Since she had looked out over the market square and wondered what the hell would happen next?

Two elderly men with impressive moustaches made a show of not watching her as they sat either side of the fireplace taking tea. A uniformed waiter was serving them; it looked like a snapshot from some long-distant past. Her long-distant past.

In stark contrast, Felix, the *Roots* director, dressed in a Che Guevara tee shirt, puffa jacket, beanie hat and ripped-knee jeans was kneeling on the floor hunched over a monitor with the cameraman looking on, watching the images on the screen. 'I think actually we're probably done down here,' he said. 'We'll need to make the move upstairs and set up up there.'

Natalia glanced at him. 'Okay, great – I'll just need to sort that out.'

Once upon a time that would have been Helen's cue to head back to her dressing room or slope off for a coffee while she waited, but she had no idea how *Roots* worked and so Helen stayed where she was.

Across the foyer the longcase clock chimed the hour. Helen didn't like to think how many years it had been since she had last been in the Billingsfield Arms. It felt like a different lifetime; back then she remembered being intimidated by the quiet grandeur, remembered not being sure what to do or what to say and the worry of being asked to leave.

She could still vividly remember what it felt like creeping up those stairs, all the while waiting for the porter to ask her just where she thought she was going, hurrying along the corridors, checking the room numbers, each passing minute making her increasingly anxious. Looking back on her younger self it seemed like back then Helen had been afraid all the time, always waiting, eyes wide open, for the sky to fall in on her.

Helen glanced up at the ornate staircase almost expecting to see her younger self up there at the top, looking back over her shoulder, wondering what the hell she was doing and wondering where to go next.

'Are you ready to go up to your room, madam?' enquired a male voice, which brought Helen sharply back to the present.

Christov, the porter, was a tall blond man with a heavy Eastern European accent, closely cropped hair and a warm open expression. He had been standing around throughout the filming, and had already loaded her luggage onto a trolley at least three times at Felix's behest. Now he hovered, awaiting instructions.

'What do you think?' he said in an undertone. 'You think maybe we make a break and leave them to it? I don't know about you but I have many things to do other than standing here listening to them all moaning. Although I am enjoying the look on Ms Mackenzie's face.' He nodded in the direction of the receptionist. 'She looks like she is kissing the stinky herring.'

Helen checked out Ms Mackenzie and then looked up at him and laughed. It was an apt description of her expression.

'Maybe we should high-tail it out of here?' he said. 'Like they say in the cowboy films. Get the hell out of Dodge? I can bring you up some sandwiches, and cake and a pot of tea? You have got other things to do, yes?'

Helen nodded.

'They said you are doing a show here tomorrow.'

'That's right, at the Carlton Rooms. I'm doing a one-woman show; songs, monologues – jokes, you know, stories about my life,' said Helen. 'And this too,' she nodded towards the film crew. 'They're making a television programme about me, for *Roots*.'

'I know the programme.' He nodded. 'Busy time for you then. These people,' he said, pointing towards the crew. 'They are your friends?'

'No, not exactly.'

Felix was still deep in conversation with Natalia about which suite would give them the best look. Natalia was nodding earnestly while ticking things off on her clipboard. Ms Mackenzie was still wearing her fish-kissing face.

'I really like the balcony,' Felix was saying, his hands working independently to reinforce what he was describing. 'And that big cream-coloured sofa. Is that in that room, or do all the rooms have them, a sort of corporate look? I was thinking maybe we could get something in?'

Ms Mackenzie pulled a face.

'Remind me again, is that the room with those big prints on the wall? Like big flowers? I'm thinking that has got to be the one –'

Natalia's nodding quickened. 'I agree, and the natural light is great in there too.'

'Can we get a different sofa?'

Natalia stared at her clipboard and then at Ms Mackenzie.

It seemed as if the only person who hadn't been into her room yet was Helen.

'Maybe we could get something a bit funkier in there? Less last year –'

Ms Mackenzie started to protest.

'I'd like to shoot Helen on the balcony, looking out over the water, something moody and reflective we can use as ambience and cutaways between segments. Helen all alone, contemplating the past. You know how this stuff works. And it'll make a great neutral space for the interviews that we don't do at the theatre. Like the anonymity of life on the road –'

'So do you want to go and set that up now?' asked Natalia, not that Felix seemed to be listening.

'Maybe we could go down to the quay this afternoon before the light goes. You know the bit where the new arts centre is, by the warehouses? I was thinking more coat-collar-turned-up-against-the-wind shots. She's got great bones for that sort of moody look. Now, do we want to shoot her going up in the lift, because if we do we've got to do it now, or wet her coat down for continuity?' Felix paused and, glancing around, caught Helen's eye, although Helen guessed that Felix didn't actually see her.

Truth was, for a director, once you got past the early excitement and then all the starry pretensions, the massive but fragile egos, the drunken, the drugged, the whole diva thing, wheeling an actor out in front of the camera, saying the right words at the right time, was just a job. And she had no doubt that as far as Felix was concerned actors were part of the furniture, noisy, difficult, opinionated parts perhaps, but still ultimately something to shuffle in and out of shot.

'Can we get a spray bottle or something from somewhere?' Felix was saying to no one in particular. 'And do you think we can sort out the sofa? Those stains are going to show up on camera.'

Ms Mackenzie reddened and waved him closer. 'Can you please keep your voice down? I mean we're delighted you're here but —'

'How delighted?' Felix snapped back quick as a rattler.

She stared at him. 'I'm sorry?'

'I said, *how* delighted are you to have us here? You see we're all starving.'

'There's a café in Dougland Terrace,' she began, helpfully pointing towards the doors. 'Just round the corner to your left; you can't miss it.'

'No chance we could eat here, then?'

'Of course. The Talbot Room is open all day, or I could get one of the waiters to come and take your order.'

Felix smiled. 'Gratis, is that? On the house?'

Ms Mackenzie visibly stiffened. 'I'm terribly sorry but I don't think so — I mean, I could check with the duty manager for you but it's not our policy —'

Felix leaned in closer and smiled wolfishly. With his bright red hair it made him look like a demented ferret.

The *Roots* team had sent a taxi to pick Helen up from the station and filmed her on the ride up. Felix had let Natalia do the talking while he peered at Helen thoughtfully, as if she was an interesting sculpture or piece of furniture that he was trying to get the measure of.

'I'm really looking forward to working with you,' he said. 'Jamie and Natalia have been telling me all about you. I mean what a journey; what a story. We've got so much to work with here, and you have a real presence, Helen – a real presence, and great facial architecture – I had no idea. The photos really don't do you justice.'

Helen had smiled and nodded and murmured her thanks, not altogether sure what the right response was to a compliment on her facial architecture. And then she had noticed that his attention had moved on – obviously the pull of facial architecture could only last so long.

At the moment Felix, over by the reception desk – having fallen foul of the Billingsfield Arms freebie policy – was weighing up the pros and cons of carrying on with filming or stopping for something to eat.

'It seems like a natural place to take a break to me,' he said, speaking to the crew rather than Helen. 'And you'll get housekeeping to sort out that sofa?' he said to Ms Mackenzie.

'I'm almost certain that there are no stains on our soft furnishings,' she began. 'And I'm not sure that we can move –'

But Felix had moved on. 'Apparently there is a café just round the corner. How about we take half an hour now, and then, if the sofa's not sorted, move on to the next location –' he glanced across at Natalia. 'Which is where? The theatre?' He glanced around at the crew for confirmation. 'So, café then? It's not looking like we're going to get much in the way of comps from the ice queen behind reception there. I would have settled for a plate of fucking ham sandwiches for God's sake.'

Ms Mackenzie glared in their direction; she had frosted over considerably since her big moment on screen.

'So you don't want to go upstairs?' Helen said.

Felix and Natalia both swung round.

'Oh God, I'm so sorry,' Natalia blustered. 'I thought you'd already gone up, Felix and I have been here a while, doing a recce, your suite – the best sofa, you know –' She giggled and blushed, which made Helen wonder if maybe she fancied Felix. 'Would you like to go upstairs and see your suite, take a look around, get unpacked? Get settled? Are you hungry? I'll get them to organise some food for you – and then are you okay with what we're doing this afternoon? You have got a copy of the schedule, haven't you?'

Helen smiled. Natalia talked to her as if she might be senile. 'I'm fine; you do understand that I've got a live show tomorrow night, don't you?'

Felix and Natalia glanced at each other. 'Well, yes,' said Natalia after a second or two.

'And that's not something we can mess with,' said Helen firmly. 'We've got a full house, and I have to be there for a technical run-through, sounds checks, lighting –'

Felix nodded. 'Okay, okay, we get the picture; not a problem. That was one of the reasons why we got you here today. Obviously we're going to want to talk about how it all started. Road to stardom and all that. And we talked to your agent and he said it would be fine to do that in the theatre?'

Helen nodded. 'I know, and I'm okay with that. But I'll still need to spend time there getting ready for the show.'

'Oh yes, of course, obviously,' said Felix, without a shred of sincerity.

'So let's get you some food; would you like room service or would you prefer to have something in the restaurant?' Natalia asked taking her arm, making as if to guide her towards the stairs. 'Apparently the chef here is really good.'

'Don't worry, I'm sure I can sort it out,' said Helen, disentangling herself. 'You go and eat with the crew. It'll give me a chance to get my bearings.'

Natalia hesitated. 'I'm not sure –'

'I've got some calls to make.'

Natalia looked her up and down. 'You sure you'll be okay with that? I really ought to stay with you. It's our company policy.'

Helen smiled ruefully, wondering what Ruth had told Natalia about her drinking habits.

'I'll be fine. What time are we going to start again?'

Natalia glanced across at Felix. 'What time?'

Felix broke off the monologue he was subjecting the

cameraman to on the importance of ambience, and glancing at his watch said, 'Say three quarters of an hour? But don't worry, we'll come up and find you when we're ready.'

'Is that okay?' Natalia asked, brightly.

'Fine,' said Helen.

Finally given the go-ahead, Christov guided Helen towards the lift. He grinned. 'So you, you're like a big TV star then, eh? ?'

Helen laughed. It wasn't quite the deferential approach she might have expected and she was glad. 'Not really, not these days, but thanks for asking.'

Christov pulled a comic sad face. 'That's a big pity. I was hoping that you might help me to get my face onto the film.' He struck a pose to make the most of his profile and then indicated the crew, as the lift doors closed behind the two of them. 'I was hoping that meeting you, this might be my big break. I sing too, you know, you like to hear me sing maybe?'

Helen smiled. 'I'm not sure that singing to me would help further your career.'

'But you can pull strings.'

Helen raised her eyebrows. 'Not any worth pulling.'

He looked hurt. 'That's a big pity. Okay, so maybe now is not the moment, but before you leave you listen, yes? You like Frank Sinatra?'

The lift made silent stately progress to the third floor, the doors gliding open like oiled silk as they reached their destination.

'You're really planning to sing for me?' she laughed as the lift doors re-opened.

'I think it would be a very good idea. What about your husband? Is he coming? I have seen him in the newspapers, very pretty, maybe you both like music. I will sing for you both, something lovely – Dean Martin maybe. You know him?' Grinning, he burst into the opening bars of 'That's Amore'.

Helen took another look at him and laughed. 'Thank you, that is wonderful. Now where do you recommend that I eat?'

'You think so?' Christov said brightly, rolling the luggage trolley ahead of him and unlocking the doors to her suite. 'I like them all, Sinatra, Sammy Davis Junior, Dean Martin and that Mack the Knife song –' he shimmied his hips and sung a line or two of the chorus, 'it's very good, very good indeed. They don't write songs like that any more – Beyoncé, 'Single Ladies' – what is all that?'

'Food?' Helen prompted gently.

'Oh yes, well the food is good here but me, I would go to the Belafonte. It's a little bar and restaurant on Porter Street, opposite the chemist, not so far away, you can walk – and not so pricey but nice music, very good food. If you go there tell them I sent you, my cousin Gregori, he runs it. I sing there sometimes.' He flung open the doors of the suite. 'They open for lunch too. I could ring, get you a nice quiet table if you like for tomorrow night after the show. Or maybe for tonight, after you have finished with the filming? Now here we are, what do you think? You like it? It's one of our nicest rooms.'

Beyond the double doors the suite was bright and modern. The pale yellow sitting-room walls were hung with huge modern abstract prints and large mirrors, while the wall opposite the main doors was dominated by French windows framing a view out over the quay, the river, and a balcony set with a small table and chairs.

Helen went over to look at the view. It was a long time since she had strayed into an urban landscape. Today in the rain the old Billingsfield quayside looked more forlorn than inviting, with the river rolling by, battleship grey, under the cloudy midday sky; although there was something oddly beautiful about the stark postindustrial dockland. High-rise flats crowded out the far skyline, and were high enough up for their windows to catch the insipid afternoon sun. Some of the waterfront warehouses had been converted into flats too, while great swathes of the quay and adjoining buildings had been given a facelift. There was a row of little bars and shops fronting the waterside, making those that were still empty seem all the more forlorn. It felt like a lifetime since she had last seen this view.

'Would you like me to give you the guided tour of our luxurious facilities?' Christov was saying, as Helen, lost in her own thoughts, stared out over the choppy slate-grey water.

'No, thank you,' she said, catching his voice on the periphery of her hearing. 'I'm sure I'll be able to find everything. Thank you.' He didn't make any move to leave. 'Thank you,' she repeated.

'I will leave you the room service menu,' he said, sliding a leather-bound booklet onto the table alongside her. 'I've put everything in your bedroom. You used to live here?'

'In Billingsfield? Yes, that's right. Although it was a long time ago now.'

'It's not always easy to come back to a place. But anything you want, anything at all – just ask for me, for Christov. I am almost always around somewhere. I will help.'

'I'll remember that.' She smiled, handing him a folded bank note. 'That's very kind, thank you.'

But still he didn't move, and for a moment Helen wondered if he was expecting a bigger tip, but instead his brow furrowed. 'You know, you look very sad, I would say pensive, you want that I should go and get that girl? The one with the hat?' Slipping the money into his pocket he mimed Natalia's body posture with uncanny accuracy.

Helen shook her head and, smiling, straightened up, making an effort to shake off the disquiet that had dogged her since she stepped off the train earlier. 'No, I'm fine, really. I was just thinking about how many years it is since I've been here, and how many ghosts I might be stirring up by coming back.'

Christov nodded. 'For everything there is a time, maybe now is the time for this, you know? Time to bring your ghosts out into the light, time to pull their teeth.' He

104

grinned as he did another graphic mime. 'You shouldn't worry, things are seldom as bad as you make them up here in your head,' he said, tapping his temple. 'We all do it, making mountains out of mouses.'

Helen smiled. 'Molehills.'

'Yes, and those too. Get some food, eat, have a cup of tea, you will feel better. You want me to send tea up? With those little sandwiches and cakes. That woman downstairs, she told me that this is where you started your career.'

Helen nodded. 'That's right.'

'Chance for me too then,' said Christov brightly, before finally leaving to the strains of 'Strangers in the Night.'

Christov was right; Helen did feel better after eating and was ready for Natalia and the crew when they came upstairs to collect her.

The streets of Billingsfield unfurled themselves like a great colourful banner beyond the windows of the limousine that the *Roots* team had hired for the shoot. If they had wanted to make discreet progress this definitely wasn't the car to do it in. Helen glanced out of the car window as they slowed down at the traffic lights outside the hotel. People stared at the car.

The crew, Felix and Natalia had crammed themselves into the jump seats while Helen had the back seat all to herself. Helen was conscious of them all watching her, as if they were all poised waiting for her to perform.

Natalia, clipboard in hand, leant forward. 'What we'd

like is for you just to talk – give us your impressions, your feelings – recollections of life when you lived here. We're going to drive around, take in some of the places you're familiar with –'

Helen nodded.

'It's been a while since you've been back here, hasn't it? Can you tell us about the last time you came home?'

'It was for my dad's funeral.'

'And when was that?'

Helen took her time before replying, trying to work out exactly how many years it had been. 'Ten years or so, maybe more like fifteen,' she said, after a few moments.

Helen could see from Natalia's expression – a very slight raise of the eyebrows – that she was undoubtedly thinking that she had barely been out of junior school fifteen years ago.

'You were on TV by then, *Cannon Square* was getting record viewing figures and you were a household name. I imagine it must have been quite an emotional home-coming for you, meeting up with all your old friends while you were back here?'

'I didn't really catch up with anyone,' said Helen flatly. 'My dad had always been a pretty solitary soul. He didn't have many friends. I think his sister came – she died a couple of years later – one or two of his neighbours. One of the men he used to work with and a couple of the women from the nursing home that he went into towards the end.'

'And you?'

Helen nodded. 'That's right – and me, and Arthur.'

'Your agent?'

Helen nodded. 'That's right. Although I think we were still married then.'

'You were married to Arthur?' asked Natalia, doing a double take in amazement.

'Don't tell me you missed that?' Helen laughed. It was obvious from Natalia's expression that she had. 'We were married for years.'

'But you got divorced?'

'Eventually.'

'And you still manage to work together? I mean he still manages you, doesn't he?'

Helen laughed. 'In a manner of speaking, he does, yes. It was just that we didn't get on as well married as we did as agent and client. I really truly love Arthur, he just made a terrible husband – almost as bad as I did a wife. But we've always been friends. Good friends.'

Natalia was frantically writing herself another note. 'I am amazed we didn't pick that up,' she said.

'So you're saying that when you came back you didn't take the time to go round and see your old friends?' asked Felix.

Helen shook her head. 'No, no I didn't. I know it sounds strange now but I was up to my eyes in work at the time. We came back for a flying visit.'

'So you didn't even go and see Harry?' asked Natalia.

Helen smiled wryly. 'No, not even Harry. I probably should have done. I meant to, but I was right in the middle of filming a new series of *Cannon Square*. I think I was getting ready to do a live show as well. We were pushed for time. So many things had changed by then, and Dad was gone. My life was focused elsewhere.' She turned her attention back to the view from the window. 'It felt a bit like by coming home for the funeral I was closing the final pages of a book.'

'So are you saying there was no one here to bring you back?'

'That's right.'

Outside the earlier downpour had washed away the listless urban dust, making the colours of the buildings seem unnaturally sharp and bright in the sunshine, the lines of the shop facades and town houses crisp and newly drawn, as if her brain was reinventing and repainting the whole place, making everywhere brighter and showier just to show her what it was she had missed all those years.

'And your dad died in a nursing home?'

Helen nodded. 'He'd been ill a little while. I didn't realise how bad he was. I organised some help for him but –' Helen stopped.

'He was sicker than you thought?' prompted Natalia.

Helen nodded. 'I had no idea how ill he was, but it was just like him not to say anything,' she said softly, turning her attention back to the view. 'Things move on.'

The strange mix of the memories, the amazingly familiar and the completely alien landscape gave Helen an odd sensation in the pit of her stomach. The market square was framed on all four sides by shops and offices, with a road running all the way around and exits on each corner, and a statue of one of the town's most famous sons in the centre, set into a fountain.

The stalls were closing down for the day, people busied themselves, hurrying between the cars, crossing the roads, slowing the traffic to a crawl. Helen even recognised one or two of the stallholders – the fish man and the flower man, apparently unchanged after all those years. But behind them – where once there had been council offices, crammed into an ugly grey concrete box that looked as if it had come straight out of Stalinist Russia, there was now a stunning new high-tech office block and parade of stylish shops. She felt displaced and slightly out of sync.

'Isn't that a bit of a cliché?' pressed Felix. 'Things move on?'

'Being a cliché doesn't make it any less true,' said Helen with a sigh. 'I was busy, Harry was busy –'

'Busy?' said Natalia, leaning a little further forward.

Helen laughed at the two of them. 'What is this? Good cop, bad cop?' Neither of them spoke.

'All right,' Helen continued, holding up her hands in a gesture of surrender. 'I didn't go and see Harry because by that time he was with someone else.'

'And that hurt? Did you think he might wait for you?'

Helen made the effort to smile. 'No, of course I didn't think he'd wait for me. We were both young, and he is the sweetest man but –' Helen hesitated, not wanting to have what she thought about Harry aired on national television. 'I was married to Arthur by that time, so no, of course I didn't expect him to wait for me. But it changed things between us.'

The words didn't seem anywhere near big enough.

'Him being with someone else?' said Natalia.

Helen nodded.

'We thought we'd drive past the theatre while we've still got the light, and do a bit to camera there, with all the posters and things,' said Felix.

Helen nodded.

The car fell silent as they pulled away from the lights.

Natalia craned around. 'It's around here somewhere, isn't it?'

'Yes, about another hundred yards. It's just up there on the right,' said Helen, pointing. 'On the other side of the next set of lights.'

'Brilliant,' said Felix. 'Can we pull in there?' The driver nodded. Moments later they pulled up on the pavement outside the Carlton Rooms.

'I know it might seem a bit disjointed,' said Felix. 'But you know how it works – it'll all come together in the edit. So if we can just do a whistle stop here, that'll take the pressure off when we come back tomorrow for the show. I'm thinking we'll film you getting out of the car and then if we can just follow you up the steps to the main doors. Is that okay?'

The cameraman was nodding, but Helen was already opening the door, getting out of the car and staring at the front of the old theatre.

'Can we just do that again?' Felix was saying. 'I'd like to get that – the whole looking up at the name in lights thing.'

Helen stared up at the showy facade of the Carlton Rooms. They had her photo up on the billboards and her name printed on a huge banner above the main doors in three-feet-high lettering. It gave her an odd feeling.

'Can you tell us what it was like last time you were here?' Natalia asked. 'I'm right in thinking this is where you started your career in show business, aren't I?'

Helen nodded. 'Saturday March 15th. I was seventeen,' she said wistfully, wondering where all the years had gone.

SEVEN

'Come on, come on, can you get yourself up here, girls? You're the Wild Birds, aren't you?' asked one of the stage hands, waving them up the steps towards the stage.

'That's us,' said Helen. 'Harry Finton said that we should come round here to do our sound check.'

'Well, he was right about that, but we need to get a move on,' the man said, leading them into the wings. 'If you'd like to get yourself down the front there, then Tony will sort you out. We've got your music. If you want to leave your coats and bags over there out of the way, I'll keep an eye on them; they'll be fine.'

Helen felt the tension in her stomach beginning to ease. She took a minute to run her hands over her hair and straighten her clothes. 'Thank goodness Harry was able to sort something out,' she murmured in an undertone to Charlotte.

If Charlotte had heard her she didn't show it and certainly didn't reply: instead she took a deep breath, squared her shoulders, and painting on a thousand-watt smile, breezed out onto the stage, with Helen trailing in her wake.

Helen hadn't completely recovered from Charlotte's bad-tempered outburst. Charlotte had always been hot-headed but she had never behaved like this before – Helen hated the way that Charlotte had spoken to her. How could they have known each other all this time and she not have guessed how Charlotte really felt?

Far from being empty, the stage was a hive of activity. Men were hurrying to and fro carrying boxes, tables and pieces of scenery. There was a scattering of people sitting in the front seats of the auditorium, while other seats were stacked with coats and bags. In amongst all the rest of the activity, a local TV crew beavered about setting up lighting and cabling.

'Hello, where do you want us?' said Charlotte, to no one in particular.

Helen hadn't been quite sure what to expect but it certainly wasn't the noisy hubbub that confronted them. A man was hammering something into one of the walls by a fire exit. Members of the TV crew were busy setting up a camera in one of the boxes, and on stage another man was fixing cables along a track inside the footlights, calling out for instructions from the crew as he went.

'Where would you like us?' Charlotte called again, , projecting her voice out into the void as she crossed the stage. As she moved a spotlight clicked on, and then another, apparently following her progress. Charlotte swung around to look at Helen and grinned.

'How about that, then? This is more like it, isn't it?' she said, executing a perfect pirouette. 'On stage, in the spotlight. This is where we should be. I belong here . . .'

Helen wasn't altogether convinced.

'That's fine,' shouted a man in the wings, who was blissfully unaware of either Charlotte or Helen. He was calling to someone deep in the darkness, way up above the tiered seating. 'Can you just try three and four now?' he continued.

'Wild Birds?' asked another man. He was standing in the aisle by the front row of seats and was dressed in a shirt, tie and jeans, his jacket slung onto the seat behind him, and from his expression, his concentration for the most part appeared to be on the sheaf of papers he had clutched in his hands.

Charlotte nodded. 'That's right, that's us. Wild by name and wild by nature,' she said.

'Really? Well, don't tell the lads in the band that, will you?' He laughed, barely giving them a second glance. 'Right, well, let's get this sorted out then, shall we ladies? We haven't got an awful lot of time. So –'

Charlotte giggled. It sounded horribly hollow and false. 'So are you Tony?' she asked, all breathy and little-girly. She was making a real effort to make him notice her.

'That's me. Why, what have you heard?' Tony said, writing something.

'Harry said that you'd let us have –' Helen began but Charlotte was already ahead of her.

'Oh, you'd be surprised,' Charlotte purred.

This time the man did look up, and grinned. 'Probably all true,' he said. 'And more besides. Now if you could get yourselves down the front here, please, ladies. What's your name?'

'Kate Monroe,' said Charlotte, wiggling provocatively.

'Well, Kate Monroe, you and you friend will be out there on the apron for your number,' said Tony, waving them down towards him. 'That's down here in front of the curtains. They'll be closed behind you because we'll be setting up for the magician while you're singing.' He swung round. 'Can we get the bloody curtains shut, somebody?' he shouted, and then he beckoned Helen and Charlotte even further forward to where the man with the cables was now busying himself setting up two mike stands.

'Right. Now if you could just come a bit closer, and stand together, and you, love – yes, you –' he beckoned Helen into the middle, 'that's great – the compere will announce you – *ladies and gentlemen*, well you know the score – and then if you could get yourselves down here. Vince will have sorted out the mikes by then, won't you, Vince?' The man sorting out the stands raised a hand in acknowledgement.

There was a swish and creak and slowly the curtains closed behind them.

'So if you can get yourselves out and stand there –' He pointed to a taped cross on the bare, scuffed boards. 'That's centre stage,' he said, in case they couldn't guess. He turned his attention to someone up in the lighting gallery. 'Do you think we have a spot for these two young ladies, Frankie?'

There was a momentary pause and then a click and suddenly Charlotte and Helen were caught in a great halo of brilliance. Helen blinked, blinded by the glare, while Tony continued. 'We've got a cabinet, two tables and some sort of mummy thing to bring on while you're doing your number. Bloody heavy they are, so sing loud. Shame you aren't a rock band really,' he laughed.

Helen held up a hand to block the light and looked down at him, wondering if he was joking. She was too nervous to be able to tell. He winked. She suspected the wink was meant for Charlotte, who made a great show of winking back. Helen knew that she was trembling and hoped that no one else could see.

'Right, now our resident keyboard genius, Ed-the-fingers-O'Keefe, will be playing for you. So he'll do a bit of an intro to get you onto the stage and then as soon as you're settled just give him the nod and he'll go into your song and you're away. So, you okay with that, ladies?'

Charlotte nodded. 'Sounds fine to me.'

In the orchestra pit below them a plump balding man with a comb-over was seated at an electric organ. He was sweating and dabbing at his face with a limp paisley handkerchief, the spotlight reflecting on his shiny bald pate. He glanced up at them and smiled. 'All right, girls,' he said. 'You'll be fine. There's nothing to worry about, nothing at all, just follow me.'

'You'll be in safe hands with Ed. He's been doing this since before you pair were born – although take my advice, watch him, and don't go anywhere near him when he's out of that pit,' Tony said with a sly grin.

'What are you telling them about me?' said Ed, aping offence. 'What sort of thing is that to tell anyone? You take no notice, girls. He's all mouth that one; you can trust your old Uncle Eddie. Now let's have a quick run-through, shall we? Settle those nerves. Show these lads what you're made of. How about we do a little something to warm up?' He raised his hands above the keyboard and a burst into a chorus of "I do like to be beside the seaside."

Charlotte's lips formed into a pout of displeasure.

'Come on, Ed,' said Tony. 'We haven't got the time to bugger about.'

'I was just trying to get them to relax,' protested Ed.

As her eyes got used to the lights Helen could just pick out Harry sitting a few rows back next to a plump woman with a notebook and pen who looked as if she might be interviewing him. Harry was looking very earnest and self-important. As Ed struck up with the opening bars of their song Harry looked up and grinned at her.

Helen was so nervous and distracted by Harry that

the music took her by complete surprise and rather than come in on the first note she stood there with her mouth open, while Charlotte thundered on alone.

'Oh for God's sake,' snapped Charlotte, glaring at her.

Tony rolled his eyes and looked heavenwards. 'Whoa there, whoa,' he shouted to Ed and then turned his attention to Helen. 'Presumably you're going to be doing more than just standing there catching flies, are you, love?'

Helen blushed furiously and nodded. 'I'm so sorry,' she began, feeling increasingly anxious. 'I didn't mean to, I wasn't ready.'

'We noticed,' said Tony. 'Anyway, don't be sorry, love, let's just give it another go, shall we? Why don't you come on again? Actually why don't you come on from back stage to the front, have a bit of a practice, and as soon as you're settled Ed will start the intro. All right, you got that?'

Helen, blushing furiously, nodded.

'Great, now I don't like to rush you, ladies, but we're on the clock here and I'm doing you a favour fitting you in at all – so, if you'd just like to get yourselves organised.' He made a wafting motion with his hands. 'Off you go. Let's see if we can't get this show on the road.'

'And don't you *dare* bugger it up this time,' Charlotte hissed under her breath as they walked back towards the wings.

Helen blinked back tears as Tony announced them. 'Ladies and gentlemen – the Wild Birds!' while Eddie played a few bars of their song. Charlotte didn't even look at her as they walked back onto the stage. This time Helen was ready.

'There you go, you see; not bad at all, that was much better. Just a bit of first-night nerves. It happens to the best of us. All you have to do is get down here and hit your mark, and relax,' Tony said, giving Helen and Charlotte an impromptu round of applause, as the music for their number faded away. 'You sound great. Really good – that was great. Okay.'

He stepped into the shadows by the orchestra pit and picked up his notes. 'Anyway, we need to be getting on,' he said. 'Why don't you two pop off and get yourselves sorted out for the show. You have got costumes, presumably, have you?'

'Oh yes,' Charlotte gushed. 'I had them designed and made specially – they're really amazing.'

Tony nodded indulgently. 'Well, that's good.'

Helen bit her lip. She felt hot, faint and slightly sick.

'Right. And you're happy?' Tony said to Ed, who was still seated at the keyboard.

'As a sand boy,' Ed said, running his handkerchief over his sweaty brow. 'And Tony's right; you sounded great, girls. Well done.'

'Good, well in that case off you go, we've got half a dozen more acts to run-through before the show. Do you know where to get changed?' Before either Charlotte or Helen had a chance to reply, Tony said, 'Vince here will look after you, won't you, Vince? Show you where to go, if you need any help –'

The man who had sorted out their microphones, and who was now standing in the wings, raised a hand and waved. He was a scrawny man with a gingery complexion, close shaved head, and was dressed in a black tee shirt and matching jeans. He made his way over with a swagger.

Charlotte turned to beam at him. 'That's great, thank you,' she purred.

'My pleasure,' said Vince. 'Nice song. You did really well; bit nerve-wracking being out there on that great big stage. You done much singing?'

'Only at school –' Helen began.

Charlotte glared at her, stopping the words in her throat. 'Quite a bit actually – charity things, small events mostly. Nothing quite like this.'

He nodded. 'Well, you came across really well – if you'd like to follow me. You two ladies local, are you?'

Charlotte nodded. 'We most certainly are,' she said, all pout and eyelashes. 'But we don't intend to stay local for much longer.'

Helen looked away and glanced down into the first few rows of seats. Harry was nowhere in sight. Everything seemed slightly too loud and in too sharp a focus. She swallowed hard, trying to quell a wave of nausea that rippled through her.

'Right, well I'll just show you where the dressing rooms are – you've got bags round the back here? Your friend's looking a little pasty. All right are you, sweetheart?' asked Vince.

'I'm just a bit nervous that's all,' said Helen, swallowing again. 'I'll be fine. I think I'm just going to go and get a bit of fresh air.'

'Take no notice of her,' Charlotte said, glaring at Helen. 'Any excuse for screwing things up, aye? She likes to make a scene, don't you, Helen?'

'Excuse me,' Helen mumbled and, breaking ranks, hurried away behind the curtains.

'See what I mean?' she heard Charlotte say. 'She's always been a bit of a drama queen. Likes to be the centre of attention does our Helen.'

With her stomach clenched into a tight unforgiving knot, Helen hurried across the stage, out behind the curtains, snatching up her bag and coat as she went, making for the stairs, dodging the stage hands, and finally – gasping for breath – pushed her way out through the fire exit at the very back of the theatre and ran into a small yard beyond.

Helen didn't look back; she didn't expect Charlotte would be coming out to see how she was.

In a little courtyard which backed onto the main car park, people were standing around under the awning of a mobile tea wagon, eating, smoking and chatting. As she hit the cold, wet, late-afternoon air Helen dry heaved, looked around in panic and then, with seconds to spare, stumbled across the yard and threw up into a rubbish bin bolted to a sign requesting people not to litter. She had barely eaten all day and her stomach protested as she retched again, relieving her stomach of what little it contained. Her arrival and her impromptu floorshow had stopped everyone dead in their tracks. As she made a show of composing herself, conversation resumed.

As Helen pushed her hair off her face, a man in a corduroy jacket, who had been standing chatting to a young woman by the tea van, ambled over to her.

'Are you all right?' he asked, as Helen wiped a hand across her lips.

She nodded. 'Yes thanks, I'm okay. I'll be fine,' she said breathlessly. 'It's just been one of those days . . . or maybe it was something I ate. It's nothing really. Thank you.'

'Doesn't look like nothing to me,' the man said, pulling a handkerchief out of his pocket and handing it to her. 'Here, would you like this?'

Helen nodded and took it gratefully. His female companion, who had a duffle coat wrapped around her shoulders like a cape, covering a leotard and thick tights, grimaced as Helen wiped her face and hands, though before Helen could hand it back, the man held up his hands and said, 'No big deal, you can keep it, sweetie – your need is greater than mine. You want me to go and get anyone for you?'

'No –' Helen began. 'I'm okay. Honestly.'

The man didn't look convinced.

'Have you been drinking?' asked the dancer, grinding out a cigarette under her foot.

Helen shook her head. 'No, of course I haven't been drinking. I'm one of the acts for tonight.'

The woman still didn't look convinced, while the man laughed. 'The two aren't mutually exclusive,' he said. 'You wouldn't be the first person by a long way to roll up steaming drunk before going on for a show. A lot of people can't get up there without being stocious.'

'Well, I'm not one of them.' Helen glared at him. 'I just told you, I am not drunk.'

'If you say so,' he conceded. 'Although if you're not drunk then that was one hell of an entrance. It should really get the judges' attention. Do you do anything else or is that the only party piece you've got?' He was smiling.

'I'm a singer,' said Helen indignantly, doing her best to say it with some confidence. 'I don't know what came over me. I've never been sick before when we've sung. I think it's probably just nerves. It's all been a bit stressful today, getting here and then we were late and the girl I sing with is –' Helen shut up when she realised that they were both staring at her. 'Sorry, I'm running on, aren't I?'

The dancer eyed her up and down. 'You haven't got a bun in the oven, have you, sweetheart? That can take you unawares too, you know,' she continued, conversationally. 'Morning sickness comes on all of a sudden, and don't you take any notice of that "morning" crap, sick all day long I was with my little' un. Morning, noon and night. Bloody exhausting, I can tell you. You want to go and see the doctor. Get yourself checked out –'

'Of course I'm not pregnant,' gasped Helen, reddening furiously. 'It's just that I'm worried about the show, that's all – and getting everything right – and it looked like it was all going to go wrong, and this is a really big chance for us, that's all. I just don't want to mess it up . . .' her voice faded away.

'God, I know how that feels; it sounds like stage fright to me,' said the dancer, sagely, lighting another cigarette. 'You want one?' she asked, offering Helen the packet.

Helen shook her head. 'No thanks, I don't.'

'Suit yourself; I find it helps my nerves. It happens to most of us at one time or another. You'll get over it.' The dancer grinned. 'Or then again maybe you won't. Some people never shake it off; even big stars, not just the minnows like us lot. You see them in the wings come show time, white as a sheet. I saw one man last year with a bucket. Great big bloke, he was – he didn't look like he was afraid of nothing.' She took a long pull on her cigarette. 'Funny old things, nerves.'

Helen, still feeling a little queasy, nodded and kept her lips pressed tight together. She didn't plan to tell anyone that her nerves had got nothing to do with singing or their act but much, much more to do with Charlotte and how horrible she had been, and the fear that everything that had gone wrong was all her fault. Maybe Charlotte was right, maybe she *was* useless. Maybe she should just go home and let Charlotte get on with it on her own; she seemed so at ease on stage. Helen had no doubt at all that Charlotte would be fine on her own. Just fine.

Another great wave of nausea rolled through her. Helen swallowed hard. The dancer eyed her up sympathetically. 'You want to try to plan ahead; dry toast, that's what I always have, two rounds of dry white toast, fills you up and settles your stomach a treat,' she was saying. 'Take it from an expert. Anyway I've got to be off and get changed.' She turned towards the man. 'See you tomorrow then, Arthur?'

'Bright and early, Rita. Are you bringing Alfie along as well?'

The woman nodded. 'Yeah, I've got to really, I've got no one to look after him for me tomorrow, but it'll be fine. He'll make a great rag-a-muffin – and besides it's high time the little bugger started to pay his way, the price of his shoes.'

The man laughed. 'Start them young, that's what I say. How old is he now?'

'Five,' the woman said, and then nodding towards Helen as she made her way inside, added, 'See you again. Take it easy, kid – you want to pace yourself.'

When she had gone the man turned his attention back to Helen. 'Do you want a cup of tea?' he asked. 'You look like you could do with something.'

Helen looked up at him and then hesitated, thinking about all the salutary tales she had been brought up on, all those dire warnings from her teachers about taking things from strangers. The thought must have shown on her face because the man grinned at her.

He had nice eyes.

125

'Don't worry,' he said, making his way back over to the tea wagon. 'You'll be quite safe with me. I wasn't thinking of whisking you away into the white slave trade, or anything half so exotic. About the only thing I can run to at the moment is a bacon sandwich. Now, what do you want with it, a mug of tea, coffee?'

'Tea, please.'

'Do you fancy a jam doughnut as well?'

Helen realised that she was starving. 'Yes, please,' she said, reaching into her bag.

'It's all right, put your money away – my treat,' said the man, pulling out his wallet.

'So what do you do?' he asked, as he handed her a steaming mug and a doughnut in a brown paper bag.

'I work in a toy shop, in town, Finton's Finest Toys,' she said. He waited and she reddened. 'Oh, I see what you mean, you mean what am I doing tonight? I'm a singer,' said Helen, sipping the tea gratefully. 'Me and my friend; we do mostly pop and folk and stuff.'

'Great. And have you ever done any acting?' he asked.

Helen shook her head before taking a bite out of the doughnut, carefully nibbling around the jammy centre, knowing even as she did that she had managed to get powered sugar all over her nose. 'No, well not now – I used to do a lot of drama when I was at school. It was really good fun, I loved it. I was in lots of plays and things, but I don't get the time any more, not since I started working full-time, so now we're both singers. Me and Charlotte. Charlotte's my friend, the one who I sing with, although she's still at school. Sixth form. I mean Kate not Charlotte, Kate Monroe. That's her stage name. We thought it sounded better – you know – to have stage names. Sorry, I'm rambling again, aren't I?' Helen said, self-consciously.

The man laughed. 'Don't worry, it's probably just the nerves,' he said and pulled a flyer out of the holdall he had slung over his shoulder. 'I was wondering if you might be interested in this? They're shooting this big historical film down on the quay tomorrow morning, and up along the stretch to the castle. It's called *Leaving Home* – it's about this family who go off to America to make their fortune, and I know they're still looking for extras for the crowd scenes. Rita and her little boy are going. Me too. It's easy money and it's good fun, and they feed you really well . . .'

Helen glanced up at him. 'It sounds great and thank you, but I'm not really an actress.'

'And you don't go off with strange men either?'

Helen reddened. 'That wasn't what I meant.' She didn't say that he seemed really nice or that she quite liked the way his eyes crinkled up when he laughed.

'It doesn't matter if you're not an actress,' he was saying. 'You don't have to be. It's all crowd stuff, background and atmosphere mostly. They're shooting a market scene tomorrow – there'll be loads of people milling about – to be honest it's money for old rope, a lot of hanging around mostly.'

'I'm not sure,' Helen began, glancing down at the flyer.

The man shrugged. 'Fair enough, please yourself. I'm

not going to twist your arm, but it was just that I thought you might be interested, that's all. You can keep the flyer. Pass it on if you can think of anyone else who might be interested. The more the merrier.'

Helen took a better look at the flyer. 'Actually I think I heard about this. Wasn't it in the local paper?' she asked. 'Are they shooting it by Castle Hill as well?'

He nodded. 'Yeah, they're closing the road tomorrow and that bit of street between the quay and the Excise House, in the old part of town,' he said, extending his hand, 'My name is Arthur by the way. Arthur Frankham.'

She smiled up at him. 'Pleased to meet you Arthur, I'm Helen –' she stopped and thought about it a split second. 'Helen Redford.'

'Is that your stage name?'

Helen grinned and nodded. 'Yes it is, does it sound daft?'

'No, not at all, it sounds great, actually. So, pleased to meet you, Helen Redford,' he said, shaking her hand firmly. His handshake was warm and firm without being bone-crushingly fierce. 'How are the nerves now?'

Helen considered for a moment and then laughed, 'Fine. I think they've all gone.' Not only were they gone but she could feel a funny little spark arcing between them, and was almost certain that Arthur fancied her.

'Jam doughnuts and a mug of tea, my own patent cure,' he was saying.

'So are you an actor?' she asked, taking another sip from her mug.

'No, well not really,' he said. 'I do odd bits in film or TV. Crowd stuff, walk-ons, a few lines here and there mostly. It's not exactly a career, but the way you get on in this business is as much about meeting the right people as talent, so it's a good way to get your face known. In real life I'm a writer.'

'Really?' said Helen, genuinely impressed. 'Wow, that is amazing. I've never met a proper writer before. Should I have heard of you? I mean are you famous? Have you had anything published?'

Arthur laughed, 'No, not yet – and okay, to be honest the acting thing is not just about making connections, I need to eat sometimes too.'

Helen smiled. She had no problem understanding that. Harry's dad, her boss, deducted her rent and share of the bills for the flat from her wages for working at the toy shop, which was good, but didn't leave much over for things like food or clothes. She had worn the same shoes all summer and now had blown the budget on the sandals that Charlotte had insisted they needed for tonight's show. Even without the shoes, by payday things were always tight, which made her reconsider Arthur's suggestion. Payday was still a week away and all that she had left in her side of the kitchen cupboard was half a packet of Weetabix, two tins of beans and a one-man Fray Bentos steak and kidney pudding. Helen took another look at the flyer. 'And they pay you *when* exactly?'

'If they take you on? At the end of the day, cash in

hand. No messing about. And they pay you for the whole day whether they use you or not.'

A bit more money would certainly help. She hadn't paid Charlotte for her costume yet. 'Okay, thanks, I'll think about it,' Helen said, tucking the flyer into her bag.

'If you do come along can you tell them that I sent you?' As he spoke Arthur handed her a business card. 'That's me,' he said, running a finger under the name.

'Arthur Frankham,' she read aloud. 'It doesn't say that you're a writer on here.'

'No, I know. That was my idea. I do other things and this way I didn't need to have more than one set of cards printed.'

Helen nodded. 'So what sort of things do you write?'

'Mostly science fiction but I'm thinking about setting up as an agent.'

'What, for books, like a literary agent?'

He laughed. 'No, not for books. I can barely sell my own stuff let alone anyone else's, so no, not for books. For actors, extras mostly I think. I've done quite a lot of work for films and TV over the last two or three years and I've made quite a few really good contacts, people I could work with, people who need extras and – well, it's early days yet but it's just an idea I'm kicking around.'

Helen smiled. 'Sounds like you've got it all worked out.' She tucked the business card into her bag alongside the flyer. 'And it would help you pay the bills till you get a big film deal for one of your books,' she added.

130

Arthur beamed. 'I like your style, Miss Redford. Maybe I should sign you up; you could be my first real client.'

Helen grinned right back at him. 'Maybe you should,' she said, 'I'm a great prospect.'

Arthur nodded. 'You know, you might be right. How about another doughnut?'

Helen looked down; she hadn't realised she had eaten the one he'd bought her. 'Don't mind if I do,' she said.

Arthur waved to the girl in the tea van. 'Same again,' he said, pulling out his wallet. 'And have one for yourself.'

It was about ten minutes later when Helen went back inside, feeling much better. It wasn't to last.

'Where on earth have you been?' snapped Charlotte, who was standing in the corridor that led backstage. 'I've been looking all over for you. I thought you'd done a runner. Why didn't you tell me where you were going? Harry's just done an interview with the *Billingsfield Times* about us. The woman he was talking to thought we were really good, despite your cock-up. Harry said she's doing a big feature on all the local acts in the show. I sent him off to look for you. She wants to talk to us and do a photo of us in our costumes before we go on.' Charlotte sighed. 'I can't believe you just buggered off like that, Helen.'

'I didn't bugger off, I was only outside,' protested Helen, glancing back over her shoulder. 'You saw me go. I was talking to this guy who is –'

'Never mind who you've been talking to. We need to go and get ready. And you'll never guess who I've just seen?'

Helen waited; she was fairly certain Charlotte was going to tell her.

'Well?' demanded Charlotte after a second or two, 'Aren't you going to at least *ask* me who it was?'

'Okay, who did you see?'

'*Leon Downey*,' Charlotte said triumphantly.

Helen pulled a face and shook her head. 'Leon Downey? I don't know who that is. Am I supposed to know him?'

'Oh come on, don't tell me you've never heard of him,' said Charlotte, with frustration. 'Vince, the assistant stage manager, you know, the one Tony said would take care of us and who set up the mikes? He pointed Leon out to me and told me all about him. Apparently he came in while we were singing and sat up near the back so he could watch us. He's heard all about us apparently, isn't that *fantastic*?'

Helen stared at her. 'But I don't understand. How could he have heard about us, Charlie? We've only ever sung at school concerts or at home. We didn't even go to the audition.'

Charlotte dismissed her concerns with a flick of her hand. 'I don't know how he heard about us, do I? I'm just pleased that he has. Vince told me Leon's got about four acts he really wants to take a look at while he is in town and we are one of them. *Us,* Helen, me and you.

the Wild Birds. Isn't that brilliant? He's a top agent apparently, and *really* well connected. Vince said he'd put in a good word in for us, say how professional we were and everything. And then there's the reporter Harry met, she was raving about us as well; it's got to be good news.'

Helen stared at her. None of the things she was saying about Leon Downey rang true, but Helen didn't dare say that to Charlotte.

'Anyway,' Charlotte continued. 'As I was coming off stage just now Leon Downey was *there* waiting to talk to Vince and he smiled at me, like *really* smiled and then he sort of nodded his head.' She paused. 'What do you think? I mean this could be *it*, Helen,' Charlotte giggled. 'If someone like Leon Downey spots us and thinks we're good it's got to be a good sign. I *knew* signing up for tonight was a great idea. This could be our big break – bright lights, big bucks, fame and fortune here we come. I can hardly wait for the show –' She paused. 'What's the matter, aren't you excited?'

Helen stared at her. 'Yes, of course I'm excited, but some man smiling and nodding at you isn't exactly the same as being discovered, is it?'

Charlotte's expression hardened. 'Oh, that's right, I might have known you'd say something like that. You always look on the black side of everything, don't you, Helen? Being seen by Leon Downey is a lot better than anything you've come up with so far.' She took a breath. 'Anyway, I think to be honest it was me he was really interested in. Vince told me that he thought I'd got real stage presence.'

'But we're a duo, Charlie,' said Helen.

Charlotte smiled thinly. 'At the moment we are but things can change,' she said. 'Anyway I need to ring my dad and get changed into my costume. The photographer said he wants to take some shots before we go on stage. And Vince said I could use the phone in the main office as long as I didn't take too long. I'll see you upstairs.'

'Wait a minute,' said Helen, pulling out the flyer that Arthur had given her. 'A man gave me this just now while I was outside. There's a film company making a film on Castle Hill. They're looking for extras. If we turn up on the set tomorrow morning then maybe they'll take us on. It's all day. And it says on here that there might be more work for them. The money's good, and it's for a proper film company. I thought maybe we could give it a go.'

Charlotte took the leaflet from her, quickly scanned the text, and then screwed up her nose. 'Have you actually read this?' she asked.

Helen nodded. 'Yes. It sounds all right to me and it's cash in hand at the end of the day.'

Charlotte stared at her. 'Are you serious?' she said. 'They want people on set at *six* o'clock tomorrow morning.' She shook her head. 'Six on a Sunday morning? You have got to be mad. There is no way I'm getting up that early on a Sunday morning for anyone. This isn't for people like me, this is for cattle, Helen. People who can't do any better for themselves. You just don't get it, do you? They don't want people with talent turning up for this kind of thing, they want window dressing, cannon fodder. Go here, stand there, look happy, look sad, look oppressed; I don't think so. No, this is where I should be, in a proper theatre, up on the stage – out in the spotlight, on TV. I want to be a star, Helen, not herded around dressed up as a peasant. They probably want you to go barefoot, you know – so no, I really don't think I'll be doing that, thank you. Here, you go if you want to.' She slapped the flyer back into Helen's hand. 'I'm going upstairs to ring my dad.'

'But it's a proper film, and it'll be extra money,' said Helen in a tiny voice, as Charlotte walked away.

Charlotte glanced over her shoulder. 'That's just the point, Helen, I don't want *extra* money,' she said, turning back. 'That's the real difference between you and me, isn't it? What I want is for someone like Leon Downey to sign us up and save me from Billingsfield and teacher training college and a life with playground duty and times tables and my dad looking over one shoulder telling me what he thinks I ought to do, while he cops off with someone barely older than I am. I want to be famous, Helen, and to have *serious* money, that's what I want, not chicken feed. Not *extra* money but *big* money – do you understand?'

Helen nodded. What else could she do?

'So you do what you like with your flyers and your crowd scenes in crap films. I'm going to phone my dad. I'll see you upstairs,' said Charlotte.

'What about Harry?' Helen called after her.

'What about him?'

'Shouldn't we wait for him?'

Charlotte pulled a face.' Harry is a big boy, you know. I'm sure he can take care of himself. You just want to concentrate on getting ready, getting down here for the photograph and most of all getting out on that stage and getting the song right. You know I could have died with shame out there when you screwed it up. How many times have we rehearsed that one? It must be hundreds. What on earth were you playing at?'

Helen felt the colour rising in her cheeks. 'Nothing. It was just nerves, that's all.'

'It was embarrassing and it was stupid, that's what it was. Thank God Leon Downey didn't see *that*. We want to come across as professionals, Helen, not rank amateurs. Now I'm off. I'll see you upstairs.'

Helen watched her go. There were still lots of people milling around going in and out of the theatre and up and down to the dressing rooms. She couldn't see Harry anywhere.

Just as Helen was about to give up and head upstairs to get changed, Ed, the man who had played keyboards for them, wandered in from the theatre, sipping from a can of lemonade. As their eyes met he smiled, waved, and headed over towards her.

'You okay, petal?' he asked. 'Can I help? You're looking a bit lost.'

'No, I'm fine, really. I'm just going to go upstairs and get ready.'

'You know, you did okay in there.' His comment stopped her from walking away. 'And you've got a good sound and a nice look –'

'Thank you,' Helen said, feeling self-conscious. 'I felt awful because I messed up the introduction.'

'You don't want to worry about that,' he laughed. 'Don't be so hard on yourself. No one died, did they? It happens all the time. You don't want to make a habit of it, but nine times out of ten if you do it during a show as long as you just keep on going and don't panic or let on something's gone wrong, then most people in the audience won't even notice. And at least you and your mate can sing. A lot of the big names we get coming here can only mime. And they don't always do that well.' He paused and looked her up and down. 'You're all right now though, aren't you?'

Helen nodded. 'Yes, I'm fine. Still a bit nervous. I don't usually mess things up,' she began.

Ed waved the words away. 'You just need to forget about it. It was no big thing, honestly. So, where's your friend got to?' He glanced around.

'Charlotte? She's gone upstairs, do you want me to go and get her?'

He shook his head. 'No, actually it was you I wanted to see. You know, you've got a really good voice. Have you had any formal training, like lessons or anything?'

'No, I just really like singing.' Helen shifted her weight, uncomfortable with the compliment. 'But thank you,' she muttered.

'I'm not being kind. You should have lessons,' he said. 'You're the one with the voice; it sticks out a mile –' He grinned. 'Although I suppose you probably already know that, don't you? Your friend's got more front, and that's the trouble. These days, trust me, having talent isn't anywhere near enough. Here –' he dipped into his pocket and pulled out a business card. 'This is a friend of mine; she's really good. She gives singing lessons. She could help you.'

Helen glanced down at the card. It was thick and heavily embossed, and the name had a string of letters after it. The quality of the card spoke volumes, and what it said was that whoever this woman was, she spoke very nicely and charged the earth.

'That's really kind, thank you, but I don't think – I mean, I can't really afford lessons at the moment,' Helen said, handing the card back to him.

'No, you keep it,' said Ed, waving her away. 'And you ring her; if you can't afford the fees then she'll work something out. I know she will. I know that she's got a couple of bursary schemes running at the moment and she is extremely well connected. She'll get you in front of the right people if she thinks you're worth it. Call her, tell her that Ed from the theatre told you to ring . . .'

Helen stared at him. 'But we're a duo,' she said lamely. 'Me and Charlotte.'

Ed nodded. 'I know, but your mate is going to get what she wants just by elbowing her way to the front of the queue. She's that sort and there's no doubt she's got the look, but you, you need to learn how – and if you ask me, you've really got what it takes. Trust me. I've seen a lot of kids coming through here over the years.'

'I wouldn't trust a word he was saying if I were you,' said another man on his way out of the auditorium.

Ed swung round. 'Vince –' he said. 'I might have guessed.'

Vince grinned at Helen. She recognised him as the man on stage earlier, the one who had been sorting out their microphones. The one who had told Charlotte about Leon Downey.

'Well if it isn't the missing Wild Bird. Flew the coop, did you?' He laughed at his own joke. 'I'd stay well away from Eddie here if I were you, sweetie. Trying to get you some free singing lessons, was he? Same old Eddie. You want to watch him.'

'Stop it,' snapped Ed.

Helen looked from face to face, unsure which of them to trust. Vince grinning like a Cheshire cat or Eddie, sweating and portly, busy dabbing his face with his huge paisley handkerchief. Feeling deeply uncomfortable she said, 'I've really got to go. I'm sorry but I need to get changed for the show.'

'You heard what I said, just ring her,' said Ed, nodding towards the card Helen was holding. 'She's really good,' he said, heading off towards the exit, pulling a packet of cigarettes out of his pocket.

'You want to be careful around him,' said Vince in a low voice as Ed vanished through the double doors. 'A bit of a funny one, is Eddie. You know what I'm saying?' he continued, tapping the side of his nose.

Helen nodded mutely. Every instinct she had told her she needed to be careful around both of them. She turned to head upstairs, but Vince was too quick for her, and grabbed hold of her elbow.

'Whoa there, hang on a minute, sweetheart. What's the rush?' he said. 'Don't run away. I don't bite, you know, and besides I wanted to talk to you. We were just wondering if you and your friend might like to come out for a drink with us after the show? Only just round the corner, at the Anchor. I told your mate I'd have a quick word with Leon about the pair of you. And he's very keen to meet up –'

Comprehension dawned. 'Oh, right, you mean Leon Downey? Charlotte told me about him. He's the agent?' Helen said.

The man grinned. 'Yeah, that's right – Leon Downey the agent. He was wondering if you'd like to come out with us afterwards for a drink, the two of you.'

'Her name's Kate. Kate Monroe.'

'What?'

'My friend. Her name is Kate Monroe.'

'Yeah, that's right, *Kate*,' purred Vince. 'She said. Nice name. And how about you, what's your name, sweetheart?'

'I'm Helen.'

'Helen,' he repeated. She didn't like the way he lingered over her name, it make her uncomfortable

'So he liked us?' asked Helen, trying to move him on. 'Kate said that he watched us singing.'

The man's smile widened. 'He most certainly did. And he really liked what he saw. So about this drink? You reckon your mate Kate'll be up for it?'

'I'll ask her – she's just gone to use the phone and get changed, but I'm sure she'll say yes.'

The man nodded. 'Fair enough, good.' He paused. 'See you later then, sweetheart; what did you say your name was again?'

'Helen,' she said. 'Helen Redford.'

'Well then, Helen, we'll pick you up by the stage door when the show's over. You don't want to let a chance like this slip through your fingers, do you? A talented duo like you and Kate; top agent like our Leon . . .' He winked and then made his way towards one of the maze of corridors behind the stage.

Helen watched him go. Everything about Vince made her feel uneasy – it felt like he was making a joke at her expense – but at the very least she knew that Charlotte would be pleased about Leon Downey. It looked like he really was interested in them after all.

EIGHT

A little knot of people had gathered on the pavement outside the Carlton Rooms to watch the crew filming Helen parading up and down the steps outside the main doors of the theatre. She had to have done it at least half a dozen times now while Felix got the shot he wanted.

One or two of the bystanders asked for her autograph between takes, while some were filming the whole thing on their phones. Cars slowed down to see what the fuss was about. After fifteen minutes or so Felix made an executive decision that they wouldn't actually go into the theatre until Helen was ready to go back for the sound checks the following day, so that they could film the whole sequence at the same time, which meant that Helen didn't get past the plate glass doors. Instead she stood outside peering in at the box office and the crush bar, like a child pressed to the glass outside a sweetshop. Not being allowed in almost felt as if she had been robbed of something.

Natalia caught her mood.

'Are you all right? Don't worry,' she said, sheep-dogging Helen back towards the limousine. 'There will be plenty of time for you to go in tomorrow. We've just got a couple more stops and we don't want to rush those. Okay?'

'Sure,' Helen said. 'And presumably we'll film me going around the back then?'

Natalia pulled a face. 'Sorry?'

'I'm working there, I'm not in the audience,' said Helen.

'Oh, I see what you mean, no, I think the plan is that you'll be going in through the front – those posters and things are just too good to miss.'

It had just started to rain again, and the passers-by, sensing that the show was over, began to wander away back towards the town centre and the car parks.

As the limousine pulled away from the kerb and slipped into the afternoon traffic Helen glanced back over her shoulder at the posters and the banner. How things had changed.

'Right,' said Natalia to the driver, glancing down at her checklist. 'If we go down here and turn left I think we'll come back around the one-way system.'

Helen settled into her seat to watch the familiar and the unfamiliar rolling slowly by. Once past the theatre they drove down by Billingsfield town hall and museum, and a great row of fine four-storey townhouses with stone facades and ornate porticos, that now housed solicitors and accountants, but once were the homes of the great and good of Billingsfield. At the end of the road, the car made its way into the Crescent, historically home to merchants and traders who had made their fortunes from the docks, and at the end they swung left down past the municipal park and the tree-lined avenue that took them by her old high school.

Helen leaned forward. The memories came flooding back. This was the nicer part of town away from the smells of the shoe factory and the tannery. Older children in uniform were trailing out through the school gates and across the tarmac heading for home.

'That's where you used you go to school, isn't it?'

Helen nodded. 'Billingsfield Grammar School for Girls. It was a really good place to be.'

The camera was rolling and Natalia and Felix both wore an expectant expression, suggesting that they expected her to carry on talking.

Helen pointed through the window. 'You see the pub on the corner up there, the Dog and Bucket? We used to go across there at lunch times. I know it's not very PC nowadays but the landlord used to turn a blind eye to the girls from the high school. We'd all be crammed into his back room at lunch time.'

Natalia looked genuinely horrified. 'You used to drink at lunch time when you were at school?'

'No, not drink,' Helen laughed, 'Well, yes, but we didn't drink alcohol, just soft drinks. The older girls used to go over there to play pool, listen to music, and play the slot machines. We thought we were so grown up. I remember we used to buy one drink and make it last as long as possible. I'd forgotten all about it – the landlady cooked us Pukka Pies with chips for the same price as a school dinner. Not exactly the healthy option but everyone did it in those days.'

The car slowed for the junction. The pub didn't look as if it had changed much at all since Helen was last there. Just seeing the facade brought back the smell of beer and cigarettes and the feel of the clammy leather benches, and the way the floor in the back room was always slightly sticky underfoot. There was a board propped up by the door advertising live music and good food. Helen turned to watch it go, like a ship passing by.

'We used to think we were so cool back then. It's where I first really started singing. There's a function room at the back.'

'And you sang with Charlotte Johnson there?'

'No, not then, I sang on my own the first time. It was a weekday evening. There was some sort of junior talent show thing that the brewery were running for a local charity I think, to be honest it's all a bit vague now. I've got no idea what possessed me to agree to do it. I wasn't exactly brimming with confidence in those days – but Charlotte was, and she was there that night too. We were both dreaming of escaping Billingsfield in some far-off magical future.'

145

She caught a look that passed between Natalia and Felix.

'What?' Helen asked.

'I was just wondering if we should maybe stop and have a look around?' asked Natalia. 'I'm sure the landlord wouldn't mind.'

Helen stared towards the pub.

They had been in the ladies together doing their hair and touching up their makeup, and Charlotte had said that they should maybe do something together, practise a bit, get a set sorted out, try and find some gigs. The memory was crystal clear like a snippet of film. Helen looked away, remembering how flattered she had felt.

They were in the same class at school although Charlotte had barely spoken to her before that evening, but everyone knew Charlotte Johnson was going some-where, her dad was rolling in money. It was only a matter of time before Charlotte was discovered. He'd paid for her to have singing lessons and learn modern jazz and tap. Helen blushed; she had been flattered and said yes. The Dog and Bucket was where this had all begun.

Felix glanced at his watch. 'I'm not sure we've got time now. Maybe we could do something there tomorrow?'

Helen took a deep breath. It was odd how memories clamoured for attention. Helen knew they were recording her, but she was no longer sure what were thoughts and what she was saying aloud. 'We used to practise at Charlotte's house. Her dad had got some backing tracks for her . . .'

As the car moved on there was another new view, and another new memory pushing the previous one aside. As she spoke and described what she was feeling and what she remembered, Felix and Natalia, sitting in the jump seats, nodded like therapists.

The car swung left past the park and back up Wherry Street by the bakery and back into the one-way system, and now all that Helen had were thoughts, impressions and feelings clamouring in on her. It was as if she had lit the blue touch paper to some part of her memory that she had long forgotten. This was the way she used to come into town on the bus – first as a child with her mum and dad, and then just with her dad, and finally alone. All alone. Helen blinked back the tears. Where had all those years gone? And now she knew she was saying all those things aloud because Felix was nodding more vigorously, and what was worse was she didn't know how to stop talking.

It was the mundane things that hit Helen the most; the shabby launderette on Park Terrace where she had taken her washing on Sunday mornings, the little corner shop a street away from Harry's flat that let her have things on tick till pay day. Helen backhanded the tears away. How could she have forgotten so many places, and so many people? Where were the memories coming from, and more puzzling still, where had she kept them hidden all those years?

'Do you want to stop?' Natalia was asking again, her tone smooth as silk. Helen glanced across at her. She was

147

good, and for the first time Helen got a glimpse of why *Roots* used her.

'No,' said Helen, 'I'm fine.'

How could she have left it so long?

Helen recognised where they were and guessed where they were going. A few minutes later the car pulled up on the pavement in front of a big old-fashioned double-fronted toy shop. The sign above the door read, 'Finton and Sons, Finest Toys and Games.'

'I didn't realise that we were coming here today; I thought we were going back to my old house and then back to the hotel?'

'We are,' said Felix. 'But we had a little rethink over tea and thought that rather than do all the interviews back at the hotel and in the theatre we'd stop off on the way. It gives the whole thing more of a sense of place, makes it more atmospheric.'

'It is in the schedule –' said Natalia, pointing to her clipboard. 'Here we are. Look. We said we would be meeting up with Harry.'

Helen nodded. 'I know,' she said. She didn't add that she had imagined waiting for him in the hotel room, meeting on neutral ground, a peck on each cheek, maybe a presidential-style handshake, then tea and a polite conversation for the cameras – not this. Coming to the shop straight from the theatre felt too quick; it felt as if she had been ambushed.

'We rang Harry while we were having something to eat,' said Natalia. 'He said he was happy for us to come to the shop. In fact I think he preferred it – you know, home turf. I think he's a bit nervous.'

'Well, if he's okay about it, then that's fine. I mean we don't want him to be nervous, do we?' Helen said softly. Harry wasn't the only one who was nervous. She glanced across at the crew. She had known that this moment was coming – she had seen Harry's name on the list – but now the moment was here she was apprehensive. What if he had changed, what if he was bitter or angry with her? And why the hell hadn't she rung him before now? What would it have taken to break the ice, to reach out and test the waters before today?

Helen could feel herself trembling. She couldn't remember the last time she had spoken to Harry. They had been such good friends and he would have been easy enough to find. Why hadn't she made the call before they started filming? Was it cowardice or fear on her part, or a little of both?

'You *are* okay about this, aren't you?' repeated Natalia. 'Meeting Harry was on the schedule, just not at the toy shop. I mean if it's a problem,' she let the phrase hang in the air.

Glancing up at the shop front Helen couldn't help wondering if leaving their first meeting to chance after all these years had been the most terrible mistake. What if Harry had grown into someone she didn't recognise? What if he resented the intrusion on his life; what if he hated her now? She swallowed down an unexpected flurry of tears. Why hadn't she rung him?

'I'm fine,' she said. 'It's just all a bit much. All this feels like something from *A Christmas Carol*.'

Natalia pulled a face. 'Sorry, I'm not with you.'

'The Ghost of Christmas Past?' Helen prompted.

'Oh yeah, right,' said Natalia, comprehension dawning. 'I see what you mean. Yeah, well hopefully it'll have the whole happy ending thing too. Maybe not a goose though . . .'

Felix laughed.

Not altogether reassured, Helen smiled while the crew clambered out ahead of her, and then at Felix's signal Helen stepped out of the car and crossed the pavement, surprised by just how nervous she felt. She really *should* have rung Harry, said a little voice in her head. *Why the hell hadn't she?*

'So how did you end up working here?' Natalia prompted.

'I had a Saturday job here when I was at school, and then when I left, Harry's dad offered me a full-time job –'

'You didn't think about going to college or university?'

Helen laughed. 'I did for about ten minutes, but it didn't happen, not in those days, not for people like me. But this was a lovely job. I loved it here with Harry and his dad. Some of the girls I went to school with went into nursing or teaching or working in shops but most of my friends ended up as machinists at Fulbrights making overalls. No, this was a lovely job.'

'But you always knew that you were destined for better things?' suggested Natalia.

150

'Not really, but we all dream, don't we?' said Helen. 'I bet if you asked any one of the girls who left my school what they wanted they would all have had great plans. But there are no guarantees. And I was happy here. Really happy –'

'But not happy enough to stay?'

'Being happy doesn't mean you can't do something else. Things change. I had a chance to change my life, maybe the only chance I'd ever get. There are no guarantees that those things will come along again; and so yes, I took it.'

At the shop doorway Helen hesitated. As she reached for the handle the door swung wide open, a middle-aged woman with a child in a buggy filling the open doorway. As the woman caught sight of the camera crew and then Helen, her jaw dropped and she began to bluster an apology. 'Oh, I'm so sorry,' she said. 'I didn't – oh my God – I'm not going to be on the telly, am I? Will you just look at the state of me. I'd have put my teeth in if I'd have known –'

'Cut,' said Felix, and then painting on a professional smile for the woman's benefit, continued, 'It's fine. Not a problem. Let's help you out of there, shall we?' And then glancing at the crew he said, 'Will you give us a lift here, guys?'

'I remember you, you're that woman off the telly,' the woman was saying to Helen, all the while pointing and grinning. 'You are, aren't you? You were in *Cannon Square*. I remember you. You know I used to love that programme. Eva Reynolds.'

151

Helen nodded. 'That was me.'

'Bloody hell, you wait till I tell my old man that I've seen you. Are you coming back? I've always said it's not been the same since you left. It's gone right off. All drugs and things, not proper stories –'

'I died,' said Helen helpfully.

'Oh yes, that's right. I remember now, that gas explosion. I wouldn't let that stop you though if I were you, pet. You could be your own twin sister or something. I mean they do all sorts on the telly these days. People coming back from the past in comas and things. I'd watch you . . .' She chattered on while watching the crew struggling to manoeuvre the unwieldy buggy out through the doors. 'It's a bugger getting that thing in and out of anywhere. I told my daughter to get something smaller, but you can't tell 'em. Can I have your autograph while I'm here? I'm telling you, it's never been the same after you left.'

Helen smiled and scribbled her name on the piece of paper the woman offered her, her smile fixed as she stared up at the shop windows. Despite the woman and the fuss all Helen could think about was washing the windows on Saturday mornings, and how cold the heavy plate glass had felt under her fingers on a winter's morning. Harry's father had liked her to dress the windows every week. He always said she had a real flair for that kind of thing. *Artistic, creative – you've got a real eye for display, Helen. She's a real asset, isn't she, Harry?'*

Helen smiled. Harry's father had always been kind to her. She realised now that he wanted her to marry Harry, take over the shop, keep his boy safe. But even so when Helen told him she was leaving he had done nothing but wish her well. *I knew we'd not have you here long, pet. I hoped but in my heart I knew – I'll be sad to see you go but if it doesn't work out you'll always have a job here, you know that, don't you? I had hoped that you and Harry, well, you know – but it was only wishful thinking; an old man's fancy.'*

Today there was a family of bears picnicking in one window, alongside a racetrack and railway line set out with little trains. The woman took the autograph and grinned. 'Best of luck, love, and take my advice; you want to give 'em a ring, see if they'll have you back.'

Helen smiled her goodbyes.

'Right, can we go again now that we've cleared the doorway?' Felix said briskly. 'How's the light?'

The cameraman gave him the thumbs up.

'Right, okay Helen, if you'd just like to go back to the car – everyone ready now?'

Just as Helen turned to do as she was instructed, she heard someone calling her name from behind her. 'Helen?'

She swung around. He was standing in the shop doorway, smiling at her. 'Harry?' she whispered. 'Oh my God, is that you? You've not changed a bit –' her voice crackled and broke.

The film crew were already rolling and no more than a step or two behind her.

153

Harry grinned; he still looked for all the world like the kind of man who would always have a pen handy if you needed one. He was greyer now, with a bit of a paunch, and his bright open features had thickened up so that he looked more like his father; but Helen would have known him anywhere.

'Well, fancy seeing you back in Billingsfield,' he teased. 'I thought you'd forgotten all about us.'

The sound of his voice brought a lump into her throat.

'Oh, Harry,' she said, her heart filling up with joy at seeing his face and knowing that even if he had aged he hadn't changed inside. Tears prickled behind her eyes. 'It's so lovely to see you again.'

'Is it really you?' he said softly. 'I've been waiting so long to see you again. I haven't been able to settle to anything all day. They said they weren't sure what time you'd be getting here. It's been hell waiting –' He paused, his eyes bright. 'It's been too long, Helen. I've really missed you.'

There was a moment of silence and then something cracked deep inside her and she ran towards him and threw her arms around him.

'Oh, Harry,' she spluttered. 'It's so nice to see you.'

'Now that's what I call a hello,' said Harry grinning down at her and kissing the top of her head. 'You look fantastic.' He paused. 'I've missed you –' he said as he held her tight up against his chest. 'You've got no idea how many times I've thought about this moment.'

She could hear the emotion in his voice and couldn't

154

stop the tears from trickling down her face. 'You could have rung me,' she said.

Harry laughed. 'And you could have rung me. I just can't believe you're finally here,' he said, making a show of composing himself. 'Come on, come inside, come inside. I've got cake out the back, and I've got some flowers for you. I wasn't sure about champagne but we've got tea.'

Helen laughed. 'Tea will be just fine. Let me look at you. You haven't changed a bit, you know.'

'Have you had your eyes tested recently?' he said, the grin holding fast.

The film crew followed them inside, squeezing through the doorway. Helen turned to catch Felix making throat-cutting gestures.

'We'll set up inside,' said Felix, by way of explanation. 'So we can film you walking into the shop together. Can you just give us a minute?'

'Sure,' said Helen. 'It'll give us a chance to catch our breath. You're okay with that, Harry?'

He nodded. 'Yes, of course. Is it always like this?' he asked, as the crew bustled past them to set up for the next shot.

'TV? More or less. It's not as smooth as it looks on your screen. You learn to be patient.'

He smiled down at her. 'You know, you look lovely. I can't believe you're here – I want to pinch myself.'

'So whenever you're ready,' said Felix, breaking into the conversation. 'Can we have you walking in, just naturally? What were you planning to do next, Harry?' asked Felix, as the crew settled themselves down by a display of baby dolls.

'Me? I was thinking I'd introduce Helen to her replacement?' said Harry with a smile.

Natalia said. 'Sounds good to me.'

Felix nodded and the cameraman gave them the thumbs up. 'Whenever you're ready,' Felix said.

On cue Harry guided Helen through the shop doors and over to the main counter, where a pale spotty girl watched their progress nervously. 'This is Lorna – she helps me out in the shop,' said Harry.

The girl stopped chewing her fingernails and held out a hand.

'So you've got my job now,' said Helen warmly, shaking it.

The girl looked like a rabbit caught in the headlights and for a moment or two it looked as if she might curtsey.

'I've already told her that we'll have no running away and getting rich and famous, haven't I, Lorna?' joked Harry.

The girl's colour deepened. Her mouth opened and closed like a beached halibut as she searched around for a reply. Her embarrassment was so acute you could almost touch it.

'So how have you been?' Helen asked Harry, diverting attention away from Lorna, who visibly relaxed. It was a ridiculous thing to say, given how long it had been since Harry and Helen had last seen each other, but she had to start somewhere.

'Oh, you know,' he said. 'So-so . . .' and then Harry laughed. 'Makes it sound like we only saw each other last week. Actually I'm fine, business is okay, and I'm really pleased you came back to see us at long last. How does it feel to be home?'

'Odd,' said Helen, any last lingering fears rapidly dissipating; Harry might be older but this was the gentle sweet man she remembered, the Harry she knew and loved.

'Well, it shouldn't, not that much has changed since you left. We've still always got the kettle on. Why don't you come on through to the back and we'll have that tea and cake. You're all right minding the shop, are you, Lorna?'

The girl nodded and visibly relaxed as the crew turned all their attention to Helen and Harry.

'Great,' said Felix. 'And can we cut there please? I was thinking we could maybe set up in the back room. It'll stop us being interrupted by customers as well. Is it okay if we go through and take a bit of a butcher's?'

Harry nodded. 'Sure, help yourself. Just straight through; you can't miss it.'

Felix, followed by everyone else, went through into the stockroom, and then peered around the door into the office. 'It's a bit cramped,' he said over his shoulder as the cameraman leaned in to give a second opinion.

'And, I'm thinking,' said Felix, 'that we're probably going to need some extra light in here. But it looks great in terms of texture – especially over there, all the boxes

157

and stuff – it looks like something out of the fifties. Okay, let's get a wriggle on, we're on the clock here, boys and girls. And we're going to need an extension lead for the lights.'

Harry glanced across at Helen. 'And you're saying it's always like this?'

'More or less. Give or take – although it's much easier in a studio.'

'It would drive me mad.'

Helen smiled. 'It's what I signed up for. Are you okay with all this? Please say something if it's too much, Harry. It seems a bit crazy. I don't see you for God knows how many years and then plunge you straight into the middle of all this. It's a hell of way to have a reunion. We can go back and film it at the hotel if you'd prefer? They'd just set up and film us talking –'

Harry shook his head, as the crew busily ferried things from the car. 'No, it's fine. It's quite interesting really. I've often wondered how they do it.'

One of the crew came back from the car carrying a light stand.

'Okay,' said Felix. 'I'm thinking it would be great if we just followed you through from the shop into here. You all right with that?'

The cameraman, peering down the viewfinder gave him an a-ok, finger and thumb gesture.

'Cool, so if you stand over there and then could you just lift the flap in the counter and let Helen through, Harry, and then just walk towards the camera, talking.

Anything you like, in your own time then,' Felix said, waving Helen and Harry into action.

Harry pulled himself up to his full height and straightened his tie. 'Real leading man material,' Helen laughed. 'You're a natural.'

Harry blushed. 'They said that you're going to be doing your show at the Carlton Rooms tomorrow night,' he said conversationally, lifting the counter so that they could trail through into the back room. 'It'll be just like old times, you up there on the stage. Maybe you should get Kate up there to do a number with you, I bet she'd love that – it would be just like the good old days.'

Helen stared at him. 'Kate?'

'Sorry, yes, Charlotte, although she still prefers to be called Kate. Her stage name and all that. You know what she's like. It sounds younger she reckons. She's still singing,' he said. 'She's doing quite well locally, actually.'

'That's nice,' said Helen, totally wrong-footed. Of course Charlotte was still around; why wouldn't she be? Helen hadn't expected it to be this difficult to talk about Charlotte. All these years and even her name had the power to stop Helen in her tracks. 'And you're still her manager, are you?' she said as lightly as she could manage.

Harry laughed and indicated that Helen should go through towards the back room. 'After a fashion. She's still as headstrong as she ever was, always got her own ideas and her own way of doing things, has our Kate – you must remember what she was like,' Harry said sheepishly, and then he glanced at the camera crew and

159

Natalia, who was standing behind the camera. 'I suppose you know that Kate and Helen used to sing together. They were very good. Really. I always thought they should have made a go of it as a duo.' And then turning back to Helen he said, 'Have you been to see Adam yet?'

Natalia, answering for her, shook her head. 'No, not yet.'

Helen looked from one to the other. 'Adam? I'm not with you. Who is Adam?'

'What do you mean, who is Adam?' Harry laughed, and when she didn't react his expression clouded. 'I thought that's why you had come back home, Helen. To see Adam. Adam, your son,' he said slowly.

Helen felt her jaw drop. 'My son?' she murmured.

'Yes,' said Harry. 'I assumed that's why you were here.'

'Someone please tell me we got that,' said Felix, somewhere on the periphery of Helen's hearing.

160

NINE

Backstage at the Carlton Rooms Helen tucked the business card that Ed had given her into her bag and hurried upstairs to find Charlotte and give her the good news about meeting up with Leon Downey. As soon as she opened the double doors onto the first-floor landing the noise from the female dressing room hit her like a wall. It sounded more like a gull colony than a changing room, with great shrieks of laughter and the babble of dozens of voices. The air was thick with the scent of cigarette smoke, mixed with sweat and perfume.

It was hot, too, and Charlotte was right; it was packed. The main communal changing area was so full that many of the women and girls had spilled out into the corridor, and were camping out on the benches along the walls, doing their makeup in hand mirrors and getting changed where they could, all the while

161

smoking and laughing and chattering away to each other.

Helen stood on tiptoe trying to spot Charlotte in the melee. Eventually she saw her over by the door that led out onto the fire escape. Charlotte was busy unzipping a dress carrier that she had managed to hang up over a wall light.

'So you made it, then,' said Charlotte grimly, as Helen eased her way through the crush of people.

'Sorry it took me so long. It really is crazy up here, isn't it?'

Charlotte handed Helen her costume. 'You can say that again. Did you manage to find Harry?'

'No, but I saw that man who told you he was going to talk to Leon Downey about us. Vince somebody?'

'Well, that's good.' Charlotte's eyes lit up. 'So what did he say?'

'He wanted to know if we'd like to go for a drink with him after the show.'

'Who, Vince?' asked Charlotte eagerly.

Helen nodded. 'Yes, him and Leon Downey – he said –'

But Charlotte had heard enough and was already shrieking with delight. 'Leon Downey? Are you telling me that Leon Downey wants to take us out for a drink?' she said, practically bouncing up and down with delight and excitement.

Helen nodded. 'That's what Vince said.'

Charlotte let out another great whoop that made the women around them turn around and glare at her. 'See,

162

I told you, didn't I? This is it, Helen, this is our big chance. God, that is just fantastic. I knew that we'd made an impression. What did you say? You did say yes, didn't you?'

Helen hesitated, unsure whether she should share her sense of unease. It must have shown on her face because Charlotte grimaced. 'Oh for goodness' sake, don't tell me that you said no?'

'No, of course I didn't say no,' said Helen reddening. 'But –'

'Go on, so what is it now? Oh don't tell me, you told him that you had to stay in and wash your hair? Oh no, wait. I know, you told him we *could* go, but you had to get in early because you had to get up to go to this bloody film thing tomorrow and traipse around barefoot in the mud.'

Helen cringed. 'No, of course I didn't tell him that, it was nothing like that. I just got this bad feeling about him, Charlie. He struck me as being really creepy.'

'Who, Leon Downey?'

'No, Vince, the man from the theatre. He said they would meet us after the show. Leon Downey and Vince – he was kind of shifty. It's hard to put my finger on . . .'

Helen was aware that Charlotte was staring at her. 'We're going for a drink with a top London agent and your instincts tell you that the guy who gave you the message was a bit shifty?' Charlotte snapped incredulously. 'Are you nuts? We're just going to a drink with them –'

Helen nodded. 'I thought I ought to say something.'

'Well you've said it now,' Charlotte said looking heavenwards. 'For God's sake give me strength. Just grow up, will you? It doesn't matter how shifty Vince is as long as we get to meet Leon. Don't you see? This is our big chance, Helen. The last thing we need now is for you to screw up again. We just have a drink with him, see what he has to say and take it from there.' She paused. 'Okay?'

'Okay, but I was thinking.' Helen bit her lip. 'How about if we took Harry along with us?'

Charlotte sighed. 'And just how is that going to look? Like we're kids who can't be trusted out on our own? Besides, I've got more backbone than Harry.'

'No,' Helen protested. 'It won't look like that at all. I thought maybe it would look more professional. Come on, it was you who suggested that Harry should be our manager.'

'Well, I've changed my mind since then, and anyway it was *you* who said we should wait before signing Harry up. Why don't we see what Leon's got to say first before we start involving Harry. And anyway he can be such an old woman, we'd probably be better taking my dad along.'

'Maybe that would be a good idea,' suggested Helen. 'You said he was coming to see the show tonight, didn't you? Why don't we ask him? He'd be ideal –'

Charlotte shot her a killer look. 'You cannot be serious. That was meant to be a joke, Helen.'

'But your dad is a businessman, Charlotte. He knows

164

about making deals and contracts, and all that kind of thing. He might be able to help us. And people respect your dad – Vince and Leon wouldn't try and mess us around if he was there.'

'Oh for God's sake. I really don't think so,' Charlotte snapped. 'And who says they're going to mess us around? We can handle this – or at least *I* can. I'm good at getting what I want. Oh, and remember when we're with Leon and Vince, that it's *Kate*. Kate and Helen.'

'We could always just *tell* him that Harry is our manager, say that we'd already got one – that would look professional. And Harry did get us a run-through, and the sound checks,' Helen said, clutching at straws

'This is about our *whole* career, Helen, not one poxy night in the Carlton Rooms. Our future, Helen. We don't want to saddle ourselves with Harry if someone like Leon Downey is interested in taking us on. And you said yourself that we shouldn't come to any snap decisions. No, I think we are much better going out to meet him on our own.' As Charlotte spoke she slipped her costume off its hanger. 'Anyway, we haven't got time to talk about it now – you need to get changed. That photographer wants to take some photos of us for the local paper, remember?'

Helen glanced around at the crush of other women. 'Shouldn't we go into the loo or something?'

'Have you seen the state of the loos?' Charlotte laughed. 'Bloody hell, come on, Helen, no one is going to be looking at you. Have you got a mirror with you?'

'Only the one in my handbag.'

'That'll have to do then, can you find it for me? Come on, we need to get a move on.' Without another word Charlotte shucked off her jeans and jumper and dropped them into her bag. Helen couldn't help but stare at her; Charlotte was wearing tiny, white, bikini-style knickers dotted with rosebuds, and a matching bra with underwiring, which gave her a proper cleavage. Charlotte still had a suntan from the summer holiday she had been on with her dad. They had been to Spain. She also had curves, proper curves. Helen found it impossible to look away. Charlotte looked feminine and grown-up and confident about her body in a way that Helen suspected she never would.

Completely unaware of Helen's scrutiny Charlotte pulled her costume on over her head and did a shimmy to get it down over her bust and hips. The dress was tight fitting and made of thin, slightly shiny, midnight blue fabric that clung to every last curve and, her dressmaker had assured them, would catch the light. There were sheer lace panels cut in round the waist and below that a full-flared mini skating skirt, cut to show off Charlotte's long suntanned legs.

'Is your dad coming tonight' Charlotte asked, as she zipped herself up.

'I don't know,' said Helen, feeling horribly self-conscious. 'He said he might come if he could get the time off. It depends on his shifts really.'

Helen glanced around to see who might be looking.

Her own underwear was tired and grey, certainly not something that she wanted to show off in front of a room full of strangers.

'Did you get the mirror?' asked Charlotte.

Helen shook her head.

'Is it all right if I get it?' Charlotte asked, as she flicked her hair back over her shoulders.

'Yes, of course,' said Helen, glad of the diversion. 'Help yourself. Oh and there are two new pairs of tights in there too.'

While Charlotte rummaged through her bag, Helen stepped into her costume, fully clothed, and wriggled it up over her hips, slipping her arms out of her jumper, then, pulling the dress higher, left her jumper hanging around her neck to cover as much of her body as she could, before finally slipping the jumper off over her head when her arms were in the dress. Only once her dress was on, and zipped up, did she slip out of her jeans. Charlotte didn't notice.

'My dad said he'd be here,' she was saying as she finally tracked down Helen's mirror in the bottom of the bag. 'He said he wouldn't miss it for the world. His little baby.' Her voice dripped with sarcasm.

Helen didn't like to ask if he would be bringing his new girlfriend along.

'And now, ladies and gentleman, tonight, here at the Carlton Rooms' all new talent extravaganza, we'd like you to put your hands together for our next act, two *fantastic*, fabulous local songbirds. Not only can they sing but it says here on my card that they're wild too. Ladies and gentleman, let's hear it for Billingsfield's *very own . . . Wild Birds*!' The compere's voice rose in an exaggerated crescendo, as he tried to whip up the audience's sense of anticipation and excitement.

Helen, standing in the wings alongside Charlotte, took a deep breath to quieten the ripple of nervous excitement in the pit of her stomach. The moment had finally arrived; all those weeks of practising and rehearsing, all those nights of singing along to backing tracks on Charlotte's tape deck, all for this. Helen felt slightly giddy as if her brain was full of bubbles and fluttering insects. She smiled at Charlotte. 'Break a leg,' she whispered.

Charlotte glanced across at her. Her lips were set in a tight narrow line.

'Isn't that what they say?' said Helen. 'Break a leg?'

Charlotte raised an eyebrow; if she was nervous she certainly didn't show it. 'I don't care what they say, Helen. Whatever else you do, just don't screw this up, all right?' Charlotte muttered as the applause died away. 'If you do I'll never speak to you again, is that clear?' And with that Charlotte stepped out in front of the curtains and waved to the waiting audience as if she had been doing it all her life, and made her way down to the front of the stage.

Helen, just a step behind, felt as if she had been punched in the stomach.

Charlotte, now smiling broadly, nodded an

acknowledgement to the ripple of applause and did a little bow and giggle. The compere, a tall thin man in a tightly fitting silvery grey suit strode across the stage to meet them.

'Well, good evening, ladies, and welcome to the Carlton Rooms. Don't they look lovely, ladies and gentlemen? Is it the first time you've sung here, girls?'

Helen nodded. The man laughed. 'Saving your voice for your big number, are you, sweetheart?' As he spoke he gave the audience a sly wink. 'Good move, I'd say; we don't want you to peak too early, do we, aye?'

Helen blushed. The audience tittered.

'Now don't laugh,' the man continued, teasing. 'It's a big night for you two tonight, isn't it, girls? Lots of pressure on everyone.' He tipped the microphone towards Charlotte. 'And what about you, princess? Are you all ready for your big moment?'

'Oh yes,' purred Charlotte, with a big smile and an embarrassment of breathy enthusiasm.

'I think we can all see that you're ready,' said the man. 'Down, girl.'

Charlotte batted her eyelashes, playing up to him. There was a ripple of good-humoured laughter in the auditorium. Helen wished the earth would open up and swallow her whole.

'In which case, best we let you get on with it! So, ladies and gentlemen, I give you act number six, *the Wild Birds.*' There was a little flurry of music as he made his way off the far side of the stage, leaving Charlotte and

Helen alone in the spotlight. It was a strange unsettling feeling.

Helen glanced down into the orchestra pit. To her relief Ed was there, sitting at the keyboard, and as their eyes met he smiled and gave her the thumbs up. She smiled back.

'Ready?' he mouthed, as the house lights began to fade and the spots seemed to brighten.

Helen nodded and with that he lifted his hands and began to play the introduction to their number. Helen took a breath in anticipation of the first note and hit it, strong and true, so that it rolled out into the auditorium. This time it was Charlotte who was taken by surprise and for a split second Helen saw a look of total panic on her face, and in spite of herself Helen felt a little ripple of triumph. Recovering quickly, Charlotte picked up the words and they were away.

Once Helen was singing any last remnants of nervousness evaporated and her voice soared above Charlotte's, her tone rich, deep, and strong, as she confidently hit every note, breathing life and emotion into the lyrics. Alongside her, by contrast, Charlotte sounded reedy and thinner, but Charlotte knew how to move and how to deliver a song, and as the tempo quickened and the spotlight followed their every move the audience began to clap and whoop and cheer as Charlotte began to dance to the rhythm, hands above her head, while Helen carried the tune.

A posse of young men sitting right in the front row

wolf-whistled and stamped out their approval. Helen felt a great rush of pleasure; it felt wonderful to be the centre of attention.

It suddenly struck Helen that Ed was right; she *was* the one with the talent, though even she knew that it still might not be enough. As they headed towards their big finish the whole crowd began to clap and sing along with them.

Charlotte grinned at Helen; her dancing was more flamboyant, more provocative now, and the crowd loved it. Even the men in the box from the television were whooping and cheering. Whatever it was they had, it was working. The Wild Birds had the whole audience eating out of the palm of their hand. Charlotte glanced across at Helen; her face was alight with a mix of pure joy and excitement.

Barely had the final note finished before the crowds began baying for more. The young men at the front were on their feet stamping and clapping and calling, 'Encore, Encore!' The sound of the applause echoing around the theatre was breathtaking, and so loud that Helen could feel it pressing against her chest almost as much as she could hear it.

From the other side of the stage the compere hurried on, microphone in hand, grinning like a madman. 'Well, what about that then, aye? Wasn't that something, ladies and gentlemen? Looks to me like you ladies better do an encore before we have ourselves a riot – what do you say, everyone? Do we want more?'

The crowd roared its approval; the boys in the front row stomped and whooped and cheered some more.

Charlotte, eyes glittering, glanced across at Helen and grinned. 'See, I told you,' she murmured. 'This is where we are meant to be.'

They hadn't expected this kind of response and hadn't prepared anything, so it was Helen who turned to Ed and said, 'Can you take it from the last verse and chorus?' And somehow, above the noise he could make out what she said and played their introduction again.

When their encore ended the crowd continued to clap and stamp, the sound ringing around the vaulted ceiling until Helen's ears hurt. The compere strode back on stage as they took yet another bow and held his hands aloft clapping Charlotte and Helen all the way. 'Thank you, Wild Birds.' And then turning to them off-mike, he said, 'Okay, off you pop, sweeties, you've had your moment in the sun.' And then back into the microphone continued. 'Ladies and gentlemen,' he said, 'wasn't that something, eh? What a great act. The Wild Birds.' He raised his arms towards them, rekindling the applause. 'It looks to me like those two young ladies are going to give the rest of tonight's acts a real run for their money. So let's get right on and see what else we've got in tonight's show. Next up we've got a great act for you. Ladies and gentlemen, I'd like you to put your hands together and give a big Carlton Rooms welcome to master illusionist and king of comedy magic, the Great Charlissimo.'

The crowd began to clap all over again.

Meanwhile Helen and Charlotte were so excited that they practically flew off the stage, giggling madly to each other with a heady mixture of excitement and disbelief.

'Oh my God, did you see them? *Did you see them*?' gasped Charlotte. 'Wasn't that the most amazing feeling? They loved us. Did you see those boys in the front row? They were on their feet and dancing and waving. God, that felt good. If Leon Downey doesn't sign us up after seeing that then he must be mad. Come on –' she said, catching hold of Helen's hand, 'let's go and get a drink –'

'That's a good idea; I think I saw a machine on the landing.'

Charlotte looked at her and laughed. 'Not that sort of drink, dummy. I meant a real drink.'

Helen stared at her. 'You mean like alcohol?'

'Yeah, *like alcohol*,' Charlotte said mockingly. 'You know, to celebrate the fact that we drove them wild out there.'

'But I thought we were going to go out for a drink later with Leon.'

'We are, but he's going to pick us up after the show. This is now. Let's go to the Crown on the corner. We can be back before the interval.'

Helen stared at her. 'Shouldn't we stay here?'

'What on earth for?'

'Well,' Helen hesitated; she couldn't think of a reason but it seemed odd to be leaving when all the other acts still had to do their turn. 'Shouldn't we stay and watch everyone else? The people from the theatre might want us, and what about your dad?'

'What about my dad?' Charlotte looked heavenwards. 'Oh for God's sake, Helen, stop being such an old woman. Come on! If my dad were backstage now he'd take us out himself and probably buy us champagne. We'll only be gone for half an hour, nothing's going to spoil in that time, come on.'

'Shouldn't we get changed first?' said Helen, conscious of how very short her skirt was.

Charlotte glanced down at her own matching mini dress and giggled. 'Yeah, okay, maybe you're right about that, but then again if they want us back on at the end we'll need to be in costume. Let's just go upstairs and grab our coats. It won't take a minute.' And with that she was gone and running upstairs to the dressing room.

The Crown was almost empty when they got there. The jukebox was playing in one corner, in another a couple of men were drinking beer and feeding coins into a row of slot machines.

Charlotte marched straight up to the bar and ordered for them. She was still flushed with excitement and brimming with confidence. 'God, that was amazing, wasn't it?' she said, talking over her shoulder to Helen. 'And it convinced me, if we needed any convincing, that we are doing exactly the right thing. I keep thinking about those boys in the front row. I mean they really loved us. And they were *so* cute.' Her grin widened as she paid and took the drinks from the barman. 'We need to think about what we're going to say to Leon Downey tonight.'

'Shouldn't we wait to see what he has to say <u>first</u>?' asked Helen. 'You know, like what he has to offer?'

Charlotte sighed. 'You are such a wet blanket, Helen. Okay, so how about if he says he wants to take us on straight away and that he can find us work? What are we going to say then?'

Helen hesitated. 'We'll have to tell him we need a bit of time to talk it over between us, and then we'll let him know what we decide. There's your dad and my dad and school and the toy shop to consider. It's not just an ordinary job, is it? It's digs and travel as well as wages and the usual stuff. And won't he want a percentage? Surely he's not going to expect us to make a decision like that there and then.'

As they spoke Helen followed Charlotte towards an empty table, tucked away in an alcove close to the bar.

'Yes, but he might. What would you say then? What would you say if he said we could start next week? This is the chance of a lifetime, Helen. And I'm telling you now, I'm game. What if he said he could get us into a show, or on TV? I'd be there like a shot. Anything *but anything* has got to be better than life at home and school,' said Charlotte excitedly. 'It would be so good.'

'We need to think this through, Charlie. We haven't even spoken to him yet.'

Charlotte glared at her. 'Why are you *always* so negative?'

'I'm not being negative, I'm being realistic.'

'Oh, really,' said Charlotte. 'Well, that isn't how it sounds from where I'm sitting.'

Helen felt as if she was talking to a brick wall. As far as Charlotte was concerned they'd already made it and had their name up in lights; she was talking as if being signed by Leon Downey was a foregone conclusion. Looking away Helen took a long pull on the drink Charlotte had bought and as the taste filled her mouth, spluttered furiously, almost choking. 'What on earth is that?' she snorted, wiping her mouth and staring at the contents of the glass.

'Vodka and Coke. Why? Don't you like it?' asked Charlotte, taking a swig. 'My dad lets me drink it at home and I reckon we ought to make a night of it; we deserve it, and it doesn't look like the sort of place that does champagne, does it?' She paused as if waiting for a laugh and when it didn't come, snapped, 'Oh, come on, Helen, just lighten up, will you? We wowed them. They loved us, you know they did. And don't dawdle, drink up, we've got time for another before we go back.' She took another long pull on her own glass and then waved to the barman. 'Can we have a couple more, please?' she said, indicating her glass.

The man grinned. 'Certainly can. You two look like ladies on a mission. Girls' night out, it is?'

Charlotte opened her handbag and pulled out her

purse. 'Something like that. You don't know who we are, do you?'

The man pulled a face, 'No, I'm sorry, love, I don't. Should I? Are you famous or something?'

Charlotte struck a pose. 'Oh yes, or at least we soon will be. We're the Wild Birds,' she said, taking out a five-pound note.

'And who are the Wild Birds when they're at home?' he asked, good-humouredly.

'We're pop stars,' said Charlotte, getting up to take her glass – still almost half full – back to the bar. 'You heard it here first,' she added with a sly wink. 'We're the next big thing. Everyone says so.'

'Well, there's a thing,' the man said. 'Famous, eh? And there's you slumming it down here with us lesser mortals tonight. I'm flattered. So, will you be wanting a double in there, then?'

Charlotte considered for a moment and then said, 'Why not?' Sliding the glass across the bar, she turned back towards the table. 'Do you want another one, Helen?'

Helen felt herself reddening and shook her head. 'No, I'm fine, thank you.'

'I'm fine thank you, *Kate*,' purred Charlotte.

'That your name, is it?' asked the man, pressing the glass up under the optic.

Charlotte nodded. 'That's right. Kate Monroe,' she said, offering him her hand. '*The* Kate Monroe.'

Laughing he set the glass down on the counter and

lifting her hand to his lips, he kissed it. 'Enchanté, made-moiselle,' he purred. 'Delighted to meet you. Tell you what, how about you have this one on the house? It's not often we get famous pop stars dropping in here for a bevvie.'

Charlotte giggled, while Helen looked down into her glass, cringing with embarrassment.

'Did you have to say that?' hissed Helen as Charlotte sat back down alongside her at the table.

'Say what?'

'That stuff about us being famous.'

'Well we are *going* to be famous. Don't hide your light under a bushel, that's what I say. I can feel it in my bones. Here, let's have a toast. To being famous.' She raised her glass. 'And let's not forget rich.'

Helen clinked glasses with her and sipped her drink while Charlotte babbled on and on about what she would like to do after Leon had signed them and how she saw their career panning out. Charlotte had just got to the bit where they were breaking into the American charts and had got the lead in a Hollywood film when other people began to drift into the pub. Within a few minutes a steady stream of customers was trailing up to the bar.

It took Helen a few minutes to work out that they had to be the audience from the Carlton Rooms, who were coming in to have a drink in the interval.

Charlotte had already drained her glass down to the dregs; her eyes were bright. 'Your shout,' she said, sliding the glass across the table.

Helen had barely touched her drink.

'I'm off to the loo,' said Charlotte. 'I'll have the same again. Best you get up there and get us a refill before the rush starts.'

Helen nodded. Although there was no way she was going to admit it, she had never bought a drink in a pub before, not a proper drink. There was a little crush of people in front of her, and despite the barman catching her eye and smiling there was no chance she was going to get served straight away.

'It's been really good tonight, hasn't it?' said a plump woman in front of her. She was talking to a small man who had a raincoat folded over his arm. 'I'm right glad we came.'

He nodded. 'Not bad, not bad at all. You want a Cherry B?'

The woman nodded.

'That magician were cracking,' said the man. 'Act like that, he should be on the telly.'

'Probably will be after this. We can say we saw him here first. And he was funny too, wasn't he? I wouldn't have wanted to go up there to help him. That lad was brave –'

'He loved it. And them acrobats were good –'

The woman nodded. 'And those two girls, the singers. Wild something –' She laughed as she said it. 'Wild all right. What on earth was that all about? I don't know how they got away with it to be honest. I mean it says on the posters *good old-fashioned family entertainment.*

Talk about putting on a show, eh? You wouldn't have thought they'd have let them get away with it.'

Helen edged closer, hanging on the woman's every word.

'And them lads in front of us shouting and whooping; bit much though for that time of night. Do you think they knew?' asked the woman.

The man snorted. 'Of course they did. How could they not? Let's face it, they hadn't got much else going for them.'

'Oh, dunno, they got an encore, and that little dark-haired one was all right,' said the woman as they eased their way closer to the front of the queue. 'At least she could sing. Got a nice voice on her.'

The man snorted. 'Not just a voice, eh? She was all right in more ways than one, although I quite liked the blonde m'self.'

The woman playfully slapped his arm. 'Stop it. Trust you to say something like that. I can't take you anywhere,' she said.

Helen hoped that the couple would carry on talking but as they got to the bar their conversation died. She was struggling to piece together what their conversation meant when the barman smiled at her. 'Same again?' he asked, nodding towards the empty glass.

'Just a Coke for me, please, and a vodka and Coke for –'

'Kate,' said the barman with a grin. 'Are you famous too?'

Helen was conscious of the couple being served

alongside them. 'No, not really,' she stammered. 'Not at all actually.'

He grinned. 'That's not what your mate said. Singers, she said, on the way up apparently – you and her, the next big thing.'

Helen pulled out a handful of coins from her purse and slid them across the counter, willing him to shut up.

'You singing round the corner tonight, are you?' said the woman who Helen had been eavesdropping on.

'No,' Helen said quickly, trying to make herself as inconspicuous as possible as she took the drinks from the counter. 'We just popped in for a drink.'

'That's a shame,' said the woman. 'They've got a really good crowd in there tonight. Full house near as damn it. It's a talent show. And they've had some really good acts on there, haven't they, George?'

The man who was sipping the froth off his pint nodded. 'And some bloody dire ones, and these girls – these singers – well, you should have been there,' said the man, directing his remarks towards the barman. 'They had these skimpy little costumes on.' He began to mime the outline.

'Yeah,' said his female companion. 'We were sitting halfway back but you couldn't miss it. You could see right through them. Clear as day.'

'Not that you could hear anyone complaining,' said the man with a loud guffaw. 'Well, at least not any of the blokes.' The woman slapped him again, and he laughed.

Helen stared at the two of them, feeling the colour

rush to her face, and then quickly she looked away and scuttled back to the alcove, glasses in hand.

'You took your time,' said Charlotte, taking her drink. 'I thought you'd gone home with the barman. He's a bit of all right, isn't he? I was just sitting here planning what we're going to do with the prize money.'

'The prize money?'

'Come on, keep up. From tonight, stupid,' said Charlotte, sipping on her drink. 'It's five hundred pounds if we win. How much do you reckon it would cost us to fly to America? Maybe we should go and have a look in the travel agents on Monday.'

Helen stared at her. She was sure she could still hear the little man with the raincoat discussing their costumes at the bar. She looked at Charlotte, who was grinning from ear to ear and still talking about flights to Hollywood.

TEN

In the storeroom at the back of the toy shop Helen stared at Harry. 'Harry, will you please tell me what on earth you're talking about?' Helen whispered, as if somehow Felix, Natalia and the rest of the TV crew might suddenly be hard of hearing.

He swallowed hard, his face reddening. 'I'm so sorry, Helen. I suppose I'd assumed that you were okay about this. I didn't mean to drop you in it. I didn't realise it was still supposed to be a secret. I just thought – well, you know, as you're here, as you'd come back –' He looked around at the crew, a study in discomfort.

'Harry, this isn't helping,' said Helen.

'I'd assumed that's why you'd come back to Billingsfield after all these years. I thought that you finally wanted to talk about it, and to see Adam again. Get it all out in the open. Get to know him. I mean we've all seen *Roots*, isn't that how it works?' He looked from face to face, looking for all the world as if he hoped someone was going to spring to his defence.

'I still don't know what you're talking about, Harry,' Helen said.

'Adam,' he repeated.

Helen shook her head. 'I have no idea who Adam is.'

'Please don't say that,' he said.

'But it's true, Harry –'

'Sorry,' he mumbled again. 'We've done our best by him, all these years, we really have – I just thought . . .' Finally, looking anxious and tearful, the words dried in his throat.

From the corner of her eye Helen could see Felix making frantic *keep it rolling* gestures to the cameraman. If Helen wasn't almost certain that it would end up being broadcast she would have turned round and slapped him.

'Harry,' Helen said, very slowly in case there was some chance he had misunderstood her. 'I haven't got a son. I've never had a son. I haven't got any children. I've never had children.'

Harry shifted his weight. 'No, well I mean I know that's the party line, and that's what everyone else thinks. So no, not officially, but we both know you have really. And don't get me wrong, I'm not judging you – I can understand exactly why you did it. You gave him up for adoption, and we adopted him. Me and Kate, Charlotte – Kate. She sings at the Bull on a Saturday night, keeps her hand in. I was hoping you might do a duet with her,

184

you know, for old times' sake.' He said it as if trying to lighten the mood; he looked around again expecting confirmation, his expression pained and growing more so. 'He's expecting you.'

Helen stared at him. 'He's expecting me?' she whispered. 'You told him that I was coming?'

'Well, of course I did,' said Harry. 'I thought that was the whole point of you doing the programme. A big reunion after all these years. I told Adam that you probably wouldn't be here until tomorrow; Natalia thought that was best, so you could get yourself settled.'

Helen turned to glare at Natalia, who looked away mumbling something noncommittal.

'And I have to say that I thought it was all a bit strange doing it now, and doing it on the telly,' Harry was saying. 'But then again what do I know? You're the star, and I thought – oh I don't know – the thing is, Adam has got lots of questions. It's obvious that he would have really. It's been so hard all these years. He knows all about you obviously, as much as we could tell him. We both understand that you really wanted him to have a stable family life, Helen. And you needn't worry, he has. We did our very best by him. Kate told me all about it – and it must have been so hard for you to give him up, even if it was for the best. He is a lovely, lovely person, but bringing him up in a proper family, doing right by him, that was the main thing.'

Helen stared at him. 'Oh, Harry,' she whispered. 'I haven't got a son. Adam's not mine.'

Harry paused, looking increasingly uncomfortable, and pressed on as if she hadn't spoken. 'Kate told me that you'd offered to help support him right from the start, but that she had told you no, that if she was going to adopt him then she was happy for us to do it on our own. I've said to her several times over the years, why don't you just ring Helen, not for us but for Adam's sake, get her to give him a bit of a leg up – get her involved in his life, you know, fundraise for the school or maybe give the prizes on sports day or something, but she's always been adamant. And Adam's just the same, but then I always think he doesn't want to go against his mum – I mean, like upset Kate, you know. Anyway I understand that you gave up a lot, but we have always done our best by him. Always.' Harry was more self-assured now, on safer ground. He smiled at her. 'We've always loved him.'

'I don't know what to say,' said Helen.

'There's nothing you need to say, not to me. But Adam, I know he would really like to talk to you. He's always been a credit to us, to you, to all of us,' Harry said. 'He's a real hard worker – a good boy – not been a day's trouble in his life. We didn't want to tarnish your reputation by letting on, that's what Kate always said and I'm all for that – and I don't think we have. We've always kept up our side of the bargain, Helen. But if *you* feel now that the time is right, well, that's your decision.' He smiled. 'I suppose times are different now, aren't they? And if you want to tell people now then that's up to

186

you, but I want you to know that we've always kept it to ourselves.'

Helen shook her head. 'Harry, stop this. We need to talk to Kate, this is ridiculous. Felix, can you please stop filming. All this is crazy,' she murmured. 'My reputation? Harry, you have to believe me. I haven't got a son.'

'National treasure – people's sweetheart.' Harry smiled warmly at her, his voice reassuring. 'I mean I'm sure people would understand – just one little mistake, it could happen to anyone – but then I've always thought you were never like the rest of them.'

'Harry, please – just stop.'

Helen stared at him. His expression was full of compassion and kindness. She could see he was trying to convince her it was all right to confess, that he understood.

'How old is Adam?' Helen asked.

Harry frowned. 'You don't remember how old your own son is?'

'Harry, I've already told you *he's not my son*.' She looked around the interior of the storeroom, piles of toys stacked from floor to ceiling, wondering what she could say to convince him. 'Where's Kate?' she said after a second or two.

'Ah, well you see, that's the thing,' said Harry. 'She's in Spain at the moment. I don't know if you know but her dad got married again and retired out there.'

Helen stared at him. 'And?'

'She's been over there for ten days to visit him. When *Roots* contacted us, Kate said she didn't want anything to do with the show or any of this,' Harry lifted a hand to encompass the film crew. 'I was really surprised, you know, especially given how she usually feels about being in the spotlight. Anyway, Kate thought it was a cheap shot –' he nodded towards Natalia. 'I'm sorry about that, but Kate was adamant. She said that we'd brought Adam up this far and she couldn't see how it would help anyone airing your dirty linen in public. She said she was amazed you'd agreed to it and she was really, really anti us getting involved.

'I don't think I've ever seen her so angry, Helen, and you know she's got a temper on her; but this was something different. She was worried about Adam, and you. But I thought if you'd agreed, that maybe it was high time it was all out in the open. And Adam has always wanted to know about you. So when I got to the shop the next day I rang Natalia back and here you are.' He paused. 'I know Adam has got all sorts of questions, and he has been playing in a band for years. And the woman in charge at *Roots* said that maybe if –' He looked pointedly at Felix and Natalia.

Helen swung round and glared at Felix. '*That maybe if what?*' she snapped.

Felix made cut, cut gestures to the crew.

'Don't you dare cut,' growled Helen to the cameraman. 'I want this on tape. Do you understand? What did the woman at *Roots* tell you, Harry?'

'Nothing – nothing at all,' Natalia interrupted.

This time it was Harry who looked outraged. 'That's not true and you know it. You and your boss said that if we let you use the story you'd put Adam's band in the programme. A proper feature. You promised. I mean why did we bother filming the band if you're not going to use it?'

Natalia looked from face to face.

Helen felt a great surge of fury. 'You mean you and what's-her-name back at head office agreed to whatever it took to get Adam in the programme?' said Helen. 'Tell me I'm wrong, Natalia!'

'It was a gift, and Ruth agreed with me. She backed me every step of the way with this,' said Natalia. 'It was just too good a story to ignore – we all knew that. We had no idea about Adam, but as soon as Harry told us about him we knew we had to go with it.'

'You told them?' said Helen to Harry, incredulous.

He nodded. 'Yes, from the way they were talking I assumed that they knew all about him. Natalia was saying it would be about family secrets and abandoned children, and I presumed that they meant Adam.'

Helen stared at him, feeling tears prickling her eyes. 'Oh, Harry, they didn't mean Adam. They meant *me* – me and my mum. I don't know what's going on here, but we need to talk to Kate. I don't know whose son Adam is but he certainly isn't mine. I never had any children.'

For a moment Harry looked as if he might protest, and then the facade crumpled. 'Oh my God,' he whispered, eyes bright. 'What have I done? How can he not be yours? All these years I've always thought –' He stared at her. 'God, I'm so sorry. In that case whose is he?'

'We need to talk to Kate,' said Helen gently.

Harry nodded. 'She'll be home tomorrow. When we arranged the filming *Roots* thought it would make good TV if we could have Kate's reaction when she arrived back – you know, once you were here.'

Helen glanced at Natalia. 'So this whole filming schedule has been arranged around Adam and Kate?' she asked. 'All those dates and all that nonsense about scheduling issues, was about *this*? You know I've arranged my tour dates around the filming, don't you. I've arranged it all so that you can film a son I never had?'

Natalia, her face ashen, nodded. 'Ruth thought it would be like a grand finale. We're going to send a car to the airport for Kate.'

'Telling her what exactly?' asked Helen.

'Nothing,' said Natalia. 'Harry said that she usually has a local cab company to pick her up when Harry and Adam are at work, so she won't think it's odd if they're not there to meet her. It'll just be a different firm as far as she is concerned.'

'And who else knows about Adam?'

'The production team. The guys back at the office, obviously, and we've been putting a trailer together. Adam's band are really good,' said Natalia.

Helen stared at her. 'I can't believe you; this is complete madness. You're messing around with people's lives. Why didn't you run all this by me first?'

'Because that isn't how we work. We knew you'd

kept this hidden for years and we wanted a genuine reaction on camera. It's what people watch *Roots* for, those big emotional moments. And I'm just going with what they told me at head office,' Natalia said. 'I think we all just assumed it would be a big reveal, lots of hugs and tears and then happy ever after. I mean it might take some bridge building but we have people, counsellors and –' Seeing Helen's expression, Natalia's attempt at the hard sell faded. 'I'm just saying,' she said, 'We do a lot of this kind of thing –'

'*This kind of thing?*'

'Bridge building.'

'This isn't about bridge building, this is completely and utterly irresponsible. These people are my friends.' Helen looked at Harry. Kind, gentle Harry. 'My friends,' she repeated. 'People I care about.'

'I appreciate what you're saying, Helen, but when it came to Adam, Harry said that Adam has always known that you are his mother,' protested Natalia. 'It wasn't going to come as any big surprise to him. We weren't going to tell him anything he didn't already know.'

Helen glared at her. 'Yes, but the problem is that it isn't true. I'm not his mother, am I?'

'We didn't know that,' Natalia said weakly. 'We really didn't.'

Helen sighed and then looked at Harry, who looked so distraught, she thought he might burst into tears.

'What have I done?' he murmured. 'What on earth am I going to tell Adam?'

191

'We can sort this out,' said Helen taking his hand. 'We just need to talk to Kate.'

'There's got to have been some sort of misunderstanding,' Harry said lamely.

Helen nodded. 'Kate will be home soon. We'll talk to her then.'

'She told me Adam was yours, and you know –' he paused, a bright tear rolling down his cheek. 'I believed her, and if I'm honest I was glad, because I'd always loved you, Helen, you know that. Even after all these years. I kept imagining what it would be like if you and I – if Adam had been ours and we'd been together. I kept hoping that you would come home. Having Adam in our lives was like having a little part of you in my life every day.'

Helen stared at him; the words made her heart ache. 'Oh, Harry,' she whispered, watching more tears well up in his eyes, and then very slowly, she put her arms round him and held him close. 'I've missed you so much,' she said, and it wasn't until the words were out that she realised how true they were.

ELEVEN

And the Winners are –

'Ladies and gentlemen, I'm sure you'll agree that we've had a real night to remember here at the Carlton Rooms' first ever talent extravaganza. What a great show it's been, hey, folks?' said the compere in his tight grey suit. 'But it's not over yet. While our panel of judges confer, Eddie Grey and the fabulous house orchestra, along with our very own Carlton Room singers, will be serenading us with a medley from the sensational Abba. Take it away, Eddie!' There was a ripple of applause through the auditorium as the opening bars rolled out through the sound system.

Meanwhile backstage the tension was almost unbearable; everyone was on tenterhooks waiting for the judges to make up their minds. Helen had found herself a quiet spot to perch, while Charlotte was pacing up and down the corridor like a caged tiger, gnawing away at her thumbnail. Other people were pacing with her or smoking. It seemed as if none of the acts had been given their own dressing room. One man was sitting in a corner distractedly ripping the programme for the show into ever smaller and smaller pieces. Hardly anyone was talking to anyone else, any conversation reduced to a low intense anxious murmur. Only the acrobats looked relaxed. There were about a dozen of them all dressed in white singlets and tight, white, pencil-slim trousers. They were sitting on the bottom of the stairs playing poker.

'How can they be so calm?' snapped Charlotte to no one in particular.

'Because they've got a job to go to next week; they're booked solid through till Christmas next year for some sort of international show,' said one of the dancers, who was leaning up against the fire doors puffing away at a cigarette. 'I was talking to one of them earlier. The cute one with the curly blonde hair.' She pointed. 'They came over on some sort of a cultural exchange from Russia. They only do this sort of thing for a bit of publicity, and a bit of beer money if they win.'

'You think they'll win?' asked Helen.

The girl shrugged. 'Who knows. Depends on what the judges are looking for, really. And anyway you and your mate did ok, didn't you? The punters loved you. Weren't they baying for more?'

Charlotte, breaking off from pacing, grinned. 'Yeah, that was us, we had to do an encore. Only encore in the whole show.'

'There you go then, sounds like a shoo-in to me,' said the girl.

Charlotte, for once, came over all coy and self-effacing. 'I'm hoping that'll go in our favour. I mean we *were* the only ones who got one, it's got to count for something, surely?'

The girl nodded. 'You'd think so, wouldn't you?'

'What about you?' asked Helen, hoping to turn the spotlight away from their performance in case someone mentioned the real reason they had been so popular.

'Me? I'm not expecting to win nothing really,' said the girl, taking a long drag on her cigarette. 'I'm just hoping to get some more work out of it. I've met some people and there's a bloke here looking for dancers for a show at the Corn Exchange. You want to go along, I've got his card if you want to give him a ring. They're doing auditions next week and then it's straight into rehearsals.'

'Thanks, but actually we're going to have a drink with an agent after the show. He's from London. He came down to see us specially,' said Charlotte smugly. 'But thanks anyway.' And then she giggled. 'He'd be mad not to sign us up after getting that encore. What do you say, Helen?'

Helen made a noncommittal noise, she couldn't bring herself to meet Charlotte's eye. The last thing she wanted was to have to explain to her what the couple in the bar had said. Since coming back from the pub she had kept her coat on.

'Oh, don't take any notice of her,' said Charlotte

casually, taking the cigarette the dancer offered her. 'She can be a real wet blanket.' Charlotte let out a long sigh. 'God, how much longer do you think they're going to be?'

As if on cue, one of the stage hands came out into the corridor wearing a set of headphones. 'Hi, folks. Can I have your attention, please? Can we have you all ready to go back on stage,' he said beckoning them towards him. 'The judges are coming back at the end of this number, so if you can make your way onto the back of the stage – and let's keep the noise down . . .'

Helen could hear the singers behind the heavy curtains as they crept across the stage to their places. All the various acts, sheep-dogged by the crew, arranged themselves around the back of the stage in a horseshoe. They were barely settled when the final song came to an end; the audience began to applaud and after a few more seconds the voice of the compere came over the PA.

'Well, wasn't that something, ladies and gentlemen? Let's give the boys and girls a warm hand and Eddie, take a bow – great stuff. What a performance. Now behind these curtains we've got all the contestants from tonight's show and I know there are a lot of very nervous people back there, so without further ado let's get those curtains open and see the fabulous acts that have given us all so much pleasure tonight.'

As the curtains glided open there was a great volley of applause. Charlotte turned on her most radiant smile and waved. Helen was hoping that as they were all huddled together no one would be able to see through their costumes.

'And let's get our chair of judges, Mr Andrew Steinman, out here – and for those of you who don't know, Andrew is one of the top impresarios in the country, and we're truly delighted that he's here with us tonight to help judge the competition. Yes, come on up, Andrew,' said the compere warmly. 'Up you come.'

As the introductions and preamble rolled on Helen felt her pulse rate rising and tension building. How much longer were they going to be before they finally announced the results? There were rounds of thanks and self-congratulatory back-slapping and then finally the compere said, 'And now we have come to the moment we've all been waiting for. Andrew, would you please tell us the results of tonight's first ever Carlton Rooms talent extravaganza? Eddie, a drum roll if you please . . .'

An expectant hush fell over the whole theatre as the drum rolled and the man opened up the golden envelope that he had brought up onto the stage with him. 'I have to say it's not been an easy task. The standard tonight has been –'

'Oh for God's sake just get on with it, will you?' mumbled Charlotte, as the judge blathered on.

Finally the impresario pulled out a card and read, 'In third place we have . . . Tania-Anne Crosier and her fantastic dance troupe, *Fire and Ice*.'

The dancers on the far side of the stage whooped and hugged and bounced around like demented rabbits, while one girl executed a perfect flick-flack across the stage as the troupe leader sashayed down to the front to shake hands with the judge and collect a cheque.

Charlotte caught hold of Helen's wrist. 'God, this is so awful, isn't it?' she said, her voice tight with excitement. She held up her other hand to show Helen that her fingers were firmly crossed. 'Come on, come on. Second or first, first or second,' she murmured, closing her eyes as if making a wish, 'Come on, come on. We have to win this. We do, we do – I'm planning that trip to America.'

Helen looked back at the judge, who was standing on the apron in a halo of light. 'And in second place,' said the man, 'we have the pop group, *The Nice Guys*.'

'Well done, lads,' said the compere. 'If you'd just like to come down here and take a bow and collect the cheque.'

From amongst the crush, four young men appeared and ambled down to the front to a hail of applause. They held their hands above their heads, grinning like loons, doing the walk of champions.

'Nice Guys and Wild Girls,' whispered Charlotte. 'Sounds great, doesn't it? I can see the headlines in tomorrow's *Argos*.'

'And *finally* in *first* place,' Andrew said, milking the crowd. There was another drum roll. 'And a very deserving winner of tonight's competition . . . we have the *Great Charlissimo!*'

Even in the midst of the stamping and clapping and

wild cheers of approval Helen could hear Charlotte gasp with disbelief.

'What? How could we *not* have won?' Charlotte growled. 'How come we didn't win? He's a bloody magician. This is just plain ridiculous. The audience loved us. It's a fix. It's got to be, they were baying for more, you heard them! We even got asked to do an encore. Didn't the judges see that? Didn't they?'

Helen had no answer.

Charlotte rounded on her. 'I don't believe this is happening. They loved us,' she repeated.

'I don't know what to say,' murmured Helen.

'Why doesn't that surprise me?' growled Charlotte.

Everyone else on stage looked a little crestfallen too, but were all still clapping the magician before taking a final bow. As Helen grabbed hold of Charlotte's hand she could feel Charlotte shaking with fury. As they came back up from the second bow, Helen spotted Vince standing in the wings watching them. He was grinning and waving and then, tapping his watch, he pointed towards the stage door. Helen shivered.

'A bloody magician,' Charlotte snarled, stuffing her sandals into her bag. 'A bloody-sodding magician. What the hell was going on there? They loved us. They did, didn't they?'

Charlotte had been complaining nonstop since they had come off stage and showed no signs of letting up.

Helen could only nod. 'Are we going to take our

make-up off before we go out?' she asked, not that Charlotte took any notice, she was far too angry to listen to anything Helen had to say.

'My dad is going to be furious about this, you know,' said Charlotte, wrenching off her costume. 'Do you have any idea how much he donates to their bloody theatre charities every year?' She pulled her sweater on. 'A fortune, that's what he gives them. *A fortune*. Well, they won't be getting a sodding penny this year, I can tell you.'

'Will he be waiting for you?'

Charlotte nodded. 'Dad? Yeah, I told him to wait out the front, I didn't want him round here fussing about. Mind you, if he was round here now I could get him to say something to the manager. I'll just go and tell Dad that we're going on somewhere. I won't be a minute. Don't go anywhere without me.'

'Won't he mind?' asked Helen. 'You know, you going on somewhere after he's shown up to see you and everything?'

'No, of course not, why should he? I'm a big girl now, and besides he'll have what's-her-face with him.' Charlotte widened her eyes and pulled a face, miming simpering adoration. 'Since he and Mum got divorced he's been out with one bimbo after another. This new one's thick as a custard and trails around him like some sort of love-sick puppy, batting her eyelashes at him,' Charlotte dropped into a sharp caricature. '*Oooo Barry you are so clever*,' she purred breathlessly. 'This new one's a model *apparently*. Anyway, what I'm saying is he won't mind if I don't go home with him. It'll give him more time alone with Miss Spaniel-Eyes.'

Helen didn't really know what to say, so settled for, 'Well, that's good as long as he doesn't mind,' and turned her attention back to getting changed.

Harry was waiting for them both at the bottom of the stairs.

'What do you want?' snapped Charlotte, before he had the chance to speak, pulling her coat tight around her. 'Come to gloat have you?'

Harry flinched as if she had hit him. 'No, of course I haven't come to gloat. I came to help you with your stuff,' he said, looking at the bags and costumes they were both carrying. 'I managed to grab a space in the main car park. I'm on your side, remember. I was going to say how sorry I am that you didn't win. You sounded really good. I don't know why you weren't up there among the winners. And I was thinking if you hadn't got to rush off maybe we could all go out for a Chinese?' Harry smiled at Helen. 'I've booked a table. I was planning to get some champagne if you won, but maybe we could have it anyway. We could drink to winning another night.'

'Well, we most certainly didn't win tonight, did we? And we can't go for a Chinese with you,' said Charlotte. 'We're meeting an agent.'

'Really? Okay, well, that's great,' said Harry. 'And

brilliant that you made some contacts already from being in the show. I knew it would happen; you're bound to get another chance.'

Helen felt sorry for him; he was trying so hard.

'Do you want me to come with you? I can phone the restaurant and cancel our table, or we could all go there and eat together if you like. Bring the agent along. The restaurant wouldn't mind, and the food is really good there. After all, I *am* your manager.'

'No,' snapped Charlotte. 'And actually I meant to say that I was joking about the whole manager thing.'

Harry stared at her. 'Oh, right, but I thought –'

'Well, don't bother. Thanks for the lift and all that and it would be great if you could just take all the stuff back to the flat for us. Helen was right, what we really need is someone who already knows the ropes, who has already got contacts in the business. Thanks, though.' Her tone was offhand. As she spoke she handed Harry her make-up bag and the suit hanger with their costumes in it.

Harry looked bemused. 'So you don't fancy a Chinese?'

Charlotte glared at him. 'I just told you, we're meeting someone.'

'How about you, Helen? Fancy coming down to the Golden Barge with me? My treat.'

It was the perfect get-out. Helen was about to say yes when Charlotte grabbed her arm. 'Thanks, Harry, but no thanks. Helen's coming with me. She can't leave me on my own, not with two strange men, and besides they want to talk to both of us, don't they, Helen? We're a duo, remember?'

Harry nodded. 'Okay, I'll see you later. And if you need me –'

'Yeah, thanks,' said Charlotte dismissively. 'We know where you live.'

'Do you want me to give you a hand with all the stuff?' said Helen to Harry.

Harry glanced at Charlotte and then shook his head. 'No, you're all right, and besides you've got an agent to meet. I hope it goes really well.'

'See you later,' Helen called after him, as he turned and sloped off laden down with their things. As he made his way out Helen wished for all the world that she was going with him.

'Why were you so horrible to him?' she said, as Charlotte tidied her hair. 'Harry's done nothing but go out of his way to help us.'

'Oh, don't be daft. He knows that I don't really mean it, and besides, he's *yours*, isn't he? I don't want to get stuck in some Chinese restaurant between you two, playing gooseberry.' And then Charlotte turned around and looked down at the floor.

'Oh my God, don't look. I said *don't look*! He's here,' she whispered. 'Over there by the doors. That is him. That's Leon Downey.' Helen turned to follow Charlotte's gaze and caught sight of Vince and another older man making their way down the corridor towards them.

'I said *don't look*,' murmured Charlotte. 'I don't want him to think we're staring.'

'Even if we are?' whispered Helen.

'Particularly if we are,' said Charlotte.

The second man was big and balding, with a paunch. He walked with a confident swagger and was dressed in a Crombie coat, carrying a trilby in his hand. He had to be at least as old as Charlotte's dad and had an unhealthy sallow look about him despite his smart clothes. He grinned when he spotted the two of them.

'Ladies, ladies, ladies. So there you are,' he said, rubbing his hands together and smiling to reveal a great mouthful of uneven, yellowing, smoker's teeth. 'I'm delighted you decided to accept my invitation. I'm Leon Downey, and I'm very pleased to make your acquaintance.' He offered Charlotte his hand. 'And you are?'

'Kate,' said Charlotte daintily. 'Kate Monroe.'

'Well, I'm very pleased to meet you, Miss Monroe. I thought you ladies made a real impression out there tonight. Quite a performance. We really saw what you had to offer, didn't we, Vince?'

Vince sniggered. Helen, knowing exactly what they meant, blushed crimson.

Leon turned his attention to Helen. 'And you are?'

'Helen,' she stammered. 'Helen Redford.' Leon Downey's hand slid, clammy and hot, around hers.

'Well, I'm delighted to meet you, Helen,' he purred, tightening his grip fractionally. It took Helen all her effort not to wipe it when he finally let go.

'Vince and I were just wondering where you'd both got to. Thought maybe you'd got a bit rattled and decided to make a break for it, didn't we, Vince?'

Charlotte giggled. 'We wouldn't do that.'

'That's good, very good,' said Leon eyeing them up and down. 'Now how about we get out of here? We thought we'd go for a little drink first and then maybe grab ourselves a bite to eat. That sound all right to you, girls?'

Charlotte nodded. 'Lovely. I've just got to go and tell my dad where we're going.'

'Really?' The man laughed. 'You're serious?'

Charlotte nodded.

'Well, right you are then. Go on, you run along and tell Daddy,' he teased. 'We don't want him worrying about his little girl, now do we?'

Helen glanced at Charlotte. Under any other circumstances Charlotte would have turned round and snapped right back at him but this time she tipped her head coquettishly to one side and, smiling, said, 'I'll only be a minute or two, he just likes to know where I am, that's all.' And with that she headed towards the front of the theatre.

Leon nodded and pulled out a cigar from his inside pocket. 'Don't be long then, sweetheart. We haven't got all night, have we, Vince?' And then he turned his attention back to Helen. 'And how about you, darling, you got anyone you need to tell anything to before we head off for a little drink?'

Helen hesitated for a split second and then she said, 'Yes, actually I have.' And before Leon could protest she was away and hurrying down the corridor and out into the car park, praying that Harry hadn't already left. He couldn't be more than a minute or two ahead of them. She caught up with him just as he was about to pull away in the car.

'Helen?' he said in surprise, braking sharply as he spotted her. 'Are you all right?' he asked as he slid open the car window.

'No, not really,' she said. 'I just wanted to tell you that I don't want to go for a drink with Charlotte. I've got to be up early tomorrow. They're filming at the Old Quay and one of the people I met asked if I want to go. I need to be up by half past five.'

Harry laughed. 'Well don't go, then. Come on, get in,' he said, leaning over to open the passenger-side door. 'We'll go and eat instead.'

Helen smiled at him; she really liked the way Harry said *we*. 'I'd love to, Harry, but Charlotte's right. I can't leave her on her own. Not with those two . . .' Helen stared at him, unable to find the words to convey her fears. 'I really can't –'

He smiled. 'It's all right. Do you know where you're going?'

'The Anchor, I think, but I'm not certain. And then they said something about eating afterwards.' She hesitated.

'I'll be home if you need me. Okay?'

'What about your Chinese meal?'

Harry laughed. 'Don't worry about that. It'd be no fun going on my own. I'll pick up some fish and chips on the way back to the flat.' And then Harry paused, and Helen felt a funny little arc of desire ripple between them, and it made her lean in closer to the car and him lean out to meet her. As their lips touched, she shivered with pleasure and couldn't help but smile.

'Umm, that was nice,' he said.

Helen giggled. Maybe Charlotte had been right about him after all.

'I don't know what I'd do without you,' she said.

Harry kissed her again, a gentle soft kiss that made her heart do an odd fluttery thing. 'You don't have to do without me,' Harry said. 'I'll always be here for you.'

Helen pulled away. 'Thank you,' she said.

'There's no need to thank me,' he grinned. 'Now go on. If you need me you know where I'll be. Just ring.'

Helen ran back towards the theatre. She could feel her heart pumping with excitement and she had a huge grin on her face. God, was this what love felt like? She glanced back to wave Harry goodbye. He pipped his horn and blew her a kiss as he pulled out of the car park. Helen smiled; whatever it was, it felt wonderful.

As Helen was about to head back into the theatre she spotted Charlotte standing on the corner, at the front of the entrance to the theatre car park, looking into the crowd. Helen was about to call out when something stopped her. Charlotte was stalking backwards and forwards staring into the street, standing out amongst the steady stream of people pouring out of the doors, moving around her, all heading home. Charlotte had her coat pulled tight around her, her hands tucked up under her armpits. She did another circuit and then checked her watch and walked back again, and then again. It was obvious that her dad wasn't there; maybe he hadn't shown up after all.

Helen hesitated, wondering what to do. Should she go over, should she call out? Before she could decide Charlotte swung round and came scurrying across the car park back towards the stage door.

'Are you okay?' asked Helen, as she drew level with her.

Charlotte looked surprised to see her. 'Yeah, why wouldn't I be?' Charlotte said stuffing her hands into her pockets. 'What are you doing out here anyway? Spying on me, are you?'

'No, of course not. I just came over to say goodbye to Harry,' Helen said.

Charlotte laughed. 'Oh don't tell me, you were worried lover boy might get jealous if you went out on the tiles with someone else.'

Helen reddened in spite of herself, 'No, it's just that you were so rude to him and he's been brilliant to us today,' she protested.

'Oh, for goodness' sake,' sighed Charlotte, 'Harry's a big boy now and this is business. He'll understand.'

'Did you find your dad?' Helen asked casually.

Charlotte's eyes narrowed. 'You *were* out here spying on me, weren't you?'

'No, of course I wasn't. Why should I?'

'That's all right then. He's just *fine*,' Charlotte said, in a throwaway tone. 'He said we were brilliant, and he is really angry that we didn't win. He said we were robbed, he said –' Charlotte stopped. 'Actually it doesn't matter what he said. Let's go and see what Leon Downey's got to say for himself. You never know, he might be the answer to all our prayers. Best not to keep him waiting.'

Helen nodded and fell into step alongside her, wondering where Charlotte's father had got to and why Charlotte felt that she needed to lie about it.

Leon Downey and Vince were waiting for them by the stage door. Vince was leaning against the wall smoking a cigarette, Leon was puffing away on a cigar.

'Well, hello there, ladies,' purred Leon. 'I thought perhaps you'd changed your minds and run away home. So how was Daddy, sweetheart?'

Charlotte reddened. 'He was fine, thank you.'

'And so he didn't mind his little girl going out on the town, then?'

'No, of course he didn't. I told him it was business. He understands – and besides, I'm not a child.'

Leon grinned. 'Of course you aren't, poppet. Come on. Let's get out of the cold and go and get ourselves a drink, shall we? The Anchor's just down here a-ways, nice place. Have you ever been there?'

'I don't think so,' said Charlotte.

'Well, let me show you the way then,' he said, and with that he slipped his arm through Charlotte's. If Charlotte was shocked she didn't show it; if she objected she didn't say a word, and instead fell into step alongside him. Helen stared at the two of them.

'Now,' Leon said, leaning in a little closer. 'Why don't you tell me all about yourself, darling.'

Vince, walking alongside Helen, grinned. 'So you local too, are you, sweetheart?' he asked as he moved closer. Helen nodded and kept her hands firmly stuffed into her coat and her elbows tucked tight in so that Vince didn't get any similar ideas.

TWELVE

In the storeroom behind Finton's Finest Toys, Natalia, Harry and Helen were busy holding a summit meeting. The camera had stopped rolling and everyone with an opinion that counted was standing in the huddle.

'Look, Helen, you've got to see it from our point of view. You've been around long enough to know that what we've got here is good TV,' protested Natalia. 'This is just the kind of thing people love. Celebrity secrets, the whole love child angle was just too good to pass up on.' She paused. 'There's been a lot of speculation in the office about who the father might be. People love that – you know, all that "who's the daddy" stuff.'

Helen stared at her; it took her all her effort not to gather the stupid, smug, young woman up by the neck and punch her. Natalia took her silence as an invitation to continue.

'I mean everyone knows that over the years you've had relationships with some *really* famous guys –'

Helen held her gaze. 'You mean I've been around a bit.'

'No, of course not – no, that's not what I meant at all – but you can hardly blame people for trying to guess . . . Ralph Jones, Harry Lomax, Bill Farnham – it's just human nature.'

Helen had visions of them in the office, thumbing through the press cuttings, looking at the pictures, weighing up the odds, working out the dates. All this and she had had no idea that this was what they were planning. How on earth must Adam feel about it? Harry was clearly in shock.

'I'm really concerned about how traumatic this is going to be for Harry and for Adam, Natalia.'

'I know, I know, you've already said that, and I take your point, I really do,' she said, holding up her hands in defence. 'But where have you been for the last ten years? This is what we do. This is what people want now. It's all about the story, and the secrets – that's what *Roots* is famous for, for digging down and mining the juicy heart-rending kernel of the stories. You signed up for this; no one twisted your arm,' she said, sounding defensive. 'You knew what you were in for.'

'It's funny, my partner Bon said exactly the same thing. He said I knew where the bodies were buried, and you know what? I thought he was right. I was maybe expecting some revelations about my mum, but what I wasn't expecting was to work with a production company who didn't check their facts.'

'*But we did*, we talked to Kate and to Harry – it was private adoption. We even have Adam's birth certificate.'

'Showing me as his mother?'

Natalia nodded. 'Showing you as his mother, father unknown.'

'That is absolutely impossible,' Helen sighed. 'I think you should ring your boss and see what she has to say.'

'We didn't lie to you,' protested Natalia.

'What is that supposed to mean?' snapped Helen. 'You didn't need to lie to me, because someone else was doing it for you.'

'We thought this would potentially be a real happy-ever-after story.'

'You mean awards territory,' said Helen.

Natalia blushed crimson.

Harry looked as if he might burst into tears.

Helen and Natalia, along with Harry, were in a corner of the stockroom which was so cramped they were practically standing nose to nose. Without a word Helen pulled out the folded sheet of paper with the filming schedule on it and handed it to Natalia.

'We were supposed to be going to my old house and then having an early supper at the hotel,' she said flatly. 'Show me where it says we were coming to meet up with my long-lost son. Just bloody show me.'

Natalia flinched. 'Okay, okay, so it's not on the list,'

she said after a moment or two more. 'And we thought you'd know – we really did.'

Helen glared at her.

'And we had kind of assumed you would expect to come here. Working at a toy shop is part of the whole Helen Redford legend,' said Felix, who until then had barely said a word.

Helen raised her eyebrows. 'The legend?' she said, heavy on sarcasm.

'You know what I mean, it's part of the myth. The story of our heroine, homely everygirl, working in a shop out in the boondocks, who gets discovered and overnight becomes a rich and famous actress. It's the stuff dreams are made of. Everyone wants to believe in fairy stories, Helen, and yours is pure Cinderella. Even the thing with your mum, the poor little girl growing up without her mother to guide her or see her success, with a distant uncommunicative father who spends more time at work than at home. It tugs at the heartstrings. And then you get a job in a toy shop with a kind old man and his gentle handsome son. We all loved it in the office. One minute you're selling Barbie and next minute you *are* Barbie –'

Helen stared at him and then shook her head. 'I don't know how you persuade people to come on your show if you treat them all like this.'

'Because we're good at what we do,' said Natalia. 'For a lot of them it's almost like therapy. People want to find out about themselves, or have a chance to tell their side of the story, to set the record straight.'

Felix nodded. 'That's right – it's about setting the record straight, laying the ghosts to rest.'

'And was all this on your schedule too, was it?'

'Look, we're sorry, I'm not sure what else there is we can say – and we're going to your old house now, and then we'll film at the theatre tomorrow,' Natalia said.

'And you think anyone is going to care about any of that if you leave this piece about Adam in?'

'You know as well as I do, Helen – it's all in the edit, what they decide to leave in, what they decide to leave out and what order they show it. We just go with the research and what we've talked about in the planning meetings.'

Helen leaned in a little closer. 'And what else have you got planned for me? A husband I never married? A soap opera I never starred in? Oh, I know. A whole family I never knew I had.'

'I can't discuss that,' sighed Natalia. 'I really can't.'

'Don't you think that it might help if you did? I could perhaps stop you from ruining someone else's life. It's my family and my past that we're talking about here.'

'I know, but the whole *Roots* ethos is about discovery and revelations. It's what we do.'

'And you got it wrong. I thought this was going to be about my mum,' said Helen, tears of frustration making her voice crackle and break.

Natalia said nothing.

'One of the reasons I'm doing this is because I thought I was ready to find out the truth about her. I've put this off for so long – and I finally thought it was time. When I was in *Cannon Square* I kept thinking that maybe she would turn up one day, you know, just pop out of the woodwork, walk onto the set and that I'd know her and we'd have this big scene – with hugs – and she would take me out and explain everything to me. What had happened and why, and that she had always loved me but just couldn't come back. You're right, just like in a fairy story and that suddenly I'd have all the answers. Do you have any idea what it's like to have a mother who walks out on you, without so much as a word?'

Natalia remained stock-still, although Helen could guess by her expression she was probably cursing the fact that the camera wasn't rolling.

'It is agonising and stunning in ways that you can't put into words. I was six when she went. The last thing I remember is making bread with her in the kitchen. I was helping. I was standing on this little brown wooden chair. My dad loved homemade bread. You know how the smell fills the whole house? Even now when I smell it I'm straight back there, straight back to that moment, watching her knead the dough on a big wooden board on the kitchen table. She had tiny hands. She was wearing a wraparound apron and it was hot and a strand of hair kept dropping into her eyes. I can see her now – her pushing it away with the back of her hand, leaving a floury mark on her forehead. I loved her, and she kept looking at me and smiling and telling me what a good girl I was.'

216

Helen looked at Natalia; Natalia, looking uncomfortable, looked away.

'And then she was gone. And you know what? I still have no idea what happened to her. Not a clue. I'm a grown woman, and I've never been able to find out anything. Nothing. My dad never said anything about it, at least not to me, and as far as I can tell not to anyone else either. Not a word, not a single solitary word about her after she went. For all those years. He didn't talk about her, he never mentioned her again and because he didn't, no one else did either. Not friends, not family. Have you any idea what that's like? What it does to you?'

No one spoke.

'One minute my mum was there and the next she was gone, like life closed over her and swallowed her up without so much as a ripple. And the thing is that those feelings don't just end there. It used to make me wonder if it might happen again. If it could happen once, would my dad go the same way? Would I wake up one morning and be in the house all on my own? Have you any idea how afraid that makes you? I was afraid all the time, Natalia. All the time. I was *six*.'

Natalia swallowed hard, her eyes bright.

'Looking back I wondered if she died or left him; or was she murdered? Drowned? Did she run off with his best friend?' Helen stopped. 'Do you have any idea how many times I've thought about it? How many explanations I have come up with? How many excuses? How many theories? *That* was what I was hoping you would tell me about, Natalia, not this. Not something that is nothing to do with me.'

Natalia glanced at Harry and then back at Helen. 'It was because of your mum that we were really excited and interested by the whole Adam thing.'

'That's my son you're talking about,' Harry said. You would have had to have been dead to miss the pain and the anger in his voice.

Helen glared at Natalia. 'What you mean is like mother, like daughter. Is that it?' When Natalia didn't reply, Helen sighed. 'You'd better let the rest of the hobbits in,' she said. 'They'll be wondering what the hell we're doing in here.'

'I think it's best if I go out there and have a chat with them. We need to regroup –' Natalia said and then continued, 'You know, Helen, most people we have on the show find the whole experience emotionally strengthening, you know, like really cathartic. It can be life-affirming if you let it; it can be a very healing and positive experience.'

'You mean I should say that Adam *is* my son because it suits your idea of what makes good TV?' Helen glanced across at Harry, pale-faced and bright-eyed. 'Did you get all that from some sort of self-help manual?"

Natalia sucked her teeth. '*Roots* sent me on a course; 'Empathy in the Media'. Most of it was complete rubbish if I'm honest, but the American co-producers said we had to go for insurance purposes. Anyway, hold that thought, I'll be back in a minute.'

And with that she was gone.

'What am I going to tell Adam?' said Harry. 'And Kate? What on earth have I done, Helen? This is a total disaster.'

Helen took a long hard look at the place where Natalia had been standing and really wished that she had punched her.

THIRTEEN

Leon Downey was far looser with his money than with his tongue. Since the four of them had arrived at the Anchor he had bought the girls round after round of shorts, and appeared to be completely enraptured by Charlotte's increasingly wild ideas and outrageous suggestions for their bright shiny future; although Helen noticed that Leon was being extremely circumspect about exactly what his involvement might be in her master plan. Helen also couldn't help but notice that neither Leon nor Vince seemed to be drinking anywhere near as much as they were.

'And then I was thinking that we should go to America.' Charlotte was still banging on. 'I mean that's where the big money really is, don't you think? Do you think that's mad? I mean they like English things in America, don't they? Lots of singers have gone out there and done really well. Have you got any contacts in Hollywood? You know I still can't believe we didn't win tonight. I mean it was crazy. I thought it was a sure thing. They loved us. You were there, you saw them, didn't you? They went mad. We got an encore. It's got to be some kind of fix, don't you think? I mean the man who won was a magician,' Charlotte snorted. '*A magician.*' The sentences were running one into another as she downed another vodka and Coke. 'A bloody magician. That is just bizarre, don't you think?'

It was coming up to closing time and the lounge bar had steadily emptied out over the last half hour or so, until there were just the four of them left sitting around a sticky Formica table, which was tucked away just out of sight of the barmaid. Next door in the public bar people were still drinking hard, their voices and laughter rolling in through the doorway behind the counter.

It was warm in the lounge bar, there was piped music, a coal fire and carpets and a few large plastic plants set around the groups of tables making each area a little more private and intimate than the benches in the public bar. Charlotte, Helen and the two men were sitting in a corner booth. Leon sat right in the corner and had his arms stretched out along the back of the built-in leather banquette, his Crombie coat unbuttoned. He had one leg crossed over the other, his ankle resting on his knee, the master of all he surveyed. Charlotte was sitting to one side of him, all eyes, giving Leon the full benefit of her adoring smile and undivided attention. From time to time Leon made a show of patting Charlotte on the thigh.

Helen couldn't help but think the gesture looked tacky and proprietorial.

Helen sat on the other side of him, making sure she was just out of reach, but nevertheless she was pinned in by Vince, who sat on the other side of her and who, so far, had said very little. She was making a real effort to stay at the midpoint between the two of them and out of harm's way.

The table they were sitting at was packed with empty glasses, full ashtrays and all of Charlotte's dreams. Helen had decided after the first two drinks that there was no way she was going to drink all of the booze that Leon and Vince were plying them with. It didn't take a genius to work out that they were trying to get the girls drunk. So, for the last hour she had been pretending to sip her drink, and then when the men's attention was elsewhere had been pouring as much as she could into one of the pot plants standing alongside their table. There had been ample opportunity; no one was taking that much notice of what she was doing or saying. Charlotte was most definitely the centre of attention.

'So,' Charlotte said; she was talking loudly, using her hands for added emphasis. 'All the Wild Birds need now really is a decent break and a good agent like you, Leon . . . and some bookings, isn't that right, Helen? We're both ready for the big time, and we're prepared to do whatever it takes to get there.' Charlotte took another pull on her glass, missed her mouth, and giggling madly, backhanded the splash of vodka and Coke off her chin.

222

'Whatever it takes. Isn't that right, Helen?' she repeated, as she struggled to recover her composure. Her speech was getting steadily more slurred and her stage makeup was beginning to slowly creep down over her face like a colourful ebb tide.

Leon patted Charlotte on the knee. 'Well, that's just fantastic, darling, and just the kind of thing we want to hear, isn't it Vince?' he said, before getting to his feet. 'Now if you ladies will just excuse me, I won't be a moment; just got to water the horse. Vince, do you want to do the honours my son and get us another round in?' He pulled out his wallet and dropped a twenty-pound note onto the table amongst the debris.

Vince nodded as Leon made his way to the gents. 'You girls want the same again?' he asked.

Helen noticed that neither of the men's glasses looked as if they had been touched.

Charlotte nodded. 'Uhuh,' she said, licking her lips. 'Vodka and Coke for me, no ice, slice of lemon, and do you reckon they've got any crisps?' she said. 'Only I'm starving.'

'I'll ask,' said Vince, and then looked enquiringly at Helen. 'And what about you, sweetheart, you want another vodka and Coke, do you?'

Helen shook her head. 'No thanks. I think I've had enough booze. Is there any chance I could just have an orange juice, please?'

Vince grinned. 'What pretty manners you've got. If that's what you want, petal, then that's what you shall

223

have, are you sure you don't want me to slip a vodka in there for you? Or how about a gin? The drinks are on Leon, you know.' He waved the twenty-pound note around to underline the statement.

Helen shook her head again. 'No, thank you,' she said.

Vince leaned in a little closer. 'You know, sweetie, you really want to loosen up a bit, be a bit more like your mate here. Have yourself a good time. Relax, Leon Downey is a very influential man. He's got fingers in a lot of pies. Me and him have worked on all kinds of shows together over the years. Dancing, singing; it would really pay you to be nice to us. You know what I'm saying here?'

'But I am being nice,' protested Helen.

Vince's grin widened. 'Well, it don't seem much like it from where I'm sitting. Loosen up. We could be very good for you. In fact between the two of us we could open a lot of doors, get you seen by the right people, see you right. Leon's very well known and I've got contacts in every theatre and music venue in town, not to mention lots of other places, so what I'm saying here is that I'd be *extra* nice if I were you . . .' and with a leer and a wink he turned away. Helen watched Vince head over to the bar, clutching Charlotte's empty glass and Leon's twenty-pound note, wondering exactly what he meant.

'He makes my flesh creep. What do you think?' Helen asked Charlotte, who was busy licking her lips and making a show of tidying her hair.

'What do you mean?' said Charlotte; she looked as if

she was having a problem focusing. 'What do I think about what?'

'About Leon Downey and Vince?'

Charlotte curled her lip. 'I don't know. Leon seems all right to me and he's pretty free and easy with his money. I like that in a man.'

'I know, but he hasn't said anything about work yet, has he? He hasn't talked about what he does or who he represents or what he can do for us.'

Charlotte's expression hardened. 'Oh for God's sake, Helen. Give the man a chance, we've only just met him. He told me that he wanted to get to know us better.'

'Yes, I know, but don't you think he ought to be talking more about business?'

'We're having a drink, breaking the ice, I'm sure he will get around to it. He's just weighing us up, Helen, that's all – sussing us out, seeing if we're worth the investment. I mean if he signs us up we're probably talking singing lessons, maybe dancing, and then there's costumes and stuff like that. It's a big investment. He told me he wanted to get a feel for us.'

'Well, he's doing that all right; he's all over you like a rash,' said Helen. She paused for a few seconds. 'Do you think you ought to cut back on the vodka? You've had an awful lot to drink.'

Charlotte glared at her. 'For God's sake, Helen, just grow up, will you? Who died and made you Pope?' she snapped.

'I was only saying.'

'Well, don't,' growled Charlotte. 'It's just a few drinks

and it shows that we're adults. This is how business works. Okay? A few drinks, a chat – and then we get down to business. My dad does it all the time.'

Helen nodded.

A few minutes later Leon reappeared, slid onto the bench alongside Charlotte, and slipped his arm around her shoulders. 'Now then ladies,' he said, leaning in close so they were forced to follow suit. 'There's been a bit of a change of plan. I've just had a quick word with Vince up at the bar and we were thinking as it's getting late that we should head back to my hotel, maybe get ourselves some room service or a takeaway. And we can talk a bit more comfortably there. It'll be a bit more private. So what do you say?' He grinned. 'Get the chance to get to know each other better.'

'Yeah, sure, that's fine by me,' said Charlotte, nodding in agreement.

'I'm sorry, but it's getting late and I've got to get up early tomorrow,' Helen began, while all sorts of alarm bells went off in her head.

'Oh for God's sake,' snapped Charlotte. 'It's like going out on the town with Mary Poppins. It's Saturday night, Helen, and this is important. This is our future we're talking about here.'

Leon smiled wolfishly. 'Yes, indeed, ladies. Now while you two sort out what you're doing, I'll go and give Vince a hand with those drinks.' He got up and headed for the bar. He was barely out of earshot before Charlotte rounded on Helen.

'*I'm sorry but I've got to get up early tomorrow,*' she mimicked. 'It makes us sound like a couple of bloody school kids. You know that you're ruining our big chance to get him to take us on here, don't you?'

'But it's true, and if you want my honest opinion, I think they're both a pair of creeps, Charlie. They're trying to get us drunk, and why aren't either of them talking business? I don't think Leon Downey is an agent at all and I *do* need to get up tomorrow.'

'Oh for God's sake – only for that bloody film thing. And who's to say that that's not a con too? Eh? I mean that bloke you talked to could have been anyone. This is important, Helen, surely you can see that – this is our career we're talking about here.'

'How could I forget? You've been talking about nothing else since we got here, and Leon Downey still hasn't said *anything* about wanting to sign us up, or who else he's got on his books, or anything about this agency he's supposed to run, or what he does. I don't trust him.'

'Oh yeah, right, and *you're* such a good judge of character.'

'I'm just saying,' said Helen.

'He's being careful, that's all. I mean he must see hundreds of people. No, he's seeing what we've got to offer. What we're like. If Leon's going to represent us he needs to know we can work together.'

'He said that, did he?' asked Helen, her eyes on the two men who were now huddled together deep in

227

conversation at the bar. Leon and Vince kept glancing in Helen and Charlotte's direction and laughing, which did nothing at all to allay Helen's suspicions. 'I just think the pair of them are dead dodgy,' she said.

'You already said that, and you know what? I really don't care,' said Charlotte. 'If Leon Downey can get me into show business and away from Billingsfield then that is all that matters as far as I'm concerned. Do you understand?'

'You don't mean that, Charlotte.'

'Oh, don't I?' Charlotte glared at her. 'Trust me, Helen: I mean every single last word. Just don't screw this up for me, do you understand?'

'Why don't we at least ask him for his business card? We could go and see him at his offices, during the day – do it properly. Ask your dad to come with us.'

Charlotte glared at her. 'Listen to me, Miss Goody-Two-Shoes. I don't want to go running to my daddy to sort this out for me. Okay? And I wouldn't come over all Julie Andrews with me if I were you, Helen Heel. I'm not the one living with my boss's son.'

'I'm not!' Helen protested.

Charlotte just raised her eyebrows and drained the last of her vodka. 'I think you'll find that you are. I'll do whatever it takes to get on, do you understand me? *Whatever it takes.* And from where I'm sitting it looks like you did too –'

Which was the moment that Leon and Vince swaggered over. 'Righty-oh, ladies, so are we all set then? Plan is

228

we'll knock this last one back and then we'll head for the hotel, okay?' said Leon.

Helen looked up at Vince's hands. He was only carrying two glasses, Charlotte's vodka and Coke and her orange juice.

'Sounds fine to me,' said Charlotte, taking her drink. Helen accepted her glass from Vince with a murmur of thanks. She took one sip and knew without a doubt he had laced it with vodka.

'I was just wondering,' she said, setting the glass down on the table in amongst the chaos, while looking up at Leon, 'if we could have one of your business cards?'

Charlotte glared her, but Leon Downey didn't so much as hesitate before replying. 'Of course you can, petal,' he said, patting his pockets in a show of searching, and then he grinned, 'Oh, hang on a minute, no, sorry, sweetie. I'm afraid I haven't got any of the new ones with me tonight, my dear. We've just moved our office into new premises and I haven't got any with my new address on me,' he said. 'You know what printers can be like.'

'I don't mind one of your old ones,' Helen pressed, picking up her handbag. 'Or I could write your new address down. I've got a pen.'

Leon laughed. 'Well, aren't you just the Boy Scout, always prepared, are you? What else have you got in that bag of yours? Not got scampi and chips in there by any chance, have you? Only I could murder a plate of chips.'

'Me too, or how about a nice juicy steak?' chipped in Vince.

229

'Or a pie,' snorted Charlotte.

All three of them were laughing at her now. Helen could feel her colour rising.

'Come on,' said Charlotte, grabbing her coat while knocking back the drink that Leon had just brought over. 'Let's get going, it's getting really boring in here.'

Leon helped her on with her coat, all the while leering at Helen. 'Now there's a girl who knows what she wants,' he said, glancing down at Charlotte's cleavage with a grin. 'Always this keen, are you, baby? She's just the kind of girl we're looking for, isn't she Vince?'

Vince nodded. 'She should go far.'

Helen said nothing.

'Come on then,' said Leon to Charlotte, slipping his arm through hers. 'Let's get out of here. My hotel is just around the corner.'

Helen hung back. She didn't want to go anywhere with any of them, but there was a part of her which felt responsible for Charlotte's wellbeing. It was obvious Charlotte was drunk; her hair was a mess and her mascara was smudged around her eyes. Under the lights in the pub's hallway Charlotte's smeared stage makeup made her look more like a hooker than a sixth former. Not that Leon seemed to mind. As Charlotte turned towards the door she stumbled; Leon reached out and caught her. There was a split second when Helen wondered what was going to happen and then Leon pulled Charlotte close.

'You know you really are a pretty little thing,' he said, 'I reckon that what you need is someone to take care of you.' And with that he kissed her, his hands working their way up under her coat.

Helen stared at him in horror and felt an icy finger track up her spine. 'Stop it! Don't do that to my friend,' she barked. 'Leave her alone, you old lech.'

Lazily Leon looked up. 'Your friend doesn't seem to mind. Do you, poppet?'

Charlotte groaned and then giggling some more kissed him back and rubbed her body up against his.

'She's drunk. You got her drunk. This isn't right —' protested Helen.

Leon laughed. 'No one forced her to drink anything. She enjoys a drink, don't you, pet? Nothing wrong with that.'

'Come on, Charlotte, let's go home,' said Helen, trying to grab hold of Charlotte's other arm. 'It's getting late. Let's go back to the flat.'

'And who is going to give a sod about what time either of us gets home? You know my dad didn't even bother to come and watch us tonight?' slurred Charlotte. 'After all the bloody fuss he made about being careful and caring so much and not signing anything without him being there, all that yak, yak, yak, and he didn't even come to see me.' Charlotte mimed a nagging mouth with her fingers. 'Well, sod him. I'm an adult now and I can do what I like, I can take care of myself.'

'I know you can, but we don't have to go back to the hotel with them. You can stay at my place,' said Helen, hurrying after her. 'There's room on the sofa; Harry won't mind. I could go and ring him and he'll come and pick us up, or I can ring your dad if you like?'

'Oh, just bugger off, will you?' said Charlotte, shaking herself free of Helen's grasp. 'Why do you always have to spoil everything, Helen? Come on, Leon, where did you say you're staying?'

Vince made as if to take Helen by the arm but she pushed him away. 'Get off me!' she growled.

'I thought I explained to you about being nice to me and Leon?' he purred. 'Although I like a girl with a bit of fight, if you know what I'm saying?'

'You are repulsive,' she hissed.

Vince laughed. 'That's not what your mate thinks though, is it? Just look at her all snuggled up with Mr Downey. They make quite a nice couple, don't they?'

Helen shivered; she wanted to be anywhere else but here with the three of them. Leon pulled open the pub door and guided Charlotte through, while Helen slipped through quickly, bypassing any help Vince might try to give. Outside in the street it was cold and still raining. Cars cut through the puddles kicking up waves of water.

'Are we getting a cab?' asked Charlotte, looking up and down the almost deserted streets.

'You'll be lucky,' laughed Vince. 'And anyway the hotel is only just around the corner. Won't take more than a couple of minutes. Do us all good to have a little walk. Get a bit of air.'

Now that she was outside and upright Helen could feel the full effects of the alcohol washing over her, while a little further along the pavement Charlotte was swaying and giggling, still supported by Leon Downey.

'I really think we should go home, Charlie, please,' said Helen. 'I could go and find a phone box and call Harry, he'll come and get us if you like. He said he would – what do you think?'

'I heard you the first time. And it's Kate, remember?' Charlotte slurred. '*Kate Monroe*, and I don't want to go home with you to that poxy little flat. Leon here is going to see to it that my name is up in lights, aren't you, Leon?' She pointed up to a nearby building to demonstrate her point, leaning back against him.

He leaned in closer and kissed her neck. 'Whatever you say, sweetheart. Whatever you say.'

Charlotte giggled. 'I like your style, Mr Downey,' she said.

'Harry won't mind,' Helen continued. 'You know he won't.'

'And who is this Harry then?' asked Leon. 'He your boyfriend, is he?'

'No,' said Charlotte. 'He's hers. She lives with him.'

'Really? Now there's a thing; it's always the quiet ones you have to watch. Doesn't lover-boy mind you being out on the lash with another man?' said Vince, moving in closer. 'Or are you bored with boys? Fancy finding out what a man's like, do you?' He smelt of beer and sweat and cigarettes.

'Will you just get off me. I'm not *out* with you,' snapped Helen, pushing him away. 'And Harry is a man not a

233

boy. I'm only here because we thought this was a business meeting.'

Vince made a teasing whooping sound. 'Little Miss Business.'

'It is a business meeting,' said Leon, turning round to face her. His eyes were bright, his expression full of dark humour. 'And as soon as we get back to the hotel, trust me; we'll be getting right down to business, won't we, Vince?'

The tone of their voices made Helen shudder. As they rounded the corner into the market square Leon headed across the road and up the steps towards the Billingsfield Arms, with Charlotte on his arm. Charlotte was still horribly unsteady, but each time she stumbled Leon steadied her and she leant more heavily on him for support. As they reached the main doors Helen looked first at Vince and then at Leon, and knew that there was no way she was going to go inside the hotel with them.

'Charlotte, come on,' Helen pleaded one more time. 'Let's go home.' She might as well have been talking to herself.

'Why don't you go home then, sweetie,' purred Leon. 'If you can't play with the grown-ups you're better buggering off back home to what's-his-name.'

Helen glared at him, and not for the first time she felt torn between looking after herself and taking care of Charlotte. She hesitated long enough for Vince to say, 'So are you coming in or are you going to stay out here in the rain?'

234

Helen looked at Charlotte, whose expression was one of drunken contempt. 'Stop being such a wet blanket. I don't need a nursemaid,' Charlotte said, waving her away. 'You bugger off back home to Harry. I can take care of myself.'

Helen stared at her. 'Charlotte, please –' she said.

'You heard the lady,' said Leon, stepping between them. 'Why don't you just get yourself off home and don't you worry your pretty little head, your friend will be safe with us, won't she, Vince?'

'Oh yeah,' said Vince, stubbing out his cigarette. 'We'll take good care of her.'

Helen doubted it very much, but other than physically dragging Charlotte away or going inside with them there was very little else she could do.

'I'm going,' Helen said, hoping her leaving might change Charlotte's mind.

'Well, bloody well go then.'

'I need to be up in the morning.'

'Yeah, yeah, so you keep saying,' said Charlotte, waving her away. 'You run along home then, peasant,' she giggled. 'It's going to be wet and muddy tomorrow so just make sure you wrap up nice and warm.' And with that Leon swept Charlotte in through the doors, with Vince following them close behind.

Helen watched the doors close behind the three of them. It was cold and dark and quiet now. Standing on the pavement in the rain Helen felt horribly alone and vulnerable. She shivered and then turned to make her

235

way back to the flat. As Helen crossed the road a car slowed down and a gang of lads rolled down the windows and whooped and catcalled after her. As they drove off she caught sight of herself in a shop window – with her hair teased up and so much makeup on she looked like she was on the game. Pulling her collar up Helen hunched against the biting wind and hurried back to home and to Harry.

Away from the main square the maze of side streets and alleys was deserted. Her heels cracked out a rhythm on the slick damp pavements. Helen felt cold and alone, tired, drunk and sad, and it was with a huge sense of relief that she climbed the stairs up to the flat. She had barely got her key in the lock when Harry threw open the door for her. She had never been so pleased to see anyone in her life.

'There you are, thank God you're all right, I was getting worried about you,' he said, his expression a touching mix of anxiety and relief. 'You're soaked right through. Come on, get yourself inside, I've got the fire going. I'll grab you a towel.'

'Have you been waiting up?' asked Helen.

He looked a little sheepish. 'Yes and no, I suppose I might have been. I went to bed but then I couldn't sleep.' He peered past her onto the landing. 'Where's Charlotte got to?'

'I couldn't get her to come back with me.' The words broke up in Helen's mouth, and she bit her lip. 'She went back to the hotel with this man, you know, the one who told us he was an agent? I'm almost certain that he was lying, Harry. I can't believe she wouldn't come with me.'

He put his arms out and she stepped into them, grateful for the warmth and the comfort, and wondered if he was going to kiss her again.

'Come on, let's get you dry. You want a cup of tea?' he said after a moment or two. 'I've got the kettle on, and I think there are still some shortbreads in the tin.'

Helen looked up at him and laughed. 'You know, Harry, there are loads of times I dream about getting away from Billingsfield, of being rich and famous and drinking champagne from a crystal goblet, but times like this, you making tea and getting out the biscuit tin seems about as close to perfection as a girl can get.'

He laughed and guided her into the sitting room. 'I was worried about you,' he said, helping her off with her coat. 'I don't care what happens to Charlotte, but I do care about you.' He paused and took a deep breath. 'I have to tell you something, Helen. I've been thinking about it for some time now actually – I have to say something.'

Helen stared at him. 'What is it, Harry?' she said. 'Are you going to sack me? Have I got to move out? If it's about the mess Charlotte made in your room, I can –'

'No. It's not any of those things,' he interrupted.

'Are you okay?'

Harry nodded. And then he said, 'I love you, Helen.'

She stared at him, open-mouthed. In one way the words came as a complete surprise but in another it just confirmed what, somewhere inside, she already knew.

'Harry,' Helen began, but he held a hand up to stop her.

'Wait, you don't have to feel responsible for how I feel. I know I'm not your boyfriend, or at least not yet,' he said. 'I would like to be, but if that doesn't happen, then I just want you to know that I will always be your friend, and whatever happens, wherever you go, that's never going to change. I will always love you.'

It was such a big thing to say.

She took hold of his hand, feeling tears of gratitude pricking behind her eyes. 'And I love you, Harry,' she said with a certainty that she was only just aware of. 'I don't know where we go from here, but I do love you.'

He grinned. 'Well, that's a start,' he said. 'I'll go and make the tea and get you that towel. Why don't you sit down by the fire and get warm?'

Helen smiled. 'I will. I'm just going to get my pyjamas on and take off all this makeup.'

'Okay. Don't be long,' he said.

Helen went into the bathroom and washed her face, and wiped away the stage makeup. She watched the reflection of her features emerging in the mirror on the front of the medicine cabinet and wondered if Harry saying that he loved her would change anything. She hoped not and hoped so, all in the same breath. What would it be like to have a proper boyfriend and go out together and plan things together and . . . Helen made herself stop thinking about the might bes and instead concentrate on the here and now. There were a lot of other things she wanted out of life besides settling down with a steady boyfriend. In lots of ways Helen and Charlotte wanted the same things. It was just that she had a very different way of going about it.

'Are you okay in there?' Harry called.

'I'm fine,' said Helen.

Once she had stripped off her wet clothes and pulled on her pyjamas and dressing gown Helen went back into the sitting room and curled up on the sofa in front of the fire. She felt warm and safe and comfortable in the soft lamplight, a million miles away from the pub and the hotel, Leon Downey and Vince.

Feeling the tension finally start to ease, Helen closed her eyes. She could hear Harry busy in the kitchen, could hear the hiss of the gas fire and the sounds of the rain against the windows from behind the curtains. She didn't mean to fall asleep, but the combination of the heat from the fire, the long, long day and the after-effects of the booze she had had, proved too much. Helen only planned to close her eyes for a minute, just to rest them, and as she did she felt sleep coming up like a warm dark wave, pulling her down into a velvety silent darkness that felt close to perfect. It was impossible to resist. Her eyes felt so heavy that she just couldn't open them and without any struggle at all Helen let sleep claim her.

Some time later Helen woke with a start, feeling completely disorientated. It was dark and it took her a moment or two to realise she was still on the sofa in front of the fire and that someone was bending over her. She gasped with a mix of surprise and fear.

'Sorry,' said Harry, who was tucking a tartan rug around her shoulders. 'I didn't mean to frighten you, or wake you. I was just going to bed and I thought you might get cold out here.'

'How long have I been here?' Helen asked anxiously, rubbing the sleep from her eyes.

'Not very long.'

She pulled off the blanket. 'How long is not very long?'

'I don't know, maybe an hour, probably a bit longer actually. I didn't mean to disturb you. But it's all right, I was going to wake you up tomorrow so you didn't miss the film thing. I've set my alarm. Go back to sleep, I promise not to let you oversleep.'

'Did Charlotte come back yet?' she asked.

'No, I should have given her the spare key then she could let herself in. I'm wondering if she's worried she might wake us up.'

He obviously didn't know Charlotte very well, thought Helen. Her guess was that if Charlotte had wanted to come back to the flat, key or no key, she wouldn't have cared who she woke up.

'Has she phoned?' asked Helen, knowing full well that if she had she would undoubtedly have heard it.

He shook his head. 'No.'

Helen could sense Harry picking up on her anxiety.

'I'm sure she'll be all right. Charlotte is nobody's fool.

There's a good chance that she went home to her own place after the meeting finished.'

Helen stared at him; she doubted very much that that was what had happened but didn't say so.

'Ring her in the morning,' he said. 'I'll do it if you like. I was just thinking,' he continued, shifting his weight. 'As you're awake, and obviously you can say no if you want to – maybe now's not the moment –' Harry stopped.

Helen raised her eyebrows and waited.

'I was wondering if maybe you would like to come and sleep with me? I mean in my bed, not necessarily – well you know, not the other thing, unless of course you wanted to,' he grinned, 'in which case that would be fine too. Or we could just cuddle up. What do you think?'

Helen blushed; it wasn't quite what she had expected. She could feel her heart doing that odd little pitter-pattery thing and she opened her mouth to speak, although she was not altogether sure what it was she was going to say, and as she did Harry bent down so that he was kneeling beside her, his eyes bright.

She stared at him. 'Oh my God, you're not going to propose, are you?'

He grinned, 'No, at least not yet –'

'That's all right then. God, that sounds awful.' Helen stopped. 'What I meant was I'm not sure how I expected going to bed with someone would happen.'

'But this wasn't it?' said Harry. 'Sorry, it wasn't very romantic, was it? I'm just replaying it in my head and it was about as subtle as a car crash.'

Helen laughed. 'It's just fine, but there's something else you should know; I've never done the other thing, and I'm not sure I'm ready to do it. But if I were –' now it was her turn to run out of words.

'But if you were?' Harry prompted.

Helen grinned. 'If I were, I couldn't think of a person I'd rather do it with than you.'

He leaned in closer, brushing his lips against her neck. She could feel her whole body responding.

'Maybe not now, though,' she said, trying to fight the clamour in her head.

He pulled away. 'You're not offended, are you? It sounded so clumsy.'

Helen shook her head. 'I'm not offended at all, Harry. It's a lovely thing – and I'm flattered.' And with that Harry seemed to grow in confidence and he slipped his arms around her, pulled her tight up against him and kissed her properly.

'We'll wait then,' he said. 'I can wait as long as it takes. I think we'll know, don't you?' And then he kissed her again.

The sensation made Helen feel dizzy, but she made no effort to resist him. It would be so easy, so very very easy just to sink into his arms and let go. Helen had no doubt that whatever happened Harry would take care of her, and that thought, and that sense of sureness, spun through with desire, was a heady combination.

Gently he pushed her back amongst the cushions, his

kisses more insistent and hers more hungry. Perhaps she *was* ready to do the other thing after all. At which point the phone rang, making them both jump and pull away from each other as if they had been electrocuted. For a moment or two they both stared at the receiver, and then the phone rang again.

'Do you think that's her?' asked Harry, reaching over to answer it, but Helen was too fast for him. She grabbed the phone out of its cradle and was about to speak when a male voice said, 'Hello, I'm sorry to ring at such an ungodly hour, but I wondered if Charlotte is there with you?'

'*Charlotte's dad,*' Helen mouthed to Harry in answer to his unspoken question. 'Mr Johnson,' she said, trying hard to make it sound as if she hadn't almost been doing *the other thing* on the sofa.

'Helen, is that you? Sorry to disturb you so late but I was worried about Charlotte. She's not come home. Is she there?'

'I was asleep,' Helen lied.

'Oh, I'm sorry. I didn't mean to wake you up but I wanted to know if Charlotte was there with you, before I start ringing round the hospitals and police stations,' he said, adding a little false laughter. 'The thing is I haven't heard from her all evening. And I'm concerned. I thought she'd probably be back home by now. I was a bit late getting to the theatre. I know I don't have to explain to you, you know what Charlie can be like – always been a bit headstrong if things don't go her way.

I meant to be there to see you sing, but Joan, you've met Joan, haven't you? Lovely girl. She'd booked us a table at this new restaurant in Battesfield. I didn't know. I thought we were just popping in for a quick drink and nibbles. Her brother owns it; he's quite a bit older than Joan. Anyway, it was their opening night, and to be perfectly honest I couldn't see how I could get out of it, you know, not once we were there.' He was making excuses and they both knew it.

'Charlotte knew we were going. I told her I'd be at the theatre just as soon as I could. I wasn't that late –' He paused, letting the jovial facade slip. 'I can't sleep – I've been sitting here, waiting for her to come home. Did it go well?'

'Yes, it was fine,' said Helen, pulling faces at Harry.

'Right, well, that's good. Did you win?'

'No, we didn't win; we were good but we didn't come anywhere in the final three.'

'Ah, right, well, that's a shame. I did wonder when Charlotte wasn't at the theatre. It must have emptied out quite fast. I wasn't that late, not really – I tried ringing when I got home but there was no one answering the phone in the box office.' He was rambling, trying to justify why he hadn't been there to see them and why he hadn't been there to support Charlotte. 'I thought she might have rung me, you know, when you were finished, just to let me know how it went.'

Helen listened without interruption, finally the words faded.

'So is she there? I would really like to talk to her. To explain – you know –'

Helen paused, considering the options. Did she tell him the truth or did she lie? Before Helen could make up her mind Harry took the phone out of her hands.

'Hello there, Mr Johnson,' Harry sounded chipper and bright and wide awake. 'Harry here – yes, I'm afraid Charlotte's asleep at the moment – no, she's fine as far as I know. I just heard Helen get up, light sleeper, you know how it is. Used to sleeping above the shop and all that. No, no, I don't think I should wake her. Helen said she was sound asleep. But don't you worry, I'll make sure she rings you first thing in the morning. Yes, just as soon as she wakes up. Mind you, it might not be that early though – we've all had a bit of a late night here. Yes, it was a real shame they didn't win. They sounded great. No, Charlotte's fine – really – bit disappointed obviously. Good night, yes, thanks, I'll say good night to Helen for you.' And with that Harry hung up.

They looked at each other; the moment had passed.

'I've never heard you lie before,' Helen said. 'And why did you tell Charlotte's dad she was here? She's not here.'

'No, but if she's not at home then we've got a damned good idea where she is. I think we should go and get her, Helen,' said Harry, pulling his jacket off the back of the chair. 'Come on, or would you prefer to stay here and go to bed?' He laughed. 'What I meant was, do you want to stay here while I go and fetch her?'

Helen shook her head. 'No, of course not, I can't let

you go on your own. I'll go get dressed and come with you.' She got up and hurried into the bedroom, pausing at the door to smile at him. 'You are such a good man, Harry. And if Mr Johnson hadn't called –' she stopped, not quite able to bring herself to finish the sentence. 'And besides that,' said Helen quickly, 'there are two of them, you need me to keep an eye out for you. If you go on your own Leon or Vince might punch you.'

He grinned. 'You care?'

'Of course I do.'

'I'll go and get the car,' he said.

'It's not that far, we can walk. She's only at the Billingsfield Arms.'

'If Charlotte was drunk when she got there God only knows what sort of state she's in now.'

Helen nodded; he was right. She hurried into her bedroom, pulled on a pair of dry jeans, a thick sweater, and a pair of boots and then, picking up her coat, followed Harry downstairs and out into the street.

It was a horrible night. It was raining harder now. They parked the Mini on the kerb close to the edge of the market square and hurried across to the hotel. Helen shivered as a bitter wind whipped at their faces and tugged at their clothes. The sharp, icy-cold rain seemed to be driving in horizontally across the road. Beyond the pools of yellowing light from the street lights and shop fronts, the market was a dark, cavernous place. The wind chased in and out of the empty stalls, making the canvas flap and whine miserably as if something was trying to break free.

Helen, tucked tight in alongside Harry, knew that if the situation had been reversed there was no way in a million years Charlotte would be coming out on any night, let alone a night like this, to rescue her.

As if reading her mind, Harry turned and said, 'We are doing the right thing, you know that. Charlotte might not like it but she'll thank us later.'

Helen smiled up at him; she admired his optimism but doubted that Harry was right.

They scurried across the road. The main doors of the Billingsfield Arms were locked when they got there. Huddled under the portico Helen pulled her coat tight around her while Harry rang the night porter's bell and waited. After a few minutes he rang again; finally a voice crackled over the intercom.

'Good evening, may I help you?'

'I hope so,' Harry said into the speaker. 'A friend of ours is here. We said we'd come and pick her up as it's so late. Her name's Charlotte.'

'Charlotte Johnson,' Helen said quickly, in case Harry had forgotten. 'She came here earlier, for a meeting.'

The line went dead and a few moments later an elderly man, dressed in a uniform, appeared from somewhere deep inside the shadowy confines of the hotel. He peered through the glass partition to one side of the main door, looking the two of them up and down.

'Our friend should be here,' repeated Helen loudly,

mouthing the words in case he couldn't hear. 'She had a meeting with one of your guests. We've just come to collect her. Charlotte Johnson?'

The night porter nodded, all the while fiddling with the keys that he had hanging from a chain on his belt. His expression suggested that whatever it was they planned to tell him, he had heard it all before, although he had the good grace not to mention that it was well past two o'clock in the morning. As the door swung open the man looked more closely at Harry. 'I know you, don't I?' he said, eyes narrowing.

Harry nodded. 'Yes. I think I sold you a bike last Christmas. Child's Raleigh, midnight blue, white leatherette seat, and matching tassels on the handlebars. For your grandson, I believe.'

'Well, damn me, so you did.' The man grinned. 'You're from the toy shop, aren't you? Bottom of Fitzroy Street.'

Harry nodded. 'That's right. Finton's Finest Toys.'

'Well, isn't that amazing. That boy loves that bike. Come on in out of the rain. It's bloody awful out there tonight.'

Harry's smile held.

The man waved them inside. 'What's your friend's name again?' he asked as they slipped past him and into the warmth of the foyer.

'Charlotte Johnson,' said Helen. 'We both had a business meeting earlier; I went home and she came back here with the people we were meeting. I thought she'd have been home by now.' Said aloud it sounded like a lie.

'So we said we'd come over and pick her up,' repeated Harry firmly, shooting Helen a look, probably, Helen guessed, to stop her telling the man they had just turned up on the off chance they might be able to find Charlotte.

'We said we'd pick her up if she was late,' he continued. 'We don't live that far away but we didn't want her walking home alone at this time of the morning. You never know what might happen.'

The old man nodded. 'You're right there, lad. Let's go through to reception. I haven't seen anyone waiting about for a lift. Nasty old night out there, you wouldn't want to walk.' He pulled his glasses out of his top pocket and perched them on the end of his nose. 'Do you know what room the guest you were meeting was in, Miss?'

'No, I'm afraid I don't,' said Helen.

'What time did you say you'd pick her up?'

Helen could see Harry fishing around for the right answer so she said, 'We didn't arrange a definite time, but we haven't heard from her so we were getting a bit worried. We thought she would probably ring –'

'And do you know who she was meeting?'

'Yes, of course. His name's Leon, Leon Downey.'

For a moment Helen thought the night porter was going to say something but in the end he just looked fixedly at the register and said, 'And this Leon Downey, he told you that he was staying here tonight, did he?'

Helen nodded.

'And what sort of meeting did you say it was?' asked the man, casually, over one shoulder.

'Business. It was about some work. We were hoping he might take us on, give us a job.'

'A job,' repeated the porter.

Helen glanced at Harry. 'Yes. Leon Downey is an agent, in show business,' Helen said. 'And Charlotte and I are singers. He said he could get us some work.' She hesitated. *Was that what he had said?* She couldn't remember now exactly what it was he had offered them.

'Right,' said the night porter, nodding, his finger working down the list in the register. 'Well, your Mr Downey is not booked in tonight as a guest. Or at least he's not on the register.'

Helen frowned. 'I'm sure that he said he was staying here. I saw them come in –'

The night porter nodded. 'Oh, there is a good chance that he is staying here. He's just not in the register.'

'I don't understand,' said Helen.

'Oh it's an old trick – just depends on who's on duty,' the man said, turning his attention to a board behind the reception desk where dozens of keys hung from row after row of small brass hooks. His gaze worked backwards and forwards scanning the bunches rather than meeting Helen's eye. 'I don't know what Mr Downey told you and your friend, but you seem like a nice sort of girl. I'd steer well clear of him if I were you.' The man continued to scan the rows of keys as he spoke. 'I don't like to speak ill of people but if you were my daughter, well, let's just say he's not the sort of bloke you want to get yourself mixed up with.'

'He told us he was in show business.'

The porter sniffed. 'That's what they're calling it these days, is it?'

'He did say he could get us work,' Helen pressed.

The man glanced at Harry and then with some discomfort, said, 'Leon Downey runs a strip club; he calls it exotic dancing but no one's fooled. He's got a place over in Battesfield and another one over in the Canaries. Lanzarote I think. He drinks in here sometimes, always bragging about his girls and how much money he's making; too flashy by half that one.'

'But Charlotte's a singer,' Helen protested lamely.

'I'm sure that she is, pet, and I'm sure that's she's very good, and maybe he's taking her on to sing; but I very much doubt it, he's not usually looking for girls with much in the way of brains or talent if you get my drift.'

Helen stared at him. 'He told us he was staying here,' she said.

'And like I said he most probably is, but he's not booked in the register. What he's done is slipped one of the other staff a few quid and got himself one of the rooms that isn't booked for the night. It's the way some of the lads earn themselves a few extra quid on the sly. Slip the chambermaid a drink in the morning to change the room up and no-one's any the wiser. Sacked without a leg to stand on if you're caught, but it doesn't stop them. And Mr Downey is well known in here, he gets the lads into his club for nowt, a few drinks on the house, oils the wheels –'

'So what are we going to do now, then?' asked Helen.

The porter glanced at her. 'You didn't come to pick your friend up at all, did you? You came to rescue her.'

Helen reddened. 'It's so late and she hadn't come back, and I was worried about her. And then her dad rang. And Leon Downey seemed really dodgy and Charlotte wouldn't listen. She thought he could help her get on the stage –'

'Aye, well you can't tell some people. They need saving from themselves. Did you say there were two of them?'

Helen nodded. 'Vince somebody.'

'Vince Leadbetter, I know him an' all, bad as each other, those two. You were right to steer well clear.'

'So what can we do?' said Helen in desperation. 'I can't just leave Charlotte with them.'

'Do you know which rooms have got guests in?' Harry said, frantically looking up at the key board.

The old man nodded.

Helen was beginning to get impatient and even more anxious.

Meanwhile Harry's gaze followed the old man's back to the register. 'So then we just have to work out which room are occupied and which other keys have been taken?' asked Harry.

'Not necessarily,' said the night porter. 'Someone could easily have slipped your Mr Downey one of the master keys, but to be honest that's not likely. They probably just wedged one of the doors open for him. So he won't be needing a key, nor have taken one.' The man's attention moved back to the register. 'If I was to bet I'd reckon he's probably on the fourth floor. We've had a conference in this week, a few of them were planning to stay over and make a weekend of it. Check out late Sunday morning. No one's going to notice an extra room or two in amongst that lot. That's who I thought you two were. Away from home, out all hours – they lose their keys, roll in steaming drunk. Animals, some people.'

'So can we go and find Charlotte?' said Helen.

Both men looked at her.

'Well, what else am I supposed to do?' asked Helen.

'You can't just go banging on people's doors, not at this time of the morning,' said the porter. 'Place'll be in an uproar.'

A light flashed on above the reception desk.

'Is that for room service?' asked Helen. 'Leon Downey said they were going to get room service.'

The night porter shook his head. 'No, that's the front door and no, Downey hasn't ordered anything. And he's not likely to if he was blagging a room for the night. I'd have known. I'm the only porter on tonight – they'd have to be mugs to order anything, they have to sign for it, you see. Everything gets booked out against a room number.'

The light flashed again.

'Look, just hang on for a minute, will you? I'll go and see who that is and then we'll sort something out.' He grinned. 'I suppose I could always set the fire alarms off, that'd get everyone out.' With that the man picked up the phone, his concentration moving away from the two of them.

'Hello, how can I help?' There was a little pause and then he said, 'Right you are, sir, I'll be there in a second –'

As the porter headed off Helen caught hold of Harry's arm. 'Come on,' she hissed.

Harry stared down at her. 'What?'

'The fourth floor. We have got to find Charlotte.'

Before Harry could argue Helen was running across the foyer and up the stairs with Harry hot on her heels. At the top of the first flight he pointed towards the lift. 'Come on, we'll take the lift. There's no point killing ourselves,' he said, guiding her in through the open doors. 'Although you do know that the porter was only guessing about which floor she was on. He could be wrong. She could be anywhere.'

Helen nodded. 'I know, but we have to start somewhere.'

'Have you thought about what we're going to do when we get up to the fourth floor?'

'Not really. I thought maybe we could listen at the doors,' she said. 'And if not there's always the fire alarm.'

Harry did a double take and then laughed. 'Are you serious?' When she didn't answer he grinned. 'Just what I've always wanted, to be arrested loitering around outside some strange woman's bedroom. Come on, let's get going before the porter comes after us and throws us out.' And with that Harry pressed the button for the fourth floor.

The lift made silent stately progress upwards, the doors finally gliding open like oiled silk as they reached their destination. Helen felt a ripple of anxiety as she peered out into the gloom.

Ahead of them, off the landing, the hotel corridor stretched left and right; the walls lined with the same heavy wooden panels as those downstairs, the floor covered in the same dense red carpet; but whereas downstairs it looked rich and warm, in this smaller narrower space it felt claustrophobic and dark. Helen stared into the gloom. It was going to be close to impossible to find Charlotte without either help or a real stroke of luck.

'This is madness, isn't it?' whispered Helen. 'We're never going to find her, are we?'

'We will, we're here now and if she's not on this floor there are three more we can search,' Harry said and then grinned when he saw her expression. 'It's a joke, Helen, we'll be fine. Don't worry, we'll find her. She's got to be here somewhere and if she is then we'll track her down. Let's make a start.'

Helen smiled at Harry, grateful for his optimism and his unquestioning support.

'It might be better if we split up. You take this side, I'll take the other,' he said.

Helen nodded and headed off into the gloom. There had to be at least twenty or so doors along the main corridor, with others going off along passages that ran at right angles to the one they were standing in. As quietly as she could Helen moved from door to door, pressing

255

her ear close to the cracks in the frame, praying that no one came out and caught her as she crept along, listening to the snoring, the snuffling and the silence as she tiptoed along the corridor.

'Psst,' said Harry, after a minute or two. He beckoned her over. Helen hurried across to where he was standing and listened.

'What do you reckon?' he said.

Through the door she could pick out the muffled sounds of a man's voice and then someone who sounded a lot like Charlotte, although Helen wasn't a hundred per cent certain.

'I think it's her –' she paused. 'What are we going to do?' whispered Helen nervously.

Instead of answering her, Harry knocked sharply on the door. 'Room service,' he said briskly and then turning to Helen, said more quietly, 'Even if it's not them they're awake so we won't be disturbing anybody.'

There were the sounds of hurried activity inside the room and then the door opened a fraction and a rather bleary-eyed Leon Downey peered around the door at them. 'You've made a mistake, we didn't order any –'

But before he could say another word Helen barged past him, forcing the door wide open, followed close behind by Harry. Leon was completely wrong-footed. 'What the –' was the best he could manage as the pair of them burst into the room.

The only lights on were the ones on the bedside tables but they were enough to illuminate Leon, who was dressed in a grubby vest and oversized paisley boxers. Above the waistband hung a great roll of lard-white belly. He still had his socks on. His thin greasy hair was awry, his face florid and sweaty. He was certainly no Adonis. Helen could pick out various items of clothes strewn around the bedroom: shoes, a shirt and Charlotte's jeans and sweater dropped onto the carpet alongside her underwear.

On the bedside cabinets and dressing table were the ruins of a Chinese takeaway, along with the remains of a bottle of vodka, cans of beer and Coca-Cola, and ashtrays full of cigarette butts – the debris of an impromptu supper. Charlotte was in bed, with the bedclothes pulled right up to her chin, eyes bright and wide – but whereas Leon Downey looked slightly bemused, Charlotte looked furious and defiant.

'What the hell do you think you're doing here?' she snarled at Helen.

'We came to get you,' said Helen. 'To rescue you.'

Charlotte threw back her head and laughed. 'Do I really look like I need rescuing, huh? You're so much braver now you've got your little friend Harry with you. Not so brave earlier, were you?'

'I didn't want to end up back here with either him or Vince – and as for needing rescuing,' Helen said, looking first at Leon and then Charlotte, 'I'm not the one in bed with some weird fat old man.'

'Oh, for God's sake just bugger off, will you,' Charlotte snorted. 'I don't need rescuing by you or anyone else.

Who the hell do you think you are anyway, Helen? You're not my bloody mother. You've got no right to come bursting in here. I'm over eighteen, I know what I'm doing.'

'Do you?' said Helen.

'This is my big chance. You just don't get it, do you?'

'It's you who doesn't get it,' yelled Helen, finally running out of patience. 'This isn't the way you get where you want to be. And him –' She pointed to Leon Downey. 'He's not an agent, Charlotte. He owns a strip club.'

'It's a gentleman's club,' protested Leon, making a show of composing himself. 'Now you heard your friend, why don't you just bugger off before I call the manager and have the pair of you thrown out.'

'Go ahead,' said Harry, picking up the phone from the dressing table. 'Help yourself. I'm sure he'd be pleased to hear from you.'

When Leon didn't move, Helen said, 'He didn't even book this room, he slipped one of the porters a few quid so that he could stay the night.'

Charlotte turned and stared at Leon. 'Is that true?'

'Take no notice of them –'

'Is it true?' demanded Charlotte.

'Anyone with any sense does it. It's purely a cash deal, baby,' he said. 'Off the books. It pays to know the right people, that's all. And I've already told you I know *all* the right people.' And then turning to Helen and Harry, he said, 'Just get out, will you?' pointing towards the door.

'Please come with us,' said Helen.

If Charlotte was at all fazed she didn't let it show. 'I know what I'm doing,' she snapped. 'Now you heard Leon, just bugger off and leave us alone, will you?'

'You can't want to stay here with him,' Helen said. 'Your dad rang.'

'Oh yeah, and what did he want?'

Helen hated the hard icy edge in Charlotte's voice. 'To talk to you. He wanted to know where you are. He's really worried about you. He knows that he let you down tonight, Charlie. He's being waiting up for you to come home.'

'Oh, really, and there was me thinking he was off out having a good time with what's-her-name. It's just his guilty conscience talking, you know that, don't you?' said Charlotte. 'When he's got a new squeeze he doesn't care about anything else or anybody. She's twenty-two. *Twenty-bloody-two*. It's disgusting. You're just so gullible, Helen.'

Helen stared at her. She hadn't realised just how hurt Charlotte felt. 'I'm sorry,' she mumbled. 'But your dad sounded really worried and I think he was genuinely upset that he missed us singing.'

'Oh yeah, rub it in why don't you. Just because yours showed up.'

'My dad was there?' Helen said in surprise, wondering whether it was a joke.

'You didn't see him, did you? I saw him round the front when I went to find my dad. There he was, scurrying away.' Charlotte paused for effect. 'Like he always does.'

Helen reddened.

'I told your dad you would ring him in the morning,' said Harry briskly.

'Well, that was really nice of you,' said Charlotte, voice dripping with sarcasm. 'And did you tell him where I was?'

'We told him that you were staying at Harry's with me,' said Helen.

'Did you now?' laughed Charlotte. 'In that case he can stop worrying, then, can't he? Now get out.'

Helen had to give it one last try. 'Charlotte, please.'

'I'm serious, just go will you?'

'You heard the lady,' said Leon, pointing towards the door.

There was a moment of standoff and then Harry caught hold of Helen's arm. 'Come on. There's nothing else we can do, short of dragging her out of here naked.'

Helen was still reluctant to leave. Charlotte glared at her.

'Don't stay here with him. Please –'

'What's it to you, Goody-Two-Shoes?'

'You're my friend.'

Charlotte snorted, 'Just bugger off and leave me alone. I don't need friends like you. I can take care of myself, is that clear?'

With a sense of crushing defeat Helen turned away. Leon ushered the two of them out of the room and slammed the door shut behind them. Harry and Helen were standing out in the corridor when the lift doors slid open and the porter stepped out.

He looked them up and down. Helen braced herself for a telling off but instead the man said, 'So did you find your friend and Mr Downey?'

Helen was about to lie, not wanting to cause another scene, when Harry nodded. 'Yes, we did. They're in there,' he said, pointing towards the closed door. 'Number forty-two.'

The man nodded and, pulling out his passkey, knocked on the door.

'What did you do that for?' whispered Helen to Harry.

'You want her to come home, don't you?'

Helen nodded. 'Yes, but you heard what she said. She's going to be livid.'

'That's true, but at least she'll be livid and safe and away from him.'

The porter knocked again.

'What the hell is it now?' yelled Leon Downey from inside the room. 'Didn't I just tell you to bugger off out of it?'

'This is the night porter, sir. Would you like to open the door or would you prefer it if I let myself in?'

A second or two later the door opened a fraction. 'What the fuck do you want?' growled Downey.

'I think you know exactly what I want, Mr Downey. I'll have to ask you to leave the premises, or would you prefer to pay for your room?' There was a moment's pause and then the porter continued in a calm even voice, 'Or perhaps you'd rather that I called the police?'

'What's it to you?' snapped Downey.

'It's my job, sir,' said the porter. 'Now which is it to be?'

There was a moment when Helen thought that Leon was going to argue and cause a scene but in the end he just shrugged and sighed. 'Can you just give us a few minutes to get dressed?'

The porter nodded and let the door swing shut.

Helen glanced anxiously at Harry, who caught hold of her hand to reassure her. 'It'll be fine,' he mouthed.

What seemed like seconds later the door to the room was flung open and Charlotte stormed out, followed close behind by Leon Downey. Charlotte had a face like thunder, her hair all over the place, her clothes awry, her coat bundled up in her arms. She glared at Helen. 'You think you're so bloody clever, don't you?' she snarled. 'Happy now? You know you've ruined everything, don't you?'

Helen said nothing.

They all made their way downstairs in the lift in complete silence, the air so tense between them that you could have snapped it like a stick. Leon Downey spent most of the downward journey fixing his tie and combing his hair. He looked remarkably calm for a man being thrown out of a hotel in the small hours. As they stepped out into the foyer he made as if to take hold of Charlotte's arm but a sharp look from Harry dissuaded him.

'If I find you on the premises again, Mr Downey,' said the porter guiding them all towards the main doors, 'I'll have no option but to call the police, do I make myself clear?'

Downey grunted. 'Yeah, yeah, yeah. Your mate didn't say that when he took my bloody money.' At the door he turned his attention to Charlotte. 'I'll give you a bell in the week, petal, or you can ring me if you like. I've got your number right here.' He tapped his top pocket. 'Let's have a little chat about the things we were talking about, see if we can't do some business. And as far as I'm concerned you've got what it takes, sweetie, you really have. You've got my number?'

Charlotte nodded.

'You're not going to ring him, are you?' asked Helen, unable to stop herself.

'It's got nothing to do with you who I ring,' said Charlotte, pulling on her coat.

'Come on, Charlotte,' said Harry. 'Let's get back to the flat. Helen needs to be up in the morning.'

Meekly Charlotte let him take her arm and lead her back towards the car, but not before she turned to Helen and said, 'I never want to speak to you again as long as I draw breath, is that clear? Me and you and the whole Wild Birds thing, it's over – all of it. We're history. Do you understand?'

Helen stared at her and nodded, realising that in amongst the great surge of hurt the other feeling she had was one of relief.

FOURTEEN

Harry and Helen were waiting in the storeroom for Natalia to come back and give them her verdict on what was going to happen next. Helen had her own opinions.

'I wish I'd rung you before,' said Harry. 'I've thought about it no end over the years, but Kate was always so adamant. No contact, she said. I think she was worried you might take Adam away.'

'I wish I'd rung you, Harry,' said Helen,.'Not about Adam, but for old times' sake. I should have kept in touch and then maybe none of this would ever have happened. It's my fault; I was just so stunned when you told me that you had asked Charlotte to marry you.'

'Long time ago now.' Harry pulled a funny lopsided smile.

'I still remember how it felt.'

He sighed. 'We can't turn back the clock. Come on,

let's go and see what that lot are planning,' he said, and pushed open the door.

'To be perfectly honest I think we should just wrap it up here and head round to Helen's old house, get that in the can and then head back to the hotel,' Natalia was saying as Helen and Harry came out of the storeroom together. 'Time's getting on and we can't move on with this thread until Kate –' she glanced down at her clipboard, 'it is *Kate*, isn't it – until she gets back and we get the full SP on this whole kid thing.'

Helen stared at them. 'What did you just say?'

The crew, Natalia and Felix and the others, were huddled together having an impromptu state-of-the-union conference in the shop, over by the Lego display. At the sound of Helen's voice they all swung round to look at her.

Natalia did have the grace to look a little sheepish. 'Sorry about that, but let's face it – Kate is the one with all the answers here, isn't she? And we can't do any more here until she shows up. So how about we stop digging and take you back to your old house? The new tenant said she's really happy for us to film there; interiors and everything.'

Natalia took another look at her clipboard. 'And Harry here said we can go and look around your old flat if we want to – and then while we're in the car if we could maybe just take a quick look at the schedule for next week? It looks like an easy haul really; we've contacted a few old names from the good old days. And we've already picked out some great archive footage from your old shows, and the network have agreed to let us film on the set of *Cannon Square*.'

Helen stared at Natalia. 'And we're moving on just like that?'

'Well there's nothing we can do here till Kate gets home really, is there?'

Helen sighed.

'So, *Cannon Square*,' Natalia prompted.

'I haven't been back there since I left,' said Helen testily.

'Yes I know. It's a real coup. We're doing some "what was it like back then?" reminiscences with that segment – Carrie Haines, Richard Lewin, oh and Bill Duffy – the one with cancer? He's said he'd love to take part. We're going to – I think it's Acton – to film him at home.'

'He's been really ill.'

'I know, but he's such a trouper; he said he wouldn't miss recording something for your show for the world. Weren't you two a bit of an item at one time?' Natalia paused for effect. 'We did have him down as an odds-on favourite to be Adam's father. We had been hoping to tie it all up – you know, this, meeting Adam, and then meeting his dad . . .'

Helen shook her head; when it came right down to it, once you got past the cutesy floral dresses and woolly berets, Natalia had all the empathy of a great white shark.

'Anyway,' Natalia was saying, 'I think the *Cannon Square* thing was the only real query on the copy I emailed you and I just wanted to let you know that it was a go. Okay? So if we could get the wagons rolling folks –' She clapped her hand and almost at once the crew started to pack up their equipment.

'Wait – what about Adam?' said Helen incredulously. 'We can't just move on as if nothing has happened. He's expecting to meet me, isn't he? Wasn't that in your big plan?'

Natalia nodded. 'Well, yes, but we said we'd play it by ear. I thought his dad could ring him. You're all right with that, aren't you, Harry? Although to be honest I'd be far happier if we could talk to Kate before we do anything at all really. Do you think you can hold Adam off till then, Harry? It seems only right.'

'Only right?' Helen spluttered. 'What the hell are you talking about? There is nothing right about this at all. He's a person, Natalia; you can't just switch him off because it's inconvenient. Thanks to you he's waiting somewhere, expecting to meet his long-lost mother. For God's sake, woman, have you got any idea what you've done here?'

'We didn't do anything, Helen. We're just filming it,' said Natalia calmly. 'All this was going on long before we got here, you have to remember that. Okay, so I'm prepared to concede that, yes, thanks to us, it's come to a head, but none of it is our doing.'

Helen stared at her. 'Are you serious? What had you got planned on your schedule for Adam?'

Natalia looked away, so it was Harry who replied. 'We thought you could meet him at the theatre, you know, after the show tomorrow. Natalia said we could have sort of a reunion in the dressing room. It seemed like the natural place really. You're a star, and Adam and Kate both love show business – it made sense when we talked about it.' He glanced across at Natalia for confirmation, who did a funny little shimmying shrug which implied it was nothing to do with her.

'And what time is Kate due back?' Helen asked.

'Tomorrow lunch time,' said Harry. 'I really ought to go and ring Adam. He'll be on tenterhooks.'

'And tell him what?' asked Helen anxiously.

'How about you tell him that you haven't seen her yet?' suggested Natalia. Harry and Helen both turned to look at her.

'If you feel you have to ring him, that is – rather than get his hopes up,' Natalia blustered. 'We can't explain anything without the full facts. It might be easier just to wait until Kate gets back.'

'Shame you didn't think about getting the full facts beforehand,' said Helen.

'It'll be okay,' said Harry, 'I haven't told him you were arriving today. I wanted to talk to you first, but he knows you're at the theatre tomorrow. He hasn't talked about anything else all week while his mum's been away.'

Helen sighed. 'How is her dad these days?'

Harry raised his eyebrows. 'Kate's? It's difficult. His new wife's twenty-eight, that's why Kate was going out to stay with him this week; Candy is off visiting her mum and dad. Kate's dad is no dad at all when it comes right down to it. I think that's why she can be like she is some-times –' Harry paused. 'But she is much better these days, a lot less volatile – she's really mellowed over the years.'

Helen smiled; she wanted to believe him.

'Kate used to go and visit your dad, you know. Take him things, pies and pot roasts; she's a cracking cook.'

'What?' said Helen.

Harry pressed on, oblivious to any impact his words might be having. 'Oh yes, she used to pop round there at least once a week – she used to take Adam over there to see him. I always thought it was a nice thing, you know – letting him see his grandson.'

'Oh my God.' Helen felt her eyes filling up with tears. 'Is that what she told my dad, that Adam was mine?'

Harry looked aghast. 'Oh, Helen I'm so sorry, I didn't think. No, I don't know what she told him. I've got no idea.'

Helen closed her eyes and made a real effort to control herself. There was nothing she could do about any of this until Charlotte came home. And how could she possibly explain to anyone, particularly Harry, just how much she was dreading seeing her again after all these years?

'What time are you on stage tomorrow, Helen?' asked Natalia, breaking her train of thought.

'I have to be there for a run-through and technical checks in the afternoon,' said Helen, turning to face her. 'You already know that. We emailed you the times. I'm not playing whatever games you have in mind,' she said.

'I don't know what you're cooking up in that head of yours but I've got a show to do.'

Natalia looked wounded.

'And so have I,' said Felix, the director, who up until now had remained steadfastly silent. 'I don't want to break up the party, guys, but we really need to get on. I'd like to get to Victoria Street while we've still got the light.'

'It'll be all right,' said Harry, shooing Helen away. 'You go and do the rest of the filming. I'll be fine. And so will Adam.' He grinned a lazy lopsided grin that she remembered only too well. '. I've really missed you.' And with that he threw his arms around her. 'I'm glad you're back.'

Helen closed her eyes and let the sensation engulf her.

'It's good to see you too, Harry,' she said. 'It really is. I've missed you too.'

The words made her voice crack and break, but inside her head Helen's thoughts were racing. It felt like she had stepped into a hurricane.

'I'll see you tomorrow,' he said.

Helen nodded.

The crew headed out towards the car. Helen fell into step behind them, glad to be outside and wishing for all the world that they were going back to the hotel. She needed time to think. Natalia was about to speak but Helen held up a hand to silence her.

'I know I have to talk to you during the filming but I just need a few minutes to get it all straight in my head, do you understand?'

Natalia opened her mouth to reply.

'Don't,' said Helen.

Natalia sniffed. 'Take your time. Anyway, given what's happened with Adam, I really should ring Ruth to discuss the shape of what we're doing here.'

And with that Natalia picked up her bag, tucked her clipboard under her arm and walked briskly down the path, away from the car. At the corner of the street she pulled out a mobile phone and a packet of cigarettes from her jacket and, whilst dialling with one thumb, lit up. They were strange thin brown things more like a cheroot than a cigarette, which made Helen think of Arthur. Maybe now was the moment to ring him.

She pulled out her phone, realising as she did that she was hoping that there was a message from Bon, or Arthur, but it looked like neither of them had thought to let her know how they were.

Bon was in Dubai with what's-her-name. To be fair he was probably up to his eyes in rehearsals and all the technical stuff, said a calming voice in her head, the one that was trying to ignore the roar of insecurity and the worry that maybe he was up to his eyes in what's-her-name instead.

And Arthur? God alone knew what he was up to. Briskly Helen tucked the phone away; now wasn't the time. What could she possibly say to either of them? How long would it take her to explain the state that she was in?

'Are you all right?' asked Felix, as Helen settled herself in the back of the car and looked up at Harry's shop.

'I've got no idea,' said Helen with a sigh. 'I knew it

was going to be tough coming back here, and it is, but for all the wrong reasons. This is crazy.'

Felix nodded towards Natalia. 'You know she means well. She's just young and hungry. You remember how that feels.'

Helen laughed. 'I hope to God I had more compassion when I was her age.'

Felix laughed. 'Yeah, I think they breed them differently these days. This mess isn't her fault, you know – whatever was going on here was happening a long time before we showed up.'

Helen nodded, 'Yes, I know, but how we handle it is down to us. I had no idea about any of this.' She sighed. 'Maybe I should have come home earlier.'

Outside the car Natalia had started to pace up and down.

'She is just so young,' sighed Helen.

'You're right,' Felix said. 'First time I met Natalia I thought she was on work experience.'

Helen laughed. 'Easy mistake to make.'

'Made me feel like a bloody dinosaur. She's going to be good when she's had a few of the edges knocked off.'

Helen looked across at Natalia. She was jabbing the air with her fingers now and blowing great plumes of smoke out. Whatever was being said, Helen suspected it wasn't going quite to plan. Finally Natalia came back to the car.

'And?' said Felix, opening the door for her.

'Victoria Street,' Natalia said briskly, flicking the cigarette away. 'Before the light goes.'

FIFTEEN

On the short drive back from the Billingsfield Arms Hotel to Harry's flat no one spoke. The atmosphere inside Harry's Mini was icy cold. Charlotte didn't say a word when they got back to the flat and marched straight in to Helen's room slamming the door behind her. Harry went to bed, alone, and Helen curled under a blanket on the sofa for what was left of the night. She propped her clock up on the coffee table just a few inches from her head and was asleep in seconds. Helen dreamt she was being chased by magicians and Leon Downey and a man who kept tapping his clipboard and telling her that she was late.

The instant the alarm went off Helen was awake; she switched it off and slipped noiselessly out from under the blanket. Pulling on her dressing gown she tiptoed to the bathroom, and washed and dressed as quietly as she could. Helen was just about to leave when Harry opened his bedroom door.

'Morning,' he said, rubbing his eyes. 'Are you okay?'

Helen nodded.

'Did you manage to get any sleep?' he asked.

Helen nodded. 'Yes, thanks. You didn't have to get up, you know, Harry,' she said, pulling on her coat. 'Why don't you go back to bed? It's Sunday morning, no work – you can have a lie in.'

'Did you have any breakfast?' he asked, already on his way to the kitchen.

'No, but I'll be okay, I'm not hungry,' she said, following behind, not wanting the sound of their voices to wake Charlotte. 'I'll grab something when I get there.'

'You can't go out without eating something.' He pressed his hand to the kettle. 'You haven't even had a drink.'

'Stop fussing,' she said, buttoning her coat.

He raised his eyebrows. 'At least have a cup of tea and a slice of toast before you go.'

'I'll be late,' she laughed. 'I'll take it with me.'

'Okay, as long as you have something. Don't worry about Charlotte, I'll see she rings her dad and gets home.' He dropped teabags into two mugs. 'It was good of you to give up your bed for her.'

Helen shrugged dismissively. 'I don't think I had much choice. And besides, I don't think she would have been very happy on the sofa, do you? At least this way I could get out without disturbing anybody. Last thing I wanted was for her to start all over again.'

He dropped two slices of bread into the toaster. 'You could have come and slept in my bed.'

Helen looked at him and blushed. 'I didn't want to spend my first night with you with Charlotte in the next room.'

Harry grinned. 'So you haven't gone off the idea?'

Helen laughed. and slapped his arm playfully.

'You know we did the right thing, don't you?' he said.

'Not sleeping together?'

'No,' he laughed. 'Going to get Charlotte. It was the right thing to do.'

Helen leaned against the doorframe watching him work. His thick blonde hair was tousled from sleep. He was wrapped in his dressing gown, and padding around in bare feet he looked more like a twelve-year-old boy than a grown man. She couldn't help but love him.

'I'm not sure that Charlotte sees it that way,' she said.

'She will, eventually, when she has a chance to think about it. There is no way either of you ought to be mixed up with someone like Leon Downey. The man's a sleaze. I was thinking when we got in last night, how about if next week I ring round the clubs and pubs and book you a few gigs locally? I know it's not exactly the big time but it would be a start. There's that folk club in Hamble Street, they have some decent groups; or there's the Grapes by the station, they have live music most weekends. I bet I could get you a few bookings.'

'You heard Charlotte. She said that the Wild Birds were history.'

'Only because she was angry. She'll calm down, you know she will, especially if we can get a few halfway decent bookings.' Although she didn't reply, something about Helen's expression made Harry frown. 'What's the matter?' he asked.

'I'm not sure that we're up to it. Not really.'

'Don't be silly. You sound great and you did so well last night. People loved you, you know that, Helen. You heard the crowd, they couldn't get enough of you. You were the only act who got an encore. I can't work out why you didn't win.'

Helen smiled and took the mug of tea Harry offered her. 'Did you actually see us while we were singing?' she asked, sipping some of the tea down to humour him.

Harry reddened. 'No, sorry. I was backstage, but you sounded great – and no one else got an encore, did they? You were good,' he continued. 'Really good.'

Helen took another sip of tea. She didn't want to disillusion him by telling him the real reason for their encore. The silence was broken by the toaster as the toast sprang free.

'There you go,' Harry said. 'I told you it wouldn't take long.' He buttered a slice for her while she made a show of drinking the scalding tea. 'You want some jam on that?'

'No, it's fine just as it is. I've really got to go,' she said, accepting the toast.

'See you later,' Harry said. 'I hope you have a great time.'

Helen leant closer and kissed him on the cheek. 'Thank you for being such a hero, Harry. Now go back to bed, will you?'

Harry nodded and then catching hold of her arm kissed her gently on the lips. 'I'll see you later,' he said.

Helen nodded, feeling her heart pitter-patter in her chest.

She folded the slice of toast in half and ate it walking down the street in the cold, grey, half-light of Sunday morning. It felt as if the whole world was still fast asleep, tucked up against the chilling morning air, and she wondered if perhaps Arthur had been mistaken or worse still playing a bad practical joke on her. Helen hadn't realised just how tired she felt. It was cold and damp and Helen was just thinking that maybe the whole thing had been a really bad idea when she turned the corner into Castle Hill and stopped dead in astonishment. It looked as if the carnival had come to town.

The entire road was closed off with a row of metal barriers. Beyond the barriers technicians and riggers were busy setting up huge arc lights and scenery to disguise a bank of phones and sets of traffic lights. At the far end of the road, Copse Quay was dominated by a huge sailing ship, moored alongside the old Excise House; the whole place was buzzing with activity. A man was stacking barrels up on the quay, people were covering the modern road surfaces with straw and wood chippings, horses were being groomed and tacked up. Men, women and children in full historical costume were bustling around, chatting excitedly, while a man with a camera hurried backwards and forwards taking still photographs of everyone.

All along the street on the landward side a row of stalls had been set up and were being dressed with bright colourful goods, fabrics and animals in wicker baskets. Close to the water's edge people gathered around great braziers to keep warm. The whole place was full of noise and light and life.

Helen stopped and stared, trying to take it all in. Lined up in one of the side streets, away from the action, was a row of modern trailers, parked well away from the clatter and buzz of the film set, while closer to the barriers stood two bright blue double-decker buses, which were currently doing a roaring trade serving breakfasts. A posse of people, all dressed in variations on parkas and moon boots, were scurrying backwards and forwards with clipboards, busily shepherding people and props around the set.

Helen hesitated at the first barrier, not altogether sure where to go or what to do. There were a couple of policemen on security, although at this time of the morning they were more preoccupied with sipping mugs of tea and eating bacon rolls than keeping crowds at bay, but the last thing she really wanted was to attract their attention in case they sent her away again.

Helen opened her bag, desperately trying to find the flyer Arthur had given her. She couldn't remember if there were any instructions on it, maybe there was something on the back that she'd missed.

'Hello,' said a voice from somewhere close by. At first Helen didn't take any notice; she didn't think there was much chance there was anyone she knew on the set – and then she felt a tap on her shoulder, and swung round.

'Well hello and good morning to you, if it isn't my first client?' said Arthur, all smiles. He was wrapped up against the cold in a duffle coat and woolly hat. 'You found it all right then? I'm glad you showed up.' He peered at her. 'You look tired, are you okay?' Before she could answer he continued,' Mind you, consumptive is a good look on this shoot – if you could cough a bit maybe they'll give you a line. Come on. Let me show you where to go and sign in.'

He nodded a hello to the policeman who waved him through.

'Come on,' he said. 'There's someone I want you to meet. 'As he spoke Arthur pointed out one of the girls whom Helen had seen a few minutes earlier hurrying backwards and forwards with a clipboard. 'Gemma, Gemma,' he called, and then as she turned towards the sound of her name he waved her over.

The girl, who had a shock of bright red curly hair poking out from under a woollen beret, waved back and headed towards them. 'Arthur,' she said, all smiles. 'How's it going? You're about bright and early.'

'Morning, honey, you look cute as ever. This is a friend of mine,' he paused.

'Helen Redford,' said Helen brightly, holding out a hand.

'One of yours, I presume?' asked the girl, raising an eyebrow.

Arthur nodded. 'She's going to be my first client. The girl's a natural.'

'Right you are,' said Gemma with a laugh, while shaking Helen's hand. 'Well, if you'd like to come with me, Helen, I'll need you to fill in a form and then I'll take you down to costume and makeup. Have you done period stuff before?'

'No –' Helen began, but Arthur was on a roll.

'I was hoping to get Colin to see her. You know, for the thing we were talking about.'

Gemma glanced at him and laughed. 'The *thing* you were talking about? Have you any idea how many things you pair talk about during the course of a day? I lost track after the *thing* with the deep-sea trawler. Or was it the *thing* about the spaceship?'

'The staff are getting really uppity round here,' Arthur sighed. '*The other thing*. Remember?'

'Okay, okay,' she said, holding her hands up in surrender. 'I'll make sure Colin sees her. Now can you just bugger off out of my way? You may notice that you and your *thing* is not the only *thing* I've got to deal with at the moment.'

Arthur bowed. 'You are an angel.'

Gemma rolled her eyes and indicated Helen should follow her. 'Mad,' she said, shaking her head. 'So, have you ever done any period work before?'

'No,' Helen said, staying close as they made their way

through the crowds. 'I'm a singer.' She didn't add that she had never been on a film set or done any acting since school. She could see Arthur drifting off towards the double-decker buses.

'There's not a lot of call for singing around here,' said the girl over her shoulder as she pushed her way between a dozen soldiers in full period costume. 'Just stay low, don't get yourself noticed.'

'Sorry?' said Helen, running now to catch up.

'If you want more work as an extra they want atmosphere, not standouts – they don't want people, faces, that catch the camera. Mind you, if Arthur's got his eye on you maybe that's exactly what he does want.'

Helen smiled and nodded; the girl might as well have been speaking in tongues.

'What about the thing?' she asked.

Gemma snorted. 'Arthur and his bloody thing. Don't worry, I'll make sure Colin sees you and knows who you are.'

Helen smiled; she had rather hoped that Gemma might tell her what *the thing* was. 'Here we are,' said Gemma as they reached one of the trailers where a queue of people was waiting. 'If you'd like to fill in the forms then someone will take you down to wardrobe and makeup. Have you got a pen?'

'And then,' said Helen, through a mouthful of noodles, 'we had to all run away from this boat that was going to crash into the dock. I mean you couldn't actually see the boat crashing. I think they must be going to put it in afterwards; you know how they do stuff with the film. You should have come as well, Harry; it was really good fun. And I met some amazing people. They're there all next week too but I said I couldn't do anything until next weekend – you know, what with working in the shop and everything – and then I met this man, he's called Colin and –' She looked at Harry, who was staring at her. 'What?' she asked, suddenly feeling horribly self-conscious. 'What are you looking at? Don't tell me, I've got sweet and sour sauce on my face, haven't I? Or noodles in my hair.'

'No, no,' he laughed. 'I was just wondering how you were managing to breathe and eat and talk. You're glowing. You really enjoyed it, didn't you?'

Helen nodded. 'And the money,' she said, pointing to the takeaway cartons with her fork. 'I wanted to pay you back for being so brilliant last night. Thank you –'

'It was nothing,' he said.

'It was everything. You were totally and utterly brilliant with Charlotte. She paused. 'And me.'

As she watched, Harry reddened. Helen giggled. 'I don't know what I'd have done without you,' she said, taking a bite out of a prawn cracker.

'While I remember,' said Harry, pulling a piece of paper out of his pocket. 'I made a list of all the pubs and places in town that have live music. Do you want to take a look and see if you can think of anywhere else?'

Helen took the proffered piece of paper. 'Did you show this to Charlotte?'

Harry shook his head. 'I didn't get a chance to. I went out to get the Sunday papers about ten and when I got back she was gone.'

Helen took a long look at the list. 'You know what she said about the Wild Birds.'

'You were good.'

'She said that she never wanted to speak to me again.'

'We all say things in the heat of the moment that we regret. I was thinking I could ring her later and see if I can smooth things over.'

Helen hesitated for a moment, and then put the fork back onto the plate. 'Harry, I really appreciate what you've done, but I don't want to sing with Charlotte. I hated what she said to me and how she behaved, and how cruel she was, and besides –' Helen paused, thinking about the business card Arthur's friend, Colin, had given her before leaving the film set. 'I'm not sure that I want to be a singer.'

She couldn't bring herself to tell Harry yet but she had agreed to go to London the following Wednesday afternoon – which was half day closing – for an audition with Arthur.

Harry stared at her. 'How can you *not* want to be a singer, Helen? You've got the most amazing voice. Are you serious?'

She nodded. 'Yes.'

Harry shook his head. 'If you don't want to sing with Charlotte you could have a solo career. We could find someone to record you some backing tapes –'

283

'Harry, it's a great idea but it won't work. Not here, not in Billingsfield, not with Charlotte around.'

'Right, okay, I'd just like you to read from the bottom of page six,' said Colin, pointing at the dog-eared script he was holding. He had a pen behind his ear and bottle-bottom lenses in his glasses. This was the man Helen had met while filming in Billingsfield and this was *the thing* that Arthur had been so very excited about; a bit part in a pilot for a new soap opera that Colin had written and that ITV had just commissioned.

'The thing is,' said Arthur, on the drive across London to the audition, 'that this might not be going anywhere. But it's got to be worth a punt. Everyone who's had anything to do with this thinks it's good, but it's a tough market out there, although my feeling about Colin is that even if this one doesn't take off there will be other things. He's good, he's going places.'

Helen nodded. She had no idea whether Arthur was right or not but the adventure was almost enough. She'd spent the rest of the money she'd made from the day's filming on her train ticket down to London. Arthur had picked her up at the station in his little car and he had talked nonstop since then, while she had listened, as they drove across the city.

Helen was almost too excited to be nervous. Arthur had grinned at her. 'You sure you're up for this?' he'd said, and Helen had nodded. And now here she was.

Colin and three other people were sitting behind a

trestle table in a draughty church hall. Helen wasn't altogether sure who they were or what they did but they looked important – and from the number of coffee cups and the state of the ashtrays, they had obviously been there a while.

The room was cold and Colin's voice echoed back at her from between the rafters of the high ceilings. Helen shivered and pulled her coat tighter around her as her eyes moved down over her photocopy of the script.

Colin nodded. 'That's a really good look. Right, so your character Marlene is a young single mum trying to get her life sorted out, and you really need this job – I mean you *really* need it, but you don't want to let Raymond know how desperate you are.' He glanced up to see if she was listening. 'Rory here is going to read in the Raymond character. Okay, in your own time . . .'

Helen glanced across at the other man, Rory, who was sitting at the far end of the trestle table. Arthur had said he was already attached to the project, which apparently was a good thing. Rory was tall and lean and wearing a sheepskin coat over skinny jeans. He had long hair and a tan and hadn't even bothered to acknowledge her when she had come in and taken a seat. The more she stared at him the more familiar he looked. She was certain she had seen him on the television but she couldn't remember which programme.

Sitting on the stage behind the table Arthur was rubbing his hands together against the chill; as Helen took a deep breath Arthur grinned at her and gave her the thumbs up. This was it, she thought. This was the moment when everything could change forever.

'Would you like to take a seat?' said Rory, his eyes down, not even bothering to look at her, reading the words off the script.

'Thanks, I've come about the job,' said Helen. 'The one in the *Mercury*? I was wondering if you'd take me on. On a trial. I mean . . . I'm local and I've done cooking before.'

'What makes you think we'd hire someone like you?' said Rory, his voice dripping with contempt. Helen felt a great flare of indignation, unsure now whether Rory and his unnatural tan was acting, or whether he really meant it.

'Because I'm good,' she snapped back.

From the corner of her eye Helen could see one of the women behind the table scribbling something and then nodding to Colin.

When she had finished reading Colin smiled. 'Righty-oh, well, that was lovely.' And then he glanced at Arthur and then back at Helen. 'We'll let you know. If you'd like to just leave your script on the chair, and thanks for coming in. Nice to see you again.'

Helen mumbled her thanks, not at all sure how well it had gone or what they had thought. Arthur pointed towards the door. Helen headed out into the bright after-noon sunshine while Arthur stayed behind to chat to Colin.

She found a quiet spot in the alley that ran between

the church hall and the houses next door and waited, wishing for once that she smoked – at least it would have given her something to pass the time. No one else came in or out. After around fifteen minutes Arthur wandered towards her, hands in pockets, shoulders hunched forward.

'Well?' she said.

'Let's go and grab a cup of tea,' Arthur said. 'There's a café just around the corner. We can talk there.'

Helen fell into step beside him, the sense of anticipation and excitement that had been building now rapidly draining away. They hadn't liked her after all. She hadn't got it. She had come all this way for nothing.

Arthur opened the café door for her. 'There y'go. Why don't you go and grab a table and I'll get us something to eat? What do you fancy? Tea and a bacon butty?'

Helen nodded and sat down to wait while Arthur was being served. She watched him chatting to the woman behind the counter. He was nice, people liked him, and he was kind, letting her down gently. Even if she hadn't got the part it had been worth a shot, Helen told herself. She'd lost nothing by coming to London, it had been a great way to spend an afternoon, and there was still the promise of another day's work at the weekend on the film set in Billingsfield, but even so, Helen couldn't help feeling a little disappointed. Crazy, really – it was naïve to expect she'd get a part at her first audition.

Arthur came back carrying a tray with two mugs of tea and a plate piled high with doughnuts.

'Sandwiches will be here in a few minutes,' Arthur said, pulling out a chair and settling himself down. 'Right, so the good news is that they're going to start filming at the end of the month.' He took a bite out of one of the doughnuts. 'God, I'm hungry. These are really good – help yourself.'

Helen hesitated. 'So what does that mean?'

'What do you mean *what does that mean*?' said Arthur, wiping a glut of jam off his chin. 'It means that they want you to start filming at the end of the month. They're sending me the contract later in the week.'

'But –' Helen stared at him. 'Really? Are you serious? They want me? But they didn't say anything while I was in there. I thought they didn't like me. And besides, I've already got a job.'

Arthur grinned, 'Well, now you've got two, and you're going to have to make your mind up which one you want to keep.'

'But you said it was only a bit part.'

'*Was*,' said Arthur, smugly, rolling a cigar between his fingers. 'Colin and I have just been talking about that.'

SIXTEEN

Helen wished more than anything that they were heading back to the hotel. She wanted to talk to Arthur, to call Bon in Dubai, to talk to familiar people whom she could let her guard down with. There was no chance of that here.

Glancing around the car Helen knew damn well that anything she let slip in the back of the car would more than likely end up on screen. Natalia and Felix were both watching her intently. The red light was on; everything was up for grabs.

Helen tried hard to settle down, her mind was a ragtag jumble of memories, thoughts and feelings, as she replayed the meeting with Harry and watched Billingsfield town centre give way to urban sprawl. Beyond the parade of shops, the market and the faded civic splendour of the Victorian manufacturing town were the factories, built along the road side and along the river bank, and then over the bridge down past the warehouses were row after row of redbrick town terraces. Even after all these years there was still a smell in the air; the smell of poverty and decline.

Helen sighed; she had thought meeting Harry was going to be the easy part of coming back.

'We're nearly there now,' said the driver conversationally, glancing over his shoulder at Helen. She managed to smile for the camera.

The houses had all looked the same when Helen had lived in one and nothing had changed in the intervening years. She knew the names of the streets off by heart and without thinking began to recite them under her breath like a mantra, *Mafeking Row, Mafeking Terrace, Albert Street, Edward Street, Victoria Street.*

Natalia tipped her head on one side like a quizzical dog.

'It was how I used to work out when to get off the bus when I came home from school,' Helen said self-consciously, feeling her colour rise. The red light on the camera seemed as if it was staring her out, willing her to blink.

'When I first went to high school – you know how things seem so scary when you're eleven,' Helen said, by way of explanation. She didn't tell them the times she came over the bridge, clutching her satchel, watching the houses pass by, watching them get shabbier and shabbier, walking slowly back home to an empty house, wishing that someone, anyone, anything would be home to meet her. She remembered unlocking the back door, lighting the fire and then turning on the radio in the kitchen so that she wouldn't have to listen to the silence, while she peeled the potatoes for supper.

'*Can we get a dog, Dad?*' She heard the ghost of her own voice echoing back from some long-gone evening.

He had been sitting at the kitchen table reading the papers. She was on the other side, talking to the open expanse of newsprint that cut him off from her.

'*Who'd let it out in the day? You're at school, I'm at work. Wouldn't be fair on an animal.*'

'*A cat then?*'

'*Spraying everywhere, stinking of tomcats, or kittens you'd have to drown. How about a canary or a budgie? You could have a budgie.*'

'*I don't want something that has to be in a cage.*'

'*We could have it in here, in the kitchen. It could look out of the window,*' said the voice from behind the newspaper.

'*And see what it's missing,*' murmured the younger Helen as she cleared away the plates.

Helen stared out into the narrow street wondering where that memory had come from, so vivid that she could still see the headlines on the evening paper and catch the scent of mince and onions hanging heavy in the air.

The car slowed down to turn the corner into Victoria Street. It crept along the kerb at walking pace, the crew calling out the numbers as they passed the houses.

Her old home was halfway along on the right-hand side. Helen, who hadn't expected to be so moved by the sight of her old street, found herself craning forward, peering out of the window, trying to spot her house amongst the others.

Every house had a tiny front garden, a strip of grey, barren, ashy soil barely three feet wide that divided the house from the road. As they crept past the row of low redbrick walls with their tightly closed gates Helen had a sudden rush of memory, remembering her father on some long distant spring morning standing pots of daffodils out by the front door, the blooms an extraordinary show of individuality in the street's unending sameness. It was such an intense image. It must have been before her mother left; Helen couldn't imagine it would have been after.

'There,' said Felix, motioning with his fingers. 'Far side of the lamppost.'

Number thirty-six still had its wrought-iron gate, still had all its woodwork painted toffee brown with the inner window frame and glazing bars picked out in cream. Helen held her breath as the car pulled to a halt outside. It looked exactly the way she remembered it, so much so that Helen wouldn't have been at all surprised if her father opened the door and peered out from the darkness of the hall to see who it was who was parking outside his house.

Natalia pulled a face. 'Bloody hell, I can see why you wanted to get away from here,' she said.

Helen felt uncomfortable. The street looked grubby and poor. The pavements were uneven and badly patched; here and there clumps of weeds sprang from the gutter. There were takeaway trays and cans tucked into the spaces between the walls and street signs. Two small children, sitting on the kerb, eyed them with curiosity. Helen knew that Natalia was making all kinds of judgements. At the house opposite her old home the nets were ripped and a dog was busy dragging empty food cartons out of a split rubbish sack.

'How long is it since you've been home?' asked Natalia.

She felt guilty enough about not coming back without being interrogated. 'I came back for my Dad's funeral. I didn't stay for long, just a few hours really. We hired someone to clear the house. Dad went into a nursing home for the last few weeks, a really nice place over near Portlee.' Helen paused. 'He'd looked at a few apparently; he didn't even tell me he was looking, let alone going. He was like that. I only found out when I rang up and a neighbour answered. It was just sheer luck; she'd come in to check that everything was okay and pick up his post. I went to see him there but he was very frail. To be perfectly honest I'm not sure he even knew who I was. He kept calling me Amy.'

'Which was your mum's name, right?'

Helen nodded and stopped talking, the words fading as she remembered him sitting in a chair by the window of the nursing home looking out over the lawn. He had been painfully thin, and so very very still, his skin almost translucent, dry as parchment and cool to the touch.

'I knew you'd come back in the end,' he'd said, although Helen knew that those words hadn't been meant for her. So they had sat side by side, holding hands until he fell into sleep. It had been the last time she had seen him alive.

Helen looked at Natalia; those last minutes together were far too precious to share, so after a second or two she said, 'We lost contact over the years. To be perfectly honest he didn't seem to care whether we spoke or not. When I was growing up it was as if I was something to be coped with, rather than something to be loved.' A tear rolled unbidden down her face – how could she hope to make anyone understand that she felt like a kitten that he couldn't quite bring himself to drown.

'Looking back I know he did his best, but I never really felt that he loved me, and he barely talked to me. We'd sit in the evening in the front room with the TV on and he'd not say a word until it was my bed time, and then he'd say, "Come on, lass – up you go." That was it, and then when I was older it would get to ten o'clock and he'd get up and switch the television set off and go up to bed, almost as if I wasn't there.'

'And before that?' pressed Natalia. 'Before the funeral, when was the last time you actually came and stayed here?'

'I came back for the week before I left Billingsfield to work on my first TV show. *The Right Brothers* it was called. Colin Paulman wrote it. He did a lot of work on *Cannon Square* later. I don't know how many people would remember it now. Anyway I came back home to sort things, to pack, to say goodbye, I suppose. I'm sure my dad was worried that I was in some sort of trouble.'

'Because you'd left your job at the toy shop?'

Helen shook her head and smiled ruefully. 'No, because I had come back home. It worried him. I think he assumed I was pregnant. Ironic really, given the situation with Adam. I remember Dad standing in the kitchen, packing up his lunch for the next day, and him saying, "Is there anything you want to tell me, Helen, because whatever it is it'll be all right."'

The words caught in her throat. Helen glanced at the front door, wishing that her dad was still there to open it. There were so many things now that she wished she had said to him. Maybe after all these years they could have found a way to bridge the silence.

'It was such a big thing for him to say to me. He was a very quiet man, my dad – closed off. It was almost as if he was never really with you. You never really knew what was going on in his head. After the funeral I came back here. Just to look. There was hardly anything to do. It was like he had barely broken the surface of his life. Everywhere was tidy. All his bills and the receipts were all neatly filed, his bank accounts, his papers, all in order, all sorted out and stacked in shoe boxes in the cupboard in the kitchen, all with the year written on them, all in order. All the rest of it; his furniture, his clothes. What he left behind him was just the lightest of impressions, like he hadn't wanted to leave a mark.' Helen smiled, aware that the crew were completely focused on her now, probably dragging her in for a close-up.

'I used to ring him, more so when I first left home. I suppose I was hoping for some reassurance – not that he was any good at that kind of thing – but I wanted to let him know I was okay and to allay his fears, or maybe mine. When I started earning real money I offered to buy him a house. And he said, '"*Where would I go? I'm fine where I am; you put that money away just in case you need it.*" So I used to send him cheques. When they came to clear out his things I discovered that he'd put all the money into a savings account; he'd never touched a penny of it. Not a single penny.'

Helen looked up at the front of the house. 'When the house came up for sale in the nineties I bought it for him so that at least he would have some security. I got Arthur to do the actual deal, because if Dad had known it was me who'd bought it I'm not sure what he would have done. Anyway, every month Dad would send in the money for his rent. Never failed. Not once.'

'Right, great –' said Felix briskly. 'If we could cut there, that's great –and then we'll set up outside so we can see you going up to the front door.'

Natalia nodded as the crew clambered out.

Helen sat quietly staring at the door, wondering what lay behind it.

'What did you say the name of the programme was

that you left to do?' Natalia was asking, peering down at her clipboard. Helen glanced across at her, wondering if Natalia had really listened to anything that she had said.

'It was called *The Right Brothers*. About two brothers who inherited their father's factory?'

Natalia nodded and made a note. 'Yeah, that's what I've got down here, I think we've got some notes on that back at the office but we haven't got that much. It was one of those shows that no one kept much in the way of footage of. Was that with Rory Turner?'

Helen nodded.

'Didn't you go out with him for a while?'

'No, not really, he wasn't my type, ex-public schoolboy – but I never really came home again after that. It was my first big break. I moved up to London and stayed with Arthur for three months while they filmed the first series. As a lodger.'

Natalia nodded. 'So you weren't an item then?'

'No, he was going out with a writer. Joan Hastings – she did some work on *Cannon Square*.'

'But later?'

Helen nodded. 'I think it was a couple of years after, there was this moment when Arthur came to pick me up from a job and we just knew.'

'Uh huh, and what happened to it?' asked Natalia, still writing.

'To me and Arthur?' Helen asked, slightly confused.

'No, not to you and Arthur, to *The Right Brothers*?'

'We did the pilot and it got commissioned by regional, but it didn't really take off. The viewing figures were pretty dire. So they pulled it after the first series.'

Natalia scribbled something else on her pad. 'Didn't you think of coming back home to Billingsfield then, you know, when the work dried up?'

'Not really, there was no work for me here and Arthur was a good agent. He managed to get me into all sorts of things – small parts mostly, but work is work. I did some ads, and quite a lot of radio drama, and I was in *The Onedin Line*, *Juliet Bravo*, lots of the soaps – I even did a walk-on in *Coronation Street*. And later there was *Casualty* and a couple of police dramas – I can't remember the names now. And between times Arthur had me going to classes, and I always sang. I did some cabaret and some theatre.'

'And so how did you get from there to *Cannon Square*?'

Helen stared out at number thirty-six wondering what it would feel like to walk in through that front door. The crew were almost ready for her to get out of the car.

Natalia was still smiling, still waiting for an answer. '*Cannon Square*,' she prompted.

'I was doing a radio play – it was a murder mystery thing – and Freddie Maritz, the man who originated and co-produced *Cannon Square* heard me on there and asked if I'd like to come in and audition.'

Out in the street Felix was giving them the thumbs up.

'Time to rock and roll,' said Natalia, pushing open

the door. 'I'll want to run-through the *Cannon Square* story on camera if that's okay with you. Let me get out and get out of shot before you get out of the car. Okay?'

Helen nodded and waited until Natalia was out of the way and behind the camera, and then she slowly climbed out of the car. As she walked across the pavement and opened the front gate, the door of number thirty-six opened a fraction, and a pair of bright eyes peered at them from the gloom inside. Helen felt a peculiar flutter deep in her chest. A second or two later a small grey-haired woman stepped into the light and for a split second Helen's heart lurched, wondering if *Roots* had managed to track down her mother after all, and then the woman smiled at her, and the moment passed. There was no way this timid little bird of a woman was her mother, but even so her face was familiar.

'Helen, isn't it?' the woman said, before she could speak. 'You're Gordon's girl?'

Without any conscious effort the woman's name appeared in Helen's head. She felt a great judder of tears. 'Mrs Handley?' she said. Her voice sounded strange.

The old lady's smile broadened out. 'That's right. I wondered if you would remember me. I always liked this house, your dad always kept it so nice and you get the sun this side – why don't you come in, pet? I've got the kettle on. I don't think you'll find it's changed that much, though I've had it decorated, obviously. My boys do it for me these days. I can't get up a ladder like I used to – come in, come in.' She waved them all inside.

Mrs Handley smiled at a bemused looking Natalia. 'I used to live over the road,' she said, pointing to the house opposite. 'Look at the state of it now, breaks my heart. When this one came up to rent we thought we'd have a bit of a change. Me and Charlie, God rest his soul – this one's got a nice yard and it's lighter, with the sun. I've got geraniums in pots out there now, just like they do in the films. Get yourself inside, people are looking.' She waved them all past.

Helen heard what was being said somewhere out on the periphery of her hearing, while her eyes and her mind drank in the details of her old house. Her first thoughts were how much it had changed and then how nice it looked and how inviting. This was the way her home might have been if her mother hadn't left. The walls were emulsioned a warm soft yellow, there were floral rugs in the hallway over fitted carpets, and pictures on every wall. Helen looked through the open door into the sitting room – there were flowers on the windowsill, dozens of ornaments all along the mantlepiece and on every flat surface, and knitting rolled up around needles on the sofa by the fireplace.

'Of course in them days,' the woman was saying to the crew, 'this was the best room here at the front. We used to live in the kitchen and save the front room for Sundays, high days and holidays. I mean how daft is that? You can't imagine people doing that now, can you? So would you like a tea or coffee?'

Helen's concentration was elsewhere. While Natalia

and Mrs Handley made conversation, Helen wandered along the narrow hallway into the kitchen at the back of the house. The old pale green cabinets had long since gone, the pantry had been knocked out, and a run of worktops and new units lined the walls by the back door and around the corner under the kitchen window. The splashbacks were tiled with bright colours, by the sink there was a mug tree and a fat wire chicken full of eggs, and in the middle of the room was a round table set with a cruet and mats in a tidy pile. Children's drawings, photos and cards were tacked to the fridge door with magnets shaped like fish and birds. It felt warm and homely. The contrast with the kitchen in her head and this cosy room couldn't have been more stark.

Helen could barely recognise it as the kitchen she had grown up in. It could have been anywhere, and yet, and *yet* something of the old house lingered. There was a familiarity, like a hint of perfume, that hung in the air.

'Is it all right if I go upstairs?' she asked Mrs Handley, who had followed her through to boil the kettle.

'Of course it is, you just help yourself, pet. Go anywhere you like. I'll get the tea made,' Mrs Handley said. 'You make yourself at home.'

Oblivious to the camera crew Helen climbed the stairs. They were steep and narrow. Off the tiny landing were two bedrooms and a bathroom. Helen stood for a moment drinking it all in and then eased open the door into the room that had once been her parents' bedroom.

The room was painted cream now and was light and

bright with a large bed, dotted with floral cushions, dominating the centre. It could have been anywhere, certainly not the dark secret place she remembered her mother and father sharing. The walls back then had been papered in heavy floral paper, with dark red chenille curtains at the window and a matching bed throw that had stayed on her father's bed till it had finally faded and fallen to threads.

Standing there now she could still imagine it, still feel the texture of it under her fingertips, and still catch a memory of her mother's perfume. There had been times when Helen had padded barefoot across the boards, now hidden under a pretty blue wall-to-wall carpet, and clambered up into her parents' big brass bed, pursued by a nightmare, and had wriggled, small and anxious, in beside her mother.

The rush of emotion and potency of the memory made Helen swallow hard. She could see it so clearly. Her mum with her soft gentle features, her long hair tied back with a piece of ribbon for bed, propped up on one elbow to watch Helen scurry across to the sanctuary of her arms. She was smiling sleepily, while alongside her, Helen's father slept on oblivious. In her imagination her mother pressed a finger to her lips and beckoned her in. Helen could feel her arms around her and feel her mother pull her in close.

Helen stood frozen on the threshold, desperate not to lose the image or the sensation, but there was no way she could hold the two of them there. She blinked and when she opened her eyes the two of them, and the room, had gone.

Her own bedroom was no better, the memories flooding in like a rip tide the instant she opened the door. Helen stepped inside remembering sitting on a narrow bed listening to the silence from downstairs after her mum had gone, as deafening as any sound, while next door in the room adjoining hers the neighbours fought and made up like cat and dog.

The room was much smaller than Helen remembered. The walls were painted pale green now, the soft colour picking out the green in the curtains and the throws on the two single guest beds. Once upon a time the walls had been papered with pink roses on black paper that curled up at the joins; there had been pink curtains that didn't quite reach the sill and bare boards with a faded shabby rug with roses in the centre beside her bed.

Helen touched the chimneybreast, earthing herself, afraid of being swept away by the intensity of the memories and how they made her feel.

Her bed had been flanked by a chest of drawers on one side, a little desk with a lamp on the other, and a dark wooden wardrobe in the alcove by the fireplace. Nothing matched; everything had been scraped together on a shoestring.

Helen sat down on the bed nearest the window and looked down into the street below. How many nights had she spent sitting there hoping that if only she was good enough, quiet enough, clever enough then perhaps her mum might just come home? And when she didn't, trying to work out what was it she had done that had made her leave in the first place . . .

Helen heard footfalls behind her on the stairs and hardly dared turn round. Finally, she looked over her shoulder to see Natalia and the crew, and not the ghosts from her childhood, standing in the room behind her. No one spoke. Helen glanced out of her bedroom window. It felt like she had never been away.

'Do you know where my mum is?' she asked. The words sounded distant and indistinct as if someone else was saying them.

Natalia shook her head. 'I'm so sorry,' she said, 'but we don't.'

Helen felt the tears running down her face and from somewhere close by she heard a strange keening sob. It took her a moment or two to realise that she was the one who was sobbing.

SEVENTEEN

'Are you sure about this?' asked Harry as Helen lifted a pile of blouses and sweaters out of the chest of drawers and arranged them in her suitcase. 'Packing your job in is crazy, Helen – you know that, don't you? And we can't hold it for you – I wish we could – but my dad needs the help in the shop. Why don't you give it a bit more time? See if acting suits you? You could probably take a couple of weeks' holiday if you wanted. I'm sure I could sort it out with Dad.'

'Harry, that's not how it works. They want me to sign a contract. I can't say thanks very much but I'm only here for the next two weeks and then I've got to go back to my proper job.'

'I don't see why not.' Harry sat down heavily on her bed. 'I can't believe you're doing this. It's a big risk. You're usually so sensible. It's one of the things I love about you – you're usually so level-headed. I'm worried that you're rushing into this, Helen. I keep thinking that that thing at the Carlton Rooms and all the fuss with Charlotte has turned your head.'

'Turned my head?' Helen laughed. 'You sounds like something out of Dickens, Harry. I'm fine and my head hasn't been turned in the slightest and it's still as level as it ever was. Now stop fussing. I've got to give this my best shot. I know it's hard for you to understand but it's too good an opportunity to miss. I haven't done any acting outside school and I know that I'm not going to get a chance like this again. They're only taking a risk on me because of Arthur. They wouldn't give me a second look if it wasn't for him, and he's already said I can have a room at his place while we're filming.'

'*Arthur this, Arthur that* –' Harry said miserably. 'What do you actually *know* about this Arthur chap?'

Helen slapped him playfully. 'Stop it, you're only jealous, and there is no need to be. What you see is what you get with Arthur, he's no Leon Downey, that's for sure. And don't look so down in the mouth. I'll come back and see you. I will, but I've got to do this, Harry, it's my big chance.'

'What if it goes wrong?'

'Then I come home and get another job.'

'I could have been your manager, you know. I know I could get you some work. I did that list, remember? All the music pubs. It's just a matter of making a few calls.'

'This is different.'

With the two of them in her bedroom there was barely

306

room to turn round. Harry moved a pile of books to one side, lay back on her single bed and folded his hands behind his head.

'That's more or less what Charlotte said to me as well.'

'Charlotte?' said Helen, trying hard to sound as if she wasn't interested.

'Yeah, she came in the shop yesterday. I thought she was looking for you but she said it was me she wanted to see – she said that she'd got herself a job. Singing in some show.'

'But I thought she was going to teacher-training college in September?' said Helen.

'So did I, but apparently that's all changed. Anyway she said I was to tell you that she's got herself a summer season in Scarborough.'

'Please just tell me it's not with Leon Downey,' said Helen.

'I don't think so. Someone rang the Carlton Rooms after the talent show and they gave them Charlotte's number; well that's what she said.' Harry paused. 'She told me that you were missing out on a really big opportunity, and that she was really upset that you hadn't rung her. I told her that I'd pass the message on.'

Helen laughed. 'If you remember, Harry, Charlotte was the one who said she didn't ever want to speak to me again, not the other way round. I'm not ringing her, simple as that.'

But Harry wasn't going to be thrown. 'I know, but she said they really wanted to book you both, for this summer thing.'

Helen glanced around the room. She had almost

finished packing now. There was just the top of the chest of drawers to clear, her mirror and her makeup, her hairbrush and the little pot she kept her earrings in. Helen pulled a holdall out from under the bed and glanced at her watch. 'I'm sorry, Harry, but I've really got to be going. Do you mind if I leave the books here? I don't think I can carry them all.'

'Don't go yet,' he said. 'There still might be time to ring about this other job if you're interested. Charlotte said they'd hold it till the end of next week if you needed time to think about it. You can ring from here if you like.'

'That's not going to happen, Harry, I've already told you, I'm going to London, with Arthur. I'm not ringing Charlotte, and I'm not going round there, and most of all I'm not apologising for trying to save her from that creep Leon Downey.'

'I just said I'd tell you.' He rolled over onto his side, so that he was looking right at her. 'I was hoping that maybe we had a future together, you and me.'

Helen sighed. 'I know, Harry, and so did I, but it's the wrong time – I can' t, not now. I've got this one chance and I've got to grab it. Come on, move – I need to get that suitcase sorted out, my bus goes in half an hour.'

He leaned closer and stroked her face. 'Do you have to go tonight, Helen? Can't it at least wait until after the weekend?'

'I've already told Dad that I'd be coming home tonight.'

'But you hate it there. You said yourself that he's never in.'

308

'It's only till I go to London.'

'You could stay here.'

'Harry, please stop it. I've hardly spent any time at all with Dad, not for months. And yes, he is hard work, and no, he's hardly ever at home, but he *is* my dad and he's all I've got. He came to see me in the show; he never said. I just want to tell him about going to London and be with him for a while. There are lots of things I need to sort out, but I'll be back. I promise.'

'Are you going to ring Charlotte?'

Helen closed the suitcase and locked it, tucking the keys into her handbag. 'No.'

'Please stay, Helen.'

'Not tonight,' she said. 'This is really hard for me to say, Harry, but it wouldn't do either of us any good. I don't want to get hurt or to hurt you. It's better if we never start –'

'But I love you,' he said.

'I told my dad I'd be home in time for tea,' she said, trying hard not to cry.

'I could give you a lift home – just stay a little bit longer, please.'

And as she turned Harry caught hold of her and kissed her, a proper kiss; a kiss full of hope, desire and longing. It made her heart skip a beat.

Helen gasped, 'Please don't, Harry,' but she didn't resist as he kissed her again and pulled her down on top of him.

309

EIGHTEEN

At number thirty-six Victoria Street, Helen, Natalia, Felix and the crew drank tea downstairs in the front room. Mrs Handley lit the gas fire and brought out a tray set with her best china, a plate with salmon sandwiches and another of cake. The camera was off and the crew were making the most of Mrs Handley's huge homemade Victoria sponge.

Helen's hands shook as she drank her tea. She felt cold and tired. 'I really thought that you had found her,' she said to Natalia. 'I thought that's what this whole thing was about. I've never understood how someone can vanish completely.'

'We've looked,' said Natalia, as if that was any help at all. 'There was no missing persons report, no one thought her leaving was suspicious – we've checked the local hospitals, mental homes, deaths, all the public records we have available. The real problem we have with your mum's disappearance is that she doesn't seem to have confided in anyone before she left. We really struggled to know where to start looking; usually somebody knows something or at least has a clue – we all leave tracks – but we just drew blank after blank. I've done a few of these before and all I can say is that your mum didn't want to be found. She told no-one, contacted no-one, and even after all this time either no-one knows or no-one's telling.'

'Surely someone must know something,' said Helen. 'All these years, if she isn't dead, she must be somewhere. Did she move away, change her name – surely if she changed her name there would be a record of it somewhere?'

'You'd like to think so wouldn't you, but we'd have to have some idea of where she went to,' said Natalia. 'There's no central register of names changed by deed poll. You *can* register them, they call it enrolling – but it's expensive, with all kinds of terms and conditions and for obvious reasons a lot of people don't bother. There are only about 250 enrolled deed polls issued annually, whereas the deed poll service issue about 50,000 unenrolled deed polls per year; the problem is their records are confidential and not available for public inspection.'

'So she could just have gone somewhere and changed her name and you're saying no-one would know?'

Natalia nodded. 'More or less. According to the deed poll service all she would need to have done was to have it witnessed by someone independent: a friend, or a neighbour or someone she worked with.'

Helen stared at her. 'So you're saying someone must know where she is?'

'Yes, but we can't find them.'

Mrs Handley topped up the tea. 'I never met your mother but the whole street knew about you and your dad; it must have been hard for you growing up without her. Hadn't she got family around here?'

'No, or at least none that I ever really knew. My mum was an only child. I've got some vague memories of her taking me to see her mum but I can't really remember her clearly.'

Natalia pulled a notebook out of her bag and flicked through the pages. 'Lavinia Hope Thornton,' she said. 'Her husband, John, your granddad, died just before you were born. And as you said your mum was an only child. We think your grandmother had a weak heart, which was why she only had the one child, and she was in her late thirties when your mum was born. Lavinia died just before your mum left as far as we can tell – progressive heart failure.'

'Do you think that's what made my mother leave?' asked Helen.

Natalia shrugged. 'We really don't know, and we've got no way of finding out.'

Helen sighed. 'Something must have made her do it. Things were different back in those days. You just didn't up and walk out on your husband and child,' Helen said, glancing around the room. 'It was so strange when I was little; it was like she had just walked out of the door and vanished into thin air. I always remember that there weren't any photos of her around the place. Not even one of their wedding. When I came back for my dad's funeral it was one of the things I was hoping to find when we cleared the house. Photos, letters, postcards . . .'

It was Natalia now who looked expectant. 'And did you find anything?'

'No, not a thing, not really – not in the way I had hoped. He had all these shoes boxes with his filing in them, all his documents, but no photos – I did find their marriage licence; she was nineteen when she got married and he was thirty. Amelia Constance Hope.'

'And she was twenty-seven when she left?'

Helen nodded. 'It seems so young now. He always used to call her Amy. I remember him calling her once when I was with her in the yard hanging out the washing. I keep thinking that she had her whole life ahead of her. A whole life without us.'

'And you hadn't come home before then, before your dad's funeral?'

'No, I used to ring most weeks to begin with, send him little things – letters, postcards, presents – but it got harder as I got older. I needed someone to love me back and he just wasn't capable of giving me anything. It sounds so selfish now, doesn't it? But he didn't seem to care one way or the other. In the end I more or less gave up. We had a row, or as close to a row as we ever got, mostly because he was just so quiet. I told him I knew why my mum had left; why she couldn't bear to stay –'

Helen stopped, realising that everyone in the room

was waiting for her to explain the things that they couldn't fathom.

'It was *him*. Just him being himself. Who could live all their life with unbroken silence? The not talking, the one-way conversations? When I first left, to begin with, I used to ring home every week; and I called Harry too, just to let them both know how things were going and how I was. But when I rang home, Dad always made me feel as if I was intruding. Harry was always pleased to hear from me, but eventually that faded too.'

'Was that when he started going out with Charlotte? Weren't you two an item?'

Helen reddened. 'Is that what he said?'

Natalia nodded.

'I could hardly ask Harry to wait for me, could I? He didn't tell me about Charlotte straight away. I remember I rang him one night and he sounded odd on the phone; not like Harry at all. It was just before Christmas, I think, and I was in rehearsals. He sounded guarded and I said something like, 'Have I rung at a bad time? Are you busy, I can always ring back?' And he said no, but that he wanted me to be the first to know that he had asked Charlotte to marry him and that she had said yes, and he was going to take care of everything.'

'And how did you feel?' said Natalia, her body slipping into a listening posture that Helen knew damn well she had learned on a course.

'Feel?' Helen said. 'How do you think it made me

feel? To be honest I was stunned. Harry knew what she was like, and it seemed an odd thing to say. I had no idea until then that Harry and Charlotte were dating or even seeing each other, let alone so involved that they were going to get married – but you can't say that to anyone without risking hurting their feelings. I had no hold over Harry – we never really dated or went out or anything, so I pulled myself together and said something like I was really pleased for them and had they got a wedding list. And he said, "I just want you to be happy, Helen, and I want you to know that whatever happens I'll always love you."'

Helen laughed. 'It seemed such an odd thing to say. At the time I thought he'd been drinking. It makes more sense now.'

'You mean you think that they got married because of Adam?' said Natalia. 'Did you talk to Charlotte about it?'

Helen shook her head. 'No, I haven't spoken to her since the night we did the talent show together in the Carlton Rooms.'

Natalia stared at her in amazement. 'Really?'

'By the time Harry told me they were getting married we'd all moved on, we were different people with different lives. I'd just got the part in *Cannon Square*,' said Helen. How could she tell Natalia that there was a big part of her that never wanted to see or speak to Charlotte again?

'And Charlotte?' Natalia said. 'Do you know what she was doing?'

'Not really. I suppose I thought she had moved back home.'

'And you didn't think to get in touch?'

'No.'

'I know Harry said that you had some sort of falling out before you left, but you were both very young – I mean we all say things that we don't mean.'

Helen smiled. 'Not Charlotte. She meant every word.'

Natalia tipped her head to one side. 'Seriously?'

She hesitated before replying. 'When I knew that Charlotte was getting married to Harry I did try to ring her –'

'And how was she?'

Helen smiled. 'I don't know. In the end I didn't talk to her. Do you think we could wrap this up soon? I'd really like to get back to the hotel. I've still got things to sort out for the show tomorrow and I really need to talk to my agent.'

'But you're okay?' Natalia genuinely looked concerned.

'A bit shaken by everything, but don't worry, I'll be fine.'

Natalia nodded. 'Great. Okay, well I was hoping we could just run-through what you know about your mum, and also if we could talk about what life was like living here – maybe upstairs in your old room – before we go back?'

On the easy chair Mrs Handley nodded. 'Help yourself. Would anyone like more tea?'

NINETEEN

'Is that you, Charlotte?' Helen could hear breathing at the far end of the line. She waited. Whoever it was hadn't put the receiver down. 'I know you're there. I know it's you, Charlie. Please don't hang up on me. I really need to talk to you.' Helen said into the dead air.

'Well, I don't want to talk to you,' snapped Charlotte after a second or two more. 'Remember? I don't want to talk to you ever again. I told you –'

'I know what you told me, and if you don't want to talk that's fine, I just need you to listen. I spoke to Harry this evening, Charlotte. He said –'

'*Kate*,' Charlotte interrupted. 'No one calls me Charlotte any more, everyone calls me Kate. Understand?'

'Harry told me that you're going to be get married.'

'That's right. Next month. Why, were you hoping for an invitation?'

'Do you love him?'

Charlotte didn't reply.

'Charlotte – *Kate* – please say something. I need to know –'

'Why do you need to know?' Charlotte growled. 'What has it got to do with you?'

It had been the very last time they had spoken. Helen was ringing from the hotel the actors and crew on *Cannon Square* used when they were on location. Everyone else was downstairs in the bar having supper; she could hear the sounds of their laughter and conversation even with the door to her room closed.

'You're right. It's none of my business, but please just tell me that you love Harry, tell me that you *really* love him, Charlotte, and that you want to spend the rest of your life with him, and I'll be truly happy for you both – because if there is anyone who deserves to be loved it's Harry. He's one of life's good guys. You know how much I think of him,' said Helen.

'Oh I know,' said Charlotte. 'He never stops telling me how bloody amazing you are, Helen. And every time he says it I have to point out that you loved him so much that the first thing you did as soon as you got a chance was to run away. To abandon him. Like mother, like daughter.'

The words stung. 'How can you say that?' Helen gasped. 'There is no comparison.'

'I can say it because it's true. You led Harry on, all the while sneaking around getting yourself an agent, fixing up auditions – all without telling either one of us. You knew exactly what you were doing, Helen Heel; lying to me, lying to Harry, leaving us all behind just because it suited you. You ruined my life, Helen, you can't deny it – you knew exactly what you were doing – to both of us.'

Helen struggled to grab her breath. 'How can you say that, Charlotte? Stop being so melodramatic. That's rubbish and you know it is.'

'Really? And there was me thinking that we were a duo, but oh no, only while it suited you. Harry was going to get us some work, but oh no, you had other ideas.'

'Stop it, Charlotte, this is nuts. You're twisting all this round. *You* are the one who said you didn't want to speak to me again; remember the night we came to get you at the Billingsfield Arms? Remember? You're the one who didn't want to get up early to go to the film shoot. You are reinventing the past to make out you were the one that was hard done by, when we both know nothing is further from the truth.'

Charlotte didn't answer.

'So why are you marrying Harry?' asked Helen.

'So that you never get the chance,' growled Charlotte. And with that she hung up.

TWENTY

Helen perched on the edge of the queen-sized bed in her suite at the Billingsfield Arms. It felt just like all the other anonymous hotel rooms she had ever spent long lonely nights in when she was on the road or on location, not at all like the rest of Billingsfield. She was grateful that it didn't feel like the rest of the town. Here everything was neutral, rather than emotionally charged. Helen lay back and stretched, letting the bed take her weight. It had been a long day.

The TV set was burbling away in the background for company; Helen had had a long hot bath, and was presently wrapped in a hotel bathrobe. She had a cup of tea on the bedside cabinet alongside the book she had brought to while away the hours, and was planning to phone home, or in this case Arthur in Oxfordshire and Bon in Dubai.

And then there was the prospect of dinner alone or

sharing a table with Natalia who, as Natalia had been keen to point out on the drive back to the hotel, was *anxious to rebuild bridges, allay any of Helen's fears*, and discuss where they were going next with *the whole Helen Redford story.*

It wasn't a particularly appealing prospect. It crossed Helen's mind that she perhaps ought to ring Harry, but what if Adam was there with him? And what would she say if he wasn't?

Helen curled up on the bed, took her mobile out of her handbag and pulled Arthur's number up from the menu. His home answer machine cut in after the fourth ring, and his mobile was off. Helen glanced at her watch. It was still early but knowing Arthur he had gone to bed with a book. Helen smiled to herself. It was what she loved about him; it hadn't always been that way but nightclubs, parties and the whole sex, drugs, and rock and roll thing had paled pretty fast for both of them. Deep down they were both people who wanted to be home. These days Arthur's idea of a good time was to snuggle up with a good thriller and hers was an afternoon in the garden; not something she suspected that Natalia would be at all interested in.

She'd made her first real grown-up home with Arthur, choosing furniture, picking out curtains, delighted and excited that finally she had found someone who loved her and whom she loved right back. Even after they realised that the marriage was dead, even then both of them had carried on caring for each other. Loving each other. Helen hesitated, wondering if she should ring off and try again. Maybe there were things she had left unsaid to Arthur too.

Finally Helen left a message, saying how much she hoped to see him – telling him that Natalia was worse than they had both expected, telling him that even after all these years she still loved him – not that she expected Arthur would call back before morning.

Next she rang Bon's mobile and hearing his voice, so warm and so clear that he could have been standing next to her, Helen smiled and began to speak before she realised that it too was an answering machine.

'I miss you,' was all she could manage before ending the call. Helen sniffed and blinked back tears; God, this wouldn't do at all. She hated that he hadn't called or texted her. Where was he, and who was he with? Feeling sorry for herself was the last thing Helen needed, all alone and this far from home.

Picking up the phone beside the bed Helen tapped in the number for reception. 'Hello,' she said, when the girl picked up the receiver. 'I was wondering if you could help me. Is Christov the porter still on duty?'

There was a moment's pause and then the girl said, 'One moment please, I'll try and find out for you. Who should I say is calling?'

Helen smiled, 'Tell him it's the big TV star. I wanted to know the name of the restaurant that he recommended.'

There was a little pause. 'If you'd like to hold the line madam, I think he might still be here –'

A moment later Christov came on the line. 'Hello?' he said, warily.

'Hello,' said Helen. 'This afternoon you told me about a great restaurant, good food, great music? Not too far away?'

'Oh yes, I know, you are the film lady – that's right, I did. It's the Belafonte. It's in Porter Street – my cousin Gregori, he runs it.'

'I was just wondering if you would care to join me for dinner there?'

There was a brief pause. 'I have to let you know that I am very flattered and that I am also very married.'

Helen laughed. 'Me too – after a fashion – and I want to stay that way. Don't worry, I just want some company and some good food, maybe some music, no strings.'

'No strings?'

'It means without the promise of anything else – just dinner.'

There was silence. She could almost hear Christov turning the idea over in his head.

'If I've offended you,' Helen began.

'No, no, not at all. I was just thinking if I should maybe phone ahead and get us a table near the stage. I am thinking I will do my Dean Martin – I will bring the hat.'

'Don't you usually have an assistant or a PA or someone to help you with things like that?' asked Natalia, who was sitting on the floor across the dressing room from

323

Helen. Helen had an ironing board out and was busy very carefully pressing the first of her costumes for the evening's performance.

'No, not always – and besides, I enjoy it. It relaxes me.'

Natalia pulled a face. 'Really?'

It was the following afternoon and they were at the Carlton Rooms getting ready for Helen's show. During the morning – after a late start – Helen had done a series of pieces to camera about what it was like working on *annon Square*, which seemed a waste given that they planned to film on the set of the soap, and filmed a series of short pieces about Helen's memories of working in TV in the eighties and nineties, which Natalia was adamant would work better with the theatre as a backdrop.

'I came by your room last night,' said Natalia casually, picking at one of the sandwiches that they had had sent in.

Helen let the iron slide over the soft cotton lining of her outfit. 'I was out,' she said, not looking up.

'I know. I had the concierge come up and let me in, just to see that you were okay. I was worried about you. I mean it was a tricky day and I had been hoping that maybe we could've talked about how yesterday went over dinner. I mean you're not under surveillance or anything but our guests don't usually skip out on us.'

Helen stared at her. 'You let yourself into my room?'

'Well, yes, under the circumstances,' said Natalia, with

her mouth full. 'I thought you might be upset and obviously disappointed that we hadn't been able to find your mum. This stuff is always emotionally challenging.'

Helen suspected it was a phrase Natalia had paraphrased from a self-help book. '*This stuff*? Didn't you consider that an invasion of my privacy?'

Natalia shook her head, peeling away the crust of the sandwich. 'Of course not. Like I said, I was worried, Helen. I thought we had agreed we'd meet for dinner. Run through the schedule. I need you to understand that we are here to support you. I rang and then I knocked and when you didn't answer I wondered if it had all been a bit much for you, you know, what with all that business with Adam and Harry, and then going home to your old house and all that. It can be a bit overwhelming, this whole process. I appreciate that – we all appreciate it. We've had it happen before. I thought maybe you'd gone to bed, taken a downer or whatever it is they used to call them, popped a pill, you know –' Natalia pulled a face.

Helen laughed. 'Got drunk, got stoned, fallen off the wagon?'

Natalia reddened. 'Well, something like that.'

'I was never on it, Natalia. And actually we didn't arrange to have dinner. You said, "*Maybe we could catch up later*," and I didn't say anything.'

Natalia sucked her teeth. 'I thought you'd taken it as read.'

Helen said nothing.

'So where did you go to? I rang your room two or

three times. I'm supposed to be here to help you, to liaise – to mind you.'

'To mind me? To keep an eye on me, you mean?'

'If you want to put it that way then yes, but in a good way. So where *did* you go?'

'I went out to supper with a friend.'

'Harry?' Natalia pressed. 'Only I rang him and he wasn't at home either.'

Helen sighed. 'No, not Harry.'

'Only, if it *had* been Harry,' continued Natalia, 'I would be really interested to know what you talked about, given all the events of yesterday. You would have a lot to talk about. I'd have really liked to have heard his take on it all.'

'It wasn't Harry.'

Natalia stared at her.

'*It wasn't Harry,*' Helen repeated more forcefully. 'I went to a restaurant about five minutes away from the hotel with one of the porters and his wife, Ewa, who works on reception.'

Natalia looked genuinely shocked. 'Really? *Seriously?*'

'Really. And we had a great night. We all sang Elvis, Frank Sinatra, and busked Rat Pack songs with four Eastern Europeans from somewhere unpronounceable until the wee small hours and shared the best paella I've eaten outside Spain.'

'So you weren't affected by yesterday?' asked Natalia, eyes narrowing.

Helen shook her head in disbelief. 'What do you want

326

me to say, Natalia? That no, I wasn't affected at all? That I was so pleased to find out about a son I hadn't got, and a mother you can't find, that I went out and got hammered with a gang of people I barely knew? *Of course* I was affected, but the last thing I wanted to do was sit in my hotel room and brood about it, or, worse still, go out to dinner with you running through a blow-by-blow post-mortem of the day's events, or worst *of all*, filming it.'

Natalia blanched.

Helen looked across at the camera; it was still rolling. 'So did you get drunk?'

'You know, I don't know where you're getting your information from but I think you need to get someone new in. In the late nineties I went to a gala dinner in some posh hotel in London, got food poisoning and collapsed. Some smart arse with a camera took a whole roll of film of me being manhandled into a friend's car and taken to A&E. Next day it's all over the red tops – not *Helen Redford eats dodgy prawn and pukes all over best friend*, but *Soap star staggers out of gala dinner in arms of strange man*. If you look more closely at the pictures you'll see that it was Arthur – I was sick all over him and ended up spending three days in hospital on a drip. And last night I had a glass of house white with my paella – so that's a *no*, I didn't get drunk. I need to be on top of things for the show tonight; I'm not twenty-five any more.'

Helen flipped her dress over and started to iron the other side.

'I really can't believe you have to do that yourself.' Natalia's tone was gentler now, more conciliatory.

'I told you, I enjoy it.'

'Like singing in bars.'

Helen nodded. 'Like singing in bars.'

'You know you should have said something; we could have come with you.'

'To keep me out of trouble?' asked Helen.

'No, of course not. It would have given us some great footage, and it sounds like it was fun.'

'Former soap star slumming it out in the boondocks?'

'No, not at all. It just shows that you haven't lost touch with your roots, that you still see yourself as one of the rest of us. You know, the common touch –'

'I never lost touch with my roots, because in lots of ways I never had any.' Helen turned the steam up on the iron. 'I usually have a dresser when I'm touring,' she said, which was obviously the kind of answer Natalia had been hoping for earlier.

'You employ someone?'

Helen nodded. 'And Arthur arranges for me to have a driver.'

'But not for Billingsfield?'

Helen shook her head. 'No, not for Billingsfield, although yes, I could have had one if I'd wanted. I'm expecting Arthur to show up any time at all. He'll give me a hand if I need anything.'

On the far side of the room the camera was still rolling relentlessly.

'Not your partner?'

'No, not my partner. Bon's in Dubai at the moment with his show, but if he had been in the country he'd have been here. He sent flowers –' Helen said, nodding towards a huge bouquet of lilies and roses in a vase on a side table, 'and a card.'

'Don't you worry about him being away? He's leading a dance troupe; it's got to be a huge temptation, all those dancers.'

Helen smiled her best smile. 'I can't keep him chained to the bed.'

Natalia reddened. 'I meant wouldn't it be nice if he was here helping you?'

'He's not Mr Helen Redford. Bon's got his own career; I was never expecting him to stop work to pander to me. And besides, Arthur is my agent. We go back a long, long way.'

Natalia nodded. 'And you were married.'

'That's right; and that was a long, long time ago now.'

'But it must make him think. Doesn't Bon worry about Arthur being here with you?'

'No.'

Natalia rolled her eyes. 'There is no way my boyfriend would cope with having my ex around. Especially not with things like dressing and that –'

'It's business.'

'Don't you worry, though?' persisted Natalia. 'Him being away on his own – I don't want to make a big thing of it, but the press are always pointing it out.'

'That Bon's younger than me?'

'Yeah.'

'It isn't the age difference that would make him more likely to go off with someone else – it's about who we are, not how old we are.'

'Right,' said Natalia, although she didn't look convinced. 'So you don't worry about it? About him? I know I would. You're getting older all the time and he is – well, he's gorgeous.'

Helen laughed. 'So he is, but we're all getting older all the time. I don't take Bon for granted, no – but that isn't about age. And love's a funny thing – you take it where you find it, and there is nothing more unattractive than someone who is insecure and clingy and seeking reassurance all the time. Bon's with me because he wants to be. I'm certainly not twisting his arm, and okay, so it may not last forever, but I'd rather have a little of something wonderful than a lifetime of boredom and mediocrity.'

'So are you saying it's not going to last?'

Helen stared at her. 'No, that's *not* what I'm saying.' She turned the dress again so that she could iron the skirt and try not to say something she might regret to the ever-persistent Natalia. She knew that happy people, getting on well, and doing good things, didn't make good television. A life playing out like a slow car crash was a much easier way to push a show further up the ratings.

'And you don't have any other staff or anything?'

'When I was on *Cannon Square* I had an assistant

who used to sort things out for me, and there was obviously makeup and a hairdresser and all that, and we used the same girls regularly, but for these kind of things it's quite often just me.'

'I was expecting you to have an entourage, you know, like Katie Price.'

'Sorry to disappoint you.'

There was a knock at the door. 'Miss Redford?'

'Come in,' called Helen, above the hiss of the steam iron and the sound of Natalia's continued disappointment.

A young man peered nervously around the door. 'We'll be ready for your run-through in ten minutes, if that's okay, Miss Redford?'

Helen smiled. 'That's great, thank you.' She switched off the iron and glanced at Natalia. 'Do you want to go and set up in the theatre? I really need to warm up now.'

Natalia tipped her head to one side.

'My voice,' said Helen, in answer to her unspoken question. 'I need to warm up to sing and I doubt you want to film me warbling, gargling and pulling faces, do you?'

Natalia glanced at Felix who shook his head.

'Okay,' said Natalia. 'We'll cut it there.' She glanced around at the crew. 'Everyone happy? Okay, well in that case we'll see you out in the theatre then, Helen.'

When they had gone Helen hung her dress up, sat down and stared into the mirror above the dressing table. Inside, the theatre looked exactly as she remembered it when she and Charlotte had turned up for the talent show. *Billingsfield's talent extravaganza.*

Helen smiled to herself; the staff had found a copy of the original poster and hung it up above the mirror. She had forgotten what it had been called until someone from *Roots* had managed to dig out some old flyers, a press release and the photos from the *Billingsfield Echo*. There were photocopies of the pictures in a file. The boy band, the dancers, the magician who had won – and Helen and Charlotte, picked out in grainy newsprint. Charlotte had one shoulder thrown forward provocatively, her lips caught in a full blown pout, behind her Helen smiled sheepishly, as if she was almost embarrassed to be there.

Helen was struck by how very little about the theatre seemed to have changed since the last time she had been in it. The box office was just the same; they still had the same red and gold colour scheme, and even what looked like the same tired dusty silk flowers in the alcoves in the foyer.

Once Helen got beyond the entrance and the great expanse of the theatre, and arrived backstage – into the engine of the place – it was even more obvious how very little had been updated. The rabbit warren of corridors was still there, with the service pipes slung along the ceiling in strapped bundles; there were the same scuffed painted concrete floors, even the same colour paint in the dressing rooms, and there was a smell that hung in the air that took her back to the last time that she had been there – a smell of sweat and dust and floor polish mixed with the all-pervading biscuity odour of humanity, with just a hint of Jeyes Fluid and damp.

Helen picked up her hairbrush. The face that looked back at her from the mirror above the dressing table might have aged but the eyes hadn't changed a bit. She could still see Helen Heel in there, the girl who had longed for everything and feared that she would end up with nothing.

Helen sighed, fighting the flashes of *déjà vu*, and started her vocal warm-up, ignoring the ghosts that came tap-tap-tapping at her shoulders.

'If we could sort out your mike, Miss Redford,' said one of the assistant stage managers, as Helen stepped out onto the stage. 'And we're hoping to run-through the musical numbers with Oleg, is that right?' He wasn't looking at her as he spoke; the question was open and directed at everyone and no one rather than Helen in particular, but she nodded anyway.

'We've got our sound guy up in the gallery, and then we'll be needing to just do a run-through with the lights –' he pressed an earpiece and gave someone somewhere a thumbs up, and then smiled at Helen. 'We're good to go whenever you're ready, Miss Redford. If we can just test the mike for sound levels.'

Helen thanked him. Down in the orchestra pit a young man sat at the keyboard, waiting expectantly. He was looking up at her. He was tall and thin with sad, doleful eyes, and thankfully looked nothing like Ed.

'Hi, Oleg,' she said. 'You got here okay? I thought maybe you were going to come and see me in the dressing room before we came out here.'

He smiled. 'I was but they said that you had the TV crew in with you.'

'You could still have come in,' Helen said with a smile, glancing around the auditorium. 'Did Arthur book you into somewhere nice?'

Oleg nodded.

Nothing had changed significantly since she had been there before – the tiered seats, the balcony jutting forward like a lantern jaw, the claret-red walls and floors, and the tired gold paintwork – although this time the theatre was almost empty and much quieter than when the Wild Birds had had their run-through.

Oleg coughed and flexed his fingers.

Last time she had stood on this stage Helen had been barely eighteen, with her whole life ahead of her, like a ribbon waiting to unroll, and now – Helen took a deep breath to steady the little flurry of emotion – and now it was three quarters over. Where had all those years gone?

In the pit Oleg waited for her to give him instructions. She could see Natalia and the film crew watching her every move. The red light on the camera was already on, gleaming like a single demon eye in the gloom, and in the wings was a second one, between them recording every step, every breath and every facial expression.

Helen didn't plan to be rushed, giving herself a moment

or two to settle down and arrive on stage before she began. When she was set, Helen turned and smiled at Oleg.

'Are you okay?' he asked.

'I'm just great, just giving myself a minute, you know.'

He nodded. 'Of course. In your own time.'

'Can we have something just to set the levels, please?' asked the assistant stage manager, still with his finger pressed into his ear.

Helen nodded. 'One two, one two – how's that? Is that okay? Can you hear me?' she said, speaking into the darkness.

'Fine,' said a disembodied voice. 'Looking good from up here.'

Helen smiled, 'Thank God for that.' She glanced down into the pit. 'And you're happy?'

Oleg nodded. 'I'm very happy, and ready whenever you are. Where would you like to start?'

'If we could go with the first number and just take it from the top, just the way we rehearsed. Nice and easy,' said Helen. 'And if we could run the introduction as it's written?'

Oleg nodded and raised his hands above the keyboard. The sound of the intro filled the empty theatre. Helen closed her eyes and taking a steadying breath hit the first note, the song lifting her up, giving her the space to cut off the memories, and fight the almost over-whelming sense that, without ever intending to, she had come full circle. All the tension, all the thoughts, the hopes and the fears slipped away as the music filled her up.

The words and the pure quicksilver notes grew and swelled until the sound filled the dark theatre. As the first song ended Helen felt a rush of euphoria. Oleg smiled up at her, while the film crew and the theatre staff broke into a round of spontaneous applause. Helen, rather self-consciously, took a little bow.

The assistant stage manager grinned. 'That sounded amazing,' he said appreciatively.

'That was just about perfect,' agreed Oleg. 'Would you like to run-through it again?'

Helen shook her head. 'No, I think we're fine with that – I'm happy to move on if you are?' She looked up into the shadows. 'Was that okay for you?'

'Bang on the money,' said a disembodied voice.

'Okay, if we can do the second song – I'm thinking I'll come down to the front for that . . .' A single spotlight tracked her progress.

They worked on the second song and then the third, on through the programme; and as the last echoes of the last song finally faded, everyone applauded again.

Helen smiled and took another little self-conscious bow before turning her attention to Oleg. Strange how it was far harder to be applauded by half a dozen people than by a theatrefull.

'That was great,' Helen said. 'But can we just slow the ending down a little on the final number?'

Oleg nodded and played the final phrase again. 'Like that?'

'Maybe just a little slower?'

He played it again.

'That's fine.'

Oleg marked the score. 'Do you want to run through it?'

'From the last chorus would be good,' said Helen, all business and now well into her stride and oblivious of Natalia and the crew. It wasn't just that she was glad to be back on stage, it felt like she had never been away. 'I want to slow it for a bit of dramatic emphasis, kind of let it hang on that last phrase. Can you just give me my note?'

Oleg nodded.

Helen's voice had warmed up now, and she began to relax and push the melody on. Oleg smiled as her voice soared, so that the final few notes filled the hall with a lush, heart-stopping richness.

The assistant stage manager clapped enthusiastically. 'Wow, that really is amazing; I had no idea you could sing like that,' he said.

Helen laughed. 'It was where I started,' she said. 'Actually it was right here on this stage.'

'Really?' said the man.

'Really,' said Helen as, breathless and elated, she took another bow, acknowledging the flurry of applause from the people in the hall. This time, as she straightened up, Helen spotted a familiar figure sitting in one of the seats a few rows from the front – and felt the sense of renewed pleasure fade and die.

She was older, her long hair cut into a bob and expensively styled to frame her face, but even so Helen would have recognised Charlotte anywhere. For a moment or two neither of them spoke.

'Hello, Charlotte,' Helen said finally, almost in a whisper, unable to take her eyes off her or shake the chill she felt.

'*Kate*,' said Charlotte, getting to her feet and tugging her jacket tight around her. 'Everyone calls me Kate these days.'

'Where is Harry?' said Helen steadily.

'I assume that he's back at the shop. When I got in the car at the airport I knew there was something not quite right so I rang him. To be perfectly honest I wasn't at all surprised when I found out that you'd shown up here, making a mess of our lives. You never could keep your nose out of other people's business, could you?'

'That's hardly fair, this wasn't my idea,' said Helen.

'So Harry said,' said Charlotte. 'I don't know why he couldn't have just left things alone. The trouble with Harry is that he's got this highly developed sense of right and wrong. I told him when that stupid woman from *Roots* rang. I said that he shouldn't say anything, but off he went. Yak, yak, yak. He just couldn't keep his big mouth shut.' Helen could hear the crackle of emotion in Charlotte's voice. 'Why the hell couldn't you have left well alone?'

338

'We can't talk out here,' said Helen. 'Why don't we go to my dressing room? We can have some privacy there.'

'You haven't changed a bit, have you?' Charlotte curled her lip. '*Why don't we go my dressing room?*' she mimicked.

Helen stared at her; Charlotte might be older but she certainly hadn't matured. The edge and spite in her voice came straight out like the last night they had had together at the theatre – the difference was that Helen had grown up in the intervening years.

'Stop it,' she said flatly. 'I'm not playing this game with you, Charlotte. I didn't ask for any of this. I came back to Billingsfield to take a look at my own past, not yours. You either need to get Harry down here so we can sort this out once and for all, or just go home. I'm too old for all this.'

Charlotte stared at her, obviously taken by complete surprise. Helen didn't need to point out that she had come a long way since she'd last seen Charlotte.

It didn't take long for Charlotte to find her voice. 'Don't you dare tell me what to do,' she snapped. 'My life, my family, are my concern, not yours. Is that clear?'

Helen held up her hands. 'Okay, it's your call. Whatever you've got yourself into it's nothing to do with me. I'm really happy for you to just go back to Harry and that'll be it as far as I'm concerned.'

'You don't mean that,' said Charlotte.

Helen could see the look of disbelief on Natalia's face

but, ignoring it, Helen turned her attention back to Oleg. 'Thank you, that was really great. If we can do it like that tonight. Have you got everything you need?'

Oleg nodded. 'I'm fine, thank you.'

'You were better than fine; you were great,' she said. Oleg smiled, and nodded to acknowledge his thanks.

'And we're okay up there?' she said shading her eyes and looking up into the Gods. 'Fine,' said the voice from the darkness. 'If you're happy?'

Helen nodded and while Charlotte watched, she picked up her music and headed backstage.

'Where do you think you're going?' said Charlotte.

Helen kept on walking.

'Wait,' snapped Charlotte. 'You can't just walk away . . .'

As she reached the curtains Helen turned. 'I can and I will. I don't need to be part of whatever peculiar warped little game you've got going on here, Charlotte. This isn't my mess, it's yours. Bye.' With her heart in her mouth Helen made her way towards the wings. She knew she should just keep on walking; Charlotte couldn't have a conversation with someone who wasn't there.

'I'll tell everyone about Adam,' Charlotte called after her, her voice echoing around the auditorium. 'The papers will love it.'

Helen laughed and shook her head, turning back to confront Charlotte. 'Do what you like! We both know Adam's got nothing to do with me. Do you really want to hurt him by dragging his name and his life through the press? The people who know me will know the truth, and those people who don't can think what they like.'

'You don't mean that,' said Charlotte

Helen paused. This had gone on quite long enough; she was far too old to be bullied by someone like Charlotte. 'Oh but I do. And if that was genuinely some sort of threat, Charlotte, then I'll sue you,' she said as evenly as she could manage. 'There'll be DNA tests and the story doing the rounds in the national papers and the local ones. I know you've always wanted to be famous, but I'm not sure this is exactly the kind of fame you had in mind. Nor the kind of thing you'd want to drag Harry and Adam through.'

'You wouldn't,' said Charlotte.

Helen smiled. 'Just watch me. I don't want to do it this way but trust me, I will, because you're cruel and selfish, and you need to be taught that you can't mess around with other people's lives, thinking it's all right. Now if you'll excuse me I'm going to go and get ready for the show.'

Helen caught a glimpse of Charlotte rounding on the film crew. 'Did you hear that?' she snapped, camera still rolling. 'Did you? Did you get it, did you hear what she said? Are you going to show this on the TV?'

Natalia's face was completely impassive. Helen meanwhile made her way backstage, her heart pounding in her chest like a drum. One of the crew unclipped her microphone; Helen made an effort to block out the sounds coming from the auditorium.

341

When she got to the dressing room Helen closed the door behind her, fighting the temptation to turn the key in the lock, and pressed her forehead to the cold wood, making an effort to compose herself. Harry had been wrong about one thing – Charlotte really hadn't changed at all over the years.

TWENTY-ONE

Helen sat down at the dressing table and poured herself a glass of water. Her hands were trembling. It had been complete madness to agree to do the filming for *Roots* alongside her live show. What the hell had Arthur been thinking of, and why on earth had she gone along with it? Helen glanced at the clock on the wall. Arthur had promised her that he would be backstage in plenty of time for the performance – that would be his plenty not hers. She just wished that he would break the habit of a lifetime and show up early for once. No sooner had Helen had the thought than there was a knock on the door.

'Who is it?' Helen called.

'It's me,' said a familiar voice.

Helen sighed; at least it wasn't Charlotte. 'Come in, Harry,' she called.

Harry opened the door very slowly. He was still dressed

in his work clothes and stood on the threshold wringing his hands. Behind him stood a tall thin young man with swept-back hair and a face that Helen recognised; it was just that she couldn't quite remember where. His expression was one of curiosity, defiance and an uncertainty that made Helen's heart ache. So many of the things Adam believed about himself were built on sand and lies. Helen wondered just how much Harry had already told him.

'Are you okay?' Harry asked Helen.

Helen nodded. 'Please,' she said, beckoning them inside, 'Why don't you both come in and let's close the door?'

Harry looked around the room. 'I hope you don't mind. The man on the stage door let us in. We told him we were friends. Apparently our names are on his list, so he said we could come straight through.'

Helen nodded; she needed to have a word with Natalia about who exactly was on the list and who she had agreed could come backstage.

'We thought Kate might be here,' Harry added.

'She is. Or at least she was. I saw her a few minutes ago in the auditorium,' said Helen, pointing. And then turning her attention to the young man alongside him, she said, 'You must be Adam.'

He nodded. He looked nervous.

Helen smiled at him. 'Pleased to meet you. I've heard a lot about you from Harry,' she said, wondering where on earth she should begin. 'Why don't you both take a seat – please, sit down. I could probably get us some tea if you'd like some?'

Harry shook his head. 'We're fine, thank you. We just came to find Kate.'

Helen could feel Adam watching her; it was hard not to stare at him, this boy who believed that he was her son. He was in his twenties with gingery gold hair, his expression fluid and unsettled. Helen struggled to place him.

'I've waited a long time for this,' Adam said nervously.

Helen nodded. 'Your dad told me. I don't know where to begin really, Adam. I don't know exactly what your dad's told you –' she paused waiting to see if Harry would leap into the abyss, and when he didn't, she continued, 'I know that your mum and dad are really, really proud of you.' She paused. 'And they both love you very much –'

Nobody else said anything, instead both men looked at her.

'Your dad told me that you play in a band?'

'Yeah.' Adam nodded. The atmosphere in the dressing room was so charged you could almost reach out and touch it. Circling the obvious, Adam took his lead from Helen and picked up on the social chit-chat. 'We're doing quite well,' he said. 'I'm out playing at gigs most weekends. We're booked more or less right up until Christmas.'

'That's great,' said Helen.

'We've not got a contract or a manager or anything. We do a lot of covers but I do write my own stuff; maybe Dad said. I thought,' Adam said, carefully, as if testing the waters, 'that maybe I got my musical streak from you. Dad's always told me that you've got the most

345

amazing voice. They don't say that on the telly though, do they? They only go on about your acting. I've watched you for years.'

Harry was a picture of discomfort; she nodded. It was coming, the moment she had known would come in Harry's shop, the moment that couldn't be ignored or avoided. She glanced at Harry, who raised his hands just a fraction in a gesture that said, 'What can I do?'

'I was going to bring my girlfriend to meet you today. But then again I thought it might be a bit awkward, you know, the first time . . .'

Helen took a deep breath; now was the moment. 'Adam, I don't know where to start –'

But before she could say anything else there was a banging and a hammering on the door loud enough to wake the dead and a second later the door flew open, framing Charlotte. She was red-faced now, her hair less coiffured. Helen wondered what she had said to Natalia, or what Natalia had said to her.

Seeing Harry and Adam in the dressing room took the wind out of her sails; whatever Charlotte had been planning to say to Helen the words died on her lips, and instead she stared at Harry.

'What are you doing here? I thought you told me you were going to stay at the shop?' she said in a low voice, far kinder than the one she had used on Helen. 'You said you wouldn't come here, you promised me.'

Harry nodded. 'I know I did, but I was worried about you, I couldn't let you go through this on your own,

Kate,' he said. 'And then there was Adam to think about. He's been waiting all these years. You're my family, you two. I wanted to be here for you both.'

Behind Charlotte, Helen could see Natalia and the film crew desperately trying to squeeze their way past Charlotte and make their way into the dressing room.

'Why don't we all get inside,' said Natalia softly over Charlotte's shoulder. 'We don't want to have this conversation in the corridor, do we?'

Helen shot her a sharp look, but Natalia ignored her. It was Adam who looked from face to face, bemused. 'Are you going to film this?' he asked, staring at Helen as if she was responsible. 'I thought you were just going to talk about what happened and then show some stuff about the band.'

'That's right,' said Helen firmly, speaking very slowly as if the film crew were hard of hearing or stupid or maybe both. 'We're not filming it, are we, Natalia? Natalia and the crew are going to wait outside, aren't you? Because whatever needs to be said is between the four of us.'

Natalia looked indignant and began to protest. 'Oh come on, Helen, that's hardly fair. We've followed the story this far – and contractually I'm not sure –' she began.

'Well, I am.' Helen glared at her. 'I want you to wait outside, please.'

'Maybe we could pick it up later?'

'Go,' said Helen, pointing to the door.

Holding her hands up in surrender Natalia and the

347

others backed out into the hallway and closed the door behind them.

When finally there were just the four of them Helen turned to Charlotte. 'I really think that we all deserve an explanation, don't you, Charlotte?'

'No one calls me –' Charlotte began.

'I know, I know,' sighed Helen, holding up her hands to stem the tide. 'No one calls you Charlotte any more, but I remember you back when everyone did. You were a lot of things when we were friends, Charlotte, but I don't ever remember you being a liar.'

Charlotte's cheeks flared scarlet. 'How dare you –' she began.

'You have to tell Adam and Harry the truth.'

Adam frowned. 'What does she mean, Mum?' Adam glanced at Helen. 'It's all right, I already know the truth; Mum told me all about it. You couldn't bring me up. You'd just got started and got your first big job and were about to go on tour when I was born and you and Mum had always been good friends and Mum said that she'd look after me while you were away – that's right, isn't it?'

Spoken aloud it sounded childlike, naïve and compelling. Helen wondered just how many times Adam had repeated those words to himself over the years. Her eyes misted with tears. No one spoke.

'Tell her,' said Adam. 'Tell her how you looked after me, Mum.'

Finally Charlotte turned to Helen, her voice thick with emotion. 'Why did you have to come back?'

'Please, Charlotte,' appealed Helen. 'Tell them the truth.'

Charlotte closed her eyes and made a show of composing herself before turning to Harry and Adam. 'Adam, Helen isn't your mother. I am.'

Adam stared at her. Harry too.

'But you said –' Adam began.

'I know what I said,' whispered Charlotte. 'I've been dogged by what I said every day, every hour since I met Harry up in Scarborough and came back to Billingsfield, Adam. I'm so sorry, my love. You have to believe me. I didn't intend to lie to you or your dad, not for all this time but I couldn't find a way to unsay what had been said.'

Adam made a strange guttural sound. 'But you said –'

'Oh, honey I know, I know – but you have to believe me when I say that I love you both more than I can ever put into words,' said Charlotte, her voice full of tears. 'But that one little lie slipped out and that led to another lie and another one and then another, and once they were out I just couldn't find a way to get them back in again.'

Harry was staring open-mouthed at Charlotte. 'Adam is your son?'

Charlotte nodded. 'I couldn't tell you, Harry. I just couldn't. That day in Scarborough I just couldn't bring myself to tell you the truth. I didn't want you to think badly of me. I was in such a muddle when we met and when you said, *Whose baby is that?* the lie came so easily. It was so much easier to deal with if it was Helen's shame, not mine. You should have seen your face when I said

349

Adam was Helen's. I always knew that you loved her and that you missed her.' Charlotte's voice dropped so low Helen had to strain to pick out the words. 'I thought that you'd help us if you thought that the baby was Helen's.'

'Oh, Charlotte,' Harry whispered. 'Why on earth didn't you tell me the truth?'

Adam was ashen. 'I don't understand. How can you be my mum? All these years you told me I was hers,' he said, pointing towards Helen. 'All these years you've lied to me and to Dad. All these years I kept wondering what sort of woman, what sort of a mother could just walk away from her own child, *from me*. And the stupid thing was you hadn't walked away at all – you'd stayed.'

A single tear rolled down Charlotte's face.

'All these years,' said Adam, 'there was me wondering what I had done, what was wrong with me that Helen wanted nothing at all to do with me. Do you have any idea how that's made me feel? I used to try and persuade myself that it was because if she saw me, if she ever came back, she would be so filled with guilt and love that she wouldn't be able to be parted from me again – that she'd snatch me away – and how awful that would be for you and Dad.'

Charlotte flinched but Adam wasn't finished.

'I remember asking you why and you always had some explanation, some little homily to make me feel better; but most of the time I, you know, I just thought Helen couldn't care less, that she didn't love me and that she never had. And what about all those cards and presents you said came from my mum? All those well dones and happy birthdays – all those lies? How could you – do you have any idea what you've done?'

More tears trickled down Charlotte's face. 'I didn't mean it to happen like this. If Helen hadn't come back –'

Adam laughed. 'What do you mean *if Helen hadn't come back* – did you know about this, about me?' he said, swinging round to Helen.

Helen shook her head.

Adam let out a long sigh and shook his head. 'Did it never occur to you that one day I'd go and find Helen and ask her about what had happened? I've been planning it for as long as I can remember. I was waiting for the right moment but I kept putting it off because I didn't want to hurt *you* – you were so adamant, and now I know why. I'd got it all planned. What I'd say, what Helen would say – I've played dozens of different scenarios through in my head. It isn't Helen who's lied to me all this time. It's you. How could you do this to us?'

Any bluster that Charlotte had left ebbed away and she slumped onto a chair by the door. 'I love you, Adam, you have to believe me. I really didn't mean it to happen this way. I didn't think – I was working in Scarborough. I was walking along the front with you in a pram. You weren't very old, I'd only been out of hospital a little while, and you were so lovely – such a good baby – and just this tiny little scrap of a thing. I was having to keep working and I remember that day I couldn't get anyone

351

to keep an eye on you. They'd been really good about me having you backstage, they'd let me work in the box office right up until you were born, but it wasn't going to last for ever and money was so tight, and then all of a sudden, out of the blue, there was Harry walking along the prom towards me. I couldn't believe it. It was like a mirage. I was so stunned I didn't know what to say.

'Harry came straight over and started to chat and asked me about the baby. He was up there for some sort of trade thing, and I just said he was yours, Helen. Just like that. Looking back it was a stupid thing to say but the words were out in an instant, before I really had time to think about what I was saying.'

'Charlotte told me that she had been sharing a flat with you, Helen,' said Harry, picking up the threads of the story. 'She told me that you'd got this new job and were sending her money to look after Adam but that it wasn't very much and you were all struggling to manage –'

'But I'd been ringing you, Harry –' protested Helen.

'I know,' said Harry. 'But I thought you were just putting a brave face on things. It suddenly all made sense; you hadn't come home and you always had an excuse about why I couldn't come and see you. Meeting Kate it all fell into place.'

Helen stared at him. 'You thought that I was lying?'

Harry nodded.

'Oh, Harry,' said Helen.

Charlotte smiled affectionately at Harry. 'But he believed me. He's always been such a kind man. He took me out for lunch and made the man in the restaurant let us park the pram right by the table. He said he'd stay and look after Adam while I did the show, and then he took me back to this little place I was renting. I made him coffee and he just looked around and said that it was madness living there, with Adam, and that I should go home with him and that we could both look after Adam till you had finished the tour.'

Helen looked from one face to the other. 'But how did you manage to register him as mine?'

'It was easy. Right up until I met Harry on the prom-enade I suppose I was in denial about the whole thing really. I didn't see a midwife. I'd worked up until the week I had the baby.– but once I'd told Harry that Adam was yours it all seemed so simple. I hadn't registered him so when I did I just used your name, and I knew all your details. It made everything so much easier if Adam wasn't really mine –'

'And then you came back to Billingsfield with Harry?'

Charlotte shook her head. 'No, not straight away. Not for a while. But he kept coming back to see us, see if we were all right, wanting to help us, wanting to know where you were. I thought at one point that he was going to go and find you and offer you the same deal as he'd offered me, so in the end I told him that you'd met someone and it was serious and that you had asked me to keep Adam.'

'And you believed her?' whispered Helen.

Harry nodded.

Helen stared at Charlotte. 'How on earth could you do it?'

'I had to say something, Helen and it all fitted. It explained why you didn't come back to get the baby. I'd seen this thing in the paper where you'd started dating some actor and it all just fell into place.'

'Harry, how could you ever think I'd be the kind of person who'd leave my baby?' said Helen.

Harry looked uncomfortable. 'I didn't, not really – but fame does strange things to people and I could see that if you were working away, being on tour was no place for a baby –' he reddened furiously, 'and there was the thing with your mum.'

Helen stared at him. 'You mean, you thought it was history repeating itself?'

'I wasn't to know, was I? I suppose I had my doubts, I'd be lying if I said I hadn't, but Charlotte sounded so plausible and I could see that it would have been hard for you, and you were sending her money every week.'

'I was?' said Helen in astonishment.

Charlotte nodded. 'After the talent show me and Dad had this huge row, which was why I decided to leave, and then when, later, I found out I was pregnant and I wanted to come back Dad said he didn't want me there cramping his style. His girlfriend at the time was the same age as me. They're younger now . . . anyway the last thing he wanted was me rolling up with someone calling him Grandad.

'He told me I ought to get rid of it, and then when I

didn't he said the best thing I could do was put Adam up for adoption, but then when I didn't do that either he started to send me money. Every week. He felt guilty – I just think he was buying me off. And so I told Harry it was from you.'

'Your dad knows about all this?' asked Harry.

'He's always known,' said Charlotte, looking at Helen. 'You know what he's like. For God's sake, he even used to flirt with *you* when you used to come round; no wonder my mum left him. It made me feel sick. He told me right from the start that he wanted nothing to do with Adam or me. When Harry asked me to marry him, my dad said I should tell him the truth, not play Harry for a fool – but I never did think that, Harry – I didn't think you were a fool, I never have. I thought you were wonderful, I was so touched by how kind you were and how generous. My dad said that if you loved me you'd marry me anyway.' Charlotte paused, her voice crackling with emotion. 'But I couldn't take that chance.'

Harry shook his head. 'Oh, Charlotte, why didn't you tell me the truth?'

'Because I was afraid you'd leave me. I've always known that you did it for Helen,' said Charlotte. 'You thought you were rescuing Helen's baby and that one day she'd come back for him and come back for you too.'

Harry flinched as if she had slapped him. 'How could you think that? You think I'm that shallow? Bloody hell, Charlotte. You're right, I *did* love Helen. I *do* love her, but I love you too, Charlotte. I couldn't have married you if I hadn't loved you. I watched you with Adam, how lovely you were and how hurt, and I saw another side to that spiky sharp person you show everyone when you feel threatened. I saw past all that. I always have.'

It was Charlotte's turn to look stunned. 'I thought you felt sorry for me,' she murmured.

He laughed. 'Well, I did, but that wasn't what made me marry you. Do you think I kept coming up to Scarborough all those times just to see Adam? I wanted to see you; I fell in love with you, Charlotte. I loved you then, I love you now –' he looked at Adam. 'I love you both.' And with that he swept Adam and Charlotte into his arms.

Helen stayed back, the tears running down her face.

'Excuse me,' said a voice from outside the dressing-room door, 'Can we come in now?'

Helen got up and opened the door just a crack; the film crew were outside pressing themselves into the open gap like puppies trying to get into a warm kitchen.

'Can you give us a few more minutes?' said Helen, holding up a hand to stem the tide; although it was couched as a question it was obvious what the answer was.

Natalia sighed. 'Can we just get a run down of what happened in there?'

Helen glanced back into the dressing room. 'Maybe later,' she said. In the dressing room Charlotte had stepped away and was wiping her eyes, Adam looked pale and .

teary, and Harry was getting himself sorted out, patting his pockets, straightening his tie, making a show of getting ready to leave.

'Just let them in, Helen, I think we should be going home,' said Harry. 'We've got a lot to talk about, and we've no need to do it in front of the cameras.'

Adam nodded. He smiled a funny lopsided smile at Helen. 'I was hoping that we'd sort this out,' he said. 'You and me and Mum and Dad. I thought that we'd got a lot to talk about. Building a bridge, getting to know each other. I never imagined that it would turn out like this.'

Oblivious to the crew pushing their way back into the dressing room Helen nodded and put her arms around him. 'I'm so sorry, Adam, I had no idea about any of this. I never had any children – sometimes I wish –' she stopped and smiled, 'I could always be your auntie . . .'

Adam held her tight and then, pulling away, shook his head in disbelief. 'All these years,' he said, 'I thought you'd rejected me.' He glanced at Charlotte. 'I love her, you know, even though she's done all this. Does that sound mad?'

'No, of course it doesn't,' said Helen. 'She's always been your mum, Adam, whether or not she gave birth to you wasn't the thing – and you have to remember that. Your mum loved you from day one. She could have given you up and come home without you, but she didn't.'

Adam looked at Charlotte and nodded. 'It's hard to get my head around all this.'

Harry took hold of Adam's arm. 'Come on, son. Time to go home – we've got a lot to talk about.' And then turning to Helen he said, 'We'll be all right. We'll be able to sort things out. Come on, Charlotte. Let's go home.'

Charlotte moved more slowly. She looked drained and defeated. 'I just need a minute,' she said. 'You go on. I won't be long.'

The two men stepped outside.

'I'm sorry,' said Charlotte to Helen the moment the door was closed.

They were two words that Helen had never expected Charlotte to say about anything.

'I'd like to say I understand, but I don't,' said Helen.

Charlotte smiled ruefully. 'I'm not sure that I do now. Looking back it seems like a different lifetime. I was a different person then. At the time it seemed like you had it all; the talent, the voice, the big break . . .'

'I thought the same about you,' said Helen. 'Big house, rich daddy . . .'

Charlotte laughed. 'And a lot of good it did me.'

'What I've done, all the things I've done over the years,' said Helen gently. 'They didn't just fall in my lap, you know. I had to work and it came at a cost. I didn't have family.' She paused. 'And I haven't got Harry –'

Charlotte looked up at her. 'No, you haven't, have you?'

'I was really surprised when I found out you hadn't gone to teacher-training college.'

'It was so stupid,' said Charlotte. 'Talk about cutting

358

your nose off to spite your face. I wanted to show my dad and you and everyone else that I could still do it, even without you. Vince got me into this show in Scarborough – so there we are, you took your chance and I took mine – and I blew it.'

'Vince,' said Helen looking towards the door. 'Adam –'

Charlotte nodded and then blushed furiously. 'He came to find me after that night with Leon. I saw him on Sunday when I was on my way home from Harry's flat, and he said he'd heard what had happened and that maybe it had been for the best. And then he said he knew someone who'd got this show coming up, up on the coast. They were looking for girls – no funny business and I'd be able to get an Equity card.' Charlotte snorted. 'That was a lie, but the work was real enough. I was there eighteen months and I was doing quite well and then Vince showed up out of the blue. He said he wanted to take me out, said I owed him and that if he'd been my agent I would have had to pay him a percentage. He was half drunk, half joking but he wouldn't take no for an answer, so we started seeing each other. It was never going to go anywhere. He was such a sleaze. Anyway, after a couple of months, after he'd had what he wanted he just cleared off. Things weren't great on my own, but they were doable. The show was doing okay, and there was always the chance that something better would come out of it. But I wasn't eating properly, I was working all sorts of odd hours and just never felt well. It didn't occur to me that I might be pregnant. And then when I

359

realised I was, I kept thinking it wasn't happening – that if I ignored it, it would go away.'

Charlotte stopped. 'I really need to go and talk to Adam and to Harry.' She backhanded a flurry of tears away and opened the door to the dressing room. 'You know, I've missed you.'

Helen laughed. 'You were horrible to me.'

Charlotte nodded. 'Not always. I was just jealous – you always were the one with the talent.'

Helen said nothing, remembering how many times she had looked at Charlotte and her life with envy. Maybe the grass was always greener.

'Maybe we should meet up and have a proper talk, have dinner or something. I know Harry would like that,' said Charlotte. 'And Adam. I don't know if I can put it right, Helen.'

Helen sighed. 'I'm sure you can. They both love you.'

Charlotte picked up her bag. 'Good luck for tonight.'

'Thank you,' Helen said. She had almost forgotten that she was on stage in couple of hours.

'Are you coming to the show?' asked Helen.

'We're meant to, according to that girl with the TV crew we've got tickets, but we'll see,' said Charlotte.

Helen nodded. There was an awkward moment when both women hesitated, Helen could see that Charlotte was weighing up whether to embrace her or not. In the end it seemed Charlotte decided against it and turned to leave.

At the door Helen stopped her. 'Wait,' she said. 'Just

one thing – Harry told me that you used to go and visit my dad after I left.'

Charlotte nodded. 'That's right. He was really kind to me. He was so proud of you, you know.'

Helen sighed, struggling to control the ache in her chest. She didn't have any idea how her dad felt about her. All those years, all those long empty evenings, the endless silences, the awkward phone calls, he'd never once told her that he was proud of her. 'And what about Adam? Harry said you used to take him too.'

Charlotte's expression softened. 'Your dad loved seeing him. I know what you're thinking, Helen, and the answer is no. I never passed Adam off as his grandson – there are some things even I wouldn't stoop to. He knew exactly who Adam was and he knew all about me and Harry and the lie I'd told.' Charlotte paused. 'He told me that I should put things right, that it was worse for people to find out the truth than be told it – that way I could choose when I told people, when I was strong and ready. And he was right. I should have said something a long long time ago.'

And then Charlotte turned, pulling the door closed behind her, and was gone. Helen turned round biting her lip, eyes full of tears, for the first time aware that the camera was rolling.

TWENTY-TWO

Natalia, just out of camera shot, glanced down at her notes. 'So do you ever get nervous before doing a show?' she asked.

Helen, who was putting the finishing touches to her hair in the big mirror above the dressing table, leaned back and smiled. 'You're joking, aren't you? Of course I do. Who wouldn't be nervous if they'd got a camera crew following them around all day watching their every move?'

'I meant nervous about tonight,' said Natalia. 'And it's been a very emotional couple of days for you.'

Helen decided not to take the bait. It had been a little while since Charlotte, Harry and Adam had left, and Helen was doing her very best not to hold an impromptu postmortem. She needed time to think about the things that had happened.

It was hard. Natalia had got curiosity down to a finely

honed torture and no amount of telling her that she wasn't going to talk about Charlotte, Adam and Harry seemed to satisfy her; but then Arthur had turned up with flowers and champagne – better late than never – and with his arrival the tone had subtly changed.

'I do get nervous, but not as much as I used to. It used to be really bad when I first started out, but these days I'm fine, and I think a little nervous energy is good for your performance, you know, sharpens you up. And television was different – not like performing in front of a live audience.'

'And it's a big night tonight for you, isn't it?'

Helen brushed powder onto her face to kill the shine. The camera crew behind her were trapped in the mirror's reflection, the cold hard Cyclops' eye of the camera staring at her unblinking. It had been a big night in so many ways. Arthur, sitting behind them, watched but didn't say a word.

'That's right, it's the first time out for a run of one-woman shows I'm doing around the country over the next few months. I think we've got twelve dates booked in all, something like that, and it all starts here.'

Natalia nodded. 'Which is apt, as your whole career started out here.'

'It feels like a nice touch,' said Helen warmly. 'It's been a while since I've toured with my own show, and coming back to Billingsfield makes it extra special.'

'And how long is it since you've been back?' Natalia pressed. Helen smiled, wondering how many times

363

Natalia had asked her that question over the last two days. It felt as if Natalia was trying to catch her out, or drive her into a corner that she couldn't escape from.

Helen blotted her lips. 'Far longer than I'd care to remember. It feels like a lifetime since I was in this theatre. It's a lot more glamorous these days. Last time I was here I didn't have a dressing room to myself; I was sharing a dressing room upstairs with the chorus and all the rest of the female acts.'

'So, have you got anything you want to share with us now you're back in your home town in amongst all the memories, all the old faces and places?'

Helen considered her reply for a moment. It felt much worse and much better than she had ever dreamed, but Helen didn't say that. In fact she didn't say anything, because before Natalia could press her for an answer there was a sharp knock on the dressing-room door, which made them all jump.

'Supper, Miss Redford?' said a disembodied voice from out in the corridor.

'Thank you,' Helen called, and then turning to the film crew said, 'If you'll excuse me I really need to eat and finish getting ready now.' As she spoke she indicated the robe she was wearing.

There was an odd little pause. It was obvious they hadn't expected to be asked to leave while Helen got dressed. 'I thought you'd be going back to the hotel or something,' said Natalia.

Helen shook her head. 'I ordered in. I wasn't sure what

the plans were and I need to eat before I go on.' Helen didn't add that she didn't want them trailing after her; providing a running commentary on her every mouthful, her every thought, was exhausting.

Reluctantly Natalia got to her feet, the rest of the crew taking their cue from her.

'Okay, we'll cut it there then,' she said. 'Seems like a natural break. We'll leave you to it then, Helen, and pick it up later. Give you a few minutes' peace,' she added, with a chirpy little smile that didn't quite hide her annoyance. 'You that know that Felix is going to film you as you go up onto the stage?'

Helen nodded.

'And you're okay with that?'

'Absolutely fine.'

'Right, well okay in that case we'll be off. Break a leg,' said Natalia, heading towards the door.

'See you later,' said Helen, turning her attention back to the mirror. As they opened the door, a man came in with a picnic basket.

'Well, that went well,' said Arthur, who had been sitting out of camera shot in the one comfortable chair in the room. He thanked the man, tipped him and took the basket.

'You want me to be mother? What have we got?' He said, sliding the basket onto a side table. Arthur paused, catching her gaze in the mirror. 'At least you managed not to punch her.'

Helen laughed. 'It's been touch and go, and there's still time. You can eat too if you like – there should be plenty

365

for both of us. Do you want to unpack it? I just need to get my dress on.'

'I'd rather help you with that,' Arthur purred.

'Down, boy,' said Helen. 'I'm just hoping for a hand with the zip.'

'Days were you'd have a dresser,' said Arthur, peering into the top of the picnic basket. 'I think Tally might be free if you want me to book her.'

'I hate all that fussing about, Arthur, you know that. I like to keep things easy, low key, private. And anyway I've got you, haven't I?'

'You mean I'll do.'

Helen turned. 'That isn't what I mean at all.'

He smiled. 'It was here, wasn't it?' he said, glancing round. 'All those years ago. I parked round the back and wandered round to where they used to have that tea van. Do you remember? It only seems like yesterday. I keep thinking about us, about all the things we've been through together –' he began haltingly.

Helen laughed. 'Well, don't think, Arthur. Just get the food sorted out.'

'This looks good,' he said, peeling open a box. 'What's in the flask?'

'There should be chicken noodle soup, and some wraps. Oh and juice. I wasn't sure what *Roots* had got planned for me so I decided it would be better to be prepared. And thank goodness I did; there wouldn't be time to go out and get something now. I got the hotel to send it over.'

Arthur pulled a face. 'All sounds horribly healthy. Did you order any booze? How about I open the champagne?'

Helen shook her head. 'Can we save it until after the show's finished? Do you mind?'

'Of course not. Is there something sweet in here? Crème caramel maybe, or a tiramisu?' he said, sifting through the containers.

'Fresh fruit salad.'

'You're kidding me?' he said with disgust. 'I was hoping you might at least have ordered cake?'

'I didn't want anything too heavy before going on. And no dairy – not while I'm singing.'

Arthur sighed. 'Ah well, in that case I think maybe I'll pass on the picnic. Nice flowers,' he added conversationally, glancing at the bouquets arranged on a shelf that ran along one wall. 'And lots of good luck cards too,' he added, leaning in closer to peer at the signatures and salutations.

While he was busy Helen slipped off her robe and slithered into her costume.

She had had three made for the tour. This one was copper coloured, boned and cut on the bias, making the most of her slim waist and curvy hourglass figure. Not that Arthur was paying that much attention. His mind appeared to still be on the flowers. Helen laughed. How times had changed, she thought, as he peered myopically at the cards fixed to the wrappings.

'Golden boy send you flowers, did he?'

'Yes. The roses.'

'The pink ones?'

'Uhuh.'

Arthur sniffed. 'Not very imaginative. Have you heard from him today?'

'No, but he's really busy with this new show.' Helen rolled her eyes. 'And stop sounding so hard done by. You had your chance, Arthur, remember?'

'I know, how can I forget? But I was thinking perhaps we were too hasty. We're older now, we understand each other. I'm more tolerant now, more patient.'

'Well, I'm not,' laughed Helen. 'Can you stop moaning and zip me up?'

'I thought he'd get something more impressive.'

Helen laughed. 'Just tell me you're not jealous.'

'I'm not jealous,' Arthur said in a monotone. Helen slapped him playfully with the back of her hand and eased the dress up over her hips, and then she stopped.

'What's the matter?'

Arthur sighed. 'You know I loved you from the first time I saw you throwing up in that bin.'

'Oh, Arthur,' said Helen, not sure whether he was joking or not.

'By the way, I've had a call from someone in the BBC – they're looking to cast a new drama series.'

'And they're looking at me?' said Helen, swinging round.

Arthur nodded. 'Female lead. Some sort of detective thing. They'd like us to go in for a meeting end of next week.'

Helen grinned. 'That's fabulous. Do you know anything else about it?'

He shook his head. 'Not much. It was Harry Fentman, he likes to play it very close to his chest but he was very keen to find out what your commitments were. He's going to email – And a publisher called and –' Arthur paused and stared at her. 'Why don't you get changed after you've eaten?' he said. 'I'd have thought the last thing you'd want to do is spill soup down the front of that.'

'I'll be fine. They've sent napkins, and if you're that worried I'll put my robe back on. It just makes me feel better to know I'm as ready as I can be.'

'You know it's funny being back here,' he said. 'You and me, after all these years. It makes me realise just what we've missed. Have you ever thought that maybe we should start over, give it another go?.'

Helen laughed. 'It was a long time ago now, Arthur, and we didn't miss out on it so much as decide we didn't want it. Remember? You and me, it was like chalk and cheese, oil and water. I've always loved you but there is no way I want to wake up with you.'

Arthur held up his hands in surrender. 'Okay, okay, point taken, but please don't go on about how much water has gone under the bridge. Just the thought of running water makes me head for the bathroom these days. I don't suppose you get that with his nibs, do you?'

'Will you just shut up about Bon and help me to zip this up? We had our chance and it didn't work, and besides I don't know what you're complaining about, we see each other all the time. I probably see more of you than I see of Bon.' Helen paused, admiring her reflection in the mirror as Arthur fixed the hook at the back.

'My point exactly.'

Helen ignored him. 'Oh that's great, don't you think? It fits like a glove,' Helen said, running her hand down over the waist and hips

He sniffed. 'Did you ask them to put all those rhinestones on it? It looks like you're channelling Dolly Parton.'

'It could be worse,' said Helen, straight-faced. 'It could be Freddy Mercury.'

Arthur peered into the mirror surveying his own generous middle-aged spread. 'You know there was a time when I'd have cut quite a dash in a white Lycra jumpsuit.'

Helen laughed and handed him her necklace. 'Well fortunately for everyone those days are long gone, Arthur.' She paused as he dropped the necklace over her head and moved closer so that he could see to fasten it.

'I'm glad you could make it tonight,' she said. 'The last couple of days have been hell.'

'So I gather. You want to talk about it?'

Helen shook her head. 'Maybe later, but not now,' she said, resting her hand over his. 'I'm just glad that you're here.'

Arthur raised his eyebrows. 'I wouldn't have missed it for the world, you know that, don't you?' And leaning in closer still, brushed her neck with his lips. 'I just can't see why you're wasting your time with that boy.'

'Because *that boy*, as you call him, loves me.' And for a moment their eyes met in the mirror, old friends still in love after all these years. 'Stop it, Arthur,' she said. 'We did all this before, remember, and it was a disaster.'

'I love you,' he said softly.

'Sometimes love isn't enough. You can't go back. *We can't go back.*'

Arthur sniffed and pulled out a cigar. 'So where is he tonight?'

He held her reflected gaze. Helen was the first to look away. 'Don't,' she said briskly, wiping away an unexpected tear. 'You know exactly where he is. He's working his arse off in Dubai. You'd be the first one to accuse him of sponging off me if he didn't work – now come on, we need to eat.'

'No, baby, y*ou* need to eat,' he said. 'I'm not sure I'm ready for that much healthy food at one sitting and besides, I've got things to see to. And I know you like some time to yourself and time to warm up. And if you won't dump what's-his-face and run away with me then I'm going to nip off and have a smoke.'

Helen laughed, relieved that he had lightened the mood. 'I'm glad to see you've got your priorities right,' she said.

Arthur sniffed imperiously. When he had gone Helen settled down to eat her supper.

He had barely left when there was another knock at the door. Helen waited, wondering whether Arthur had forgotten something or whether it was someone with a message, as the door very slowly opened,

Helen glanced over her shoulder. 'Harry?' she said in amazement as she saw his familiar face peering round the door. 'What on earth are you doing here?'

'I'm not disturbing you, am I?' he said, without stepping inside.

Helen shook her head. 'No, not at all, but I thought you'd be at home with Charlotte and Adam.'

'I was,' he said, and then looked her up and down. 'You know, you look amazing.'

She smiled. 'Thank you. How's Adam doing?'

He shrugged. 'Not too bad. It's a lot to take in. We just need to talk it through, get it all straight in our heads. In a funny way it feels like a relief.'

Helen nodded. What else was there to say? 'And what about you? How're you doing?'

'I'm good. Really.'

'I just don't understand how you didn't guess about Charlotte and Adam.'

Harry reddened. 'I know, looking back there are lots of things that make sense now and I think that there was a part of me that always suspected, I just didn't want to risk losing what we had –'

'So what are you doing here?'

'I brought you this,' Harry said, slipping into the dressing room and setting down a suitcase on one of the chairs. 'Your dad gave it to Charlotte before he died. He wanted you to have it.'

Helen stared at him and then at the suitcase. 'And she's had it all this time?'

Harry nodded. 'I kept wondering why she didn't contact you about it, although now I know why,' he said ruefully.

'And has Charlotte looked inside it?' Helen asked.

Harry shook his head. 'No, not as far as I know. I'm not exactly sure what she planned to do with it. It's been tucked away in the spare room since your dad's funeral. I thought you'd like it and now seems like the right moment.'

Helen took a long hard look at it. It was the same plain brown leather case that she remembered from her childhood.

'He used to keep it on top of the wardrobe in their bedroom,' she said, getting up to run her hands over the smooth shiny leather. 'I always used to wonder where he'd ever been that he needed a suitcase.'

Harry took out a keyring out of his jacket pocket; it had a single key hanging from it. 'Here,' he said, handing it to her. 'I'd better be getting back home before they miss me.' He hesitated and then very gently leaned closer and kissed her. 'It's good to see you again,' he said.

Helen smiled. 'Thank you,' she said. 'For everything. I keep wishing I had come home sooner and then maybe none of this would have happened.'

Harry shrugged. 'Who knows?' he said. 'The trouble is, if you're not careful you can spend your whole life thinking about what might have been. You have to deal with what your life is, not what you'd like it to be. And I'm happy with the choices I made.'

'I had to go,' Helen said. 'You do understand, don't you?'

Harry nodded. 'Yes, although I've often wondered what life would have been like if you had stayed.' He paused. 'But you had to go, didn't you?'

'Yes,' she said softly. 'I did.'

Harry smiled his goodbyes. As he turned and opened the door a part of her longed for him to stay. 'Thank you for this,' she said, pointing to the suitcase.

'It was the least I could do.'

'How are they really?'

'Charlotte and Adam? They'll be all right – it's going to take a while but I know that we can work it out. I love Charlotte and I love Adam – neither of those things have changed.'

'They're very lucky people,' said Helen.

Harry smiled self-consciously. 'Bye,' he said.

She nodded and he was gone.

As the door closed Helen tried to quell the feelings of regret and loss and instead she turned her attention to the suitcase, wondering whether she really wanted to open it before the show or whether to wait until there was time to explore what was inside. Helen glanced up at the clock. Time was tick- tick- ticking away. She weighed the key in her hand. The compulsion to open the case was too strong to resist.

Crouching on the floor Helen slipped the key into the lock and turned it, feeling the teeth bite in the mechanism, feeling the lock give, and then she slid the little clips across so that the fastenings sprang open with a metallic thud. The sudden noise made her jump.

Very slowly Helen lifted the lid. The case was lined with checked pale cream paper and the whole thing smelt of camphor and lavender. Inside, it was filled to the brim with hundreds of envelopes and little packets all neatly tied into bundles with white cotton string. Helen picked up the first bundle and felt her heart lurch. Even after all these years, despite the fact that she had only been six when she left, Helen recognised her mother's hand-writing, rounded and childlike, across the front of the first envelope in the bundle.

The letter was addressed to her father.

Helen glanced at the clock on the dressing-room wall. How could she not look?

Very carefully Helen untied the string. There were perhaps two dozen thin, cheap envelopes in the first bundle, dated from May 1963, through until Christmas. Helen turned the first one over, and to her surprise discovered that the envelope was still sealed. Rifling through them she turned over the second and the third, the fourth and the fifth; none of the envelopes had been opened.

Taking a knife out of the picnic basket Helen slit the first one open. Inside was a single sheet of lined paper, neatly folded in two. Carefully Helen unfolded it and saw the words that had been written but never read all those years before:

Dear Gordon,

I just wish that you would listen to me and let me explain everything to you. We can't go on like this, it's killing me. Surely you can see that the reason I'm so down is because of what you're thinking. I can't bear the way you look at me and then don't say anything. Your silence and the look on your face is far worse than any amount of shouting or arguing.

I thought it would ease up after all these months and maybe get better, but as it hasn't, I thought it might be best if I went away for a few days. Maybe a bit of distance will help you see sense.

I love you dearly but you make it so hard some times.

I just want you to know that I would never have anything to do with anybody else. I thought you knew me better than that – and certainly not with Jim. He's your best friend, Gordon – and we're neither of us that sort of person. I just wish you would let me explain. But I know the more I say that there's nothing between me and Jim the more you believe there is. I know that we can sort this out. I'm staying with Lillian if you want to talk. Till I hear from you, stay safe and give my love to Helen, I miss you both so much.

Your loving wife,
Amy

Helen, oblivious now to the ticking of the clock, opened the second letter, dated a week later.

Dear Gordon,

I can't believe you've not rung or written or called round.

I'm waiting for every post to come, every time the telephone rings I think it might be you.

How is Helen? I think of you both all day, all night. This is like torture for me, Gordon. I suppose that is how you want it to feel. I can't bear to be away from you both but I can't bear you thinking badly of me all the time either. I couldn't sleep or barely eat – and I hated the way you looked at me. I couldn't stand it any more.

I can't keep living off Lillian. If this goes on for very long I'm going to have to get a job. Just for a little while till you and me sort things out.

Buntings are taking people on, casual. So I might go there.

Lillian keeps saying how I should go and see a doctor and that I'd be mad to come back to you but I miss you so much, my love. Give Helen a hug from me. If you'd just ring I'll come home.

Helen sat back and stared at the piles of letters – years and years' worth of words written and unseen, unread until now. She wondered what had possessed her father not to open them. What had he thought all those years, when the letters kept turning up week after week? And what, given that he hadn't read any, had possessed him to keep them all?

Helen began to go through the letters, pulling them out. In her haste she dropped them onto the floor, letter after letter, the sixties, the seventies, the eighties and nineties; letters for every year. There were Christmas cards, postal orders, cheques and birthday cards, airmail envelopes and gift packages – on and on until the year of her dad's funeral.

Helen sat back on her heels. She could hear the minutes trickling away. Outside in the corridor she could hear people arriving, hear the theatre coming alive for her show – but how could she possibly go anywhere without knowing what had happened to her mother?

Helen ripped open the envelopes until she was surrounded by piles of them. At the heart of each one was the same heart-wrenching truth; Amy had loved her husband, Helen's father, and she had always loved him. She loved them both and what was painfully brutally clear was that she hadn't meant to leave them for long, just a day or two, or at the longest a week or two until he came round and talked to her, said he wanted her home, said he believed her, said that he loved her.

Helen read page after page after page, drinking in all the words; the longing, the pain, the anger and eventually the acceptance that Gordon didn't love her and didn't want her back.

Finally Helen opened up the last envelope in the final bundle.

Dear Gordon,

It was so good to see you today – after all these years wasted.

Oh my love you have no idea how good it was to see you and to hear your voice. And so good to spend some time with you, even if we couldn't have long together – but once you move into Portlee we'll be able to see more of each other. I've worked there for a while now. I couldn't believe it when I saw you walking in.

I know that lots of things have changed and all this time has gone by, but I just wanted you to know that I have always loved you.

Your ever loving wife, Amy.

Helen looked at the address and felt her heart lurch.

She picked up the envelope and turned it over to check the postmark and as she did realised that there was something else inside it; a small photograph cut from one of the strips from a photo booth.

Helen stared at the picture for a moment. She had seen the face looking back at her somewhere before. It took her a second or two to place it and then getting to her feet she hurried out into the corridor to find Arthur, or Natalia or someone from the crew.

Felix was standing outside by one of the fire doors

having a cigarette. As soon as he saw her face, he said, 'Are you all right? What's the matter?'

'Where's Natalia?' asked Helen anxiously. 'Have we still got the car here?'

'Yes, sure, it's round the back in the car park,' said Felix. 'Why?'

Helen glanced down at her costume wondering whether she should change but there was hardly enough time as it was. 'Can you get it, the car – we're going to find my mum. I know where she is –'

Felix stared at her, she could see by the expression on his face that he was weighing up whether she was drunk or had finally lost it completely.

'Please,' pressed Helen. 'Just get the car. Call Natalia – whatever it takes. I know where she is.'

'Are you serious?' asked Felix.

Helen nodded and thrust the letter into his hand. Felix scanned the page and the address. 'Is that near here?'

'About a mile away, if that.'

Felix glanced at his watch, but before he could say anything, Helen said, 'I know what the time is, but I need to find her –'

'Now?'

Helen nodded. 'Yes, *now.*'

'But this is dated years ago; she might not still live there anymore and it's not even her permanent address, it says care of –'

'I think that's probably why you couldn't find her; from reading the letters it looks like she lived with a friend for years in different places. The 'care of' in the address speaks volumes. As far as she was concerned my dad could come and take her back at any time. There's a whole suitcase full of these – she's lived her whole life waiting for him to ring, to write, despite everything everybody told her. Please just get the car, will you, I have to check – I have to know.'

The sound of her voice had brought Natalia out of hiding. 'What's going on?' she said, her face folded into an anxious frown.

'I know where my mother is,' said Helen, handing her the letter. 'We have to go there.'

'Are you nuts?' said Natalia incredulously. 'There's only half an hour till the curtain goes up.'

Helen stared at her. 'This from the woman who was telling me about what makes good television. It's a mile away, Natalia, and we've got half an hour. Worst-case scenario, they hold the curtain for a few minutes – I need to find her.'

Natalia took a breath as if she was going to protest and then said, 'Okay, if you're sure about this.'

Helen nodded.

'Okay, Felix, get the camera, I'll get the car.'

'Why do we have to go this minute?' said Natalia as the car pulled away. 'Couldn't it wait until after the show?'

Helen shook her head. 'No, it can't wait – I need to go now.'

381

Natalia shrugged. 'Your call,' she said. 'Tell me about the letters.'

Helen navigated while the crew filmed. The address on the envelope was on the other side of town, out in the suburbs where the urban sprawl softened and gave way to broad verges and nicely tended gardens. Evening was coming on. Time was going fast.

Helen pressed herself to the car window watching the street names. 'Here, here,' she said, pointing. 'Belmont Gardens.'

The car swung into the street in a large arc.

'What number?' said Natalia, in a replay of the events in Victoria Street.

'A hundred and twenty six,' said Helen.

The car slowed to a crawl. 'Fifty, sixty . . .' They read off the numbers until finally they came to a hundred and twenty six, a modern chalet bungalow tucked well back off the road with a new car in the driveway. The car had barely stopped before Helen was out and hurrying up the drive with the camera crew trailing in her wake.

'What are you going to do? What are you going to say?' asked Natalia, trying to keep up with her.

Helen had no idea. As she reached the front door it opened. Helen stopped mid-stride as a woman, thin as a whip, with cropped grey hair, stepped out.

Helen stared at her. 'Are you Lillian?' she asked.

The woman nodded. 'You must be Helen,' she said. 'You look just like your mum.'

'Is my mum here?'

The woman shook her head. 'I'm so sorry,' she said. 'I'm afraid she's gone. Do you want to come in?'

Helen felt her heart sink; her shoulders slumped, the expectation and anticipation, the adrenaline that had carried her this far draining away. After a lifetime of waiting she was too late.

'I can't, I've got a show to do.' Helen hesitated. 'Do I know you?' she said fighting back the tears as she peered at Lillian's calm, even features.

Lillian smiled. 'It was a long time ago now. I used to pop by your house when you were little. Your dad wasn't keen – he always said I was flighty.' Lillian laughed. 'And he was right, I suppose. I was married and used to meet his best mate at your house. We thought if your dad found out he'd go crazy.'

Helen stared at her. 'He thought my mum was having an affair, and all the time it was you?'

Lillian nodded. 'It was awful. He wouldn't listen to her when she tried to explain, wouldn't talk about it, even when I tried to make him see sense. It went on for months and months before she finally left – I always told your mum she ought to go back and fetch you, you know, but she thought –' Lillian paused. 'She was haunted, frightened, by something your dad said, before she left. She had been really low and the doctor had put her on tablets. I mean they'd call it depression now – but anyway, Gordon said that if she couldn't cope, if she had a breakdown, that social services would come and take you away and that you'd end up in a home.'

383

Helen stared at her. 'Are you serious?'

'Oh God yes, your mum was absolutely terrified that he'd have social services after her. Him telling them she was on tablets and carrying on with some man. Things were different back then. When she first left your dad, she was sleeping on my sofa and I said, "Go and get Helen, we'll manage," and she said no. Your mum was absolutely adamant. She said, "If they see me in a state like this they'll take her away and put her in a home. I know they will – Gordon will tell them I'm not a fit mother. He will – I know he will –"

'I kept trying to tell her that he'd said it to frighten her, but she wasn't having any of it. She kept hoping that one day you'd understand and that you'd come and find her, and well, if you're here then you know. She loved you so much – I know you're in a hurry but just wait there for a minute.'

Lillian went inside and moments later came back out with a framed publicity shot that Helen had had taken way back when. It was in black and white and scrawled across the bottom were the words *Happy Christmas Amy, with love and all best wishes from Helen Redford.*

The woman handed it to her. Helen stared at the studio portrait of her younger self.

'She used to write in to the show and send a Christmas card every year when you were on *Cannon Square*,' Lillian said. 'She's still got all your thank you letters somewhere. I know she was upset but she understood why you didn't want to meet her – you must think that she just abandoned you, but it was much, much more complicated than that.' The woman laughed and shook her head. 'She's very proud of you, you know. And I always knew you'd be back one day.'

Helen, clutching the framed photo, felt the tears trickling down her face. The handwriting wasn't even hers. She had never seen any of the letters or the cards. Someone in the publicity department had sent the photo and the letters. Someone who had no idea who Amy Heel was.

'She will be really upset that she missed you,' said the woman.

'She lives here?' said Helen. 'But I thought you said she'd gone – She's *not dead* –'

'Oh no,' said Lillian, her hand flying up to her mouth. 'Oh, I'm so sorry, pet, is that what you thought? No, she's fine – she's going to your show tonight. She left about five minutes ago; you most probably passed her on the way.'

Helen looked at Natalia.

'Let's get back in the car,' said Natalia. 'Now.'

'Tell her that the cards were lovely,' whispered Helen. 'Tell her that I've read the letters. Tell her –' The words caught like dust in her throat.

Lillian grabbed her hand. 'Go, you'll be able to tell her yourself.'

They were no sooner back in the car than Natalia was on the phone. The crew filmed as the car pulled hurriedly away from the curb. Helen stared out of the window.

She felt strangely numb. Her mother was alive, and she was on her way to see Helen in her show – and more than that she loved her and always had, in fact she loved her enough to leave her behind. It was such a strange place to find herself. Helen sat very, very still, praying that she wouldn't wake up and find out that it was all a dream.

As the car pulled up at the stage door Arthur came running out of the back of the theatre, red-faced and looking anxious.

'Where the bloody hell have you been?' he said, throwing open the car door and practically dragging Helen out. 'I've been looking all over for you. The theatre manager is going ballistic. He's been talking about suing if you don't show.'

Helen took hold of his hands. 'It's all right, Arthur, I'm here now. And I'm fine. I just need to nip into the dressing room, check on my hair and makeup. I won't be a minute. And don't worry, I'm all ready to rock and roll.'

Arthur didn't look convinced. 'So where the hell have you been?' he pressed, glaring at Natalia. 'Is this down to you? I'm going to go and ring the executive producer of *Roots*. Did this lot drag you off somewhere to see someone? Ruth what's-her-name, I'll have her arse in the shredder – we've got a bloody contract.'

'It's my mum,' Helen said quietly, hardly daring to trust herself to say the words aloud.

Arthur's eyebrows furrowed. 'What about her?'

'She's alive, and she's going to be here tonight, at the show.'

Arthur's mouth opened but no sounds came out, and without waiting for him to get his act together and reply, Helen hurried past him down the corridor and threw open the dressing-room door, the thought rising up every single step of the way – her mum was alive. Here in the theatre. Finally the thought took hold and bubbled up like champagne, threatening to drown her in emotion. She grinned, closing the door behind her, and turned round.

Standing by the dressing table, in amongst the debris of the letters, the presents, the packages and the envelopes was a small, slim, grey-haired woman with tiny hands. Her hair was short and curly, framing a warm lively face; a face soft with lines and good humour. Helen stared.

It was the face Helen remembered from her long-distant childhood. It was the face she had seen at her father's funeral. The one she had seen on one of the staff from her father's nursing home. The one she had assumed was just another carer. Looking at her now, seeing the family resemblance, Helen wondered how she could have been so stupid, so very short-sighted.

Helen didn't move, barely daring to breathe in case she vanished. 'Mum?' she whispered.

Amy Heel nodded. 'I thought I'd –' she stopped. 'I mean –' her eyes began to glisten. 'I don't know where to start, Helen,' she said.

The sound of her voice made Helen's heart hurt. Helen

didn't move. 'We can start from here,' she said, her voice unsteady. 'From right now. And we can take all the time we need, but right now I've got to get ready to go out on stage.'

Amy nodded. 'I know,' she paused, tears rolling down her cheeks. 'Oh, sweetheart, I've missed you so much,' she said, and with that Helen stepped into her open arms.

'You found her then,' said a voice from behind her.

Helen swung round and was amazed to see Bon standing in the doorway and was even more amazed when she realised his comment was being made not to her, but to her mother.

'I thought you were in Dubai,' she said.

'I was, but there was no way I could let you go through all this on your own. I know how much you were struggling with the whole idea of coming back here.'

'I met him at the stage door,' said Amy, by way of explanation. 'He made them let me in.'

Bon grinned. 'She was trying to persuade them to let her through and I took one look at her and knew exactly who she was – same eyes, same mouth –' He grinned. 'I was telling your mum before you got here how we're going to be get married.' He laughed. 'Once I've asked you that is, and assuming that'll you have me.'

Helen stared at him. 'Are you serious?'

'Never more so,' he said. 'I was going to wait till my tour ended but I couldn't wait.'

'What about Libby?'

Bon smiled at her. 'What about her? She's fine, she

sends her love. The show's going really well. She can manage without me for a few days.'

Helen reddened. 'I just thought –' she stopped. What she didn't say was that Libby was gorgeous and young and he seemed to be spending a lot of time with her. To her surprise Bon sighed. 'Actually it was seeing Libby that made me want to come back even more. She's out there with her husband, Marco, celebrating their wedding anniversary – and I kept thinking this is mad – we should be doing this. You and me.'

There was a sharp tap on the door. Helen stared at Bon.

'On stage, Ms Redford, please,' said a disembodied voice.

'Just coming,' said Helen, taking one last look at the two of them before heading out into the corridor. 'You'll both be here when I get back, won't you?' she said.

Bon grinned at Amy.

'Of course we will,' he said. 'I'm hoping you'll say you'll marry me.'

Helen smiled at him. 'Why wouldn't I?' she said taking one last look in the mirror before opening the dressing-room door.

Felix was waiting outside. He gave her the thumbs up from behind the camera as the assistant stage manager smiled at her. 'All set, Ms Redford?'

Helen nodded and followed her up onto the back of the stage.

*   *   *

Slowly – almost unnoticed at first – the lights in the theatre began to dim. Tucked out of sight in the wings Helen could sense the growing anticipation and expectation in the audience. The seconds ticked by. Part of the magic of good showmanship is to make an audience wait, to hold them there a few seconds longer than feels quite comfortable, so that every eye is focused on stage. That growing sense of what is *about* to happen pushes aside all the thoughts about the drive there, the queue to get in, the day they had had before the show began. And so Helen waited.

In the auditorium someone coughed; there were the sounds of people settling back in their seats, their conversation changing from a noisy cheerful babble to an altogether lower, denser hum. There was a crackle of excitement in the air, an electric charge as tangible as a coming storm. It made Helen's skin prickle.

'Okay, Miss Redford?' mouthed the assistant stage manager, giving Helen the thumbs up. She smiled and nodded, all the while aware of every breath, every movement, every sound around her.

As the music began to play Helen closed her eyes, making an effort to control the panic that bubbled up inside. There was a peculiar fluttering fear that started somewhere down low in the pit of her stomach and rose up into her throat, closing it down, stealing her breath away and making her heart race. She knew that once she was out on stage it would be fine, but for now the panic crowded in on her, making her tremble, making the sound of her pulse ricochet around inside her skull like a drumroll. Deep breaths, calm thoughts; any second now the curtains would open and everything would be all right.

In the auditorium beyond the curtains, the audience was still and quiet now. The hairs on the back of her neck rose.

'Miss Redford?' someone whispered. Helen opened her eyes and looked up. One of the crew adjusted the radio mike onto the front of her dress and leaning closer flicked it on before tucking the wire down in amongst the embroidery. One of the spotlights reflected in the facets of the jewellery she was wearing, projecting a great arc of rainbows into the wings. It felt like an omen.

Helen smiled her thanks and she pressed her lips together, blotting her lipstick, and then ran a hand back over her hair checking it was all in place, her heart still racing, anxiety edging out all sensible thoughts.

The technician grinned. 'You look fabulous,' he whispered. Her smile held. On the far side of the stage, behind a cameraman, Arthur, her agent, raised a hand in salute, his fingers crossed. He winked at her. Behind him, deep in the shadows, Helen could just pick out Bon, with her mother standing alongside him.

A moment later the music changed to the signature tune for *Cannon Square* and as the curtains slowly opened, the deep inviting voice of the theatre's resident compere rolled out over the PA.

'Ladies and gentlemen, welcome to this evening's show. Tonight, for one night only, we would like you put your hands together and give a great big Carlton Rooms welcome to star of stage, screen and television, our very own homespun diva, Miss Helen Redford!' His voice rose to a crescendo in the darkness.

It was as if someone had thrown a switch. From the auditorium came a sound like heavy rain and then thunder as people clapped, cheered and stamped their feet, the sound filling the theatre; a sound so loud that Helen could feel it pressing on her chest as much as she could hear the noise. The assistant stage manager waved her on and as Helen stepped out into the glare of the spotlight the volume of the applause rose.

She waited for the noise to ebb and then smiled out into the expectant darkness.

'Well, hello there,' she said, pulling up the stool that was there waiting for her centre stage. 'It's been a long time coming, but it's great to be back here at the Carlton Rooms. I don't want to think about how many years it's been since I stood right here on this stage. I've been away too long.' And as she spoke the audience roared its appreciation and Helen's nerves melted away like snow in sunshine.

It had been a long time coming, but finally Helen was home.